Blood
Water

Blood Water

AN EDWARD HUNTER SPY ADVENTURE

DOUG ADCOCK

DougAdcockAuthor.com

Paperback ISBN-13: 978-0-9976867-3-9
Ebook ISBN: 978-0-9976867-4-6

Cover jacket design and maps by Cathy Helms www.avalongraphics.org
Interior Design: Tamara Cribley www.TheDeliberatePage.com

Published by Douglas Adcock
Breckenridge, CO

For Dr. Ray Kelch, my "Uncle Ray," who first piqued my interest in history and nurtured it during visits to San Francisco and London.

Dramatis Personae

Historical characters are in **bold**. Dates included where known.

Edward Hunter—protagonist

Luca Gironi— Edward Hunter's "servant" and companion. Born in Venice, but has spent 20 years or so in England serving the Earl of Leicester

SIDNEY'S PARTY

Philip Sidney (30 Nov 1554-17 Oct 1586) courtier and later poet, nephew and heir to the Earl of Leicester

Lodowick Bryskett (1547-1612)—travelling companion to Sidney

Griffin Madox—Sidney's secretary

Harry White- valet

John Fisher—servant

ENGLISH EXPATRIATES

Dr. Nicolas Simmons

Ambrose Barnes

John Hart (d. 1586)

James Randolph

John Le Rous (d. 1590)

Roger Fitzwilliams

Charles Carr

ROYALTY AND NOBILITY

Henri Valois (1551-1589)—son of Henri II and Catherine de Medici; Duke of Anjou (1566-1573); elected King Hendrick of Poland (1573-74); Henri III of France (1574-1589)

Louis de Gonzaga, Duke of Nevers (1539-1595)

Alphonso d'Este, Duke of Ferrara (1533-1597)

Robert Dudley, 1st Earl of Leicester (1532-1588) courtier, Elizabeth I's Master of Horse and favorite

VENETIAN RESIDENTS

Edward Windsor, 3rd Baron Windsor of Stanwell (1532-75)—English Catholic nobleman

Catherine de Vere, Lady Windsor (1538-1600)—his wife

Tintoretto (1519-94)—aka Jacopo Robusti, noted painter

Paolo Veronese (1528-1588) noted painter

Sebastian Bryskett (1536-91) Lodowick Bryskett's older brother

Alessandro Malpiero—Venetian senator

Stefano Picenino—Gironi's cousin, a shoemaker

SERVANTS

Christopher—Ambrose Barnes's servant

Francis—Ambrose Barnes's servant

Beatrice—cook at Pozzo della Vacca

Giulio—her son

Captain Ducasse—serves Louis de Gonzaga, Duke of Nevers

COURTESANS/PROSTITUTES

Signora Filippa—runs a Venetian bordello

Lucia—a mistress of Baron Windsor

Caterina—a young courtesan in training.

Leona, Lucetta, Maria, Giulia, Bianca, Marta—prostitutes

CRIMINALS

Tomaso Biradi—criminal kingpin in Padua.

Girolamo Rossi—Venetian kingpin in the Nicolotti area

Marcantonio Costa—Venetian kingpin in Castellani area

Emilio Carollo—pimp in Padua

DOMINICANS

Vice Inquisitor Antonio Fascetti

Brother Alberto

Brother Giuseppe

AUTHORITIES

Captain Scarpa—in charge of law and order in Padua

Corporal Molinari—official of the Romagna

OTHER

Hubert Languet (1515-1581) French diplomat who served the Elector of
Saxony, mentor of Philip Sidney

Signor Girolamo Zordan—Silk producer who owns Palladian villa south
of Vicenza

∼ Notes on the Map of Venice ∼

This map is not accurate, as anyone acquainted with the city will know. Venice contains about 150 canals and over 400 bridges. Few of the canals are shown and the only bridges included are the Rialto and the bridge by *Palazzo Foscarini* and *Carmini*, where the mock battle described in chapter 27 took place. The six *sistieri* into which Venice is divided are generally indicated. For a description of the areas from which the Nicolotti and Castellani were recruited, refer to Signora Lucia's explanation in chapter 13.

1. *Piazza San Marco*
2. Saint Mark's Basilica
3. Doge's Palace
4. *Piazzetta*
5. *Merceria*
6. Rialto Bridge
7. *Campo San Cassiano*
8. Signora Filippa's brothel
9. *Palazzo Michiel*, French Embassy
10. Tintoretto's house and studio
11. Ambrose Barnes's lodgings, later used by expatriates
12. *Campo San Polo*
13. Baron Windsor's *palazzo*
14. Zanipolo (Basilica of Saints Giovanni and Paolo); *Scuola di Sant' Orsola*
15. Stefano Picenino's shop and house
16. *Campo Santa Margherita*
17. *Mezza Luna* (Half Moon Tavern)

18. Lucia's house
19. *I Frari*
20. *Scuola di San Rocco*
21. Sebastian Bryskett's lodgings
22. *Fondaco dei Turchi* (warehouse and residence of Turkish merchants)
23. *Fondaco dei Tedeschi* (warehouse and residence of German merchants)
24. *Ca' Foscari*
25. *Palazzo Foscarini*
26. *Carmini* Church
27. *Le Convertite*
28. Dorsoduro lodgings rented by Sidney
29. Church of San Sebastian
30. Office of Cannaregio *Signori di Notte*
31. San Giorgio Maggiore
32. The Ghetto
33. The Arsenal

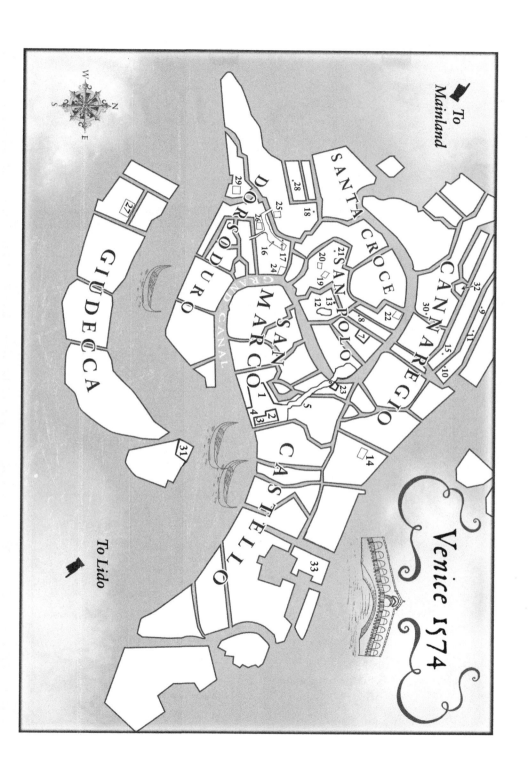

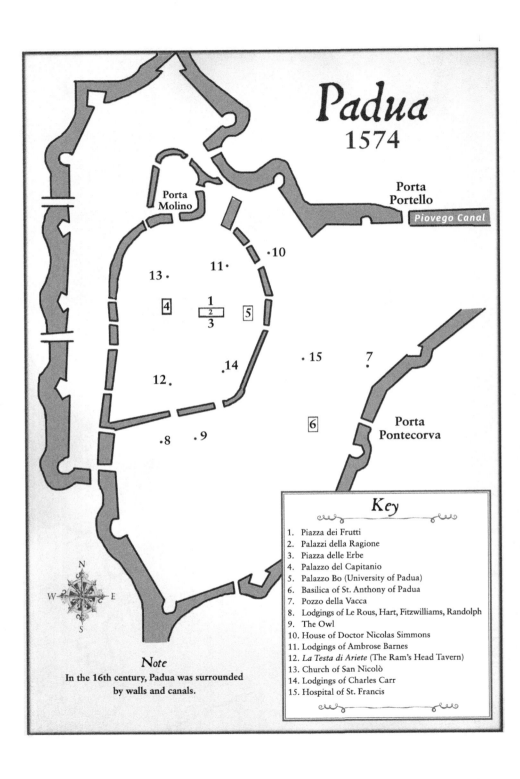

Padua
1574

Porta Molino

Porta Portello

Piovego Canal

Porta Pontecorva

Key

1. Piazza dei Frutti
2. Palazzi della Ragione
3. Piazza delle Erbe
4. Palazzo del Capitanio
5. Palazzo Bo (University of Padua)
6. Basilica of St. Anthony of Padua
7. Pozzo della Vacca
8. Lodgings of Le Rous, Hart, Fitzwilliams, Randolph
9. The Owl
10. House of Doctor Nicolas Simmons
11. Lodgings of Ambrose Barnes
12. *La Testa di Ariete* (The Ram's Head Tavern)
13. Church of San Nicolò
14. Lodgings of Charles Carr
15. Hospital of St. Francis

Note
In the 16th century, Padua was surrounded by walls and canals.

Northeast Italy
in the later
16th Century

N
W · E
S

VENETO

Vicenza

River Brenta

Mestre
Marghera
Murano
Venice
Lido

Padua
↑
Piovego
Canal

Chioggia

River Adige

· Rovigo

DUCHY
OF
MANTUA

S. Maria
Maddalena

River Po

DUCHY OF
FERRARA

Ferrara

DUCHY
OF
MODENA

River Reno

ROMAGNA

Bologna

PAPAL STATES

Adriatic Sea

On Distant Shores

Tuesday, 23 February 1574, Westminster

EDWARD HUNTER'S HEART BEAT FASTER AS HE ENTERED WHAT LORD
Leicester's servant called the 'audience chamber,' as though Leicester
were royalty.

Robert Dudley, Earl of Leicester, sometimes *did* usurp the royal pre-
rogatives, when Queen Elizabeth was not present. As the queen's favorite
escort over more than a dozen years, he had at times adopted the role of
consort, much to the jealousy of others. Wearing a red, richly embroidered
satin doublet that rose high on his neck to end in a small ruff under his
chin, sporting moustaches that swept out beyond his cheeks, Leicester
exuded confidence and power as he turned from his ornately carved desk
to greet Hunter.

"Master Hunter, pray be seated." Leicester indicated a chair opposite.

"Thank you, my lord." Weak-kneed, Hunter was glad he need not
stand. The furnishings were as intimidating as Leicester himself: a
Flemish tapestry with a vibrantly colored hunting scene, crimson velvet
drapes framing the windows, a bronze statue of Hercules atop a Turkish
carpet on an oak chest.

"I remember speaking to you over a year ago," Leicester said, "soon
after your return from Paris."

His body tensed remembering those August days of terror. "Yes, my
lord." Images of mutilated bodies swam uninvited into Hunter's mind.

"I was grateful then to hear that my nephew Philip was safe."

Hunter forced his face to remain neutral, though he heard again the screams of the slaughtered. He closed his eyes and channeled his thoughts to the relief he had felt when he left France. "We were both fortunate to escape the massacre on Saint Bartholomew's Day."

"Indeed you were. Philip spoke very highly of you in his letters."

The warmth Hunter had felt when Philip Sidney accepted him as a companion, despite the difference in their station, dispelled the macabre images of the massacre, but he said, "I am not sure I deserve high praise."

"Nonsense!" Leicester flipped his hand dismissively. "Lord Burghley also praised you, and you saved Ambassador Walsingham's life at the English Embassy."

Hunter recalled that instant of fear and awkwardness and allowed himself a smile. "It was an ungraceful moment for us both. I was forced to tackle him when a man aimed a pistol at his back."

Leicester slapped his thigh and laughed. "No. It was an act of bravery. That is part of the reason you are here. Bravery, your friendship with Philip, and your uncle's constant desire to improve his fortunes."

Leicester might choose to label an instinctive act as bravery. He did not know of Hunter's failures in Paris. Nevertheless, Hunter could scarcely contain his excitement, knowing that Sidney had written Leicester to request Hunter join him in Venice. He hoped the fact that his trip might provide a profitable opportunity for Leicester and Uncle Babcock would secure their backing.

"It is my wish, and your uncle's, that you undertake a journey to Italy, both to observe my nephew Philip and to discuss matters of trade with some silk producers of the Veneto," Leicester continued.

Hunter relaxed at Leicester's words. He *would* travel to Italy. He knew, of course, that their plans were greater than mere trade. How much did either of them count on him to achieve their dreams of mulberry plantations, an English silk industry, perhaps even a royal monopoly for silk production? Leicester's words, "observe my nephew," were troubling, but he said, "It would be an honor."

Leicester pursed his lips. "I will be blunt regarding my nephew. After the slaughter in Paris, I sent a letter ordering him to return to England. He received it in Frankfurt and assured me he was safe in Protestant territory. Then he proceeded to the Catholic realm of the Habsburgs, where he protested that he lodged securely in Vienna with Hubert Languet, the Ambassador from Saxony. Alas, he did not stop there, but proceeded to

Italy, clearly violating the permission to travel Her Majesty had granted him. I have heard that he consorts there with Catholic expatriates at the University of Padua and in Venice. I need scarcely tell you that both I and his parents are concerned about this hazardous behavior."

Hunter's shoulders tensed again. Besides being tasked with luring Venetian silk weavers and their secrets to England, he was being sent to spy on his friend and report to Leicester. He dared not offend the earl but felt he must speak in Sidney's defense. "In Paris, Philip spoke with many scholars, both Protestant and Catholic."

"That was before thousands of French Protestants were slaughtered. I would have thought that would teach him some caution." Leicester's face was turning red. "I hope you will advise him well and help keep him from harm."

Each sentence from the earl was a weight of duty placed upon him. He was to be a spy, an advisor, and a protector to his friend. Hunter fought down the urge to object. He nodded, as the situation obliged him to.

"Now," Leicester continued, raising his hand and summoning a servant by the door with a flick of his fingers, "I know that you do not speak Italian well, so I am sending one of my men with you."

At the sound of footsteps, Hunter turned to see a man in his mid-thirties, dressed in a leather jerkin over a blue doublet. A brown beard covered some, but not all, of the smallpox scars on his cheeks. The servant's suspicious brown eyes weighed up Hunter.

"Master Hunter, meet Luca Gironi. He has served me loyally for over fifteen years. He not only speaks Italian; he was born in Venice and speaks their dialect as well. He is handy with a sword and has other talents that may prove useful. I can provide you no better travelling companion."

"Thank you, my lord." Hunter realized Lord Leicester was ensuring that his reports would be accurate. Not only must he spy on Sidney, Gironi would spy on him. He stood and nodded to the servant. "I thank you as well for agreeing to travel with me. I hope you will not regret it."

"I am sure I will not." A look in Gironi's eyes revealed he was also aware of the contradictory roles of servant and overseer.

Friday, 16 April 1574, Somewhere in Italy

"Damn"! He slapped his hand down on the letter and a quill flew off his engraved and gilded writing desk. He could not allow himself to approve

such an act. It would ruin his chance of promotion. What did this English idiot think he was doing? It was too late to stop his plan, but it could be thwarted. Alas, some would have to die. He silently prayed to God to forgive him. Orders must be given. He called a servant to fetch an underling.

CHAPTER 1

Plunging In

Thursday, 22 April 1574, Padua

AFTER A LONG, DIFFICULT JOURNEY, HUNTER WAS FINALLY HERE. He knocked eagerly on the door of Pozzo della Vacca, where Philip Sidney lodged. He looked forward to Sidney relating his Italian adventures, and he was sure Sidney would demand he recount every stage of his five-week journey.

A window opened above, and a boy leaned out. "*Sì?*"

"*Signor Sidney?*"

"*S'è andà a Venesia,*" the boy said.

Hunter's shoulders sank. The joyful reunion he anticipated would be delayed. He turned to Gironi. "If we ride to take the boat from *Porta Portello,* could we be in Venice tonight?"

"I believe so," Gironi said.

As they prepared to remount, someone shouted, "Hunter!"

He recognized the lanky figure of Lodowick Bryskett, Sidney's travelling companion, and the squat Griffin Madox, his secretary, advancing under an arcade. Behind them strode a man wearing the uniform of the Padovan guards. If Sidney's party had gone to Venice, what was Bryskett doing here? As he drew closer, Hunter made out a bandage beneath his hat.

"Sidney was taken by violence last night," Bryskett said without preamble. "Come, you can ride with us." He shouted a string of orders in Italian to the boy at the window.

Hunter's head spun. Disappointment turned to panic. "You are hurt, Lodowick. What happened?"

"A blow to the head, but they patched me up at the hospital." He turned as the boy opened the door. "Madox will explain while I collect weapons and water."

Hunter faced Madox eagerly.

"Pray forgive Lodowick's blunt greeting," Madox began, "but he is keen to set out after the miscreants as soon as possible." He took a deep breath. "Late yesterday, Master Sidney received a request that he present himself today before the Venetian magistrates. At twilight we rode around the walls to catch the night boat. We took no weapons, as they are forbidden in Venice. After a few furlongs, we saw an overturned cart, and a man called for help in righting it. As soon as we dismounted, a half dozen armed men rose from the ditches and attacked us. We were outnumbered. A big, ugly fellow gave me a glancing blow here." He touched a bump on his left temple. "When I came to my senses, I saw them loading Sidney into the cart, bound and gagged. Some set off west with our horses. Three riders and the cart headed south."

"Was he badly wounded?" Hunter asked. He glanced at Gironi's troubled face. This was not the news either wished to send back to England.

"I'm not sure," Madox said.

Bryskett barged out the door, wearing a sword and carrying a flask of water and a brace of pistols. "No sign of Captain Scarpa?"

"No," Madox said.

"Are you badly hurt?" Hunter asked Bryskett.

"They mended me at Saint Francis's Hospital. I came to my senses just as the captain arrived. He promised to meet me here." Bryskett turned and spoke in Italian with the guard who hovered behind him.

Hunter shivered with fear for his friend and fear his mission to keep Sidney safe had already failed. Though he and Gironi had come to trust one another on their journey south, might Gironi write his master blaming Hunter for a delay in reaching Padua before Sidney's capture? "Our horses are fresh, Luca, and you speak the dialect. Shall we start in pursuit?"

Gironi shook his head. "I do not know the country south of here."

So Gironi was reluctant to be responsible for Sidney's well-being. He could mention this to Leicester if need be.

Bryskett addressed them. "The captain knew where the thieves would sell our horses. He has gone to retrieve them. He also sent three scouts ahead to inquire and guide our search."

"Pray they reach Sidney before these rascals do him harm," Hunter said.

"Amen." Bryskett said. "But if they meant him harm, they would have done so yesterday."

"I pray you are right."

"How are you armed?" Bryskett asked.

"Much as you." Hunter nodded at his horse. "I carry a brace of pistols, and Luca has another."

"Good." Bryskett turned to Madox. "You had best stay here. Look after Fisher and White when they come out of hospital." Madox appeared more relieved than disappointed.

They turned at the sound of hooves. Two mounted men appeared, leading a string of horses. Two of them whinnied, greeting their owners.

"*Capitano*," Bryskett called out.

As they spoke, Gironi translated for Hunter. "The captain says the horse trader was grieved to surrender the mounts and gear, but he preferred that to being arrested. He wonders what is so special about this Englishman, but he has his orders. He will allow us to ride south with him and two of his men. Our party will be eight or nine strong."

"How many men attacked you?" Hunter asked Madox.

"I'm not sure. Seven or eight. But only three rode south with the cart."

"Then we will be more than a match for them." Perhaps his first letter to England could report success at protecting his friend.

"We have lost enough time," Bryskett said, strapping his pistol holsters to his horse. "When we find Sidney, he will need his mount, so we shall lead Ned." His face clouded for a moment, and he added, "And we might need to ride him if one of ours goes lame."

Hunter tensed. Bryskett had imagined they might need to fetch Sidney's body home on his horse. His heart raced as he and the others mounted. At a frown and a nod from Captain Scarpa, they set off at a fast trot. Hunter longed to spur Dancer to a gallop, but he feared they might have a long way to go.

His fears proved prescient. As the miles and hours passed, Hunter's buttocks and thighs ached. He ground grit between his teeth and blinked dust out of his eyes. At the same time, his spirits cautiously rose. Innkeepers and tavern boys they questioned reported that a cart such as

Madox described had stopped, and they had served food and drink to the driver and his companions. The farther that cart had traveled, Hunter reasoned, the more likely that Sidney still lay alive in it.

Captain Scarpa sighed with each indication that the extent and expense of their search would increase, but he led them on with professional determination. At the toll booth by the Adige bridge, he finally released a stream of invective. Gironi provided an expurgated version. "Must we go farther yet? Why did they not stop near Padua and demand a ransom? Now we must change horses. More expense. I hope your Master Sidney is worth it."

They rode on.

Outside Rovigo's walls, the owner of the stable smiled and waved as they approached. The party dismounted and walked stiffly inside, while grooms scurried about their horses. Over the bread, cheese, and wine, Scarpa speculated about Sidney's disappearance. Why were the abductors continuing a long, hard ride farther south? The captain had not thought his scouts would need to change mounts. His superiors would question the expense. They would soon arrive at the frontier with the Duchy of Ferrara. Surely the cart had halted before then or turned aside. Perhaps his scouts had already caught up with it. If not, the man-thieves were still hours ahead of them.

Bryskett bit his nails during the captain's speculations, then said, "Their Lordships trusted him into my care, yet I could not command him. I fear this man-thieving is connected with his foolish dash to Genoa and Florence."

"What?" Hunter exchanged looks with Gironi. Lord Leicester's worries about Sidney were proving well founded. "When did that happen?"

"Last month. I'm not surprised he didn't tell you about it."

"I have had no letters from him in over a month. What happened?"

"He was staying with the French Ambassador, Monsieur de Ferrier. We had come back to Padua, and he was to follow. When he did not, I returned to Venice, where the ambassador told me Sidney had accompanied his courier to Genoa and Florence. I was overcome with anxiety. To ride into states allied with Spain... He could have been grabbed and loaded on a Spanish galley. Or suppose his horse had run down someone. How long would it be before the Inquisition asked the authorities to turn an English heretic over to them?"

Had Bryskett reported this escapade to Leicester? Unlikely, given the trouble it would cause him. "Indeed, he did foolishly hazard himself,"

Hunter agreed. Was his journey connected to his consorting with Catholic expatriates?

"We knew not where to send a messenger to call him back." Bryskett exhaled strongly. "When he returned, he did apologize. Yet he argued that no harm had befallen him, and he had gained the pleasure of seeing the great dome of Brunelleschi, Michelangelo's statue of David, and other works much talked about."

"And you fear this capture is connected to his excursion?"

"I don't know. Though Her Majesty's license to travel did not include any Catholic states, after we travelled to Bavaria and Austria without incident, he pressed to visit Venice. He argued that the pope's reach was weak there, and we would be safe. But his reckless ride may have caused enemies to consider he was more vulnerable outside the boundaries of the Republic."

"What enemies?" Hunter asked. Did Bryskett count the English Catholics in Padua as enemies?

But at that moment a stableman entered to say that their horses were ready, and Captain Scarpa stood with a resolution that signaled they would mount immediately.

"Enemies may not be the right word," Bryskett said. "It is complicated, and now we must ride."

As they entered Rovigo, one of the scouts, looking haggard and dispirited, rode to greet them. After he spoke to Scarpa, the captain exploded in a string of exclamations.

Gironi's face registered shock as he turned to Hunter. "They told an innkeeper at dawn that they were headed to Ferrara. Scarpa says we will not ride out of Venetian territory and should turn back."

Hunter spurred his mount toward where Bryskett was already remonstrating with Scarpa. "Tell him we must rescue Sidney," Hunter urged, frustrated that he could not speak Italian.

"I am," Bryskett said.

Scarpa snapped words that silenced Bryskett for a moment.

"Sidney is the nephew of Queen Elizabeth's favorite, almost her husband," Hunter argued, exaggerating. "Does he want to be responsible for the death of someone so close to the queen? Will the *Signoria* be pleased when Her Majesty asks why Venice did not do all it could to save him?" Gironi translated immediately. Hunter detected a hint of doubt in Scarpa's face, and he pressed on. "Surely the Duke of Ferrara will also be anxious to oblige Her Majesty."

Bryskett added something in a milder tone, perhaps assuring Scarpa his persistence would be rewarded.

Scarpa glanced from Bryskett to Gironi to Hunter. He exhaled loudly, nodded, wheeled his horse, and set out at a brisk trot.

Hunter hoped his argument would hold until they found Sidney. He gave thanks that they had changed horses, as Scarpa pressed them onward for almost two hours without a break. Perhaps this was his revenge for being pressured into continuing the pursuit. The heat and choking dust increased, and Hunter's legs and backside ached. Finally, they reached the River Po.

On the far side of the ferry, a guard wearing a tunic emblazoned with the arms of the Este rulers of Ferrara approached Captain Scarpa and spoke quickly, while his companion ran to a nearby tavern. Scarpa frowned and the tone of his questions became menacing. The guard sputtered apologetic answers, then gestured behind him to where a man approached whose bearing clearly expressed authority. Scarpa and his party dismounted to meet him.

Captain Caselli of Ferrara and Captain Scarpa introduced themselves, exchanged respectful greetings, and entered into a lengthy dialogue. Bryskett and Gironi edged close, trying to overhear. At one point, Hunter caught the word *morto*. He drew a breath in shock, but Bryskett held up a hand. Hunter waited impatiently.

When the Ferrara Captain finished, Gironi explained, "The cart passed here before noon. They claimed to be taking the body of a Bolonese man back for burial and waved a paper with Venetian seals requesting passage."

Hunter's heart beat faster. "Could it be that Sidney is dead?"

"Their captain doesn't think so. When our scouts explained they pursued men who had captured an important Englishman, their captain questioned his guards carefully. They admitted they had taken only a quick glance in the cart. He sent two of his men to accompany our scouts in pursuit."

"I pray to God their captain is right."

"He argues that if Sidney were dead, they would not continue across frontiers, but discard his body."

Hunter was still troubled. "Unless they need to prove his death to someone who hired them."

Worry creased Gironi's face.

Bryskett interrupted. "Do not be so melancholic. We must continue to hope. Mount up."

The advance party had done its job, as guards at Ferrara's gates waved them around the city and pointed them on the road south to the frontier with the Romagna. There, the men sent from Ferrara stood beside one of Scarpa's scouts at the border hut. He reported that the cart and riders had passed only a few hours before. The officer on duty, Corporal Molonari, had allowed Scarpa's other scout to ride into papal territory with one of his men and now stood ready to accompany their party. Scarpa gave a withering glance at Hunter, no doubt regretting the need to cross into yet another territory.

"Like the Ferrarans, they want to make sure we get up to no mischief," Bryskett commented.

"Did the man-stealers say anything about Sidney?" Hunter asked.

"The same story, a bit embellished. They were carrying a body to Bologna and feared he might have died of plague. That kept the guards from looking."

Hunter bit his lower lip. "He must be weak by now."

"They have surely given him sustenance," Bryskett said.

Corporal Molinari led the pursuers on. Half an hour down the Bologna road, a friar stepped from behind a dilapidated building and signaled them to a halt. After a brief word, Captain Scarpa jerked upright in his saddle. He called to his party in an excited voice and spurred his horse down a narrow road on the right. Hunter's heart raced. They must be close to their quarry.

At the top of a low rise, Scarpa reined in. Broken-down farm buildings spread out below them. The captain barked an order. Hunter saw the guards draw weapons from their holsters and he did the same, winding the mechanisms and priming both his pistols. Scarpa gestured to each side, and his guards spread into a line. Hunter, Bryskett, and Gironi took their places on the right. All rode forward at a walk, pistols at the ready.

A hundred yards from the buildings, all dismounted. The Padovan guards on the left side advanced cautiously to what had been a farmhouse. They slowly circled it, glancing behind each wall and through windows, then turned and waved the others forward.

Now it was the turn of Hunter and his companions to investigate the crumbling outbuildings on the right side. Bryskett and Corporal Molinari sidled toward what might have been a cow house on the far right. Hunter and Gironi crept toward a smaller shed. As they approached, a rustling caused Hunter to flinch and raise his pistols. Out of the corner of his eye, he sensed Gironi do the same. He stifled a laugh as a large rat scuttled into the weeds. He and Gironi exchanged sheepish glances. Hunter signaled to Scarpa that all was clear. He, in turn, pointed to the large barn before them.

A sagging roof still clung to the rafters on the left side of the barn, where half a large wooden door hung askew, but only weather-beaten timbers remained atop the right side. Hunter scanned the gaps in the stone block wall for a glint of sun on a pistol barrel, but he saw nothing. On his right, Bryskett edged closer, pausing every few feet. The Padovan guards did the same on his left.

Hunter heard a low moaning. A glance revealed the others had heard it too. Was Sidney in pain? He walked quickly ahead, but Bryskett hissed, "No. It may be a trap."

Together, pistols at the ready, they advanced. Captain Scarpa darted ahead and flattened himself against the wall next to the doorway. He stole a glance inside. His head snapped back to face the men, eyes and mouth open wide in shock. Disregarding Bryskett's warning, Hunter dashed to the doorway. Through the dust motes swirling in the slanting sunlight, he discerned four bodies covered in blood. Another lay in a dark corner. For a moment, he could make no sense of what he saw, but cried out, certain that Sidney had been slain.

CHAPTER 2

Murky Depths

A MUFFLED CRY ANSWERED HUNTER'S WAIL OF ANGUISH. AS HIS EYES adjusted, he made out the form of Philip Sidney, his head and shoulders leaning against a pile of roof tiles, his mouth gagged, and his hands and feet bound. Dust and grime covered his hose and doublet. Ignoring the shouted warnings behind him, Hunter leapt over the corpses of the abductors, dropped his pistols, and knelt next to Sidney. Their eyes met in relief and affection.

"Thank God you are alive. Are you hurt?" Hunter fumbled to untie the gag, avoiding the bruise and scratches on the left side of his face.

Sidney shook his head. When the knot was loosened, he gasped, "Water."

Hunter turned to call, but Bryskett already knelt beside them and lifted a leather flask to Sidney's parched lips. Hunter drew his knife and cut Sidney's cords.

"I am relieved to see you, Philip," Bryskett said in a shaky voice.

After a long draught, Sidney replied, "And I you—both of you. I am well, save for scratches and"—he touched his face—"a tender cheek."

Captain Scarpa and Corporal Molinari loomed over them with troubled expressions. Scarpa asked a question in Italian.

"Let me take another drink and I'll tell you what happened. Lodowick, you can translate for the captain." Sidney lifted the flask to his mouth, and then pulled himself onto a large block of stone. "You must already know that the men lying here drew me in a cart for almost a day. The young fair-haired one gave me bread and water late last night and in the early morning, but it must have had a potion, for I swooned and was unaware for many hours."

"They needed you to be so when they passed the frontiers," Hunter said.

"Frontiers?"

"Yes. We are in the Romagna. They carted you through Ferrara."

"I had no idea," Sidney said. "I thank God you followed so far." He took another drink. "When I awoke, they bound me again and carried me to this barn. They talked softly to one another, and I could make no sense of their words. Perhaps the potion still held me in thrall. I feared they were planning the best way to kill me, but my confused mind asked why they had not done so. Soon a half-dozen men in helms and breast-plates arrived, and my captors greeted them. They shared some wine. I could not understand what was happening. It seemed they intended to turn me over to those armed men, but suddenly they drew knives and slit the throats of my captors."

Hunter studied more carefully the corpses behind him. Each throat had indeed been slashed open. The nearest one's face bore a surprised expression. Why was Sidney involved in this ghastly business?

Sidney continued. "The armed men gazed at me and spoke, and I feared they would slay me as well. They appeared to reach a decision. Two lifted me, leaned me against those tiles, and spoke in a comforting tone. Then they rode away, taking the cart and horses of my captors. I have been lying here nearly two hours, as flies gathered about the corpses, wondering whether I had been left to starve, when I heard movement and speech outside. Thank God you came."

Hunter's body relaxed. "And thank God you avoided the fate of your captors." Drop by drop, questions about who was responsible for the capture and the killings began to fill his mind as worry for his friend drained away.

Scarpa, who had waited patiently, tapped Bryskett's shoulder and demanded he relate all Sidney had said. After he heard the account, he conferred with Corporal Molinari and gave orders to his guards, who began the grisly business of loading the bodies onto horses.

Bryskett explained. "We are going to an inn a few leagues hence, where we can take supper and rest for the night, while that papal guard rides to get help. A coroner will have to come to investigate, the corporal says."

Sidney rose stiffly and brushed the dirt from his doublet and hose. "I fear I will not give him all the answers he wants, as I have many questions myself."

"Did you recognize any of those who took you?" Hunter asked.

"None. Nor any of their murderers. But they wore helms like these guards." He nodded to Molinari's men.

Hunter turned to Bryskett. "Can you ask..." he began.

Bryskett frowned and shook his head.

Yes, a question linking the *romagnoli* guards and the murderers would be ill advised now. Hunter told himself he must be patient.

As they walked to the main road, Sidney placed his arm around Hunter's shoulder. "I am overjoyed to see you, Edward. I have been looking forward to your arrival. I did not think it would occasion your coming to rescue me. You have saved my life."

Though thankful for Sidney's affection, Hunter said, "I am only one of many. You must thank Lodowick and Captain Scarpa and his men."

"I shall. But for now, let me rejoice in our friendship."

To relieve his embarrassment, Hunter introduced Sidney to Gironi. "Your uncle loaned me Luca for this journey."

Sidney looked doubtfully. "Do I know you?"

"You may not remember," Gironi said, "but I saw you as a young scholar back from Shrewsbury, visiting your uncle."

"But you spoke Italian to the captain."

"Venetian actually. I was born in Venice," Gironi explained, "but my father sent me to a cousin in Antwerp to apprentice with a locksmith."

Hunter smiled. Gironi had skipped over the details he had told Hunter on the journey south. He had been apprenticed to a locksmith in Venice but had been spirited away to Antwerp after he had been discovered with his master's half-clothed daughter.

Gironi exchanged a quick glance with Hunter, then continued. "When Lord Leicester and the English forces came over to Flanders to fight the French, I ran off to join them. I did your uncle a service opening chests after the Battle of Saint Quentin. I have served him ever since."

"I have looked forward to sharing Padua and Venice with you," Sidney said to Hunter, "but perhaps Gironi can tell you more of Venice."

"It has been almost twenty years since I was in Venice," Gironi said. "I daresay much has changed."

"I will be grateful to hear all you have learned here in Italy," Hunter said. Perhaps talking about experiences other than his capture might divert his friend.

"And I to hearing about your travels hither," Sidney said.

They reached the main road, where they encountered Scarpa's third scout and his *romagnoli* companion, riding north toward them. The young scout first smiled to meet his comrades, then raised his brows in puzzlement at Scarpa's questions, shook his head vigorously, and raised his hands in a helpless gesture.

Gironi explained the exchange. "Scarpa thanked him for leaving the friar to direct us to the barn. Marco, the scout, said he did not speak with any friar, and he had found no one further south who had seen the cart, so he came back to find us."

"Then how did the friar know a party was in pursuit of a cart and riders? What did he say to Scarpa?" Hunter asked.

"You must ask Scarpa that," Gironi said, "though I would not do so now."

Scarpa was riding his mount around the partly collapsed building where he had seen the friar. From his expression, it was clear the cleric was nowhere to be found. He spurred back to the party and barked an order. His men, leading horses laden with corpses, started walking south.

"We are going to the inn," Gironi said.

Sidney and those who had ridden with Scarpa were the only patrons of the inn. The supper table buzzed with questions, posed and translated in English, Italian, and Venetian.

"Why did these dregs of Padua," whom Scarpa recognized and named, "snatch a notable Englishman and cart him here?"

"They must have been hired by someone who wished him harm," Bryskett answered. "But was that someone in the Romagna, in Padua, or in Venice?"

"Someone who had enough skill to forge a Venetian seal on this passport." Scarpa held up the folded document with its dangling seal. "We found this in the barn."

"How can you tell it is counterfeit?" Bryskett asked.

Scarpa pointed as he explained. "This is smaller than the proper seal, the lion's eyes are but slits, and its wings have too shallow an angle."

"May I see that, Captain?"

Scarpa passed the document to Bryskett. Sidney and Hunter leaned in on either side. Hunter concentrated to commit the details to memory.

"I swear this is the same as on the summons you received yesterday," Bryskett said.

"It certainly looks the same. I must have lost it when we were attacked," Sidney said.

Hunter said, "It makes sense that the same hand was behind the letter that led you into the ambuscade and this document presented by your captors."

Bryskett handed it back and told Scarpa their suspicions.

Scarpa nodded and asked, "Does Master Sidney have enemies in the Veneto?"

Sidney put down his wine with a dry laugh. "I must, it seems, but I'm at a loss to know who. Certainly not Philip, nor Otto, nor Johannes."

"I would scarce imagine German Protestants," Bryskett said. "But you have also spent time with many Catholics."

"Well, we *are* in Italy, Lodowick," Sidney replied. "I suppose you are objecting again to the English students at the university. Do you suspect my cousin Richard? He is halfway to Vienna by now. Certainly not Roger or James. And John—I have never met a merrier fellow. How could any of them have plotted my capture by those *bravi*?"

Hunter longed to know the surnames of those Sidney mentioned. They must be the Catholic students on the list Walsingham had given him, those the Earl of Leicester had charged him to investigate. Sidney's dismissive attitude worried him. "You may be too trusting, Philip. In Paris, you were convinced for a month that I was Paul Adams, then for a day that I was a Catholic traitor."

"I was wrong," Sidney said, "but I was right to trust you."

"But he was a spy all that time," Bryskett pressed.

Sidney threw up his hands. "I cannot distrust everyone I meet."

"Well," Hunter said, "someone certainly wishes you ill. Trusting too far did not serve us well in Paris." Why was his friend so unwilling to consider he had enemies?

"You cannot compare the hostile mood of Paris with Venice," Sidney argued.

Scarpa asked what the Englishmen were saying, and Bryskett explained.

"There are men I can question when we return to Padua." Scarpa sighed. "But even if we discover who lured Sidney to be captured and drew him hither, we still have to explain who murdered his captors and left him to be found."

"Did their helms not mark them as servants of the Romagna?" Bryskett asked.

"Our friend Corporal Molinari said such helms and breastplates are common," Scarpa said. "Any nobleman might equip his men with such gear."

"So, Sidney has a mysterious enemy *and* a mysterious savior," Bryskett said, switching to English and relating Scarpa's information. "Perhaps when Corporal Molinari returns with the coroner, we may learn more."

"What did the friar say to Captain Scarpa?" Hunter asked.

"The friar only asked if they sought a *careto* and riders, then pointed the way," Bryskett reported.

"What sort of friar was he?"

"Ah, you are not familiar with the clothing of different orders. This was a Black Friar, a *domini canis*, a hound of the Lord."

A Dominican, the order that made up the primary staff of the Inquisition. "The ragged friar was not an impressive representative." Hunter tried a different line of questions. "Scarpa said he could question men in Padua when he returned," Hunter said. "Can you ask him who?"

Bryskett shook his head. "Not if we want to stay on his good side. We cannot question him too closely on his investigation."

Sidney turned to him. "Lodowick, pray let us retire. Though I would know more, I can scarcely stay awake."

Sidney and Lodowick retreated to their chamber. Though Hunter regretted he would be unable to ask Sidney privately why he resisted speculation on who had ordered his capture, he was suddenly aware of his own exhaustion. Questions must wait.

Friday, 23 April 1574, An inn in the Romagna

The morning brought more disappointment. Hunter was unable to speak with Sidney alone. The bruise on his friend's face had turned a darker shade, and Bryskett reported his shoulders and hips were also bruised from his ride in the cart. The small beer was sour and the bread stale. As Hunter was finishing breakfast, he heard the clop of horses' hooves and the jingle of reins.

The stable lad burst in. "They are coming!"

All strode to the door. Riding toward them was Corporal Molinari, and by his side two in Dominican robes, one thin, tall, and young, his companion shorter and older. A half-dozen men followed them. Bryskett seized Sidney and Hunter by their elbows and pulled them inside.

"I had not imagined the coroner would be a cleric," he said, "and a Dominican to boot. We are not in Venetian territory, but a papal state."

Hunter realized what he was saying. In Venice, the Inquisition's influence was diminished by the Republic's desire to remain on good terms with trading partners in Protestant Europe and the Ottoman Empire. But here, the ruling prince was the pope himself, and the Inquisition reported directly to him. Three English Protestants could be seized and tried as heretics. "What can we do?"

"Remain calm. I am not here of my own free will," Sidney reasoned. "And both of you have come to rescue me. We must be as polite as possible." Despite his recent experience, Sidney seemed convinced nothing bad would happen to him.

Captain Scarpa and Corporal Molinari accompanied the Dominicans into the inn. Scarpa paused and pointed to Sidney. Beneath the taller Dominican's eyebrows, which joined to make a dark line, his hawk-like stare sent a shiver down Hunter's spine. The cleric nodded to Scarpa and proceeded to the stables with his attendants.

"What was that?" Hunter asked.

Sidney swallowed. "I hope he merely asked who had been captured"

The three friends gazed into the courtyard. The tall Dominican stood at a distance from the corpses in a stall while his shorter companion, who must be the coroner, poked at the bodies and ordered his men to lift and turn them over. Beside him, a thin clerk took notes. After a cursory look, the taller Dominican turned, and the Englishmen drew back.

The innkeeper whisked the Dominicans, Scarpa, Molinari, and the scribe into a smaller room. He invited the *romagnoli* attendants to enjoy a glass of wine with Gironi and the Padovan guards. Sidney, Hunter, and Bryskett stood uncertain, clearly not included in either group.

After some time, Scarpa and Molinari came out. Scarpa spoke to Bryskett, who reported, "The tall one is a vice inquisitor; the short one, the infirmarian from a nearby priory. They would like to interview Sidney now. I can come to translate."

Hunter and Sidney exchanged worried looks. That the officials were Dominicans was bad enough, but one of them held an important office in the Inquisition.

"Very well," Sidney said. Both entered, but Bryskett returned almost immediately. "They are speaking in Latin and have no need of me."

"What is the inquisitor asking?" Hunter asked.

"He wants to hear Sidney's story of his capture."

"Let us hope there are no questions of religion."

While anxious minutes passed, Scarpa ordered his men out of the bar and into the stable. Gironi strode over to Hunter and Bryskett. "The actions of the man-stealers are Padua's problem, so far as the vice inquisitor is concerned. The master of a close priory is content to bury them for a generous contribution from Scarpa. Because he has no desire to carry them back, he agreed. They will load the bodies on a cart."

Sidney returned, but shook his head at his friends and remained silent while the vice inquisitor, the coroner, and the scribe strode out of the inn. Scarpa and the servile innkeeper followed.

Hunter could hold his curiosity no longer. "What did the inquisitor ask you?"

"He wanted the story of my capture and transport here," Sidney answered. "He asked if I knew who might want me captured. He asked me to describe the men who murdered my captors. He asked how long I intended to remain in the Veneto. He seemed more interested in disposing quickly of an irritating annoyance than of discovering who was responsible for those bodies."

"Honestly?"

"He said, 'We have your description of them, and the appropriate investigations will be made.'"

"Did he ask about religion?" Hunter asked.

"He said he assumed that I was one of those Englishmen who did not recognize the authority of the pope."

"And you said?"

"That he was correct. Why lie?"

Bryskett sucked in air. "Your rash gambol across Italy has emboldened you too much. Do you forget what just happened to you?"

"My capture was obviously not the work of the vice inquisitor. He reminded me we were in papal territory and recommended that we stay here for as little time as possible."

"Let us heed his words," Bryskett said.

Gironi chimed in. "Captain Scarpa plans to leave as soon as the villains are buried. We should sleep in Venetian territory tonight."

Sidney spent the ride to Santa Maria Maddalena telling Hunter of his visits to Heidelberg, Frankfurt, Strasburg, Bratislava, and Vienna, and the notables he had met in those places. Although Sidney mentioned meeting Hubert Languet, whom they had known in Paris, both he and Hunter avoided speaking of the slaughter they had witnessed there. Instead, Sidney recalled the celebrations they had attended together and the days when Hunter had shown him Parisian sights. He now was eager to introduce Hunter to Venice and Padua in the same fashion. Throughout his narration, Hunter continued to worry. Although Sidney was in no danger now, in the company of Captain Scarpa and his men, would he be safe back in Padua? He had been attacked there once. Though those men had been slain, others might attempt another assault. Would he take greater precautions? Keeping his friend from harm might prove more difficult than he had thought.

"Pardon me," Sidney interrupted his thoughts. "I have been speaking without a rest. What have you been doing since we bid farewell in Paris?"

Hunter suppressed his worry about Sidney's welfare, instead confessing to a more boring eighteen months than Sidney, resting in Hertfordshire, then working for his Uncle George Babcock in London, writing letters and contracts. He related his adventures and misadventures during his journey south with Gironi.

At the inn in Santa Maria Maddalena, Hunter drew Bryskett aside. "You mentioned 'enemies' yesterday. I have had no chance to ask you whom you meant."

"I did say that 'enemies' was not the right term. The attack on us has led me to consider everyone again. The German and Polish nobles we have met in Venice are all Protestants with titles. They have no reason to envy Philip or oppose his religion." Bryskett paused and firmed his lips.

"Philip said as much. What about the Catholic expatriates?"

"That is another story. They are jolly enough when Philip shares a drink or a meal, but any of them might be jealous of his circumstances— his wealth and position. Though they seem to ignore it, the fact that he is a Protestant links him with forces that oppose their religion. He can return to England, while they are trapped in exile, far from their families."

Hunter frowned. "You have given me things to consider, but are any of them reason enough to capture and transport him?"

Bryskett sighed. "Unlikely."

"Do you believe it would be safest for Philip to leave Italy?"

"Of course I do," Bryskett said. "I argued against our coming, but I am not the deciding voice."

"Will you urge him anew to leave, now that this has occurred?"

"I have tried in vain before now. Perhaps he will listen to a new voice. Will you try to persuade him?"

Hunter hesitated. He had not yet seen Venice, that fabled city floating on the water. He had promised to negotiate silk contracts for his uncle and the Earl of Leicester. Of course, the earl had engaged him to ensure the safety of his nephew. If any harm came to Sidney, silk bargains would account for nothing. "I will try."

Hunter joined Sidney in his room, glasses of wine on the table between them. "How long do you intend to remain in Italy?" he began.

"Through the summer." Sidney eyed him warily and sipped his wine.

"Considering the jeopardy you just escaped, would it not be wise to leave sooner?"

"You sound like Bryskett and Languet."

So as not to appear in league with Bryskett, Hunter retreated from the topic of leaving Italy. "You said earlier that Languet taught you much in Paris and afterwards."

"Yes. I owe him a great deal. He has immense knowledge of modern politics and insight into the motives of men. He introduced me to many at the Imperial Court in Vienna, found me an Italian tutor there, supplied me with letters of introduction to men in Venice, wrote me a program of study, and he sends a letter every week with suggestions of books I might read."

"Your face suggests you might welcome a little less advice." Hunter swallowed a mouthful of wine.

Sidney nodded. "Hubert means well, but I believe he wants to shape me into a leader for the Protestant cause in Europe. I have a high regard for him, but my travels have allowed me to escape from parental oversight, and I am unwilling for him to become my substitute father."

Hunter sensed an opening. "You said Languet found you an Italian tutor. Was he therefore a more understanding father?"

"After I made clear to him I meant to come to Italy, he relented."

Hunter lowered his head and looked at Sidney like a teacher to a pupil. "Did you tell him of *all* your Italian travel plans?"

"No. Not even Bryskett knew about my journey to Florence."

"He believes that your capture was related to that excursion."

Sidney placed his glass on a stool. "I do not see how it could be."

"Dear friend, do you intend to dismiss all dangers until you meet a fatal one? *Someone* wanted you carried south to the Papal States. Is that not sufficient reason to ride out of Italy?"

"That someone wanted me in papal lands must be true." Sidney raised an objecting forefinger. "But someone likewise wished to release me."

"That is even more mysterious, I agree."

"If I leave Italy now, neither mystery will be solved," Sidney said.

He had struck one of Hunter's weak spots. To leave a mystery unsolved was like a burr on his saddle. Nevertheless, he said, "Better an unexplained mystery than a dead friend."

"You are exaggerating," Sidney said. "If someone wanted me dead, my attackers would have killed me."

Hunter tried another tack. "Bryskett worries about your friendship with the Catholic expatriates at the university."

"That again." Sidney snorted and looked away.

"But your passport forbids you from communicating with English exiles."

Sidney faced Hunter again, and his eyes grew serious. "Edward, I know that my uncle is not supporting your journey so that you may amuse yourself with me in Italy. You are to investigate and report on me. I would have mentioned this before, save that *your* watcher, Luca, has been with us until now."

"I told you I am acting as an agent for my uncle, to obtain supplies of raw and finished silk." Hunter looked into Sidney's accusing eyes and sighed. "But you are right. I am to report to your uncle. But, as you said of Languet, he means well, as do I. We do not want you to come to harm."

"I did not urge you to join me here to substitute for my father and uncle."

Hunter sighed. "You spoke of escaping, but you will always be the son and nephew of honored families. Your position is assured. I haven't the luxury to choose a vagabond life. If some ill befalls you, I fail in my mission. As a second son without prospects, I will be doomed to copy land contracts to the end of my days."

"God forbid. I have no wish for you to be blamed for my mistakes, but your fear is not reason enough for me to leave Italy." Sidney threw up his hands. "We were both in greater peril in Paris than here. I would have stayed at Penshurst if I had sought total safety."

"Now you are the one exaggerating," Hunter said.

Sidney pressed his argument. "What safety can be assured if I leave Italy? I may fall from my horse in Saxony or be captured by pirates in the Channel. No, I have striven too long and hard to gain a little freedom to go running back to the arms of my family now."

Hunter pressed in return. "Would leaving Italy force you to admit your uncle and Languet were right?"

Sidney's brows clouded with anger. "And suppose they were?" He closed his eyes and composed himself with a deep breath. "I cannot deny my pride is involved. I shall stay at least a month. You must agree there are mysteries to solve."

Hunter ignored the invitation to agree. "What will you do now to ensure yourself against an attack?"

Sidney ticked off points on his fingers. "I shall certainly be more on my guard. With you and Gironi here, I will have two more companions to travel with. I will ask Captain Scarpa if an officer might observe our lodgings daily. Do you have further suggestions?"

"Will you take an oath that if any further danger appears, you will leave Italy?"

Sidney took another draught of wine. "I swear that I will consider it."

That appeared to be as much as Hunter could wring from him. He felt relieved, wanting to explore Italy himself. His relief was short lived. He imagined Sidney suffering a fatal end and himself confessing to Lord Leicester that he had failed to force his nephew to safety because he wished to see Venice. He vowed he would stay near his friend and would question the expatriate Catholics closely.

"So," Sidney folded his arms over his chest, "what will you do concerning your promises to my uncle?"

"I must write him. I have given my word to do so and, as you note, Luca will do so if I do not."

Sidney nodded.

"But I can share what I am going to send. I did not promise my letters would be secret."

Sidney smiled. "I would be grateful. But it is best I write first to tell of my unfortunate adventure and assure him I am well."

Hunter was relieved. "I am glad." A cloud of doubt quickly followed. "Will you tell him of your gallop to Florence? Bryskett and Gironi may reveal it."

Sidney sighed. "I must. But I shall stress how I regret my folly and will not connect it with my capture."

"*He* may make that connection."

"I cannot help that. I shall also stress the care you and Bryskett took to rescue me."

"Thanks. I will also say that I encourage you to abandon Italy."

"Do so. I can present myself as the obstinate youth."

Hunter cast a mischievous glance. "That should not be difficult."

Sidney gave a dry laugh. "Upon second thought, I may say nothing praising you."

Hunter smiled in his turn. "While you take extra care, I intend to discover what I can of your capture. I know you trust those you have met in Padua and Venice, but I intend to look at your acquaintances with new eyes, and I ask you to do the same."

Sidney bit his lip, then nodded. "Very well. We are agreed that someone wishes me ill, and he is best discovered; that we shall consult over letters to mine uncle; that I shall mount better guard upon myself; and that I shall consider quitting Italy if I am attacked again. Let us shake hands to seal our bargain."

CHAPTER 3

Surface Reflections

Saturday, 24 April 1574, Padua

LATE IN THE AFTERNOON AT PADUA'S PONTECORVO GATE, CAPTAIN SCARPA left them. Though he could not spare a man to guard their residence, he promised to report what he discovered of those who had captured Sidney.

At their lodgings at Pozzo della Vacca, Sidney and Bryskett had scarcely had time to relate their adventures to Madox and White when the door burst open and four young men burst in, calling "Philip!" almost in unison.

These are the Catholic students I am to appraise, Hunter thought, as each one embraced Sidney and Bryskett and declared his relief at their safe return.

Sidney pried himself loose, "Gentlemen, I thank you for coming to greet me."

"We aim at more than that," said the shortest of the group, a man of light brown hair and a thin beard along his jaw line, wearing a modest brown doublet and trunk-hose. "We will treat you to supper at the Owl."

"I am grateful for your offer," Sidney protested, "but our housekeeper Beatrice is preparing a special meal in honor of our return and I am weary from my journey, both to and from."

"Then we must have your company on the morrow," the short man said, "but, if you are not spent completely, could you tell us what happened to you?"

"I have force enough for that," Sidney replied, "but I must first introduce Edward Hunter, recently arrived from England."

All turned toward Hunter.

"Edward, this is Jack Hart, from Oxfordshire." The short man who had issued the invitation extended his hand. His grip was firm. "Jack has introduced me to the music of Andrea Gabrielli in San Marco's."

Hunter chalked up another item that would concern Lord Leicester. Hart had convinced Sidney to attend services in Venice's Catholic basilica.

"Hart smiled. "Those who cannot sing or play must listen."

"And this is Roger Fitzwilliams," Sidney said, "a Yorkshireman."

Hunter's heart raced. Might Fitzwilliams know him from his work as a spy during the Northern Rebellion? "What part of Yorkshire are you from?"

"The West Riding, near Leeds."

Hunter relaxed. His time in Yorkshire with the Spranklins had been near Thirsk, forty miles away. He took in Fitzwilliams's tall figure, full curly beard and moustache, long, thin nose, thin eyebrows, and the silver buttons on his black doublet. His bearing declared him to be a proud man. His handshake was less firm than Hart's.

"And James Randolph," Sidney continued, "from Gloucestershire."

Randolph had a high forehead, crowned with thick, black hair. His chin was clean shaven, and his spotty moustache showed he had had difficulty growing a beard. As if to make up for that, he sported a large black patch of hair beneath his full bottom lip. His eyes looked wary, rather than friendly, and he offered his hand with some reluctance.

"Last of this rabble," Sidney said, eliciting laughter, "is John Le Rous, from Suffolk, and a Doctor of Civil and Canon Law from the University of Padua."

Le Rous's red hair and beard accorded with his name. He wore a lion-tawny doublet and venetian breeches. His broad face lit with a smile as he shook Hunter's hand warmly.

"Did you receive your degree recently, Doctor Le Rous?" Hunter asked. His companions laughed.

"Just John, if you please. My friends laugh because they are not used to my being addressed by my title. I received it in seventy-one, but I am not welcome back in England just now, and I have found Padua agreeable."

Le Rous's comment suggested he did not miss his family or feel trapped in Italy. Hunter moved him mentally down his list of suspects.

"Gentlemen, let us sit round the table." Sidney gestured. "You see that Madox and White, who have already heard this tale, and Bryskett, who was forced to live it, have prepared jugs of wine to help you endure my narrative."

The expatriates seated themselves on a bench opposite Sidney. Bryskett sat to his right, saying, "I am here to correct errors in his story, and to stress how he frightened us to death."

"Surely I am not responsible for your fright, but rather the villains who carted me off," Sidney objected.

"Granted, but still I must relate all those hours when Philip was sleeping, and we were busy riding in pursuit," Bryskett said.

Madox filled their cups and sat to Sidney's left. "If that is the case, I will have to tell what occurred when you both were unaware."

"Please, sirs," Fitzwilliams said, "tell us your story, rather than bickering."

While Sidney, Madox, and Bryskett narrated their story, Hunter sat observing the expatriates.

James Randolph kept casting wary glances at Hunter. Why was he so uneasy?

Roger Fitzwilliams added exclamations—"How dare they?" "What insolence!" and "Low-born beasts"—that suggested he would never stoop to speaking to such rogues as apprehended Sidney. Was he protesting too much? Could a gentleman find a middleman who would contract ruffians, keeping his hands clean?

Jack Hart exhibited the most concern for Sidney's health and well-being, asking, "How could you endure such an ordeal?" and advising, "You must rest for several days."

John Le Rous cleaned the fingernails of one hand with those of another, then repeated the process. Was he particularly nervous just now, or was this a constant habit? Were those pieces of wax he dislodged? Could he be the forger of Venetian seals? Le Rous moved back to the top of the suspect list.

Their exclamations of concern all seemed genuine, as Bryskett spun out the story of pursuit, occasionally calling on Hunter to confirm or expand on a point. Sidney inserted his groggy understanding of what had happened during the journey. When he described the killing of his captors, all the expatriates displayed confusion.

"I expected Scarpa's men rescued you," Le Rous exclaimed, "not strange armed men." His companions agreed.

"And you never saw the armored rescuers again?" Fitzwilliams asked.

"Never," Sidney said.

"Could they have been following you?" Hart asked.

"From Padua?" Bryskett said. "No. Scarpa's scouts would have caught up with them. No one we questioned as we rode south mentioned such a force. We believe they came from within the Papal States."

"Why would papal forces kill those man-stealers?" Hart asked. "Did you ask the authorities there?"

Sidney laughed. "Such authorities as we met were not to be questioned by us." He told of his encounter with the vice inquisitor.

"I am glad you returned to Venetian jurisdiction safely," Hart said. "Despite my faith, I do not wish to see my Protestant friends burned."

"I believe the vice inquisitor you describe is Antonio Fascetti," Fitzwilliams announced.

Everyone turned in his direction.

"How do you know this?" Randolph asked.

"Doctor Simmons spoke to me of him." Fitzwilliams smiled with the satisfaction of knowing more than the others. "Though he is the vice inquisitor, Fascetti is effectively in charge in Bologna, as Inquisitor Morandi is very ill."

Hunter filed away questions to ask Fitzwilliams later: Did he have personal communications with the Bologna inquisitors? Whom did he think might have hired the men who captured Sidney? Who was Doctor Simmons?

His thoughts were interrupted when Randolph asked, "Master Hunter, pray tell us why you have come to Padua?"

Before he could answer, Sidney said, "I met Edward in Paris, where he was an agent promoting the establishment of an English Staple in Rouen. We sheltered together in the English Embassy during the Saint Bartholomew's Day Massacre."

The expatriates lowered their eyes. Despite the fact that Pope Gregory had issued medals to celebrate the massacre, these Catholics appeared reluctant to applaud the slaughter of thousands of French Protestants.

Fitzwilliams looked up first. "A deplorable incident, but you must admit that the Valois dynasty faced a *coup d'etat*, and that any ruler is justified in defending himself."

The other expatriates looked up, heartened by his explanation.

Hunter had heard this defense before, but did not believe its premise, that King Charles IX faced a rebellion. However, he needed to gain the trust of the expatriates if he were to discover their own thoughts, innocent of not, regarding the legitimacy of Queen Elizabeth. Yet he could not sheepishly agree. "I grant you a prince must defend himself, *or herself*, against threats," he paused to make sure his hearers absorbed how the defense could be used by both sides, "but I think a prince could arrest rebels and try them, rather than launching the slaughter of thousands of innocents throughout the country."

Hart and Le Rous nodded.

Fitzwilliams pursed his lips. "Yes. The reaction was lamentable."

"Princes must weigh how the rabble will react to their acts," Hunter said. That should appeal to Fitzwilliams's disdain of the lower classes.

"Indeed," Fitzwilliams agreed.

"I cannot conclude that King Charles made his throne more secure," Bryskett said. "The Protestants rule the Midi now, in defiance of him."

"I regret if my question caused us to dispute religion or politics," Randolph said, "but I still hope to discover what brought you to Italy, Master Hunter. Was it merely your love for Philip?"

"That certainly is the major factor," Hunter said. "But both our uncles hope to promote the production of silk cloth in England. I am to contact silk producers here to obtain a supply of thread." His uncle's other wishes must remain hidden.

"Vicenza produces more thread than Padua," Randolph said. "Do you intend to go there?"

"I have the names of several of what the Italians call *setaioli* to contact in Padua and there."

Sidney yawned.

"Gentlemen," Hart said, "we have already tired Philip for too long. We must thank him for the wine and the story of his capture and bid him good-bye."

The expatriates rose and offered their thanks and farewells. As Sidney accompanied them to the door, Hunter knelt by Le Rous's chair and picked up small pieces of pale wax. By adding red dye, one could produce sealing wax.

After he closed the door, Sidney turned to Hunter. "Well, do you believe my friends to be the dangerous influences that my uncle, and perhaps Bryskett, fear them to be?"

"I would be foolish to pronounce a judgment on such short acquaintance," Hunter said. "I hope to speak with each of them further during my stay. My love for you is such that I wish to make sure none of them hides a secret design."

Sidney shrugged. "You must satisfy yourself."

"I thought you agreed to look at your acquaintances with new eyes." Hunter opened his palm. "Le Rous flicked bits of wax from his nails. What do you make of that?"

"If you combine candle ends for economy, you might catch wax in your nails. That is no evidence he produced false seals."

Hunter frowned at the facile explanation.

"We agreed that whoever wishes me ill should be discovered," Sidney continued. "I thought *you* were undertaking that task. I never agreed to distrust my friends."

Hunter bristled. "I trusted that with you I need not play the lawyer. Should I have written down our bargain and examined every tittle?"

Sidney placed a hand on his shoulder. "Do not be crusty with me. I swear that, if you find evidence against one of them, I shall mark him as untrustworthy."

Hunter kept his shoulder tense. "I should hope you will. They all arrived at the same time. Had they met together to consult before they came?"

"They live together. Or rather, Hart, Fitzwilliams, and Randolph live in a house Le Rous rents." Sidney sniffed. "But it seems the supper must be done. Let us eat and go to bed."

Hunter could not object to Sidney's suggestion. After Sidney's party was seated at table, the smiling Beatrice carried in two roasted capons with pride and her son followed with a platter of carrots, peas, and spinach. When Sidney complimented her, her cheeks flushed red. After she retired to the kitchen, Hunter continued with his questions. Sidney explained, between bites, that Fitzwilliams was particularly interested in the Roman Catholic hierarchy and that Doctor Simmons was an Englishman who had graduated from the University of Padua over a decade before and now tutored candidates in civil and canon law. No, he had not been aware that Randolph had a particular interest in silk production. He considered Gabrielli's music beautiful and believed attending Mass with John Hart at San Marco had no more damaged his spiritual welfare than Hunter's attendance of Catholic services in Paris when he was a spy. Sidney finally requested an end to interrogation, saying his brain was too tired to answer more questions.

In their chamber, Hunter asked Gironi "Luca, why were you tardy for supper?"

"I contrived to care for the horses when the guests arrived," Gironi said. "Servants can tell you much about their masters."

Hunter nodded approval. "What did you learn?"

"The four men share two servants. Master Le Rous rents a house owned by the Soranzos of Venice, near Santa Maria del Torresino. The others are his boarders."

"Sidney told me most of that."

"All were at the house at the time of the attack on Sidney's party."

Hunter grunted. "I would hardly expect them to assault Sidney themselves."

"Of course. When I broached the subject of who the attackers might be, they suspected Tommaso Biradi's men. He controls a number of *bravi* for hire and can be found at *La Testa dell' Ariete* near the ghetto."

"An excellent bit of information gathering, Luca," Hunter said. "I must visit the Ram's Head."

Gironi raised his eyebrows. "You, sir? From what the servants said, a gentleman would not frequent such a disrespectable tippling house. It will be better if I have some drinks there."

Hunter had to agree. Though Hunter's Latin and the services of a guide from Magdeburg had served them in German states, Gironi's skill in Italian and Venetian was now more important.

Sunday, 25 April 1574, Padua

Beatrice, moving with surprising speed for one with such a substantial frame, served a breakfast of fried eggs and freshly baked bread the next morning. The gentlemen of the party were still in their shirts and trunk hose when John Fisher announced that one Master Barnes had arrived.

"Barnes?" This was not a name Hunter had been given in England.

"Another of Philip's Catholic student friends," Bryskett said, with a disapproving face. "Wealthy enough to rent lodgings inside the city walls, near the *Palazzo Bo*."

"All true," Sidney said. "But let us not keep Ambrose waiting." He nodded to Fisher to show Barnes in.

All rose to greet their guest, a thin young man, slightly taller than either Hunter or Sidney, with a high forehead, serious blue eyes, and full lips.

"Philip," he exclaimed. "How delightful to see you well, with"—he touched Sidney's cheek—"only minor damage. Pray excuse my early arrival, but I had to assure myself that the reports of others were true." He shifted his gaze to Hunter.

"Ambrose Barnes, this is my friend Edward Hunter, newly arrived from England," Sidney said.

"Pleased to meet you," Barnes said. "You must be the one seeking *setaioli*."

Hunter raised his eyebrows in surprise. "You are well informed."

"I spoke with Fitzwilliams and company at the Owl last night."

"Good," Sidney said with relief. "Then Bryskett and I need not relate our adventure."

"Roger and Jack painted the picture in broad strokes but did not include every detail."

"Nor can Philip," Bryskett said. "He was sleeping most of the time."

"So I hear," Barnes said. "But I pray he will be kind enough to entertain my questions."

"I shall," Sidney said, "but let us sit. Have you broken your fast? Beatrice was out early and purchased a delicious loaf."

Barnes waved away the offer and sat with Sidney, Hunter, Bryskett, Madox, and White, while Fisher cleared the table.

Gironi caught Hunter's eye. "The nags will want to break their fast as well," he said, heading to the door. Hunter nodded consent.

Sidney spread his hands. "Ask away, Ambrose."

"First, I wonder that you did not recognize any of those who captured you," Barnes said.

"I had little time to do so before I was stunned. When one gave me bread and water, it was the middle of the night. The only time I had to observe them was when we stopped in the Romagna. I remember a scar on the forehead of one man with thinning hair and a black beard on another, but they kept distance from me. Then the others arrived, and my captors were killed."

"We did not spend a lot of time looking at the corpses," Bryskett said. "But Captain Scarpa recognized them and said he would investigate."

"Did he say whom he would question?" Barnes asked.

"Tommaso Biradi," Bryskett said.

"Aaah." Barnes's syllable indicated recognition.

This was the second time Hunter had heard the name. "Does he arrange captures?"

"They say that no crime takes place in Padua without his knowledge," Bryskett explained.

"Have you any guess as to your saviors?" Barnes asked.

"None," Sidney said.

"Perhaps they had a feud with those who captured you."

Sidney shook his head in doubt. "Do rogues travel so far from Padua to carry on feuds?"

"If his captors took him all that way," Bryskett put in, "it can only be they were hired to transport him to papal territory."

"That makes some sense." Barnes sounded unconvinced. "But as it is clear someone means you harm, Philip, I urge you to appeal to the Council of Ten for permission to bear arms in the Veneto."

"Do you think they will grant such a privilege to foreigners?" Sidney asked.

"I do not know," Barnes said. "But last night Captain Scarpa's report would have reached Padua's *podestà*. Today it will be on its way to Venice. It will be a strong argument in favor of allowing you to bear arms. I suspect the Ten will be embarrassed by your capture. If you care to write a request in your best Italian, I can have one of my servants take it to Venice overnight on the *padovane*. The Ten meet on Wednesdays. You may be invited to appear before them then.

"Master Barnes has made an excellent proposal," Bryskett said. "Although, as your best Italian is plagued with errors, I suggest you write in Latin."

Sidney nodded. "I will do it—and in Latin."

"I assure you my Italian is similarly plagued," Barnes said.

Though impressed with Barnes's suggestion, Hunter wanted information. "This Biradi you speak of. Why would he want Sidney transported to the Romagna?"

Barnes smiled. "Biradi would not care one way or the other. He arranges what others pay for."

"Who in Padua might employ him? Has Philip insulted some Italian gentleman?"

"Have you offended someone, Philip?" Barnes asked.

"Me?" Sidney threw up his hands. "I swear I have not."

"An Englishman, then?" Hunter asked.

Barnes's face clouded over for a moment before he recovered and turned to Bryskett. "I do not wish to accuse anyone falsely, but one Englishman is known to haunt the Ram's Head."

Bryskett nodded. "Charles Carr."

"Surely he would have no grudge against me," Sidney protested.

"Who is this Carr?" Hunter asked.

"Over a year ago he lodged with Le Rous, Fitzwilliams, Hart, and Randolph." Sidney sighed. "But I fear he was too fond of gambling and drink."

"And loose women," Bryskett added.

"He withdrew from the university," Sidney resumed, "and, after forgiving him many debts, Le Rous finally asked him to leave his house."

"I believe he now lodges near the ghetto," Barnes concluded.

Hunter mentally added Carr to his list of suspects and began to consider ways to engage each of them. Could he ask one or more of them to show him part of Padua, instead of Sidney? Could Randolph introduce him to silk dealers? Might he ask Fitzwilliams more about clerics? What questions might discover any envy of Sidney's wealth or position?

The bells of Saint Anthony's Basilica began to chime. Barnes straightened up. "It is time for the late Mass. I must bid you farewell."

All walked to the door with him.

"Thank you for your visit and your advice," Sidney said.

"I was pleased to meet you," Hunter added.

As Barnes and his servants led their horses toward the basilica, Hunter asked Gironi, "What did you learn?"

"Neither Christopher nor Francis are happy to be in Italy, to start."

"Why?"

"Simply missing their home. They do not speak the language, the food is strange, the merchants cheat them—the usual complaints."

Hunter shrugged. "But about Barnes?"

"He does not complain about being here. Though they were loath to speak ill of their master, when I pressed, they admitted to being perplexed. He is not the same man they arrived with last autumn. His humors change by the week. A month ago he was choleric and shouted at them for little cause. Last week, he was sanguine and full of joy. Yesterday he appeared melancholy. They set it down to bad air rising from the river."

"So they are physicians, are they?"

"If so, their patient is a mystery to them."

"What was his humor in England?"

"Sanguine, they said."

"Well, Barnes promised one of them could take Sidney's request to bear arms to the Council of Ten."

Gironi nodded his approval. "Seems a good idea, after what has passed."

CHAPTER 4

Paddling About

Monday, 26 April 1574 Padua

SIDNEY AND BRYSKETT ESCORTED HUNTER ABOUT PADUA DURING THE morning, pointing out the tomb of Antenor, Padua's Trojan founder, and the enormous clock on the entrance to the *Palazzo del Capitanio*, where Captain Scarpa's office was. In answer to Hunter's questions, Bryskett indicated the ghetto to the south, and the general direction of Barnes's lodgings to the north. They strolled through the *Piazza dei Frutti* and the *Piazza delle Erbe* and met James Randolph at midday at an eating house. He conducted them around the *Palazzo del Bo*, indicating the crests of famous families and exclaiming on the virtues of the university housed there. He offered to show them the university's botanical gardens, but Hunter claimed he was exhausted and needed a rest. In reality, he wanted to return and hear what Gironi had learned at the Ram's Head.

"The patrons were morose," Gironi reported. "As sour as their wine. They said some friends had been killed somewhere south of Ferrara. They did not know the details. When I asked the names of their companions, it almost sounded as though Master Sidney had been taken by evangelists—Matteo, Marco, Luca, and Pietro. The last one ruined the set."

Hunter gave a mirthless laugh.

Gironi continued. "Master Biradi, the chief criminal, left town suddenly to visit a sick aunt in Verona, or perhaps Bergamo. Luigi, my informant, was uncertain. Two of Biradi's underlings were not so quick; Scarpa arrested them as horse thieves. The others found a sudden need to visit friends out of town, like their master."

"Excellent work," Hunter said. "You gathered more useful information in a few hours than I did all day."

"Ah, but you no doubt absorbed more culture, history, and architecture."

"So I did, but just now I would prefer to discover who aims to harm Sidney. Did Luigi mention that?"

"No. He seemed not to know what the slain men were doing in the Romagna."

"Did you ask for Charles Carr?"

"He was not there today."

A rapping downstairs caused them to leave their chamber. At the door, Harry White took a message from Barnes's man Christopher and handed it to Sidney.

"I am in Master Barnes's debt," Sidney exclaimed. "The Council of Ten requests that I present myself Wednesday afternoon, to expound my request that we may go armed about the Veneto."

Wednesday, 28 April 1574, Venice

Hunter stood in the middle of Saint Mark's Square, agog. Before him stood the basilica, its arched entrances surrounded with sparkling mosaics and statues honoring Venice's guilds and seasons, its four bronze horses so life-like he expected them to leap into the piazza, and rising above them yet more arches, angel statues, and cross-topped domes. To his right, two stories of evenly spaced arches supported the shimmering pink and white majesty of the Doge's Palace. Nobles in black robes huddled and walked together before it in Venice's political center, the vague area known as the *broglio*, where alliances and bargains were agreed. Farther to his right towered the red brick *campanile*, with Gabriel balancing on its peak. At its base stood Sansovino's gleaming new *Loggetta*. He turned slowly, followed marching arches and construction around to San Geminiano at the square's west end, then traced more arches on the north side back to the clock tower, with its "moors" waiting patiently above Saint Mark's winged lion for the hour to arrive so they might strike the bell.

"I am duly impressed," Hunter said. "Such splendor, such beauty, such wealth. No wonder the 'Most Serene Republic' is renowned throughout Europe."

"It is enough to make you believe all the boasting the Venetians do," Sidney said.

"You are not convinced?"

"That theirs is the ideal form of government, a republic that combines the advantages of monarchy, aristocracy, and democracy?"

"Well, that is hard to gauge from architecture," Hunter admitted.

"But the buildings are meant to impress, and they do. You have yet to voyage up the Grand Canal. The palaces there rival those of any nobleman in Europe."

Around Hunter swirled men of many countries: Turks whose turbans bobbed back and forth as they walked, merchants whose apparel marked them as German, Jews with their yellow caps. As well as the guttural sounds of German, phrases in Greek, Latin, French, and several dialects of Italian floated toward him. A swirl of black and white robes caught his eye, and he froze.

"What is it?" Sidney asked.

"A pair of Dominicans."

Sidney followed his gaze. Two friars, one two heads taller than his rotund companion, walked briskly toward the clock tower. "Yes. But you should not worry here, in the heart of *La Serenissima*. The last time we encountered the 'hounds of the heretics' it was more dangerous, and we rode away unscathed."

"Your 'all is well that ends well' philosophy worries me," Hunter said. "Give me something to write your uncle that shows you will be cautious."

Sidney cocked his head in a superior attitude. "You may tell him I am requesting the Council of Ten grant permission for me and my servants to bear arms in Venetian territory."

Hunter admitted defeat for the moment. "And when are you to appear before the Council?"

Sidney looked up at the *Torre dell'Orologio*. "Before the moors strike three, Bryskett and I must be on our way. I expect we will face a good deal of suspicious looks and waiting. I will leave you in Luca's capable hands."

"And my brother should be along soon," Bryskett added.

Sidney and Bryskett walked across the *Piazzetta* and through the *Porta della Carta*, beneath a carved doge kneeling before Saint Mark's lion.

Beside him, Gironi smiled. "All so familiar, yet so different. Much remains from twenty years ago, yet new buildings have risen and old disappeared." He shook his head. "But we may not spend all afternoon staring about the piazza. When you meet Bryskett's brother, I hope to search out if my cousin Stefano is still at his shop."

"I pray you have a joyful reunion." As the moors on the clock tower began to strike, a tall man strode from the entryway beneath it and headed for the central flagpole. He turned in profile to scan the crowd, and the ridge of his nose was a duplicate of Lodowick Bryskett's. "I will wager that is Sebastian."

"I shall not bet with you," Gironi said. "The resemblance is too great."

Sebastian Bryskett broke into a smile when he saw them approach. "Good day. You must be Edward Hunter."

"I am," Hunter took his hand. "And this is my man, Luca Gironi."

Bryskett raised his eyebrows. "Gironi? You are Italian, then?"

"Si," Gironi said with a smile. "I was born here, but I have lived the last seventeen years in England."

"Your background is much as mine," Bryskett said. "My father came to England at the time of King Henry, but from Genoa. Do you still have relatives here?"

A cloud crossed Gironi's face. "I am unsure. I know my parents both died some years ago. I may have a cousin in Cannaregio. I hope to make enquiries today."

"Yes," Hunter added. "Madox and White took our cases to Sidney's lodgings in the French Embassy at *Palazzo Michiel*, so we are unencumbered."

"Good," the senior Bryskett said. "Gironi, you may enquire after your cousin now. I can take charge of Master Hunter and deliver him to his lodgings before sunset."

Gironi started to turn away, then turned and asked Hunter, "Sir?"

Hunter hesitated a moment, as Gironi's status had drifted from servant to guide and indispensable translator since they had reached the Veneto. "I am agreeable."

"Then I will take my leave." Gironi headed to the gondolas rocking at the end of the *Piazzetta*.

"My brother's message said Master Sidney wanted to show you the wonders of Venice himself," Bryskett said, "so I shall introduce you to some things he will not."

"What might those be?" Hunter asked.

A sly smile crossed Bryskett's face. "You shall see. Do you not relish surprises?"

"The pleasant type."

"I assure you they will be pleasant. Let us set forth." Bryskett led him through the gateway beneath the clock tower.

As they wound their way through crowds on the *Merceria*, Hunter lagged behind, staring at shops displaying luxuries and the varied arches and columns rising above them. Bryskett paused at the top of the Rialto Bridge, to allow Hunter to take in his surroundings. Before him palazzi rose on either side of the Grand Canal, each façade an impressive combination of arches, windows, and balconies in an array of styles. Sebastian named the families who dwelt in each grand house, then named the various craft plying the Grand Canal. Gondolas wove their way between *batele, sandoli, caroline*, and *peate*. On the opposite side, Sebastian pointed out the murals of Giorgione and Titian on the side of the *Fondaco dei Tedeschi*. When they descended to the San Polo side of the Rialto, Hunter continued to dawdle near the vegetable and fish markets.

"Pray follow, or you will be lost," Bryskett chided. He led Hunter through zigzagging lanes to a smaller bridge. Hunter stopped to scan the buildings on either side of the canal.

"If you stop on every bridge in Venice, you shall never get anywhere," Bryskett said.

"Pray remember this is all new to me, Master Bryskett," Hunter said. "I have never seen buildings such as these, rising from the water as if by an enchantment."

"Ah, the Queen of the Adriatic has seduced you, has she?"

"I certainly marvel at her beauty."

"If you have an eye for beauty, I will show you more," Bryskett said. "Pray follow."

They soon emerged into an open space, crowded with small groups of people. "*Campo San Cassiano*," Bryskett announced. "The Venetians call it *Campo San Cassan*."

Hunter had not seen so many well-dressed women as wandered about the campo. "I thought..." he began, about to say that patrician wives were kept behind closed doors.

A loud laugh pealed forth from a young blonde in a red dress and a yellow scarf. Her companion, a young man, guffawed at his own jest.

"Oh..." Hunter said.

"Yes," Bryskett said. "You are in *Carampane*. Did you think these patrician wives?"

"For a moment," Hunter admitted.

"The sumptuary laws of *La Serenissima* are passed in an attempt to make sure you will not confuse honest matrons for prostitutes, but they are passed in vain."

"These are the famed courtesans of Venice, then."

"Courtesans? No. These are the *meretrici*, or *cortigiane di lume*, prostitutes who will accept most clients. They are a cut above the *puttane*, the whores who frequent the alleys of the district and hang out their wares at the *ponte delle tette*."

"I have heard of that," Hunter said.

Again, a flash of black and white attracted Hunter's gaze. A tall Dominican straightened up after ducking under the low beam of a narrow alley on the east side of the campo. When he turned sideways, his receding chin and forehead and his prominent nose made an arrow pointing down at a young woman in a faded yellow dress, her head covered in a brown shawl. He grabbed her by the arm, pulled her forward, and roughly turned her away from Hunter. The shorter Dominican waddled up on the other side, and together they marched the girl up an alley leading to the Grand Canal.

"I saw those two in Saint Mark's Square, shortly before we met you," Hunter said.

"Clerics are some of these ladies' best customers." Bryskett frowned. "But they usually prefer to arrive after dark and take their pleasure indoors, rather than leading the women away."

A brunette in a green gown approached, swaying, but Bryskett waved her away. She turned with a pout. "We can pass the *ponte delle tette* later if you wish to view breasts."

"Perhaps." Hunter was curious but chided himself for his lascivious desires. "Where are we going now?"

"Signora Filippa's." Bryskett plucked his elbow and led him to the left.

"Is she a courtesan?"

"Not exactly."

"What does that mean?"

"She has several women in her *casa*," Bryskett explained as they crossed a bridge. "But not such as you just saw, who parade themselves on the squares and esplanades. Her clients come to her, and she feels free to turn away any who do not seem the right sort."

"And what sort is that?"

"Of the right degree. Sober. Healthy."

Perhaps he and Sebastian were the right sort. "And what are we to do there?" Hunter asked with trepidation.

"I will simply introduce you, unless you are in the market for more."

Hunter had not known a woman for two years. He had imagined an encounter with a Venetian courtesan, in which he acted a confident and carefree part, but now guilt and shame struggled with that dream. "An introduction will suffice."

"Her ladies are known for their musical talents, as well as," Bryskett raised one eyebrow, "the other. And they speak several languages."

"In truth?"

"Indeed. Helena is Greek—well, Corfiote actually. One girl is from Dalmatia, another from Austria—it is good for business if a woman can speak to her clients in their own language."

"Any speakers of English?"

"You shall see."

They continued until they stood before a doorway flanked with columns twisting up to tracery under a pointed arch. Bryskett knocked and a small window in the door opened.

"*Son 'Bastiano.*"

The door swung open. A huge man with a bristly beard and moustache gestured them in, eyeing Hunter with suspicion.

"*Zuan, ti presento Signor Hunter. È inglese,*" Bryskett said.

"Good day," the giant said.

Hunter laughed in surprise.

"That may be the limit of his English," Bryskett said, leading him upstairs to the *piano nobile*.

A woman in a light blue gown floated onto the landing above them and greeted them, also with an English "Good day." Her light brown hair was coiled high on her head. She wore a pearl necklace and earrings. Her lips were painted bright red and her cheeks rouged. The wrinkles near her eyes and mouth revealed her age. Above her welcoming smile, her brown eyes measured Hunter.

Bryskett introduced Signora Filippa and spoke to her further in Venetian. She exclaimed something about Lucia, whoever that might be, and led them down a corridor to a large reception room, or *portego*, with windows overlooking a canal. Its furnishings reminded him of the Earl of

Leicester's reception chamber. Porphyry vases sat on a carved and inlaid chest, rich red and blue patterned carpets from the East covered the floor, and green velvet drapes framed the windows.

Signora Filippa left them surveying the *portego* and crossed to a door on the right side of the corridor. In a tapestry on that side of the *portego*, a naked Danaë lulled on a couch while a shower of small gold coins, actually Jupiter in disguise, fell on her voluptuous body. Light danced up through windows onto this tapestry, as well as one on the left wall, on which leering satyrs and coy nymphs danced. Beneath that tapestry an actual woman lay on a couch, in an imitation of Danaë's posture, but wearing a pale red gown over a low-cut white bodice. Her small bare feet dangled off the couch. A mane of curly blonde hair framed her broad face. She smiled sweetly at the men and half closed her eyes, a sleepy but hungry lion. Hunter's stomach churned.

"Leona is a favorite of the German merchants," Bryskett said.

Hearing her name, Hunter realized he was not the first to notice the animal resemblance.

"But you do not have to stumble today in either German or Italian. This afternoon, Lucia is visiting. She speaks English well, as she has spent several years in a special relationship with Edward, Baron Windsor. She no longer stays with Signora Filippa but has set up on her own. Let us grant her the title of *cortigiana onesta*, an honest courtesan."

Sidney had mentioned Lord Windsor as an English nobleman he had dined with. They turned at the sound of female laughter. Signora Filippa emerged from the door at the right with a tall blonde woman in a gown of dark blue silk and a shorter adolescent girl in a cream gown. Hunter was struck by her beauty. High cheeks, a petit nose, tender pink lips, and wide eyes in perfect balance. Her blonde hair was braided and coiled on top of her head.

The tall woman advanced with a noble bearing and spoke, "I am Lucia, and this is Caterina. Your happy arriving gives Caterina a chance to practice your tongue." She looked at Caterina expectantly.

Caterina's face flushed. "Good day, gentlemens," she stammered.

"Good day to you," Bryskett said. "We have not met before."

Hoping to assuage the fear he saw in Caterina's face, Hunter said, "*Bon giorno, Caterina.*" She visibly relaxed, and her face glowed.

Lucia clucked her tongue. "No, no, sirs. If you speak Italian, she cannot try her English. To be kind, overlook her errors."

Hunter glanced at Bryskett and said, "We will surely do so."

An awkward silence followed, and Lucia looked expectantly at Caterina. She swallowed, gestured to the couch and padded stools beneath Danaë, and said, "Pray sit."

Lucia smiled.

They crossed to the couch and the men sat on the stools with a clear view of the women and the naked princess in the tapestry above.

Again, Lucia glanced at Caterina, who asked, "You want drink? White, red wine?"

Lucia smiled again and both men ordered red wine. Filippa called to a girl to bring the drinks, and, to Caterina's relief, Lucia spoke. "Signor Hunter, is this your first time in Venice?"

"It is."

Lucia looked at Caterina. "Your first time in Venice," she parroted. "What things you like?"

"What things *do* you like?" Lucia corrected.

Caterina winced as though berating herself for the mistake she had made. "What things do you like?"

"The buildings are beautiful," Hunter replied, and added, "and so are the people."

Caterina smiled back. The serving girl arrived with glasses of wine— tiny ones for the women, larger goblets for the men.

Lucia advised Hunter on the palaces and churches he must visit. He worked hard not to stare at Caterina, but even when he was attending Lucia, he was aware he was not looking at her. Finally, he asked Lucia, "How long has Caterina been learning English from you, signora?"

"She has been with Filippa," she turned to the matron with a questioning tone, "three, four months?"

"*Quatro*," Filippa said.

"So four months," Lucia said. "She has progressed well, but she needs practice." She cast a meaningful glance at Hunter.

Yes, he was attracted to Caterina. Had he met her at a ball, he would not hesitate to spend time in her company. He knew the unwritten rules of ordinary wooing, but here, there would be no wooing. Bedding her for payment was a certainty. What were the rules here?

"But you have not heard her sing," Lucia continued.

As if on cue, the servant brought a lute and handed it to Caterina. The tautness in her face vanished. She plucked the strings, turned a few pegs, plucked again, then turned to the men with a smile. "I know no English song," she said apologetically.

"Yet," Lucia added, glancing at her. "But I am sure you gentlemen are accustomed to Italian songs."

Lucia spoke a title to Caterina, who began singing and accompanying herself. Her voice was clear and pure, her range amazing, and the emotion with which she sang moved Hunter, though he understood few of the words—*heart* and *love* and *never*. He guessed from her sad face that the song was about unrequited love. Beauty shone through every emotion he read—sadness, shyness, uncertainty, joy. When she finished, all her auditors applauded. Caterina blushed.

"Now you know why Filippa welcomed her," Lucia said.

"Indeed," Bryskett said. "She might serve a nobleman to entertain his guests."

A frown passed over Lucia's face. "Filippa would not surrender her easily."

Filippa gestured to their empty glasses. "More?"

Bryskett looked at Hunter. "I fear we must be going. Master Hunter has not yet seen his lodgings." He reached for his purse. "What do we owe for the wine"

While Bryskett paid, Hunter addressed Caterina. "It was a pleasure meeting you." He turned to Lucia. "And you."

Lucia turned to Caterina, who said, "Thank you, kind sir."

"And I thank you as well." Lucia said.

They rose together, and Filippa ushered the men down the stairs. Zuan directed them to a door opening onto a canal and hailed a nearby gondola.

Sidney and his party had already arrived at the French Embassy in *Palazzo Michiel*.

"How was your interview with the Ten?" Hunter asked.

"Brief. They asked that I recount my adventure. With Bryskett's help, I did so. They furrowed their brows and shook their heads. As they had the report from Padua before them, they had few questions. We are to return tomorrow for their decision, but I feel it will be positive."

"Where did my brother lead you?" Lodowick Bryskett asked.

"I met Signora Filippa and some of her charming ladies." Hunter judged that was the best term to use.

Sidney frowned and cast an unfriendly eye toward Sebastian. "Yes. He did the same for me. Though Lodowick sometimes mocks me for my virginity, I have no desire to return home with the French disease. I may already be in enough trouble with my family. Have you written my uncle yet?"

"Only a brief note saying we arrived safely, and you were well, as I promised you."

"Gramercy, Edward. I must relate my misfortunes myself, though I have not yet mustered up the courage to do so." Sidney sighed. "But, as we must stay in Venice another day, I may show you some of its marvels."

"The entire city strikes me as a marvel. Amazing palaces seem to float on the water. Sebastian named their owners as our boatman rowed us here."

"I grant you that Venice, on its surface, is memorable," Sidney said. "Yet it saddens me."

"Saddens?" Hunter asked. Both Brysketts failed to react. They had heard Sidney's comments before.

"One cannot walk the streets without being approached by harlots."

"That is because you are so handsome," Sebastian said, but received only a cold glance.

"Every turn?" Hunter asked.

"Well, I admit I exaggerate. But there are also the beggars, the shopkeepers constantly calling you to buy their wares, the men arguing prices during church services, the loot stolen from Constantinople displayed on the basilica, as though theft is a matter of pride. The city has a soul of greed beneath a façade of honor and piety."

"Even they admit they are Venetians first, then Christians," Lodowick Bryskett said. "I attribute your melancholy humor to the vapors from the lagoon."

"You may be right," Sidney said. "I know I find more happiness in Padua."

"I know a partial cure for melancholy," Sebastian said. "Let us sit and sip some wine."

They pulled stools around a table while John Fisher poured. When Gironi returned with a sober expression, they invited him to join them.

"Did you find your cousin?" Hunter asked.

"I did," Gironi said. "Stefano's shop is not far from here, near *Palazzo Longo*. He greeted me as the prodigal son, though he had no fatted calf."

"Why so solemn, then?" Hunter asked.

"I had not realized it showed. Stefano's recital of family deaths, and the smell of leather in his shop, reminded me of all I have missed since I left." Gironi smiled. "But he did offer to make us both new shoes after our long journey."

"Good."

"Not free of course, but for a reduced price. After all, Stefano is Venetian."

Thursday, 29 April 1574, Venice

Sidney's mood improved the next morning as he pointed out the architectural features of the palaces along the Grand Canal. Gironi added information, identifying buildings which were new to him. They stopped in the Biondi bank so Hunter could redeem his note of credit for Venetian coins. They dined at an inn near the Rialto, where Sidney indicated passing prostitutes to add evidence to his statement of the previous night.

The afternoon found Hunter and Gironi in *Piazza San Marco*, watching Sidney and Bryskett enter the *Palazzo Ducale* again. This time, Hunter waited for them to reemerge after what they hoped would be a brief meeting with the Ten. He strolled along the palace arcade, from column to column, attempting to identify the carvings on each capital. After arriving at the corner with sculptures of planets and signs of the zodiac, he turned to gaze out across the lagoon at San Giorgio Maggiore. Alighting from a gondola on the bank before him were the Dominican pair he had seen twice the day before. "Luca, this is my third sighting of those two."

"Well, there is a monastery on San Zòrzi Mazor, and another at Zanipolo," Gironi replied.

"Where?"

"Pray forgive me. Those are the Venetian names for San Giorgio Maggiore and Santi Giovanni e Páolo."

Hunter nodded. "Yesterday I saw the friars in the campo of San Cassiano, leading away what I judged to be a prostitute."

"That friars and prostitutes are together is no surprise," Gironi said, "but that usually happens at night."

"That is what Sebastian said."

Gironi pondered a moment. "Perhaps one of them had found she had the French disease after mounting her, and he was taking her to the

Ospedale degli Incurabili before he went to pray hard and consult a physician for a course of mercury."

"Halloo, my friends," came a voice behind them. Sidney and Bryskett approached, smiling. Sidney announced, "I have a patent from the Ten to bear arms—not only myself, but Bryskett, Madox, White, and Fisher. I trust there will be no more attacks."

"Wonderful news," Hunter said. Now he could write Lord Leicester more details about Sidney's safety. And he could return to his detection of what lay behind Sidney's abduction.

CHAPTER 5

Testing the Waters

Saturday, 1 May 1574, Padua

As Hunter and Gironi climbed, their nostrils were assailed by foul smells: cooked onions, urine, ordure. Hunter knocked on the door and heard an "*Un momento.*" From the sounds, a man relieved himself in an already filled chamber pot and struggled into hose and breeches. In a moment, the door opened. A short man, his dark hair disheveled, unshaved for days, wearing a stained shirt and ashy venetian breeches, stood blinking at them. Beyond him stood a low bed with rumpled covers and a single stool. "*Si.*"

"You are Charles Carr?" Hunter asked.

Carr appeared surprised to hear English. "Yes. Who might you be?"

"My name is Edward Hunter and this is my servant Luca Gironi. I am a friend of Philip Sidney, whom I believe you know."

Carr nodded. "I do. How might I serve you?" He seemed reluctant to invite them in. Considering the sour odor wafting from the room, Hunter was glad of it.

"Do you know what chanced to happen to him?"

"I have heard he was taken and carried past Ferrara by felons."

"He has asked me to speak with his friends to see if they can guess a cause." Hunter was uncertain whether calling Carr a friend was accurate.

Carr shook his head. "I cannot."

"Excuse our disturbing you," Hunter said. "I hazard you have not broken your fast."

"You are correct."

"If there is an establishment nearby, I am willing to play your host while we become better acquainted," Hunter offered.

Carr's eyes lit up. "Allow me a moment to don a doublet."

Hunter and Gironi exchanged glances. The prospect of a free meal produced an enlivened Carr. The trio descended to street level.

"Luigi's is nearby," Carr said, heading to his right.

As they walked, Hunter began his probe. "When did you first meet Master Sidney?"

"Soon after his arrival last November. I was lodging with John Le Rous then."

Hunter followed his lead. "But you now lodge alone."

"I wanted independence," Carr said. "Le Rous and Fitzwilliams objected to the hours I kept."

So that was his justification for moving to the miserable garret: no mention of lack of money. They arrived at Luigi's. Carr entered and ordered bread, cheese, and wine. Gironi said he and Hunter had eaten.

"And you, Master Hunter. How long have you known Master Sidney?" Carr asked.

Caught off guard for a moment, Hunter quickly recovered. "We met in Paris less than two years ago, when he began his tour of the Continent. We had the misfortune of being there on Saint Bartholomew's Day." In spite of himself, images of corpses on the street assaulted him. He shuddered and closed his eyes for a moment.

"Yes, Sidney mentioned that, but he would not furnish us any details." Carr's eyes narrowed. "Will you?"

Now on the defensive, Hunter said, "I prefer not to stir those memories." Why had he mentioned the massacre?

Carr gave a smug smile and bit off another piece of bread.

Hunter needed to gain the advantage. "My man Luca learned that those who captured Sidney frequented the Ram's Head, as you do. Did you know them?"

Carr chewed thoughtfully for a moment. "The Ram's Head has many patrons. I may have spoken with one or two of the men at some time."

"Which ones?" Hunter pressed him.

Carr raised his chin in offense. "May I ask if Master Sidney has asked you to conduct this interrogation?"

Perhaps Hunter had pushed too hard, but now was no time to back down. "As a matter of fact, he has. He is still recovering from his ordeal," he lied, "and he seeks to know who is behind it."

Carr grunted.

"I understand the men are petty criminals who work for Tommaso Biradi." Hunter continued.

Carr raised his eyebrows, took a deep draught of his wine, and wiped his mouth. "It appears you know so much you need little information from me."

"Did any men at the Ram's Head speak of Sidney, or of riding to Ferrara?"

"No."

"I thought you might help your friend by relaying whatever you know about Biradi or the men who work for him."

Carr gave a mirthless laugh. "If you knew Biradi, you would know that would be unwise."

"Do you fear him?"

"Anyone with a brain fears him."

"Did Master Sidney offend him?"

"Not that I know. You must ask him yourself."

Hunter judged it best not to reveal he knew that Biradi had fled. Instead, he put on a bold front. "Perhaps I shall."

Another smug smile from Carr. "I wish you luck."

Hunter would get no useful information from Carr. He and Gironi stood. Carr thanked him for the breakfast, and they bid farewell.

As they walked away, Hunter said, "Clearly he knows more than he would tell."

"Perhaps if you agreed to buy him meals for the next month, he would be more forthcoming," Gironi suggested.

Hunter chuckled. "Money may be the way to move him, but his reticence regarding Biradi is unlikely to change. It appeared honest fear to me." The clock on the *Palazzo del Capitanio* chimed eleven. "The morning progresses well. Doctor Simmons said we might call between eleven and noon."

The servant introduced himself as Zòrzi and led them to a room filled with papers and books. A man in his forties turned from a desk and stood as they entered. Sharp eyes stared out from a thin face framed by a heavy beard with touches of gray at the temples and chin. "*Salve.*"

"*Salve, dottore.*" Hunter introduced himself and his servant.

"Yes. I remember Master Gironi from his earlier visit." Simmons waved them to a seat. "He said you are new to Padua and wished to make my acquaintance. Do you need tuition for the university examinations?"

"No, sir," Hunter said. "I came to Padua at the invitation of Philip Sidney."

Simmons nodded. "A virtuous young man. John Hart introduced us."

"Perhaps you heard of his recent misfortune."

Simmons frowned. "Alas. Yet *accipere quam facere praestat injuriam.*"

"True, yet I am sure Master Sidney has no intension of injuring others as a result of his own injuries. However, his capture proves someone bears him enmity and, as a dear friend, I am seeking to discover who endangers his safety. After all, *nonne amicus certus in re incerta cernitur?*" Simmons was not the only one who could offer Latin maxims.

"He *is* fortunate to have such friends in his need," Simmons said. He blinked several times. "I fear I do not know Master Sidney well enough to discover his enemies."

Another statement of ignorance, but at least it had not been in Latin. "You do know his friends, however. You mentioned John Hart."

An expression of annoyance crossed Simmons' face, quickly replaced by a bland smile. "Yes. I am helping him and Roger Fitzwilliams prepare for doctoral examinations in canon and civil law. Both know Master Sidney more closely than I. Perhaps they will be better able to assist your investigation."

"They also could think of no one behind Sidney's capture." Though tired of the morning's fruitless interviews, Hunter ventured another question. "Ambrose Barnes mentioned Tommaso Biradi as a man who might know of those who ordered Master Sidney seized."

Simmons stiffened and his eyebrows rose. "He might indeed know of any criminal enterprise undertaken in Padua." He smiled. "Yet I do not think it would be wise to ask him to reveal his knowledge."

Another warning, yet Hunter pressed ahead. "How would one go about contacting Master Biradi?"

"I am told he frequents *La Testa dell' Ariete.*" Simmons sniffed. "But I am sure no gentleman would enter there."

"Perhaps I must, if I am to learn who wishes Master Sidney ill."

"You would do so at your peril."

"Can you think of no one else who might know of a plot to harm my friend?"

"Any one of the ruffians for hire in Padua might know. The difficulty would be in convincing them to reveal that knowledge. Whether from fear or loyalty, they will say naught but mum."

"Well," Hunter rose. "We shall trouble you no more."

Simmons stood as well. "Is Master Sidney taking measures to keep himself from further harm?"

"The Council of Ten has granted him permission to bear arms in Venetian territory."

Simmons nodded. "I am glad to hear he is taking precautions. I wish you luck unravelling this mystery."

"I shall indeed need luck," Hunter said when he and Gironi stepped into the street.

"And help," Gironi said. "I will make another visit to the Ram's Head."

"Simmons said one would visit there at his peril."

"He said *a gentleman* would enter there at his peril. I have entered and returned unscathed." Gironi smiled.

"You must nevertheless be on your guard. Let us buy food at the market and then visit Captain Scarpa."

Their interview with Scarpa proved unproductive. The arrested horse thieves would say nothing about who had ordered their actions, and both endured whippings. When it was clear they would not speak, a friend appeared to return the money they gained from selling the horses and to pay their fines. The captain assumed the funds had come from Biradi. He had spoken to other denizens of *La Testa dell' Ariete*, but all had pleaded ignorance.

Upon his return to Pozzo della Vacca, Sidney handed Hunter a letter from his uncle. He must have dispatched it soon after Hunter left.

"He hopes I have arrived safely and asks for the responses from silk producers," he announced to Sidney. "After a day without accomplishment, I am reminded of another task I have not done." He did not share the rest of the letter. Uncle Babcock reported that the Fleming in Canterbury, who claimed he could weave whole silk cloth, could only produce fringes and ribbons. Returning with an Italian weaver was essential. Had he discovered a source of mulberry trees? Did he know if silk flies could withstand the voyage? Captain Connors and the *Adventure* were due in Venice in early August, and he was to board, with whatever or whomever he had managed to acquire.

"We have both suffered a day of less achievement than we hoped," Sidney said. "I strove with Petrarch, and Petrarch vanquished me."

"Come, come," Bryskett said. "Your translations were not that bad. And you said that reading his verse inspired you to imitation."

"Perhaps I will gather the nerve to try sonnets in English someday," Sidney said, "but not today."

"I offer you both the consolation Bacchus affords." Bryskett transferred cups from a cupboard to their table.

They sat and drank. If Hunter must pursue his uncle's quest for a cheaper source of raw silk and probe other possibilities, he could use that quest as an opportunity to speak with Randolph alone. "Master Randolph seemed to know of silk merchants. Perhaps he can introduce me to someone here, or in Vicenza."

CHAPTER 6

Wading

Tuesday, 4 May 1574, Padua

RANDOLPH WAS EQUALLY PLEASED TO INTRODUCE HUNTER TO PADUAN silk producers and to exhibit his ability to translate English to Italian and vice-versa. The first two *setaioli* they visited, however, sent their wares to relatives in Lyon, and expressed reluctance to deal directly with Englishmen. The second suggested a silk producer in Vicenza who had a connection with London. Was he on Uncle Babcock's list? He would have to unearth that piece of paper.

Hunter and Randolph stepped into a tavern for refreshment before approaching a third *setaiolo*. As they ate, Hunter questioned him. "Are there laws I do not know that make these merchants reluctant to deal with me?"

"Venice has many laws regarding silk," Randolph said. He listed various restrictions regarding where certain fabrics could be woven, what duties had to be paid to import silk cloth into Venice, and where various qualities of silk might be sold. "Though whether the laws are enforced is another matter. These merchants may have settled conduits of trade and eschew anything new."

"The *setaiolo* we just spoke with suggested enquiring in Vicenza. You did as well."

"They are further from the watchful eyes of the Venetian Silk Guild, and closer to trade routes north. I believe some already deal with London mercers, but I know not which ones. I would escort you, but my studies and my purse argue I must stay."

Hunter chewed a bite of lasagna. A trip to Vicenza might work well. Gironi could accompany him as a translator and venture into the forbidden realms of enticing weavers to England and transporting trees and worms. "On another matter, it has been over a week since Sidney's escape from his capture. Have you heard any gossip as to who may have been behind that deed?"

Randolph considered. "Those students who boast of their associations with the criminals of Padua report that the men killed in the Romagna worked for Tommaso Biradi."

"Is Charles Carr one of those?"

"Well, he is no longer a student, nor does he boast, though he associates with those who may engage in unlawful activities."

"Could Carr have hired some of them?"

Randolph chuckled. "He is more likely to be in debt to them than to hire them."

"Does Carr or anyone resent Sidney's wealth or birth?"

"Carr bears Sidney no grudge. Nor does anyone envy him. Whoever hired those rogues remains a mystery."

Another blind alley. "You cannot guess?"

"Philip is such a pleasant fellow, who could wish him ill?"

"Someone did. He is, after all, a Protestant, and the relative of a Protestant leader in England."

Randolph's features tightened. "Does that mean every Catholic is a suspect, or only we English Catholics?"

Hunter had pushed too far to retreat. "I do not wish to offend, but would any English Catholic here benefit from Sidney's disappearance?"

Randolph's eyes and tone were icy. "We are Philip's friends. We would mourn, not profit, from his disappearance. Your questions confirm what I suspect. You have come to Italy for reasons besides silk. As I have answered your queries, will you now answer mine? Has the Privy Council sent you to spy upon us?"

This was the reason behind Randolph's suspicious looks. Hunter struggled for a statement that was neither a lie nor the whole truth. "His uncle is worried about his friendship with Catholics, I admit, but I am not come as a spy to report to the Privy Council."

"You may assure his uncle it is unlikely Philip will find his way to papal allegiance, but would it be terrible if one Protestant chose toleration over persecution?"

Hunter considered arguing that Queen Elizabeth already had a policy of toleration but thought it better to agree. "Toleration is to be wished, on both sides. But my questions about who wishes him ill remain. Someone paid those criminals to capture Philip."

Randolph leaned back, mollified. "Perhaps you should consider who will inherit if he should die."

"His younger brother Robert. He is but a boy, incapable of plots and in school hundreds of miles away."

"You did ask who would profit. Certainly no one here."

"I apologize. I grasp at straws." Hunter needed to make amends. "Allow me to buy you another wine before we visit our last *setaiolo*."

Their final visit proved lucky. Signor Lovato, though satisfied with the trade channels for his silks, directed Hunter to Signor Zordan, a *setaiolo* who had purchased groves of mulberry trees, built a villa designed by Palladio near Vicenza, and was eager to find new markets.

Tuesday, 11 May 1574, On the road to Vicenza

"While you were successful contacting *setaioli* in Vicenza and collecting invitations, I made little progress with the English expatriates." Hunter recounted his conversations as he and Gironi rode.

John Le Rous earned money by translations into English, Italian, French, and Latin, and tutored candidates in civil and canon law. These scholarly pursuits, along with the rent from his boarders, allowed him to make a living. His modest income and apparel led Hunter to believe he was unlikely to have hired *bravi* to attack Sidney. Unlike Randolph, he took no offense when Hunter hinted English Catholics in Italy might desire harm to Sidney because of his uncle's vigorous Protestantism. After considering that possibility, Le Rous suggested that their parents in England might do Leicester more harm than students in Italy. He, too, doubted Carr's involvement and regretted turning him out. He hoped to find an Englishman among the new students to replace him, but Barnes and the two others who came recently were all wealthy enough that they need not share lodgings. He began to list the economies he had to make. He mentioned buying cheaper tallow candles and using fewer of them. Remembering Sidney's comment, Hunter asked him directly about the wax under his fingernails, and Le Rous admitted to saving the butt ends of candles and melting them together. He refused to hazard a guess of who might wish harm to Sidney.

John Hart denied any knowledge of Sidney's attackers and changed the subject to art and music. He had fallen in love with Italy's architects, sculptors, and painters. Hunter recognized several that Sidney had mentioned: Palladio, Sansovino, Titian, Tintoretto, and Veronese. Hart said he had guided Sidney to choose Veronese as his portraitist. He insisted on walking Hunter to the church of San Sebastian and explaining the virtues of each Veronese fresco. In the end, Hunter had to admit that reforming the English church had resulted in the loss of inspiring art, but he argued that discarding the abuses of Catholicism was worth that loss. They agreed to disagree.

Hunter appealed to Fitzwilliams's vanity, encouraging him to disparage any of the other expatriates. Though he looked down on Carr for his dissolute ways, he dismissed the idea that he had hired Sidney's attackers, and would not entertain the suggestion that any other expatriate might have done so. When Hunter asked, he denied having met Vice Inquisitor Fascetti, but explained he was curious to observe the politics of the Catholic hierarchy, secular and regular, and the contentious relationship between Venice and the Holy See. He bragged about meeting the Patriarch of Venice, and the Venetian Inquisitor.

Hunter and Gironi spotted Vicenza's Bissara Tower in the distance but turned aside to take the road to Villa Zordan.

Hunter continued. "Fitzwilliams said he was surprised I did not ask him who might have killed the man-stealers. I had to admit to myself that I had been so focused on finding a link between Sidney's captors and an expatriate that I had not questioned any of them about who might have slain the rogues. Fitzwilliams had a supposition, however. He believed Sidney's enemy was someone in Bologna. This unknown enemy hired *bravi* through Biradi. Their killers were the servants of that enemy, who slew the man-stealers so they could not say anything which might lead to that enemy."

"I am unaware of any Italian enemy of Lord Leicester. And why didn't the killers take Sidney with them? Fitzwilliams's idea will not hold up," Gironi said.

"I thought the same but did not dispute with him. I was busy chiding myself for not asking the others to account for the murders. I must do so if I contrive occasion to speak with them privately again."

"At least you have eliminated two suspects, Le Rous and Carr," Gironi said.

"I am not sure about Carr. He may not have hired those men himself, but he could have been acting for another. Fitzwilliams's interest in the Catholic clergy might extend to aiding their fight against heresy. Hart's connection of art and religion could lead him to an act that furthered Catholicism, despite his friendship with Sidney. All the residents of Le Rous's house could have combined their funds to hire cutthroats and now shield one another with their denials."

"So, you have not eliminated anyone, then."

"No."

As they approached the Villa Zordan, they passed workers picking leaves in mulberry groves. Hunter's thoughts turned to the task ahead. In addition to Gironi serving as translator, he must rely on him chatting with workers. Though they had discussed their past lives as they traveled from London to Padua, and he trusted him, he had not revealed the secret part of his trade mission. Now he must.

"You look troubled," Gironi said.

"Well, you know that I search for a source of silk thread for my uncle's project."

"What exactly do you mean by project?"

Hunter squirmed. "I did tell you that he knows of silk weavers who have come from Flanders to Canterbury and hopes they may weave whole silk cloth."

"You did say so." One side of Gironi's mouth rose.

"There are other plans I...well...I did not tell you."

Gironi smiled. "You mean enticing an Italian weaver or two, digging up mulberry trees, and grabbing a box of worms to voyage to England."

Hunter gaped.

"Did you think the earl would not confide in me, especially as I am the one who must speak with the craftsmen and peasants. Do not worry, Signor Zordan knows only that you are eager to seal a bargain for his silk."

Another reminder that, although Gironi was more a companion and collaborator than his servant, his first allegiance was to the Earl of Leicester.

Zordan greeted them in the central hall of his villa, decorated with frescoes of ladies and gentlemen peering out from painted pillars and gods reclining on its ceiling. Hunter was relieved to find their host could speak French, which allowed Gironi to leave and speak with the workmen.

Zordan took pride in showing Hunter every room of his villa, each decorated with mythological paintings by Zelloti. He served an impressive supper and spoke of art and music, speaking names Hart had mentioned. When Hunter broached the subject of silk, Zordan declared that all discussions of commerce must wait until they toured the workrooms of *barchesse* that formed the symmetrical wings of the villa.

Wednesday 12 May 1574, Near Vicenza

The following day, as they walked through room after room of the north wing, watching workmen pull trays from shoulder-high racks and scatter mulberry leaves among the ravenous silkworms, Hunter realized he must abandon his uncle's scheme of transporting the creatures to England. The voyage was longer than their life cycle and supplies of fresh mulberry leaves would be impossible to obtain.

Back at the villa, Zordan and Hunter negotiated a price for two wagonloads of silk thread. Zordan suggested the ship collect the thread at Chioggia, a fishing village south of Venice, where Venetian authorities were less strict and more open to bribes. Though evading laws gnawed at his conscience, Hunter agreed to write to his uncle outlining the price difference between loading at Venice and Chioggia. He was sure which option Uncle Babcock would approve.

Sunday, 16 May 1574, Padua

The rest of the week in Vicenza had produced no better offers. Gironi's conversations with weavers failed to find any that were discontented enough to leave family and friends for an uncertain future in a wet, distant land. The one promising note was that Gironi had found peasants willing to sell him mulberry trees in buckets, though Venetian law forbade it. He hoped to strike a similar bargain with peasants closer to Chioggia.

The bells of Saint Anthony's Basilica pealed as Hunter and Gironi dismounted, tired and dusty, at Pozzo della Vaca.

Sidney opened the door to welcome them. "Well, the prodigals return."

"Hardly prodigal," Hunter said. "The inn we found cost only four soldi, and we received just what we paid for."

"Amen," Gironi sighed. He led their horses behind the house.

Sidney smiled. "I hope you have not returned with fleas."

"I cannot pledge surety for that," Hunter said, "but I will surrender my clothes to Beatrice to be cleansed."

"That will suffice. But you must cleanse yourself."

Hunter laughed.

"Take off your boots and wash the dust from your throat with a cup of wine."

Lodowick Bryskett clomped down the stairs. "Well met, Edward. What news?"

Hunter sat his feet on a bench and flexed his bare toes. "I thank you for your welcome." He told them of his mercantile adventures in Vicenza, omitting Gironi's activities. "And what have I missed in Padua?"

Bryskett and Sidney exchanged looks.

"But little," Sydney said. "I heard a few of Zabarella's lectures on Aristotle's theory of the soul."

"Have you seen your English friends?"

"Yes. We dined together last Thursday. Most said you had spoken with them as though you were a sheriff."

"They did?"

"James Randolph thought you suspected one of them had hired the rogues who made off with me."

Hunter remained silent.

"Ah, so you *do* suspect my friends." Sidney's brows knit.

"If you can supply me with other suspects, I will speak with them."

Sidney shrugged. "The entire episode is a mystery to me."

Bryskett interjected. "Roger told us a pimp was found dead in the marketplace the day Edward left. Biradi is suspected, of course."

"Yes, and Ambrose Barnes has disappeared. They assume he went to Venice without telling them," Sidney added.

Bryskett rose. "Another letter came for you, and one for Gironi." He handed both to Hunter.

His uncle's hand. Perhaps he had written each week, eager for news. "Have you heard from your uncle, Philip?"

"He has had no time to receive my letter confessing all, nor yours and Gironi's corroborating my tale."

"Did I hear my name mentioned?" Gironi entered the room.

"You did." Hunter held up his letter. "You have a note here."

Gironi scanned it. "My cousin hopes I might visit him again soon. He feels our last meeting was too brief."

Hunter read his own letter. "It seems we must go to Venice soon. My uncle writes that the *Adventure* is about to sail. He asks that I obtain finished silks from the Morea to add to its cargo." And Caterina was at Signora Filippa's.

CHAPTER 7

Buoyant

Wednesday, 19 May 1574, Venice

HUNTER AND GIRONI WOUND THEIR WAY ALONG THE *MERCERIA* FROM *Piazza San Marco* to the Rialto. This was looking familiar to Hunter. Perhaps he would soon be able to make his way around this labyrinth of a town. Signora Filippa's was over the bridge, through the market, and then... Well, he would take a gondola. But he must first attend to business. He pulled the piece of paper from his sleeve as they emerged into a campo.

"Ventura," Hunter read aloud. "Opposite the *Fondaco dei Tedeschi*." Hunter looked around. "The Rialto Bridge is on our left. I think—straight ahead."

"Good, you are getting your bearings," Gironi said.

They located the shop in the shadow of the huge German trading building. A young man in the yellow cap required of Jews greeted them. After introductions, Gironi voiced their interest in *fior di morea* silk. The young man ushered them into the shop, seated them in a small room surrounded by brightly-colored silk hangings, and offered them a new hot drink called *cha*, made, he explained, by pouring water over the dried leaves of a plant grown in the East. Hunter sipped the slightly bitter liquid with trepidation. Perhaps some might like it, he decided.

An older man, most likely the father of the young Ventura, emerged from a back room and greeted them. Hunter mentioned Uncle Babcock, but the name did not register with the elder Ventura. Perhaps another merchant had given the name to his uncle. After pleasantries, the elder Jew pulled aside a deep red velvet cloth to reveal skeins of raw silk. He picked each one up as though it were a precious treasure, and recited its exotic name, besides the *fior di morea*, he presented *coronella, cipriota, giana, candiotta, politia, salona* and *rocalica*, offering each one for Hunter to touch. He explained their origins in parts of Greece and Albania under Turkish domination and extolled their qualities. When he paused for breath, Hunter asked the price, but the older man smiled and waved away his request.

"We will get to that later," Gironi translated. "His family also imports silk from Persia that he wants you to see."

This would take longer than Hunter had anticipated.

After considerable time viewing and touching an array of silk threads, among which Hunter could barely detect any difference, the elder Ventura finally deigned to mention prices. The *fior di morea* his uncle had requested was a medium-priced silk. As negotiations proceeded and Hunter mentioned larger quantities, the price per skein dropped, with the proviso that there might be a change between this day and early August, when the silk would be delivered for loading on the *Adventure*. Hunter reached a tentative agreement within the limit his uncle had stipulated. If he wrote soon, he should get a reply by mid-July.

By the time Hunter sealed the bargain with a handshake, it was late afternoon.

"My cousin's shop is not far from our lodgings," Gironi said. "Shall we share a gondola?"

"I think I shall wander a bit, to see more of the wonderous buildings in the city," Hunter lied.

"Be careful. It is easy to become lost."

"I can always find my way to a canal and summon a gondola," Hunter said.

"As you wish. Shall we meet at Sidney's lodgings just after sundown and search out an eating house from there?"

"Agreed."

It was already later than Hunter had hoped. He did not want to take wrong turns and waste time reaching Signora Filippa's. His desire and his conscience had waged battle since that first day in Venice. Each time he envisioned Caterina, his desire won. It had been over two years since he had known a woman. After the gondola bearing Gironi disappeared, he hailed one for himself and told the gondolier his destination. The man nodded with a leer and pushed off.

Caterina began to sing. She closed her eyes and the tightness around them vanished. Her lips shaped the syllables without effort. Her fingers plucked the strings delicately. Her voice soared. Her body swayed as the music flowed from her. She was beautiful. She strummed a final chord and looked toward Hunter, the nervous uncertainty returning.

He smiled and applauded. "It was lovely."

"Sorry. I know no English songs. Can you teach me one?"

"I have no talent of singing," Hunter said.

Signora Filippa entered the room and placed glasses of wine on the table in front of them. She gave Caterina a look that caused her to put down her lute and cross to sit on the couch next to him. "I leave you alone. Know one another better," she said. Caterina was not the only one learning some English.

Hunter and Caterina sat staring at one another. She flashed a nervous smile.

Hunter smiled back. Uncertain what to do, he lifted a glass and said, "To a lovely lady with a lovely voice."

Caterina took her glass. "Thank you."

Both drank, then returned to gazing at one another tentatively.

"I want to please you," Caterina began.

"You have done so already."

"But I must do more than sing." Worry creased her forehead and she shifted closer to him. "You like to kiss?"

Of course he would like to kiss this beautiful young woman, but he preferred other circumstances. He hesitated.

Her eyes clouded with fear again. "You think I am not pretty?"

"I think you are beautiful," he said. "It is just...this is my first time."

Her mouth opened and her eyebrows shot up. "First time with a woman?"

"No." Madame Moreau had helped him over that hurdle. "It is..." He waved his hands to indicate the room, the velvet drapes, the gilded furniture...

"Ah, you no come to a"—she searched for the right word—"a house before."

"Not…this kind of house."

She nodded. "Then I must try more to please you."

"Looking at you pleases me."

She glanced at the door. "Madam Filippa will ask, 'Was she good?'"

"She heard you sing and play," Hunter said.

"Yes. But she teach me to please men. I am the girl for the English, she say. I must learn speak English, sing English, do things the English gentlemens like."

"Englishmen are like other men."

She smiled. Her eyes invited him. "Then kiss me."

He leaned forward and kissed her gently on the lips.

She moved closer and cradled his head in both hands. "Can you kiss more warm?" She opened her lips.

He kissed her again and her tongue was busy in his mouth. He felt himself stir.

"You like?"

"I like that very much." He clasped her shoulders. "I like you very much."

She sensed his reluctance. The tightness returned to her face. "You say, 'but'."

"But I do not feel right…" he began.

Her mouth quivered. "No say you not want me."

"I do, but…" How could he explain that she should not be what she was?

"No say 'but'. Madam Filippa will ask did I please you—please you with my body. If I no please, she be mad."

"But do you want to be here?"

She looked blankly, then understood. "Our farm poor. I have no dowry. Madam Filippa is cousin to my mother. She say, 'Take her. Teach her. She is pretty. Can sing pretty. In Venice she be more than servant.'"

He realized the choices she had faced. He wanted to say being a servant was an honest choice, but he knew how the students of Padua treated pretty servant girls.

"I am here little time. Five month. Madam Filippa not happy. One English gentleman not like me. Say other girl better."

So, he was a test. Each man she saw was a test for her. Would she be allowed to stay at this 'respectable bordello,' with a chance to rise to the status of a desired courtesan? If she failed too many tests, she might be thrown out to the life of a street whore. Who had that other Englishman been? "Will you sing another song?"

"If you kiss me."

He did, with more enjoyment.

She fetched her lute and returned to his side. "This song about kisses. I sing verse, then la-la-la, then kiss. I sing again, two kisses. Sing again, three kisses. Yes?"

"I understand." He took a large swallow of wine as she nestled close to him.

The song progressed as she described, with more and longer kisses after each verse. After six verses, she loosened her bodice. "Now song say breasts soft and want kisses." Hope mixed with fear in her vulnerable eyes.

As she sang, her firm young breasts swelled against the loose bodice. Indeed, they did long to be kissed. Hunter's desire grew faster than his guilt. If he did not intend to couple with her, why had he come here? Fornication and adultery were sins he had already committed. Would paid sex be any worse? A beautiful young woman whose life was pleasing men was offering herself to him. He sang, "La-la-la," along with Caterina, then his lips met the softness of her breast.

It was twilight when he left Signora Filippa's. He turned down Zuan's offer to summon a gondola, choosing instead to walk. Sebastian Bryskett had mentioned a *traghetto* at the *Fondaco dei Turchi*, which was not far away. His afternoon with Caterina weighed on his mind. He basked in memories of her voice, her face, her soft flesh, and the ecstasy of his release. Immediately his spirit plunged with the conviction he had defiled her and himself. He had allowed his lust to overcome what he knew to be right. He had justified his desire in the moment. Yet why had he gone to Signora Filippa's? Could one defile a prostitute? No, not a prostitute, a courtesan. Did those Venetian labels make a difference to God? Why did he always consider these questions after he had acted? He would pray for forgiveness.

He followed Zuan's directions and reached the *traghetto* landing stage with self-congratulation for not getting lost. He paid the ferryman who poled him across and stepped onto the shore. North should lie the French Embassy, but they had not taken the gondola from this place earlier today. Well, he could enquire his way if he needed to.

Twenty minutes later, he had to admit he was lost. Had he missed a turning to the left before he crossed the last canal, or perhaps it was the next one? It was growing dark, and the few shops he had passed were closed. He saw no gondolas along this stretch of canal. He turned and began to retrace his steps along the *fondamenta,* as they called an embankment.

With no warning, he was grabbed from behind and lifted from the ground, his arms pinned at his side. He kicked out, but a second man grasped his legs tightly and growled a threat. He saw only the man's back and his red hair.

"Help!" Hunter shouted. "*Secours!*" Why had he not learned the Italian word?

A third man struck him in the face and clamped a hand over his mouth. He gave orders, and the others turned Hunter so lamplight shone on him. His assailant, a coarse-faced man with a broken nose and a scar over his left eye, studied him, then said, "*Non xè lu.*" He drew a dagger from his belt. Terrified, Hunter struggled, but the giant behind him held him tighter, and the scarred man struck him on the right temple with the hilt of his knife. Hunter's world went black for a moment, then he was aware of someone pulling at his waist. When his eyes focused, the scarred man held his purse and nodded toward the canal.

Hunter's body swayed back and forth three times in his assailants' grip, then he was flying through the air. The cold water enveloped him as he sank beneath the surface.

CHAPTER 8

Going under Once

Hunter sputtered to the surface, his mind immediately clear. The water around him stank. It was high tide, before the currents swept the refuse of the city into the lagoon.

His wet clothes pulled him down. A terrifying night in the Seine swirled through his mind. No, he must not panic. Swiveling his head from side to side, he spotted steps on his right leading from the canal. The trio who had assaulted him strolled along the *fondamenta*. Perhaps they thought he could not swim and would drown. They obviously did not care, nor fear arrest for their deed. He stroked through stinking water to slime-covered stairs. As he pulled himself onto the embankment, a door opened. His calling had roused someone.

A young man wearing an apron covered in paint splotches ran toward him, asking an excited question.

"I don't understand," Hunter said.

"*Tedesco?*"

"*No, inglese.*"

"Ah!" The young man helped Hunter to his feet. Foul water dripped from him.

"Domenico!" a voice called from further down the *fondamenta*, followed by a question.

The boy answered as he guided Hunter past statues of turbaned men toward a lighted door. Holding it was an older man with a full gray bread and moustache, sunken, concerned eyes, and bushy brows. He also wore a paint-spattered apron. He and the boy spoke as they motioned Hunter inside.

Hunter gestured to his wet clothes, not wanting to ruin any of their furnishings. The older man waved away his concern and pointed to a chair. The room was brightly lit with candles. All around him were paintings of various sizes: portraits, saints, gods and goddesses. Was this Veronese's studio? The paintings did not resemble those he had seen at San Sebastian.

The elderly painter presented him with a small glass of liquid. "*Graspa.*"

"*Grazie,*" Hunter replied. After the putrid water of the canal had threatened death, he could use some water of life. He tossed back the strong-smelling drink.

The boy was at Hunter's shoulder with cloths he might use to dry himself. Using gestures, the painter and his apprentice encouraged him to disrobe and dry himself. After hesitation, Hunter did so. From the works of art, it was clear they were used to seeing naked men and women. The boy took his clothes to another room, where splashing indicated he was rinsing out the canal water. Hunter was suddenly aware he had lost his hat.

The painter handed Hunter a large cloth to wrap himself in and asked a question. Clearly it meant "Who are you?"

"Edward Hunter."

"Jacopo Robusti."

The name was not familiar, but then the wealthy merchants of Venice kept many artists busy. Not all were famous, Hunter reasoned. Still, judging by the number of canvases on easels, this painter had many orders.

"*Dove vivi?*"

Hunter understood. "*Palazzo Michiel.*"

Robusti nodded in recognition. He indicated the glass and asked "*Un'altra?*"

"*No, grazie.*"

Robusti took the glass as the boy returned with Hunter's clothes, wrinkled and twisted from wringing. There was no alternative to donning these damp garments.

Robusti said something ending with the words *Palazzo Michiel* and indicated his assistant. It was clear the young man would take Hunter to Sidney's lodgings.

"What happened?" Gironi exclaimed.

Hunter explained briefly and asked Gironi to reward the apprentice for seeing him safely to their lodgings. After the young man left, Gironi called a servant to strike a fire in the hearth and fetch a blanket. For a second time, Hunter stripped off his cold, damp clothes. They still smelled of the canal, but less strongly.

"Three men?" Gironi asked. "Tell me again what passed?"

Hunter recounted his assault in more detail.

"And the man said, 'It's not him.' Who do you think they were searching for?"

"Ah," Hunter exclaimed, forming a theory. "My clothing marks me as an Englishman. They were looking for one who lives nearby. This must be another attempt to capture Philip. I am the same stature and frame as he. I have been confused with him before, by some ladies in Paris."

"That makes sense."

"When we return to Padua, we will search out this Tommaso Biradi at the Ram's Head and ask him questions."

"Will you walk into a den of thieves?" Gironi asked.

"You did."

"But I was perceived as a local." Gironi paused. "Perhaps we should ask Bryskett or Sidney to accompany us."

"What? And deliver the quarry into their clutches!"

Gironi sighed. "I admit that is a bad idea. I simply thought we might need more strength."

"The larger the group, the more likely they would think we came for a fight. It would end in a riot," Hunter said. "What will they do to two of us, kill us?"

"That is not impossible," Gironi rejoined. "It might have happened to you tonight."

"I thought so when the leader drew his dagger, but he was only after my purse."

"How much did you lose?"

Hunter paused a moment. He had paid five scudi at Signora Filippa's. "My purse held some two hundred soldi."

"Do you have more here?"

"No. In Padua. I must to the Biondi bank tomorrow."

"In those clothes?" Gironi gestured to the pile on the floor.

Hunter sighed. His soaked clothing might dry by the morning if hung by the fire, but they would still smell. "Pray rinse my garments in fresh water again before you hang them to dry."

"I shall, but you must wipe the canal stink off your body. I will ask Alberto to bring a basin and a rag. You must be hungry. I shall ask him to fetch us fish pies and wine from an eating house."

"And some *grappa*," Hunter added.

Over supper, Hunter gave Gironi details of his rescue. When he mentioned the painter's name, Gironi exclaimed, "Jacopo Robusti! You were succored by Tintoretto! His paintings are in churches and scuole all over Venice."

"Tintoretto! Why did he not say so?"

"It is not his proper name, but a nickname. That boy must have been his son."

Thursday, 20 May 1574, Venice

The following morning, Hunter regarded his mangled doublet and breeches with dismay. A trace odor of canal water lingered. His shoes remained damp. He should have packed another set of clothes. "Can your cousin recommend a launderess who can redeem these garments?" he asked Gironi.

"Of course. But you must wear something while that redemption takes place." Gironi looked him up and down. "Stefano is about your size. You may borrow his clothes to visit the bank and search out Ambrose Barnes. I will trace your foot and take that drawing as well, as he may have shoes to fit you. Shall I ask him to recommend a draper and a tailor as well?"

Though the twisted clothes might be improved, they would never look as good. Hunter had planned to buy a new suit in the Venetian style while he was here. Why not now? "Pray do. If I might borrow clothing and credit, convey my thanks. And may I prevail upon you to purchase a linen shirt and black hose?"

When Gironi returned, Hunter donned his new shirt and cousin Stefano's humble attire. The shoulders were a bit tight, and the waist of the breeches somewhat large, but they would serve for now. The shoes were an excellent fit. He visited the Biondi bank, then hailed a gondola and handed him the address of Ambrose Barnes's Venetian residence in *sestiere* San Marco. As Hunter approached his lodgings, a narrow two-story building in need of replastering, a servant backed out of the door, pulling a barrow filled with boxes.

"Good morrow, fellow. Is your master within?"

The big man loosed his hold on the handles of the barrow and straightened up with a start. "No, sir." His eyes darted nervously past Hunter, as though searching for others.

"When will he return?"

The servant stood frozen and speechless for a moment, then raised a finger to summon Hunter close. "I beg your pardon, sir, but my master has changed houses."

Hunter stood perplexed. Why this move? Why whisper this news? "Is he at the new house?"

"Yes, sir."

"May I accompany you thither..." Hunter's pause begged for his name.

"Christopher, sir."

"Christopher. I can assist you with this cart."

The servant stood uncertain for a moment. Hunter sensed he wished to refuse but dare not offend this gentleman who knew his master. "You may come with me, sir, but I will need no help with this load."

Hunter followed Christopher as he tilted and wheeled the barrow expertly over two bridges. He hailed a *peata*, and its two boatmen helped him aboard with his load. The *peata* maneuvered into the Grand Canal, then turned right to enter the narrower canals of Cannaregio. After a left turn, Hunter recognized the turbaned statues he had seen the night before.

"Our new house is not far," Christopher said. After passing under a bridge, the boat glided to a stop at the end of a narrow street. "It is the third house on the left. You need not wait while we lift the barrow."

Hunter proceeded to the door indicated and knocked. After some moments, a servant, shorter than Christopher, opened the door a crack and stammered, "Who—uh—*chi è*?"

"I am Edward Hunter. Pray ask Master Barnes if I might have a word with him."

"One moment, sir." The servant hesitated, then closed the door.

An unusual and rude precaution, Hunter thought. Did Barnes fear theft here in Venice?

Barnes himself opened the door a crack, recognized Hunter, then swung it wider, peered up and down the street, and saw Christopher. "Pray enter, Master Hunter. Francis, come help Christopher with his load."

Barnes led Hunter into a central room with benches and a table. "I am surprised to see you in Venice. What brings you here?"

"Business," Hunter replied. "As you may recall, I am to arrange the purchase of silk for my uncle."

"Ah, yes. Did Master Sidney accompany you?"

"No. But I must thank you for him. Your suggestion to appeal to the Ten for permission to carry arms was successful." That should start the interview on a positive note.

"I was pleased to be of service," Barnes said. "Pray take a seat."

Hunter sat. Thumps and banging told him the servants were unloading. "I am still attempting to make sense of the attack on Sidney."

"We spoke of that before, just after the attack," Barnes said. "Francis, pray pour us cups of wine before your next load. Did you talk to Charles Carr?" He sat with firm mouth and brows creased.

"Yes, I did. He pointed to Tommaso Biradi but denied any knowledge of who might have engaged Biradi and his men to capture and transport Sidney."

"Did you believe him?"

"I am uncertain."

A look of concern passed Barnes's face. "I can only tell you again that *I* have no knowledge of that affair."

So every expatriate had said. "Have you any guess of who killed his captors, or why?"

"No."

Hunter switched tactics. "I looked for you earlier at your lodgings and was fortunate to encounter your servant. Why have you changed your abode?"

Barnes's eyes hardened. Perhaps he had been too direct.

"A man may choose to engage lodgings for many reasons—cost, proximity to notable places, healthful air, the rank of one's neighbors..." Barnes left it to Hunter to take his pick and made it clear that his reasons were none of Hunter's business.

Francis arrived with wine.

"What brought you to Venice? I thought you attended lectures at the university."

"Business brought me here." Barnes's tone indicated that this was none of Hunter's concern either, and he would not expand his answer. "I beg pardon, but I am confounded by your attire."

So, Barnes could also switch tactics. How much should Hunter reveal? An account of his assault might pry other information loose. "I was forced to borrow an artisan's clothes after being attacked last night and thrown into a canal."

Barnes's eyes and mouth opened wide. "Where?"

"In fact, not far along this same canal, near the statues of the Moors."

Barnes's face changed from hostility to fear for a moment. "Pray tell me more."

Hunter related the assault, watching Barnes closely. He showed growing interest and shuddered at the mention of a dagger. When Hunter said he swam to nearby steps, Barnes asked, "You can swim?"

"Yes."

"A useful skill in Venice. You were lucky to escape with your life."

Hunter continued, "I believe the ruffians mistook me for Sidney."

Barnes relaxed and pondered a moment. "Then whoever was behind taking him by force persists, and now seeks him in Venice as well."

"That is what I fear."

Barnes nodded. "Then I understand why you continue your enquiries."

"In light of the assault I suffered, have you any further thoughts on who might be behind this?"

Barnes pursed his lips. "I have heard Biradi's reach is long, and there are similar men here in Venice."

"Do you know the names of any of those?"

"I have heard men speak of Rossi and Costa with fear. Perhaps someone hired *bravi* through one of them."

Hunter noted the names, wondering how Barnes had heard them. "Do you know where such men are to be found?"

"There are many low tippling-houses in Venice where criminals loiter."

"I shall have to ask at one."

Again fear crossed Barnes's face. "Take care. Such men as Costa and Rossi do not take kindly to those who want information about them and their deeds."

"I am sure you are right." Hunter was unsatisfied with Barnes's answers but judged that pressing him further would gain nothing. "I hope to see you soon in Padua."

CHAPTER 9

Dangerous Waters

Saturday, 22 May 1574, Padua

"WELL MET! WELL MET!" SIDNEY EXCLAIMED. THEN HE LOOKED HUNTER up and down. "Did you need to pawn your clothes to pay for a boat back?"

Hunter laughed. "No, no. But it is a lengthy story."

"Then pray enter and tell us all."

Hunter and Gironi seated themselves with Sidney's party, to share in a meal of roasted veal. Hunter told of his negotiations for silk thread, the assault, and his rescue by Tintoretto. Gironi interjected comments whenever he felt Hunter had overlooked an important detail.

"I know not what part of your tale should cause me most amazement," Sidney said.

"I vote for his ignorant befriending of Tintoretto," Gironi said. "Assaults are commonplace."

After their laughter, Bryskett said, "But you have yet to explain your apparel."

"I wear the clothing of Luca's cousin, Stefano," Hunter said. "And shoes newly fashioned by him. A tailor promised me a new suit by Wednesday next."

"I am more interested in what makes you think these ruffians mistook you for me," Sidney said.

"I grant you I am much better looking," Hunter smiled. "But your lodgings are in the neighborhood, you have already been attacked once, and we are much the same size. Does it not make sense that whoever was behind the first attack still seeks to do you harm?"

Sidney sighed. "I wish the Ten's permission to bear arms had included you."

"I would still have been one against three," Hunter said.

"I am surprised those odds would deter you," Gironi said, "given your plans for the morrow."

"What are those?" Sidney asked.

When Hunter hesitated, Gironi said, "He proposes to march into the Ram's Head and ask Tommaso Biradi who hired your assailants."

The table exploded in exclamations of astonishment and disapproval.

"That is folly," Sidney summarized.

"My other enquiries have borne no fruit," Hunter protested. "I shall not be deterred." He hoped he had as much resolve as he stated.

"If you persist," Bryskett insisted, "then at least we shall accompany you."

"I have discussed this already with Luca," Hunter countered. "If they wish you harm, Philip, then the greater folly would be for you to come too. And the greater show of force we present, the more likely we will provoke them. I hold they gain less honor from an easy triumph over two men than in a victory over half a dozen, so they are more likely to order us out than attack us."

Madox and White nodded. Bryskett and Sidney reluctantly yielded.

"The only possible reprieve is if Biradi has left town again," Gironi said hopefully.

"Alas, he has not," Bryskett said. "He was parading about the *Piazza delle Erbe* on the day you left for Venice, as if daring Captain Scarpa to come arrest him."

"Yes," Madox interjected. "The day that pimp was found there with his throat slit open."

"Has the murderer been found?" Hunter asked.

"I doubt much effort has been made there," Bryskett said.

"How did they know he was a pander?" Hunter asked.

"It was the common talk of the marketplace," Madox said. "His name was Emilio Carollo. A small, thin man. He was well known."

"Perhaps I might ask Biradi about that as well," Hunter said.

Gironi groaned. "As the one who must translate, I shall write my will before we go."

Sunday, 23 May 1574, Padua

Half the paint had flaked off the sign bearing the ram's head. The exterior of the tavern had fared even less well. Hunter approached with a determined step, though his heart raced.

"Are you sure?" Gironi asked again.

"We have been over this before. It is Sunday morning. Many of the men will be recovering from a night of drink. It is full daylight. What better time to approach Master Biradi?" Hunter reasoned.

"Never might be a better time," Gironi said.

Hunter took a deep breath. "Let us enter." He pushed against the taphouse door, and it swung open. From the full daylight outside, they entered a twilight interior. As his eyes adjusted, Hunter approached the bar, passing grimy tables. At one, men with serious faces beheld one another suspiciously from behind hands of cards and piles of small coins. At another, two men appeared asleep on folded arms. Gironi followed Hunter, a few steps behind. He nodded at three men drinking at a third table, perhaps acquaintances from his previous visits. The men who stood at the bar stared at them as if they were curiosities. Hunter nodded a greeting, making note of each one. A bald man with no discernible neck, and meaty arms that strained against the sleeves of his shirt, did not return his greeting. The gaping grin of the second man, a less robust fellow, revealed a few yellow teeth behind scarred lips. The third man, who seemed amused, leaned on the bar as if he had already consumed several cups. No one here with a broken nose.

"*Sì?*" the thin man behind the bar asked.

Hunter hoped his voice would not crack. He spoke in the lowest pitch he could. "I would like to speak with Master Biradi."

Hearing non-Italian words, but recognizing the name Biradi, the men at the tables raised their heads to observe this oddity. Laughter greeted Gironi's translation. Several stools scraped across the floor as men stood.

"*Sì, Signor Biradi, per favore,*" Hunter said.

"*Ah, l'inglese parla l'italiano,*" the barman said, causing more laughter.

"*No, devo tradurre,*" Gironi said.

"*Tu chi sei?*"

Hunter understood. "*Sono Edoardo Cacciatore*—Edward Hunter."

"*Mi chiamo Luca Gironi.*"

The barman played to his audience as Gironi translated. "So, you walk in unannounced and expect to talk to *Signor Biradi.*" He pronounced the name slowly with a strong English accent that produced guffaws. He pointed to his right. "Perhaps you should just walk through that door and demand an audience." The barroom dissolved in an uproar of laughter.

Hunter pressed on, with the necessary delays while Gironi translated. "Tell him Master Edward Hunter humbly requests a few words."

"About what?"

"Master Sidney."

"Sidney? Sidney? Who is that?"

"The man taken from Padua by Matteo, Marco, Luca, and Pietro."

At the names of the slaughtered men, the room fell silent. The barman and those standing at the bar stared hard at Hunter. The air of comedy vanished.

The barman muttered something and entered the solid door with iron strapping he had indicated earlier. Hunter concentrated on controlling his breathing, aware that every eye was upon him.

In a few moments, the bartender returned. Behind him strode two men radiating menace. They signaled Hunter and Gironi were to follow them into what must be the inner keep of Biradi's castle.

As they entered, Biradi stood. He was a stocky man of about Hunter's height, with black hair, full lips, and piercing eyes beneath heavy brows. His beard and moustache were carefully trimmed. He wore an embroidered satin doublet. He gestured for them to sit opposite him, where cups of wine had been poured. "*Sior 'Unter, bevi qualcosa.*"

"Thank you." Hunter thought it best to stick to English.

Behind Biradi, at a small desk filled with papers, sat a wizened man with spectacles. Several seals and sticks of red wax stood beside his inkpot and quills. The source of Sidney's summons, Hunter thought. With a wave of his hand, Biradi shooed the secretary and the larger men from the room. The parley began, with Gironi translating for each.

"You asked to talk with me?" Biradi began.

Hunter dived in. "Yes. I wanted to ask who paid to hire the men who captured Philip Sidney and carted him to the Romagna."

Biradi's heavy brows shot up in disbelief. He uttered a mirthless chuckle. "Why would I know?"

"I understand you know everything of a certain kind that goes on in Padua."

"And you expect me to tell you, if I happen to know?"

"I hope you might."

Biradi gave his mirthless laugh again. "Did you ride after this Sidney?"

"Yes."

"Did you see the men whose throats were cut?"

"I did."

Biradi appeared to consider his next question. "Did they look as though they had put up a fight?"

"No. They looked as though they had been taken by surprise."

"Did you see what happened?"

"No. My friend Signor Sidney saw it and he told me."

Gironi's face blanched as he translated Biradi's next statement. "I should like to speak with this Sior Sidney."

Hunter's heart pounded. Might Biradi hold them and demand Sidney turn himself over? He had been a fool indeed to come. After a deep breath, he said, "Signor Sidney told me all he saw in detail. Perhaps I can exchange my information for what you know about who hired his captors."

Gironi's wide eyes asked Hunter if he truly wanted to say this. At Hunter's nod, he turned and translated.

Biradi's eyes became cold granite. "Do you think you are in a position to bargain?"

"I hoped I might get something for my information."

"You might be allowed to leave alive," Biradi said.

CHAPTER 10

Blood Water

HUNTER HAD OVERPLAYED A WEAK HAND. HE SWALLOWED. "WHEN Matteo, Marco, Luca, and Pietro reached a barn in the Romagna with Sidney, they unloaded him and waited. Soon other men arrived. The Paduans greeted them as though they were expected. Those who came offered them wine and laughed with them, then suddenly grabbed them and cut their throats."

Anger flared in Biradi's eyes. "What did those men look like?"

"They wore helms like this." Hunter indicated the shape with his hands. "And breastplates."

"Any devices?"

"No. No identifying badge."

"And their faces?"

"Signor Sidney said he remembered little. Some had beards, some not."

"How long after the murders did you arrive?"

"Within hours."

"And what happened then?"

Hunter sensed he must supply every detail he could remember. He told how the Paduans had been loaded onto horses and carried to an inn. He described the visit of the vice inquisitor and coroner the following day.

Biradi listened and nodded. His face hardened, but the anger did not seem directed at Hunter. Finally, he asked, "Do you know the name of the vice inquisitor?"

"Antonio Fascetti, I believe," Hunter said.

Biradi seemed satisfied. "You may go." A mirthless chuckle. "You did not touch your wine."

Hunter lifted his cup and sipped. Though Gironi's hand twitched in impatience, Hunter hesitated, searching for something nagging at the corner of his mind. Then he remembered. It was hazardous, but they had survived so far, and he would probably never have a chance to meet Biradi face-to-face again. "Do you know who killed the pimp Emilio Carollo?"

When he heard the name, Biradi shouted and slammed his fist on the table. No need for a translation of that anger. Hunter sat frozen, expecting the door behind them to burst open and strong hands to grasp his shoulders, but instead Gironi grabbed his arm. "We must leave now and never return." He pulled Hunter through the door and across the barroom at a run, as its patrons laughed in derision.

They did not stop until they reached the *Piazza delle Erbe*.

"'Sblood, Hunter, were you trying to get us killed?" Gironi asked between breaths.

"Not really." Hunter caught his breath. "I always intended to ask about Carollo, and I knew I would never have another chance."

"If you are dead, you will never have a chance to do *anything* again!"

"If you shout, everyone will look at us," Hunter warned.

Gironi rolled his eyes to the sky and jerked his head toward a stall in the shadow of the *Palazzo della Ragione*. He ordered two *grappe* and threw back his glass. "Now, what did you learn from that mad adventure that you did not know before?"

This was not how a servant was supposed to talk to his master. Of course, Hunter was not his master, the Earl of Leicester was. He was addressing Hunter as Leicester's deputy. Hunter swallowed his pride with his liquor. "Well, it is clear that the men killed were Biradi's men..."

"We knew that."

"...and that he is very unhappy that they were killed..."

"Also predictable."

"...that I gave him the first details he had received..."

"Perhaps."

"...and that the death of the pimp Carollo is connected."

Gironi stood speechless for a moment. "How do you reckon that to be true?"

"Biradi was angry about the death of his men. When I asked about Carollo, he might have dismissed it, if it were a separate matter. And

Carollo's death was quite public. His body was found here in the marketplace, with his throat slit like those in the Romagna."

"Yes."

"If it had been just a disagreement with a pander who was withholding money, I suggest he would simply have disappeared. But Biradi was sending a message."

"To whom?"

"I'm not entirely sure. If the pimp was a go-between, the message might be for the person who contracted for the attack on Sidney. He might blame that person for the deaths."

"Why not kill him directly?"

Hunter shrugged. "Perhaps Biradi didn't know who he was, and he squeezed the information from the pimp before killing him."

Gironi sighed. "You may be right, but I am not sure it was worth hazarding our lives."

Hunter slapped his thigh.

"What now?" Gironi asked.

"Is there a way to find out which girls Carollo pandered for?"

Gironi snorted. "Until an hour ago, I could have found that out at the Ram's Head."

"Ah, yes," Hunter said. "But if your friends at the Ram's Head would know, then Charles Carr would. We could ask him."

"Now? Why this sudden interest in Carollo's whores?"

"Who would know better whom Carollo spoke with in the days before Sidney was taken? Once Carr hears of our conversation with Biradi, he may be less willing to name them."

"I would have thought one harrowing interview in a day would be enough."

"I do not think Carr near as frightening as Biradi."

"No, he is not, but you do not need me to speak with another Englishman."

Hunter had asked much of Gironi. As Lord Leicester's man, he could portray Hunter as either brave or foolhardy in their encounter with Biradi. He needed his good will. "That is true. I shall buy you another *grappa* before tracking down Carr."

Fear flashed across Gironi's face. "Promise you will not follow him to the Ram's Head."

Hunter threw up his hands. "If he is not at his dwelling, I shall return to Pozzo della Vacca."

No one answered Hunter's knock at Carr's garret door. Perhaps he would find him at Luigi's. Besides, he was hungry. His guess proved correct. Having consumed a few goblets, Carr was less guarded and willing to display his knowledge of Carollo. Hunter consumed an eel pie and a cup of wine while Carr spoke with regret of Carollo's demise. He rated him an excellent, good-natured fellow—for a pimp.

"Can't say I approve of a man making his living off a woman," he opined. "She ought to be able to do business for herself."

Hunter detected an opportunity. "Did you know any of his women?"

Carr smiled with an air of superiority. "I have *known* several of them." He winked. "As the Bible says."

Although Hunter found no mirth in the comment, he gave a brief smile to encourage Carr. "How many worked for him?"

"Four or five. Let me see." Carr rested his hand on his chin and looked at the ceiling. "Maria, Lucetta, Giulia, Bianca, and—I can picture her, but—yes, Marta."

"Would you know where to find these ladies?"

Carr leered back at him. "Lonely, are you? Well, it's hard to know who has taken them in now that Emilio has met his end. Of course, Lucetta disappeared before that, about the time I first met you. I have heard Giulia is the property of Roberto Fontana, at the Pope's Arms just across the Ponte Molino." He laughed. "She is a jolly roll in the hay, a right plump wench." He looked at Hunter for a reaction. "Not to your taste? Maria might have gone to Signora Soranzo. I think a cousin of hers worked there."

"Where?"

"Oh, out past the Prato somewhere. I never went there myself."

"What does Maria look like?"

"Long brown hair. Firm tits. A pretty face. No smallpox scars."

Those were two names Hunter might ask for, in the two locations Carr had named. "What about Bianca and Marta?"

"I have not heard."

"And the girl who left before?"

"Lucetta? I understand she went to Venice."

"A difficult place to find someone," Hunter said. But he knew ladies there who might have heard of a newly arrived prostitute. "Any idea where in Venice?"

"None."

"What did she look like?"

"A slight girl. Red hair. She didn't appeal to me."

Hunter recalled the glimpse of a thin red-haired girl in *Campo San Cassiano*, being prodded along by two Dominicans. Perhaps, but Venice must have many red-haired prostitutes. "May I buy you another drink?"

Carr smiled. "I have earned that by giving you all the information about the girls."

"Edward," Sidney pronounced his name with a concerned tone when he opened the door and looked him up and down as if to satisfy himself that his friend had suffered no harm. "Luca told us of your encounter with Biradi."

Hunter shrugged. "We escaped without wounds."

"Now you sound like Philip." Bryskett joined them at the door. "You make a good pair of gamblers." He motioned both toward the table and called to Beatrice for another cup of wine. To Hunter's surprise, John Hart sat there.

Hart rose to greet him, adding his expressions of concern for Hunter.

"Pray swear you will not venture alone again on such a dangerous mission," Sidney insisted.

"I was not alone," Hunter said. "Luca was with me."

"And he is above, resting after the fright you gave him," Sidney said.

"Were *you* not afeared as well?" Bryskett asked. The sparkle in his eye suggested that Gironi had told him so.

"Terrified," Hunter admitted.

"Then why..." Bryskett began.

Hunter looked squarely at Hart. "I could find no answers to who paid for the attack on Philip, so I asked the man who clearly knew."

Hart remained silent, but his expression evidenced innocence and ignorance.

"And you were the one who presumed to instruct me on avoiding danger." Sidney gave a smug smile. "Luca said you found no answer at the Ram's Head."

"Not directly. I am convinced, as everyone thought, that the attackers were directed by Biradi, that he was unhappy at their murders, and that he may be seeking to punish whoever instigated the affair."

"Luca said you suspect the pimp Carollo was involved," Sidney said.

"Biradi's anger and the manner of Carollo's death led me to believe that."

"Did Carr confirm your suspicions?" Bryskett asked.

"I did not ask him to connect Carollo to Biradi, but I discovered some of the women he controlled. I hope they will know more of Carollo's actions."

Sidney clicked his tongue. "Surely Carollo did not hire the soldiers who slew my captors. Do you plan to delve again into perilous places?"

Hunter hesitated, reluctant to admit his intentions.

"Your pause shows you do," Sidney said. "I implore you to allow one of us with a license to bear weapons to accompany you. Biradi has long arms. Because you escaped today may not warrant you will be so lucky tomorrow."

Hunter scanned the worried faces around the table. He had to acknowledge the wisdom of Sidney's suggestion. "I pledge to do so. As Lodowick speaks Italian, he might serve me as well as Luca."

"I will be glad to attend you," Bryskett said, "though Gironi's Venetian may yield better results."

"Two companions will provide greater safeguard," Sidney said. "And I am willing, though a poor linguist, and loathe to visit brothels, to bear you company as a third."

"You advise me to avoid danger, yet you run toward it yourself," Hunter challenged.

Sidney smiled. "It takes a wise man to keep his own counsel."

Hart seemed about to burst. "I hope you might both be more cautious. I was troubled to hear of the assault upon you in Venice, but amazed that you met Master Tintoretto."

"The circumstances were regrettable, but the meeting propitious," Hunter said.

"Do you think that you might be welcome if you returned with friends?" Hart asked.

Returning to thank the painter again for his kindness would not be amiss. As to a request to include friends, the worst that might happen was a refusal. "I would be willing to send a letter," Hunter said.

"This coming Sunday, the choir will perform a new work by Gabrielli at San Marco," Hart said. "You are welcome to join us."

Hunter had several reasons to return to Venice. He had just promised to attempt to introduce his friends to Tintoretto, he hoped to ask Barnes more questions, he wanted to enquire about the red-haired Lucetta, and of course there were the warm caresses of Caterina. "Thank you. I shall."

Tuesday, 25 May 1574, Padua

Hunter's visit to the Pope's Arms in search of Giulia, accompanied by Gironi and Bryskett, yielded no useful information. Although her new pimp had profited from Carollo's death, he was terrified rather than guilty when discussing the murder. Giulia, also clearly frightened, said Carollo spoke to an Englishman, but she described Carr.

At Signora Soranzo's, a little silver convinced the madam to allow the men to speak with Maria. Yes, Carollo had spoken with Englishmen. She knew Carr intimately, but she did not know the identity of the second *inglese*, only that Carollo had spoken with him some months before. Bianca and Marta had left for Venice as soon as they heard of Carollo's murder. They were with Signora Francesca at the Castelletto. Lucetta had also left for Venice, just after the Dominicans visited Carollo.

"Dominicans?" More evidence that Lucetta was the girl he had spotted in *Campo San Cassiano.*

"Yes," Maria said. "They argued with Sior Carollo, though I could not hear what they said through the wall."

"Can she describe...?" Hunter began. But at that juncture, Signora Soranzo entered, fear clearly written on her face. The offer of more money could not prise any more from them.

"There is truly danger when whores fear someone more than they desire money," Gironi said to Bryskett.

Hunter was wrapped in his own thoughts. Maria's memory of an unknown Englishman was evidence Carollo was a go-between with Biradi. He should have asked her when the Englishman spoke with Carollo. Dominicans visited Carollo about the time he and Sidney had returned to Padua. Lucetta left for Venice then. Likely she was the same woman he had seen with friars his first day in Venice. A Dominican had directed Scarpa to where Sidney lay bound, then disappeared. The vice inquisitor, also a Dominican, questioned them in the Romagna. The rest of the whores had scattered after Carollo's killing, probably fearing Biradi. These events seemed connected, but he could not tie them into an understandable bundle.

Thursday, 27 May 1574, Venice

Hunter strolled along the canal, humming to himself. Things were working out well. His new suit needed only minor alterations, and the tailor promised it that afternoon. After he had thanked Gironi for his help, he dispatched him to Tintoretto's studio to request a meeting tomorrow afternoon, by which time Sidney, Bryskett, and Hart should arrive. As Gironi would then go to his cousin, Hunter was free to visit Caterina. To avoid the gondolier's knowing smirks, he had directed him to the campo before the church of San Stae. Another turning to the left and right, and he stood before the door of Signora Filippa's. Zuan answered and accompanied him up the staircase to the *matrone*.

"*Buongiorno, Signora Filippa*," Hunter said. "*Caterina, per favore*."

"*Occupata*," Signora Filippa said.

Hunter frowned. He had been imagining various erotic encounters with Caterina for over a week. Discovering her with another client deflated his desires. Did one have to schedule appointments?

"You wait?" Signora Filippa enquired.

Hunter hesitated a moment. The idea of Caterina with another man so soon before she welcomed him into her arms was distressing.

"*Un'altra fanciulla?*" she asked.

"No." It was Caterina he had dreamed about, not just any woman. "*Aspetto*."

"*Vin?*" Signora Filippa asked.

"*Sì. Rosso, per favore*." Hunter sat on the couch under Danaë and studied the satyrs and nymphs on the tapestry opposite. The nymphs' young, firm breasts reminded him of Caterina's. He shifted his attention to the woven flowers beneath their feet. As Signora Filippa placed his wine on a stool, he heard a scream down the corridor. He leapt to his feet.

"*Aiuto!*"

Caterina's voice! He sprinted down the corridor, following the shouts to a door on the left, through a small anteroom, and into a chamber. As he wrenched the inner door open, Caterina, holding a petticoat to cover her nakedness, fell into his arms. Behind her, equally naked, face snarling, the tall Dominican Hunter had seen weeks before grabbed her right arm.

"No!" Hunter shouted, batting away the friar's hand. Teeth clenched, he drew back a hand to strike the friar for whatever he had done to Caterina, yet she leaned against him, sobbing, blocking his movement.

The Dominican retreated, spitting out a string of curses and retrieving a garment to cover himself.

Signora Filippa was at Hunter's shoulder, pushing past him. She glanced from Caterina to the Dominican and barked a question. The monk snarled an answer as Caterina wept.

Hunter felt moisture on her back. He held his hand up, red with blood. "Look!" he shouted, turning his palm toward Signora Filippa.

Now it was the *matrone's* turn to loose invectives on the Dominican.

While they argued in the bedchamber, Hunter wrapped Caterina in her petticoat and guided her through the antechamber into the corridor. Other courtesans swarmed around them, expressing shock and sympathy. They separated Caterina from Hunter and ushered her further down the hall.

Freed from the need to care for Caterina, his anger swelled again. How dare the Dominican wound this fragile violet? He charged back into the bedchamber, fists clenched. The friar had pulled his tunic over his head and regained a bit of dignity. "What did you do to her?" Hunter demanded.

Signora Filippa held up her hand. Hunter stopped, glaring at the friar. A hand on his shoulder spun him around. Zuan, the huge doorman, spoke to him in soothing tones. The *matrone* moved next to Hunter, her voice also calming. Against his will, Hunter allowed himself to be guided into the reception area. "What happened?" he demanded.

Signora Filippa motioned him back to the couch he had occupied. "Wait." She disappeared down the corridor.

Zuan remained with Hunter. Why wasn't he throwing the friar out? Fuming, Hunter swallowed his glass of wine. His leg quivered up and down with impatience. "What is happening?" Zuan smiled back, uncomprehending.

After a while, Caterina emerged, escorted by Leona.

"Caterina!" Hunter rose and enveloped her in his arms. "Caterina, are you all right?"

"Yes." She sniffed.

"What did he do?"

"He have little whip. He want I beat him. I say no. He ask again. Again I say no. Then he beat me." She started to cry again.

"The brute." Hunter looked over her shoulder as Signora Filippa entered the room. "What is happening to the friar?"

Caterina spoke briefly with the *matrone*, then turned back to Hunter. "Leona will serve him."

Hunter was dumbfounded. Evidently Signora Filippa was unwilling to lose a customer, and Leona was willing to offer more violent services than Caterina. "Is Signora Filippa displeased with you?"

Caterina's forehead furrowed.

"Is she angry with you?"

Caterina glanced at her *matrone*. "I think no. Friar not say he want beating. He should."

Signora Filippa appeared to understand and nodded.

Hunter held Caterina close. This was not the time to fulfill his lust, though he could not describe how he felt now as mere lust. Yet how could he allow himself to care for a courtesan? He kissed her gently. "You must recover from this attack."

She continued to nestle in his arms. He looked at Signora Filippa for help. She stepped to Caterina and held her by the shoulders. Caterina reluctantly pulled away from Hunter and allowed her *matrone* to steer her toward the rooms down the corridor.

A Man of God, indeed. That was the friar Hunter had seen in *Campo San Cassiano* on his first day in Venice, herding the woman he was now certain was Lucetta. Was he taking her somewhere to be his mistress? Had he threatened Carollo, then arranged the pimp's murder to take Lucetta? Was he a partner with Biradi? Hunter was halfway back to his lodgings when he remembered he had not paid for his wine.

Friday, 28 May 1574, Venice

Hart practically bounced as they left the studio. "Did you see the way the light struck the Madonna he was painting? Such ability! Such speed! He can render both the divine and the profane. How can I thank you, Edward, for this?"

Happy to have pleased his friends, Hunter said, "I was glad for the chance to thank him again for helping me."

"Your misfortune has proved our good fortune," Sidney said. "I almost regret having Veronese paint my portrait, rather than Tintoretto."

"And I regret counseling you to do so," Hart said. "At the least, may I buy you a glass of wine, Edward?"

"Only Edward?" Bryskett asked.

"Fine, fine," Hart said. "All of us."

"There is a tavern past the statues of the moors," Gironi said.

"Did you not say Ambrose Barnes had his lodgings near here, Edward?" Sidney asked. "If it is not far, we might search him out and invite him to join us."

In the company of others, Barnes might reveal what business kept him so long in Venice, and why he had moved. "He does lodge nearby. I believe it is the first turning after the next bridge."

The third on the left, Hunter remembered. When he raised his hand to knock, he realized the door was ajar, the frame splintered. Pushing it open slightly, he called out "Master Barnes!" He turned to the other men. "When I was last here, Barnes took great care to secure this door." He called again.

"Something must be amiss," Sidney suggested. "Let us enter."

The five moved tentatively down the short corridor, calling out. No answer. The room with table and benches looked much as it had the day Hunter and Barnes had spoken, but books from a shelf lay scattered on the floor. They discovered the other rooms were in shambles. Mattresses had been stripped from beds and torn open. Chests had been emptied. Food had been pulled from kitchen cupboards, strewn about the floor, and crushed underfoot.

"A clear robbery," Sidney concluded.

"Could Barnes have returned to Padua, and his lodgings burgled?" Bryskett asked.

"We must report this to the *Signori di Notte*," Gironi said.

"Lords of the Night?" Hunter asked.

"Literally, yes," Gironi said. "In this case I mean the agents who work for the Night Lord in this *sestiere*. If you gentlemen wait here, I shall find a gondola to take me to the authorities. It will be best if you do not order the scattered things." He left the others looking uncertainly at one another.

Hunter noticed a folded sheet of paper protruding from a book on the floor. As the others examined the contents of an upturned chest, he perused it. The writing made no sense, then he realized he was looking at a message in cipher. He opened his mouth to tell the others, then reconsidered. If this were a letter from Biradi, it might prove Barnes was behind the attack on Sidney. Or it might be a method the Catholic expatriates, including Hart, used to communicate with one another.

"What..." Sidney began, pointing at the letter, but his question was cut short by a cry from outside. Gironi was calling them. Hunter stuffed the coded letter inside his doublet as they rushed from the house.

"Come! Come!" Gironi stood at the north end of the narrow street, opening onto a canal. He pointed down at a gondola. They ran to him and surveyed the scene. A brown stain discolored the pavement by the gently rocking gondola. On its foredeck lay a body clad only in a bloody linen shirt, its head turned from them. A pale hand crusted with dried blood dangled over the side.

"Today is far from *Serenissima*," Gironi said. "These are waters of blood and death."

"Pray see if we recognize him," Hunter said. A glance at the others showed they shared his premonition.

Gironi transferred his weight onto the gondola's gunwale, shuffled forward to reach the body, grasped the shoulders, and turned the corpse onto its back.

The men uttered a collective gasp. Ambrose Barnes lay before them, his throat roughly cut on one side, a stab wound in his chest.

CHAPTER 11

Grasping at Straws

HUNTER'S HEAD SWAM FOR A MOMENT WITH IMAGES OF THE MAN HE HAD killed in Paris, of piles of corpses in its streets. When he opened his eyes, he focused on Barnes. Could he have been attacked by those who sought to harm Sidney, as they had mistaken him? Or had Hunter's attackers thought he was Barnes the week before? Could this have been merely a robbery Barnes interrupted? Where were the servants Francis and Christopher?

Hart stood overwhelmed and distraught. If there were a conspiracy among the expatriates, he was not a party to it. "We must take him back to Padua," he said.

"No," Gironi said. "The *Signori di Notte* must investigate first. We must not move him until they come."

"Shall I go fetch them?" Bryskett asked.

Gironi climbed from the boat. "It were best I went. I speak Venetian."

Hunter continued to stare at Barnes's pale face. The slit throat, though a botched job, resembled the murders of Biradi's men and the pimp Carollo. Had those who had slain Sidney's man-stealers slain Barnes? The *romagnoli* butchers were not likely to be in Venice. Was this another warning by Biradi? For whom?

"Look," Bryskett pointed at an approaching boat, filled with armed men, a red-and-gold Venetian banner at the prow.

"We need not seek the *Signori di Notte*," Gironi said. "A captain of a *barche longhe* comes to us."

"Who are they?" Hunter asked.

"Special authorities who report directly to the Council of Ten. We must mind our manners."

The long boat pulled in behind the gondola and three men wearing red coats with winged-lion crests climbed out. Behind them, a tall slim man with broad shoulders spoke excitedly, gesturing first at the gondola, then to the skies.

"The gondolier," Gironi explained.

The interrogation took over an hour. The officers questioned each man. They clambered into the gondola and inspected the body. They marched back to Barnes's lodgings, ordered everyone to wait outside, then reemerged with more questions.

They returned to interrogate the gondolier, sitting despondently beside the canal, forbidden to board his own boat, while Gironi eavesdropped. He had been sleeping in his boat the night before. Sometime in the early morning, shouting aroused him. He saw one man pursued by three. They grabbed the man right in front of him and knocked him down. One man told him to flee or they would kill him. He did not hesitate. It had been too dark to see the faces of the attackers or their victim. The most he could say is that one man was larger than the others. The victim was insensible, but still alive when he fled. Fear kept him away until late morning, when he began to imagine his boat might have been stolen and went to the authorities.

The officials from the *barche longhe* conferred. They would report this as a burglary and murder and turn it over to the *Signori di Notte*. The Englishmen could take their countryman to Padua for burial. They might also take any of his belongings that remained in his lodgings, as the officers had listed them. The *Signori di Notte* would contact the landlord to discover what was owed and would send word to the *Palazzo Michiel*.

"Sidney and I will fetch a sheet to wrap the body," Hunter said. "Can you Italian speakers arrange a boat to Padua?"

At Barnes's lodgings, Hunter pulled the coded message from his doublet. "I found this in one of these books." He indicated them with his foot.

Sidney stared and screwed up his brows. "A message in cipher? Do you think this might point to Barnes's killer? Should we not tell the *barche longhe* captain, or the *Signori di Notte*?"

"Neither them nor Hart, if you please. One of the books may be the key. I shall explain in Padua. Let us take the bed-clothes to the canal, then return to pack his belongings."

Saturday, 29 May 1574, Padua

All were tired after a restless night on the barge, at first trying to make sense of Barnes's death and robbery, then fitfully sleeping among the cargo of cloth and dried fruits, as far from the corpse as possible.

Hart took on the task of attending to the body, delivering the news to the expatriates, and making arrangements for Barnes's funeral and burial. The others walked stiffly to Pozzo della Vacca, following a cart with Barnes's possessions. After depositing the chests and eating a few slices of bread, they hurried to Barnes's Padua lodgings, Hunter anxious to arrive before the expatriates did and expecting to find at least one of his servants there. Instead, this door too had been forced, its bolts and lock dangling on broken pieces of wood.

"This is no accidental concurrency," Hunter said.

"Most likely it happened last night, while we were on the boat," Sidney guessed.

"We may look forward to more long hours of speaking with Captain Scarpa," Gironi said.

"We should search inside." Hunter pushed the door open. "Barnes may not have been the only victim."

They found no bodies, but rooms in similar disarray to those in Venice. Dried beans crunched underfoot in the kitchen. Two plates and a cup lay broken on the scullery floor. Linens and hangings had been stripped from the beds; the mattresses slit open. Whatever chests of clothing had been there had been carried off. A desk lay tipped on its side, its top ajar, its interior empty, and ink splattered on the floor.

Their investigation was interrupted by the arrival of Hart with Le Rous, Randolph, and Fitzwilliams. Exclamations of surprise filtering up the staircase caused Hunter and his companions to descend.

Hart shook his head in disbelief. "How could misfortune strike him in both cities?"

"This is no haphazard act." Fitzwilliams said. "Not misfortune but intention."

"Are his lodgings stripped clean?" Le Rous asked.

"Even more so than in Venice," Hunter said. "No bed linen or curtains, no cooking pots, only a few broken plates."

Le Rous headed to the kitchen.

"Are his servants missing?" Randolph asked.

"They are," Sidney answered.

"Then we must ask the guard to search for them," Randolph said.

"Servants would have no need to break in the door," Fitzwilliams said. "This is the work of criminal villains."

Le Rous returned to the main hall. His head swiveled around as though taking inventory. "Everything of value is gone: serving bowls, spoons, candlesticks, chairs, fire dogs, bellows... Did you find any clothes?"

"No," Hunter said. "Nor the chests that held them." The items missing from the Venice lodgings were lighter and easier to transport. That argued that the destination of all Barnes's valuables was Padua.

"There will be little to sell," Le Rous said.

"Sell?" Hart asked.

"He will have left debts," Le Rous said. "And you spoke to us of the funeral costs."

"But we all agreed to contribute toward those," Hart said.

"But we did not know then that he would leave nothing," Le Rous objected.

"I am willing to bear a share of the costs of burial," Sidney said.

Hunter felt the unspoken pressure of the group. "And I."

"We can count on Simmons to contribute when he learns of this," Randolph said.

"But not Carr," Le Rous said.

"I believe Baron Windsor knew his family," Fitzwilliams said. "We might send a message to him in Venice. Perhaps he will wish to attend the funeral."

And contribute as well, Hunter thought. Each man seemed true to his character: Randolph suspicious of the servants, as he had been of Hunter; Le Rous concerned about money; Hart sympathetic and generous; and Fitzwilliams eager to demonstrate superior knowledge. The expatriates became absorbed in the practicalities of paying for Barnes's funeral. Though each seemed surprised to discover the robbery, none appeared particularly grief-stricken by the man's death. Perhaps he had been wrong to rush to these lodgings instead of accompanying Hart to see their reaction to news of the killing.

"How much did you reckon the expense at San Nicolò?" Le Rous asked.

"Father Antonio mentioned six ducats," Hart replied.

"Then our share would be less than one each," Le Rous said.

Fitzwilliams stated Hunter's suspicion. "Biradi is behind this. He is behind many crimes in Padua."

"So everyone says," Randolph said. "But why this one, here and in Venice?"

"Barnes was not shy in displaying his wealth," Fitzwilliams said. "Anyone who does so makes himself a target."

Randolph returned to his earlier theory. "Perhaps his servants worked with Biradi and harbor with him now."

"Perhaps his killing was not part of Biradi's plan, only theft." Fitzwilliams scowled at Hunter. "Now we cannot ask what he knows."

"I certainly cannot," Hunter said. "But he would be unlikely to confess a crime to us." He spotted an opportunity. "Are any of you aware if Barnes owed a debt to Biradi?"

All the expatriates denied any knowledge.

"Might he have needed money and been forced to borrow?" Hunter pressed.

All shook their heads.

"He spoke of buying glass vases in Murano," Le Rous said. His eyes lit with an idea. "Did you find any ledgers or account books?"

"We did not," Hunter said.

"Pardon me, gentlemen," Gironi interjected, "but I should go to the *Palazzo del Capitanio* and report this theft. It would be best if someone stayed here to answer enquiries."

Le Rous looked at Hunter and Sidney. "I fear it must be you who first discovered the burglary here and in Venice."

Hunter knew he was right, though he longed to retreat to Pozzo della Vacca and begin deciphering the letter. "I shall stay. Will you gentlemen make final the arrangements for the funeral and send us word?"

"We shall," Fitzwilliams promised.

After the expatriates left, Sidney asked, "Do you still believe my friends to be behind the attack I suffered? Or your attack? Or Barnes's?"

"I am constructing a case now that mostly absolves them," Hunter said, "yet I must decipher the letter I found to be sure."

"You said you would enlighten me," Sidney said.

"One of Walsingham's decipherers explained one method of making a cipher. Two people agree on a book. They specify a place to begin a substitution of letters or symbols. When one receives the enciphered message, he can open the book to that place, substitute a letter from the book above each letter in the cipher, and read the message," Hunter explained.

Sidney nodded. "And your case?"

"Barnes was behind the attack on you. He somehow engaged Biradi to capture you and bear you into papal territory. When Biradi's men were killed, he was angry with Barnes and sought revenge. The men who attacked me were Biradi's men and mistook me for Barnes, not for you."

"Why would Barnes seek to harm me?"

"I don't know."

"Biradi should seek revenge on those who killed his men, not on Barnes."

"Yes, if he knew them," Hunter admitted. Sidney was quick to prick holes in his theory.

"What about the robberies?"

"They would conceal the true reason for the killing." Hunter paused. "Or perhaps Barnes *did* owe money to Biradi, and this was one way to collect."

"Before, you thought Carollo's death was connected," Sidney said.

"I am not sure now," Hunter said. "Unless he conveyed messages between Barnes and Biradi. If Biradi did not know who hired his men, he might have forced Carollo to tell him, then ordered the killing of Barnes." He could not account for the Dominicans, though he would not point that out to Sidney.

"A moment ago, you suggested Biradi knew Barnes because Barnes owed him money. Now you suggest he didn't know Barnes and had to find his identity from Carollo," Sidney said.

"I admit my case needs refining."

Sidney snorted. "At least you now think better of my friends."

Gironi appeared at the door with Captain Scarpa and two of his men. Scarpa greeted them with a wry comment and a sigh.

"He says 'We meet again,'" Gironi translated.

Monday, 31 May 1574, Padua

The Mass was over; the mourners who had gathered for Ambrose Barnes's funeral made their way out of the parish church of San Nicolò.

Hunter had spotted Edward, Baron Windsor and Lady Katherine during the service. As Sidney had promised an introduction, he edged his way toward the baron. Suddenly Charles Carr stepped in front of him. "I beg a word with you." His tone warned this was no polite request.

"Might we speak later?" Hunter asked.

"We might not," Carr said. The left side of his face was bruised and his lip had been split.

Hunter could have pushed past him, but it would not do to cause a scene at a funeral. He led Carr to one side.

"Why did you go to Biradi?" Carr asked in whispered rage. Before Hunter could answer, he pointed to his discolored face. "Do you see this? Biradi's men showed up at my place last week, saying he wanted to see me. They dragged me to the Ram's Head and shoved me into the back room. Biradi said another damned Englishman had come to see him and accused me of sending you. Said I had been seen talking to you afterwards. That's when I told you about the whores, and you never mentioned you had just seen Biradi." He finally paused.

"I am sorry my questions to him resulted in your injuries," Hunter said. "I did not think you would be the target of his anger."

"You might have warned me."

Hunter chanced a question. "Did you introduce Barnes to Biradi?"

"What?" Carr stepped back. "Why would you think so?"

Not a denial. Carr was not the only one who could answer a question with a question. "Do you think Biradi had Barnes killed?"

Despite fear in his eyes, Carr asked, "Why would Biradi have him murdered?"

"Perhaps that was not the main goal. All his valuables were taken. Could Barnes have been in debt to Biradi?"

Carr did not answer immediately. "He said, 'Damned Englishmen. You never pay your debts.' I thought he was talking about me." He looked down. "I owe him almost twenty ducats from gambling. But perhaps Barnes owed him, too."

"Did Barnes gamble?"

"No."

"Might he have borrowed from Biradi?"

"I cannot tell, and I *will* not ask." Carr's eyes blazed.

"I can only apologize again for the harm that has come to you," Hunter said.

Carr snorted and turned away. Relieved, Hunter searched anew for Baron Windsor but did not see him. Sidney approached. "I chose not to interrupt a conversation so full of heat."

"Carr had reason for his anger," Hunter said. "Biradi's men pummeled him, and he accused Carr of sending me to question him."

Sidney nodded.

"But he did say that Biradi complained of Englishmen who did not pay their debts. That supports my case that Barnes owed Biradi."

"Perhaps," Sidney said. "Before, you said Biradi was angry over the death of his men."

"Perhaps it was both. Suppose Barnes contracted your captors but would not pay when they failed to deliver you to harm."

Sidney shook his head. "I fear you would lose your case. Barnes had no motive to harm me. In fact, he suggested I petition the Ten to carry weapons in the Veneto. And my captors did deliver me to others."

"You would have made a good lawyer," Hunter conceded. "Though petitioning the Ten might be his device to divert suspicion from himself. What did you learn from Baron Windsor?"

"He knows Barnes's family in Berkshire and plans to inform them of his death. He asked if any jewelry or personal items had been found, and I told him no. He did contribute to the funeral expenses and asked if money were needed for the landlords."

"I regret that Carr prevented my meeting such a generous man."

"There should be another opportunity," Sidney said. "Baron Windsor has invited me to dinner next Friday."

Wednesday, 2 June 1574, Padua

Hunter rubbed his eyes. He hoped Walsingham paid his decipherers well. They deserved it. He stared again at the numerals IV-XXII-VII at the top of the letter. They were the clearest symbols on the page, followed by a hotch-potch of unseparated letters, which he had yet to organize into words. He dropped the page of gibberish his last effort had produced onto the mound on the floor, lifted a blank piece of paper from the pile on the desk, and began again, this time with the fourth chapter of the fourth book of *De Imitatione Christi*, rather than the fourth page of the fourth book. He counted down twenty-two lines and in seven words and began to copy the text.

Sidney opened the door behind him. "Still at it?"

Hunter replaced his quill in the inkpot and stretched his hands over his head. "Indeed I am." He sighed. "There are so many starting places these numbers might indicate—the fourth page, fourth book, fourth chapter—the twenty-second line, or word, or letter. Or the numbers could be read backwards. As the books are in Latin, I guess the cipher is in Latin. I guess repeated letters should not be considered. I guess the alphabet should be listed above the letters from the starting point. I am full of guesses."

"Pray hold," Sidney said. "I do not wish you to go mad. You have labored two days to no effect. I shall help you tomorrow if you will grant yourself a respite and accompany me to Venice on Friday to dine with Lord Windsor."

"Both your help and a respite will be welcome," Hunter replied. Another trip to Venice would allow him more than an introduction to the English Catholic nobleman. With Gironi's help, he could search out and interview Carollo's two prostitutes who had fled to the city. One might have seen Barnes or overheard the friars. Alone, he might visit Caterina again.

A clattering downstairs caught their attention.

"Ah," Sidney said, "if that is Gironi, we may dine."

Hunter straightened his papers, sealed the ink pot, cleaned his quill, and followed Sidney downstairs. Gironi sat, removing his boots.

"Good evening, Luca," Hunter greeted him. "Did you locate other sources of spun silk?"

"Indeed I did." Gironi fixed him with a wry grin. Both men knew that Gironi's trip into the countryside around Padua had a different purpose. "I shall not bore these gentlemen with the details now but inform you after we eat."

Friday, 4 June 1574, Venice

"Good morning, gentlemen," the heavily-rouged woman at the gateway to the Castelletto cooed. "What may you wish today?" Her eyes sparkled in expectation of four customers.

No subtlety here, Hunter thought.

"Assure her we only want to talk with some ladies," Sidney protested.

"In a moment," Gironi said. He switched to Venetian "We hope to speak with Signora Francesca."

"You are doing so." She smiled.

"We understand two ladies may have recently arrived from Padua, Marta and Bianca."

Signora Francesca eyed them narrowly. "They did, but two cannot serve four of you."

Bryskett laughed.

"Explain now." Sidney urged.

"We merely wish to talk with the ladies," Gironi said.

Signora Francesca raised a skeptical eyebrow. "Talk?"

"Yes."

"That would not need four of you."

Hunter realized it had been a mistake for all of them to repair to the Rialto. "You and I can speak," he prompted Gironi.

"But neither are armed," Sidney objected.

"We have daggers, which are all a woman is likely to wield," Hunter said. "Besides, you do not want to enter a brothel."

His argument carried the day. Sidney and Bryskett agreed to wait at a nearby tavern.

"*Tedesco?*" Signora Francesca asked. Why did Venetians always assume foreigners were German?

"*Inglese,*" Hunter said. They followed her up a flight of stairs to a waiting room. Its furnishings were similar to those at Signora Filippa's, but the lip of a marble vase was chipped; the corner of a faded tapestry had begun to unravel.

"I doubt she believes we only want to talk with her ladies," Gironi said. "We may have to pay the full price."

"If we find more about Carollo's English patron, it will be worth it," Hunter said.

Signora Francesca returned a few moments later, trailed by two young prostitutes. "*Marta e Bianca,*" she announced. Marta was slightly shorter, a brunette with a turned-up nose and thin lips. Bianca, as her name suggested, was pale with light blonde hair and a fuller figure. "Which of you wants which girl?"

"We wish to speak with both at the same time," Gironi said.

Signora Francesca raised her brows again. "No rough business."

"We agree to pay, though it shall be only talk," Gironi assured her.

She spoke to the two women, who giggled at the idea. "In advance." She named her price.

Hunter counted out the coins, and the *matrone* led them to a cramped room with a bed and two padded benches. The girls seated themselves on one and smiled uncertainly. Hunter and Gironi positioned the other bench opposite them and sat.

"We came from Padua," Gironi began.

The girls glanced at one another with widened eyes and their bodies tensed. "Did Biradi send you?" Marta asked.

"No. We wish you no harm. Do you fear..." Gironi decided not to repeat the name "...that man?"

"Yes," Marta said. "Carollo..." Bianca nudged her into silence.

Hunter extracted a four-soldo piece and nodded to Gironi, who said, "We are willing to pay you for information. That man threatened us as well. We promise to repeat nothing you say to him or any of his men."

The girls glanced at one another, at Hunter and Gironi, then at one another again. They appeared to reach a decision.

"What do you want to know?" Bianca asked.

"Do you know who killed Emilio Carollo?"

The girls exchanged glances again but remained silent.

"Was it—that man?"

Bianca gave a tiny nod. "We think so."

"So you left for your safety?"

Another nod.

"Ask about Englishmen," Hunter prompted.

"Why did he have Carollo killed?" Gironi asked.

Bianca bit her lips. Marta sniffed.

"Did it have to do with an Englishman?"

Both girls shared a shiver of fear again.

"Pray tell us what you know," Gironi urged. "Biradi is our enemy too." He took the coin from Hunter and rubbed it between his fingers.

Marta eyed the coin. "There were two Englishmen who spoke with Emilio."

"*Nomi?*" Hunter asked.

"*Sior Carr.*"

"And the other?" Gironi asked.

Marta shook her head and looked at Bianca, who did the same. "Biradi's men came to our house. They just asked Emilio about an Englishman."

This suggested Biradi did not know who had hired him, but Carollo did and he was the go-between. "*Non visto?*" Hunter hoped his imperfect Italian would be understood.

Neither had seen the other Englishman.

Bianca glanced at the coin Gironi held. "He spoke to another girl."

Hunter understood. "Lucetta?" he asked.

Both nodded.

"What happened to her?" Hunter asked. "Maria mentioned Dominican friars."

Gironi scowled. He raised a hand to counsel patience and put questions to the girls.

"The Dominicans came a month ago, about the time of the news that Biradi's men had been killed," Marta said.

"They talked to Emilio for a long time," Bianca added, not to be outdone.

"They argued," Marta said.

"The friars talked about danger," Bianca said, "but Emilio did not agree."

"Did Lucetta leave with the Dominicans?"

"The next day," Marta said.

"They paid something to Emilio," Bianca said. The women were clearly competing for the silver coin.

"What did they look like?"

"One was tall with a pointed nose," Marta said.

"The other short. He waddled." Bianca giggled.

Hunter struggled not to leap to his feet in excitement. That was the friar he had confronted at Signora Filippa's, the pair he had seen in *Campo San Cassiano*. "Ask what Lucetta said to them when she left."

"She cried," Marta said. "She did not know where they were taking her. They said she would be safe, but she was not sure."

"She said she would never see us again," Bianca added.

Further questions failed to produce any more useful information from the girls. They had not heard any name they recognized as an English name. Lucetta had never spoken a name either. They did not know why the friars took only Lucetta.

Hunter fished a second coin from his purse and gave one to each girl. Both promised to send word to *Palazzo Michiel* if they heard any more about Lucetta or the Dominicans.

Over the midday meal with Sidney and Bryskett, Hunter related what they had learned.

"How does this fit into the case you were building against Barnes?" Sidney asked.

"I believe he was one of the Englishmen who spoke with Carollo, whom Biradi's men were searching for," Hunter said.

"But if Barnes hired Biradi to capture me, Biradi must have known who he was," Sidney objected. "Why should his men ask Carollo to name him?"

"Suppose Barnes paid Carollo to approach Biradi, keeping his identity secret."

"Biradi does not seem the sort to deal with someone indirectly," Sidney objected.

"Unless a large amount of money convinced him to take that chance," Hunter said.

Sidney gazed into the distance and returned with a different line of questions. "You say you saw the two Dominicans they described a month ago."

"Yes. With Sebastian in the *Campo San Cassiano*, the day you spoke with the Ten. With a girl that matched the description of Lucetta." Hunter withheld the story of his encounter with the taller Dominican at Signora Filippa's. "Dominicans weave themselves into the story of your capture. A friar directed us to the barn where you were held. The vice inquisitor and infirmarian were Dominicans. Dominicans argued with Carollo and purchased Lucetta from him."

"Could they have arranged my capture or Carollo's murder?" Sidney asked.

"If those that came to Padua were in league with Biradi and brought news of his men's slaughter, why then did they warn Carollo of danger from Biradi? If they were concerned about Carollo's women, why take only Lucetta? What motive would they have for those acts?" Hunter asked.

"That is the same question I ask about Barnes," Sidney said. "You have yet to provide an answer."

Hunter sighed. "At least you accept that Biradi was likely behind Barnes's murder and the theft of his possessions."

"That does seem likely, but a man like Biradi needs no more motive than greed," Sidney said.

Bryskett cleared his throat and addressed Sidney. "We must deliver our list of what was stolen to the *Signori di Notte*."

"Will you accompany us?" Sidney asked Hunter.

Hunter had planned his excuse. "I prefer to stroll about the city this afternoon. I shall meet you at seven at Baron Windsor's palazzo. You two may go. As you have secured me an invitation tonight, I shall pay for this meal."

"I thank you." Sidney rose.

As they left, Hunter waved at the serving man. He turned to Gironi, who had not spoken since they left the brothel.

"I suppose you will want my translation services now?" Gironi asked with a sullen face.

Hunter realized he must make amends. He needed Gironi's language skills to investigate Sidney's capture and negotiate the purchase of silk. Just yesterday, he had found a peasant near Padua willing to sell them young mulberry trees. As Lord Leicester's servant, Gironi could ensure that he lost favor with the earl. "I beg your pardon for my impatience. I understood a bit of what the women were saying and became too eager to press my questions."

Gironi spoke with the serving man, who tallied what was owed. After Hunter paid, Gironi continued, "It may harm you to seize upon a few words and believe you know what is being said. Though your Italian is improving, you understand only a little and less Venetian."

Hunter knew this judgment was correct, though it irked him that an inferior addressed him so. Yet a moment's reflection told him that his feeling was flawed. Though their relationship was officially that of gentleman and servant, it was more a partnership, but he was reluctant to say so. Nevertheless, he must swallow his pride. "You are right. You are the boat I need to navigate these waters. Here, I need you more than you need me. I apologize for offending you in our interview."

"I accept your apology. But you are wrong that you need me more. You supply the funds so I may eat and travel. Your report could end my service to the earl."

"Then we must row in rhythm." Hunter continued his metaphor. Gironi's thoughts followed his. Either could end Lord Leicester's favor toward the other.

"I would not presume to advise you, but it is my duty, in this place where I can more easily read the customs and intentions of men and women, to keep us both out of danger."

"As you have done, admirably." Hunter remembered Gironi's advice to avoid the Ram's Head meeting. He stood.

"As to avoiding danger, what do you propose to do this afternoon?"

Hunter was unwilling to reveal his plan to call at Signora Filippa's. "I plan to visit the barber in the *Campo San Polo*, then I shall walk the streets of this amazing city, noting its architecture and the play of light upon the water."

Gironi regarded him dubiously. "Sounds quite poetic."

"Tonight may be one of the few times I need not impose upon you to be my translator. At Baron Windsor's palazzo, we all will speak English. It is near *Campo San Polo*, so I will not become lost. You may spend a long afternoon and evening with your cousin."

Gironi smiled. "Very well. I will expect you and Master Sidney to return to *Palazzo Michiel* safely this night. Pray do remember the word "*Aiuto.*"

"Pray remember to ask cousin Stefano about unhappy weavers."

"I shall." Gironi took his leave.

CHAPTER 12

Swimming in Circles

To avoid a lie, and to look his best for both Lord Windsor and Caterina, Hunter visited the barber on the south side of the *Campo San Polo*. From there, he followed landmarks—a bakery, a bridge, right at a bookshop, then over another bridge—to Signora Filippa's. The distressed *matrone* answered the door herself.

Hunter heard shouting from above. A middle-aged man, a well-to-do merchant by his dress, but with hair unkempt and clothes disheveled, flashed into view at the top of the staircase. He turned with a stream of invectives and waved his fist at an invisible opponent. Zuan stepped into view, advancing with slow menace. Though the merchant continued to rant, he retreated down the stairs. Hunter placed a hand in front of Signora Filippa and guided her behind him.

As the merchant reached the bottom of the stairs, Zuan barked a warning. The merchant cast an angry glance at Hunter and the *matrone*, then scuttled to the canal entrance. He halted, did his best to restore his pride by adjusting his clothes and donning his hat, and stepped onto the embankment to summon a gondola.

Signora Filippa thanked Zuan. She turned to Hunter with her hostess air. "Caterina?"

"Si, signora."

She led him up the staircase. As they reached the top, several women vanished into rooms on either side of the central corridor. She directed him to the *portego*. "Pray wait here."

Her English vocabulary had increased by a few words since Hunter's last visit. It was keeping pace with his command of Italian. A moment later, Caterina drifted into the room, graceful and beautiful.

"Master Hunter." She smiled and curtsied.

"Caterina." He smiled and nodded to her.

"I learn a English song," she said with excitement. "Will you come hear?"

"Yes." Hunter followed her to the chamber where he had seen her with the Dominican.

"Pray sit." She indicated a padded bench.

Hunter stepped closer. "First, are you well? Here?" He touched her back.

"Yes. It is heal," she said.

He smiled. "Healed. I am glad it is healed."

"It is healed," she repeated, now less worried about her errors than when he first met her. "Thank you for your help."

"I could not allow the friar to hurt you," Hunter said. "Who was he?"

"Fra Alberto."

"Has he come back?"

"No." She looked down. "Leona blame me."

"You were right to refuse his perverse desires."

Caterina screwed up her face. "Perverz?"

"Evil. Wicked," he explained.

She nodded.

"Just now, Zuan threw another man out." Hunter invited her explanation.

"He had foul..." she searched for a word, "*sboro.*"

"*Sboro?*"

"*Liquido nel pene,*" she explained. She pointed at his loins.

Despite their previous intimate encounter, Hunter blushed. "Foul liquid in his penis?"

She nodded. "Foul liquid, and foul sores. *La mal francese.*"

Now he understood. Sebastian had said Signora Filippa only allowed clean customers, trying her best to protect her girls from the pox.

"Pray sit. I will sing." She retrieved her lute from a table and tuned it. "Now a English song." She played four verses of "The Lady Greensleeves," her voice as rich and beautiful as he had remembered it. He noted she omitted a few words.

Hunter applauded. "That is the best I have heard it."

"You know?"

"Yes."

"There is more, but I do not know yet." She replaced the lute and sat beside him.

He reached for her. Their embrace was long and their kiss deep. Desire overcame him. He unlaced her bodice and kissed her breasts. Unbuttoning his doublet, she matched the heat of his desire, or so it seemed. It was her business to act thus, he told himself, but another portion of his anatomy did not care. She unlaced his venetians, grasped his stiff penis, squeezed the shaft, and pulled. She lowered her head and sniffed the small drop of semen that appeared.

As he realized this was the method courtesans used to ensure their clients were not diseased, she took his penis into her mouth. Hunter's mind reeled. This had never happened to him before. His excitement swelled. Caterina moved her hand and head up and down quickly. He was unable to control the spasm in his loins. As he released, he feared Caterina might find the taste of his seed loathsome. "I am sorry," he panted.

She looked confused. "Did I not please?"

"Very much," he said.

She smiled.

Hunter thrashed through the tangled underbrush of his emotions: sensual joy at his ejaculation, guilt at again defiling this girl, jealousy that she had done the same for other men, a longing to take her from this life of sin. "Do you...Do you do this often?"

She nodded. "Seed in the mouth will not make a baby," she explained.

"Does that satisfy most men?"

"No. They want me in bed."

He held her close and repeated her name. Like waves, the perils of her profession crashed into his consciousness. Infection, violence, or pregnancy threatened her daily. And he was part of the threat, at least of pregnancy. "But before..." he began.

"My monthly courses were close," she said. "So, no baby."

He remembered she had checked him before for "foul liquid." But how long could her luck continue? He held her by both shoulders and looked deep into her eyes. "Do you want this life?"

She paused a long time before she answered. "It is the best I can live."

"Could you not sing and play for a nobleman?"

Her eyes showed she had considered this. "What nobleman?"

Tonight Hunter would dine with Baron Windsor, but he could not suggest such a thing at their first meeting. The Earl of Leicester? Was that idea folly? The earl would welcome a beautiful, talented young woman into his household, but he would probably welcome her to his bed as well. Yet, being the mistress of one man might be preferable to coupling with hundreds. Ruin was a certain end of the latter. Was he a pander to consider taking her to Lord Leicester? A few short years ago, right and wrong had been so clear. "I do not know," he admitted.

"Do you want more?" Caterina asked.

He had come expecting a different consummation, but his mixed emotions forbade further carnal acts. "No. I want only to hold you." As he did, he prayed to find a way to take her from the brothel.

"Good evening, Your Lordship. Your Ladyship." Hunter bowed.

Baron Windsor of Stanwell, a portly man slightly shorter than Hunter, with bushy grey eyebrows and thick lips above fleshy jowls, wore a blue silk doublet with gold stripes and matching trunkhose. Hunter suspected his flat cap trimmed with a braided gold band concealed a bald head. "We had hoped to make your acquaintance at the funeral of Master Barnes," he rasped, "but you were occupied. Tonight affords us a better opportunity to meet one of Master Sidney's friends. Do join us in the blue room for wine and comfits."

Baroness Windsor, her hair held high on her head by a circlet of red gems that matched the underskirt beneath her white gown, preceded them into the room.

All sat in backed chairs near small tables with bowls of sugared almonds and dried fruit. A boy appeared with a tray of glasses filled with deep red wine. One sip told Hunter that this was the best wine he had drunk in Italy thus far.

The baron launched into a discussion of political developments with Sidney, expounding how Requens replacing Alva and the deaths of Louis and Henry of Nassau would affect the Dutch Revolt.

Lady Windsor, a few years younger-looking than her husband, smiled at Hunter. With sparkling eyes, she asked how long he had been in Venice and what sights he had seen. Her position had allowed her to meet supervisors of the *Scuole Grandi* and *Scuole Piccole,* and she showered him with recommendations of which of these confraternities to visit and which paintings she thought outstanding. When she mentioned Tintoretto's ongoing work at the *Scuola di San Rocco,* Hunter considered mentioning his meeting with the painter, but the circumstances of his encounter were not likely to impress her. Instead, he nodded, agreed, and complimented her taste. Sidney had arranged his inclusion in this gathering; it was his role not to offend.

After a quarter hour, a tall servant nodded to the baron, who asked his wife to lead them to the dining table set up in the *portego.* Servants pulled out chairs and indicated with their eyes where Hunter and Sidney were to sit. Hunter stared at the two-pronged forks. He had heard the Italians used these novel utensils but had never seen one before. He would observe what the baron did.

They were served roasted capon with peas and broad noodles, and Lord Windsor muttered a blessing. Sidney asked him for news from France. He reported that King Charles's health continued to worsen. His eyes shown with delight as he related the plot between the Duke of Alençon, the king's youngest brother, and Henry of Navarre, the king's *de facto* prisoner, to effect the latter's escape. He listed the noblemen involved and their fates. "Of course, you must know many of these men, as I understand you were in Paris at the time of the massacre on Saint Bartholomew's Day."

"I did meet some of them," Sidney dodged the implied invitation to describe the massacre but took the opportunity to draw his friend into the masculine conversation. "Master Hunter was also in Paris then."

Windsor regarded Hunter as one might a servant he had forgotten was there. "How unfortunate. What occasioned your presence there?"

Hunter, copying how the baron held his meat with a fork to cut it, paused. "Then, as now, I served as an agent for English merchants."

"Ah, a commercial venture," the baron said dismissively, spearing a slice of capon.

"Master Hunter is too modest," Sidney said. "He was also on a secret mission for Lord Burghley."

Baron Windsor's eyebrows rose in reevaluation of Hunter's importance. "A secret mission?"

Hunter played to Sidney's lead. "I fear much of the service I had the honor to perform for Her Majesty must remain secret. Master Sidney and I were both Ambassador Walsingham's enforced guests during those turbulent days."

Lady Windsor's forehead wrinkled with concern. "I hope you did not witness many of the horrors that have been reported."

The image of a pile of mutilated corpses transformed their conversation into a moment of panic. Hunter inhaled and closed his eyes tightly, as he had done before to dispel such a memory. "I witnessed many sights I wish I could forget."

"They haunt me as well," Sidney said. "Though Hunter experienced more than I."

"A moment ago, you mentioned King Charles." Hunter steered the conversation from the source of his nightmares. "Did you know His Majesty honored Master Sidney with the title of baron?"

Windsor's brows rose again in surprise. "I did not. Then we are of equal rank." He smiled without pleasure.

Sidney threw an irritated glance toward Hunter before saying to Lord Windsor, "I pray you do not mention that in any of your letters to England. Her Majesty does not favor her subjects receiving honors from other monarchs."

"I swear I shall not," Windsor said.

Hunter was unsure how much to trust this promise. "I know one should not anticipate the death of kings, but I wonder about the position of King Charles's brother and heir, now King Hendrik of Poland, far from Paris."

Baron Windsor seized the opportunity to display his knowledge of European affairs. "The Poles will be reluctant to let him go after all the furor and machination that went into electing him. His departure will plunge Poland into confusion again." The baron sipped his wine. "That is what comes of electing a king."

"We cannot tell other states how to govern themselves," Lady Windsor remarked.

"Nor has England's history of an inherited crown always kept our kingdom from chaos," Sidney said.

As two servants cleared, then brought small plates and served figs with *parmigiano* cheese, the strings of a lute sounded behind Hunter, and he turned to where a lad began plucking out "The Lady Greensleeves."

"Some music should restore our spirits after this talk of death," Lady Windsor said.

Instead, the notes pulled Hunter into the whirlpool of emotions that had gripped him earlier that day. Did the lutenist play for the baron and his mistress Lucia? Had he played for Lucia, Caterina, and the other women at Signora Filippa's? Had he taught Caterina the song? Was it Caterina's fate as well to become a nobleman's mistress? Did Lady Windsor know her husband kept a mistress?

"What progress has been made apprehending Ambrose Barnes's killer?" Lord Windsor was evidently not willing to abandon the topic of death.

"The Night Lord seemed more interested in recovering the possessions taken from his lodgings," Sidney replied. "He rented them from the Contarini family."

"Ah," Lord Windsor's syllable expressed a complete sentence. Of course officials would care more about the property of Venetian noblemen than the life of a common foreigner.

"The Night Lord believed the Englishman's name was Feenelly," Sidney said.

Windsor laughed. "Barnes probably told their man *fienili*, the Italian for *barns*, and the man misunderstood."

This disagreement of names was news to Hunter. Perhaps it was confusion, or perhaps Barnes had taken lodgings under a different name to avoid being found. That would explain his move and his servants' wariness.

"I gave them a list of Barnes's missing possessions, but they had a longer list from the landlord," Sidney said.

Windsor frowned. "His murder is a crime they are obliged to investigate. I shall speak to one of the Night Lords."

"Master Hunter is investigating as well," Sidney said. "He believes a criminal from Padua may be behind the thefts and murder."

Lord Windsor turned to Hunter. "What have you unearthed?"

"As many things of value were stolen from Barnes's lodgings in both cities, it suggested that he may have owed money to someone. The criminal mentioned is one Tommaso Biradi. Rumor has it that he oversees many petty criminals. He was reported to complain about Englishmen who do not pay their debts. My theory is that Barnes may have borrowed money from him, and this was Biradi's method of collecting. His killing may have been circumstantial, due to his returning while the robbers were in his lodgings." Hunter chose not to voice his suspicions that Barnes had commissioned Sidney's attackers.

Windsor looked doubtful. "It is odd he would need to borrow from a criminal. His family is well-to-do."

Hunter saw an opening. "I understand you knew his family well."

"Yes. They own an estate, Oak Grove Manor, near Reading."

Hunter hazarded another question. "And you are co-religionists."

"We have remained faithful to both God and sovereign," Lord Windsor said with pride. "That is why Ambrose was undertaking a degree in canon and civil law at Padua."

"Yet he spent more time in Venice than in Padua lately," Hunter said.

"Venice has more to offer," Windsor said. "Though Master Sidney finds it somewhat disagreeable, I understand."

"Certain aspects," Sidney replied evasively. "It is surely more beautiful."

"I suspect it is because of the meager lodgings that Ambassador Ferrier furnished you. They are too far from the heart of the city and too near the Ghetto. I extend an invitation to lodge with us here in San Polo *sestiere*." Lord Windsor smiled graciously.

"Yes. I pray you accept our offer." Lady Windsor's face lit up. "Your wit and learning will enliven our home."

Did she consider her husband dull, or did his visits to his mistress leave her alone and bored?

"Thank you for your kindness," Sidney said, "yet you should know I have four others in my party."

"Could you not leave some of them in Padua?" Lady Windsor asked.

"I shall consider your gracious invitation. I thank you."

As they prepared to leave, Baron Windsor, by the slightest nod of his head, indicated Hunter should linger a moment near him. Hunter raised his eyebrows in question. Windsor put a finger to his lips, whispered, "For your eyes only," and slipped a small folded note into his hand.

Outside, Hunter asked, "Will you accept their invitation?"

"I doubt it. I would be forced to listen to Lord Windsor's endless analysis of affairs throughout Europe."

"I thought that was part of the education your journey will supply."

"I get enough of that from Languet," Sidney said. "His last letter echoed what Lord Windsor said, with more weight on the mutiny of the Spanish army at Antwerp."

"As a good Protestant should," Hunter said, "and staying at the home of a Catholic nobleman would give your uncle more to worry about."

"This Catholic nobleman regularly sends reports to my Uncle Radclyffe, the Earl of Sussex," Sidney said. "You and I just dined with him, and neither of us converted."

Hunter laughed. "No. I gauge it would take more time than that."

"If I do stay here, I will take along Bryskett to watch over my faith," Sidney said.

"If he accompanies you, at least *he* will not worry from a distance."

After greeting Bryskett and turning gracefully to show Gironi he had suffered no harm during his time alone in the narrow streets of Venice, Hunter retired to his chamber. He unfolded the note Lord Windsor had pressed into his palm and read:

> *Pray come to me Monday at half past 10. Calle larga Ragusei, Dorsoduro sestiere*
>
> *Lucia*

Why would the baron's mistress ask him to visit?

CHAPTER 13

Clear Pools

SIDNEY WOULD RETURN TO PADUA TOMORROW TO WITNESS JOHN HART'S examination for his Doctor of Civil and Canon Law degree. Hunter hit upon an excuse to remain in Venice and called, "Luca, pray come help me out of this doublet. I cannot unknot the laces on the sleeves." When Gironi appeared, Hunter said quietly, "Pray shut the door."

Gironi examined the laces that bound his sleeves to his doublet. "I see little problem here. What is this about?"

"I see you have laid out my travelling clothes for the morrow, but I have changed my mind and wish to remain some days in Venice."

"Oh. May I ask why?"

"You may, but I may only partially answer. Tomorrow morning, I pray you feign a cramping in your guts. I will plead that I need to stay with you and explain as well that I hope to revisit Lady Windsor and obtain a list of paintings she swears I must see."

"And the true reason?" Gironi asked.

"This is where I will provide only a partial answer. I hope that by remaining a few days, I may meet your cousin Stefano, as you have requested. If he has pointed you the way to unhappy weavers, the time may allow you to speak with them. As for me, I have an investigation I need to pursue."

"Without the services of an interpreter?"

"Yes."

"I hope you are not commencing a dalliance with a baron's wife," Gironi said.

125

"I assure you I am not."

"Very well. I know not who else you might encounter who speaks English in this city, but I will allow you your little secret." Gironi smiled. "As for unhappy weavers, Stefano said he needed time. He can hardly go to the silk weavers' guild but must search out those who may have been denied admission."

"May they not be those who lack skill?"

"Perhaps. But some are denied membership for family feuds or trade rivalry. And even a middling Venetian weaver will be better than any silk weaver in England."

Hunter smiled. "As Erasmus wrote, *in regione caecorum rex est luscus*."

"Pray do not dazzle me with your Latin. As I translate for you, you may translate for me."

"In the country of the blind, the one-eyed man is king."

"Apt," Gironi said. "Here in Venice, which do you account yourself?"

Hunter's smile faded. "At least one-eyed, I hope."

"Very well, Master Cyclops. I shall say I begin to feel queasy even now."

Saturday, 5 June 1574, Venice

Lady Windsor was surprised to see Hunter, but she offered to accompany him to the scuole she had mentioned, as her husband was elsewhere on business. Hunter wondered if the business was with Lucia. As the gondolier rowed them toward San Zanipolo, she expounded on the virtues of Vittore Carpaccio, whose paintings of Saint Ursula they were to view.

In the campo before the huge church, she pointed out Verrocchio's statue of the *condottiaro* Colleoni. Odd, Hunter thought, that Venice imported Florentine sculptors to honor those they paid to do their fighting. She turned from the entrance to San Zanipolo to a smaller building nearby, and Hunter's heart froze. Entering were the familiar forms of one tall and one short friar.

"Is that a Dominican friary?"

"No. The *Scuola di Sant'Orsola*." Lady Windsor frowned. "Though friars from Zanipolo do say Mass there. Why do you stop so suddenly?"

"Pardon me. Two friars just entered. My previous encounters with Dominicans have not been pleasant."

"But we must enter to see Carpaccio's paintings."

Hunter could not disappoint the baroness. He forced a smile. "Then let us continue."

A layman recognized Lady Windsor and greeted them as they entered. Ahead, the pair Hunter hoped to avoid turned to see who had come in. The tall friar jerked back as though struck, bared his teeth for a moment, and fixed Hunter with a stare of ice used for an implacable enemy. The shorter friar asked him a question. He tempered his expression and stooped to give a response. The shorter regarded Hunter with curiosity rather than ire. What had the tall friar said? He could scarcely have admitted to an altercation in a brothel. The tall friar flashed a look of pure hatred before the pair turned to disappear through a doorway.

"Do you know those friars?" Hunter asked Lady Windsor.

"No. I know only the members of the scuola, not the friars." Lady Windsor nodded to her right. "Pray let us go this way."

Hunter considered that, even if she knew their identities, she was unlikely to know of any connection with a Padovan pimp and his prostitutes.

For the rest of the afternoon, Lady Windsor alternately told the story of Saint Ursula and her eleven thousand virgins, praised Carpaccio's depiction of the legend, and pointed out the portraits of members of the Loredan family he had painted attending the saint.

Monday, 7 June 1574, Venice

The bells of Santa Margherita chimed half past ten. Hunter knocked on the door of the small palazzo that the old woman pointed out as the residence of Signora Lucia. At least she had not leered when he asked.

Hunter was surprised when a tall moor answered the door. He had seen a few black men in Venice, but none up close. "*Signora Lucia*," he said.

"*Nome?*" the moor asked.

"Hunter."

The guard nodded and opened the door. He was expected. As at Signora Filippa's, Lucia appeared at the top of the staircase. She wore a gown of dark green that opened to reveal a white satin bodice and underskirt. "Pray come up."

Relieved he did not have to wrestle with Italian but uncertain what Lucia had in mind, Hunter mounted the stairs and followed her into a small room. Finding it furnished with a couch and chairs, but no bed,

Hunter felt relieved. Two glasses of wine, sugar-coated almonds, and candied fruits sat on a table. She shared Lord Windsor's tastes.

"Let us sit," Lucia said, "I am glad you came."

"I was curious why you might wish to see me," Hunter said. And a bit afraid as well, he thought.

"I must first thank you for rescuing Caterina from the horrid friar. She told me about it."

"When I heard her cry, I acted without thinking."

"She was very grateful."

"She told me herself." And showed me as well, Hunter did not add.

"It is not everyone who would help a courtesan. Many people look down on us." Lucia reached for her glass. "Pray drink."

Hunter sipped and waited. Surely there was more behind her invitation than thanking him.

"I hope I might ask you some favors for a friend," she began.

"Lord Windsor?" he guessed.

"No. Sior Girolamo Rossi."

Hunter recognized one of the names Barnes had mentioned, but to be certain, he asked, "Who is Sior Rossi?"

Lucia smiled. "He is known to many in Venice. Every courtesan, madam, pimp, street walker, burglar—they all pay him a portion. Does that help explain?"

"Yes. What might a man like that ask of me?" The back of his neck began to tingle as he imagined the possible answers.

"He has questions about Sior Feenelly, or Barn."

"His name was Ambrose Barnes. What would he know?"

"He was the Englishman killed in Cannaregio a week ago, yes?"

Hunter counted. "Ten days ago."

"And his house was robbed?"

"His rented lodgings. Yes."

"And you discovered his body?"

"Yes." Hunter wondered where this was going.

"Sior Rossi heard you were attacked on the *Fondamenta dei Mori*."

"News travels," Hunter said.

Lucia smiled. "He wanted to know if you could describe the men who attacked you."

Hunter must beware; those might have been Rossi's men. "It was very dark."

Lucia regarded him doubtfully. "Sior Rossi is unhappy." She took another sip of wine.

Hunter hoped Rossi would not be unhappy with his answers. "Why?"

"A man is attacked one night, another is killed and robbed a few nights later, all in his territory, and he knows nothing about it."

"I thought Alvise Mocenigo was the doge," Hunter said.

Lucia laughed. "Of course. The Doge, the Senate, the Great Council—they formally rule Venice and all its possessions. But in fact, Sior Rossi rules many parts of Venice loyal to the Nicolotti."

"The Nicolotti?" Hunter asked.

"Ah, how little you know. Pray take some sweets. This will take time to explain." Lucia put down her wine, cupped her hands, and held them close to one another, the left above the right. "Here is Venice. It is divided into six parts—*sestieri*. From where you sit, these fingers—" she moved her left hand—"are Cannaregio, the thumb is San Marco, the wrist is Castello. The right fingers are San Polo and Santa Croce; the wrist and thumb are Dorsoduro. Between my hands is the Grand Canal."

"Yes." The geography of Venice, which had been somewhat hazy in Hunter's mind, became clearer.

"If you cut Cannaregio and Dorsoduro in two and let the Grand Canal divide the other *sestieri*, you will divide Venice in another way, between the Nicolotti on the west and the Castellani on the east."

"I still do not know who Nicolotti and Castellani are," Hunter said.

"They are rival groups. Old rivals. From time to time they have mock battles."

"Mock battles?"

"They are supposed to be mock battles," Lucia explained, "but clubs can kill a man, and those pushed into a canal can drown."

"So, Sior Rossi's territory is the Nicolotti section."

"Yes." Lucia picked up her glass again.

"Who controls the other part?"

"Sior Marcantonio Costa."

Hunter nodded. Two men dominated illegal activity in Venice, as Biradi did in Padua. "Does Rossi believe Costa is operating in his territory?"

"Sior Costa said it was not his men who attacked you, nor who killed your friend." She waited in silence.

So did he.

"Sior Rossi hoped, as you have been asking questions to many, both here and in Padua, that you might know who attacked you and who killed Master Barnes."

Hunter weighed his options. "There is a man in Padua named Biradi."

"Rossi knows of him."

"Because Barnes's lodgings were robbed in both Venice and Padua, and because Biradi was heard to say Englishmen do not pay their debts, I would guess Biradi was behind the thefts, because Barnes owed him money."

"And your attack?" She bit into a candied lemon peel.

"I believe Biradi's men thought I was Barnes. After they grabbed me and looked at me, one said I was not the right man. I can understand why he would be unhappy if Biradi's men were operating in his territory." He hoped Rossi would exert more pressure on Biradi than the authorities could, though he was unsure what might result.

"I believe Sior Rossi will be grateful for this information," Lucia said.

Hunter's thought returned to Caterina. "May I ask you some questions?"

"You have answered mine. I shall answer yours."

"You work alone here, do you not?"

"I do."

"In the service of Lord Windsor?"

"He visits me often—two days and two nights each week."

"And the other time?"

Her eyes lit up. "At other times I may make my own plans. Other noblemen visit me regularly in the evening, but occasionally my afternoons are free."

Hunter realized he had given her the wrong idea. "I do not wish to offend, but I do not ask for myself."

"You may ask for others," she said.

How had he stumbled into this pit? "I was thinking of Caterina," he explained.

She looked confused, then said, "I have no desire to become a matron. I will house no other women here."

"That was not what I was thinking," Hunter said. "She is young and beautiful and has a wonderful voice. Could a nobleman not employ her to serve him?"

Her face hardened. Could she fear that Lord Windsor might replace her with a younger mistress? "Most noblemen I know who want mistresses have them."

"I wish I could help her to a better position," Hunter said. Lucia laughed, and he blushed, realizing her interpretation.

"Well, better a nobleman's mistress than everyone's partner," she said, voicing his own thoughts.

"I wonder if she might leave Venice and come to England."

She wagged a finger at him. "No. No. You must not fall in love with a courtesan. And a courtesan must not fall in love with her clients."

"I am not in love with her." He realized he had said that more forcefully than he intended.

"If you wish for her to quit Signora Filippa's service, you would have to pay."

"How much?"

"I do not know. She is likely in debt to Signora Filippa. Gowns and food cost money."

Another idea struck Hunter. "Might I prevail upon you to ask Signor Rossi about some Dominicans?"

She frowned. "The Dominican houses are at Zanipolo and San Zòrzi, neither in Nicolotti territory."

"Is *Campo San Cassiano*?"

"Yes."

"Over a month ago, I saw two friars taking a young—" he hesitated, searching for the right word and hoping he would not offend—"*meretrice* named Lucetta, who had worked in Padua, from that campo by force. Just the other day, I saw them again at the *Scuola di Sant'Orsola*. I wondered if Rossi might have information about her or the Dominicans."

"What did the girl and the friars look like?"

Hunter described them and added, "The taller man, Brother Alberto, frequents Signora Filippa's and enjoys being whipped."

"Ah," she said. "*Fra Alberto*."

"What do you know of him?"

"From Bologna. He comes to Venice frequently to visit, he says, the friaries here, but I think he comes as much to visit Filippa's house as to speak with the brothers. Since I left her three years ago, I have not seen him."

"Do you know the name of his companion?"

"No."

"Pray ask Signor Rossi if he knows anything of the friars or the girl."

"I shall."

"How did you fare at your secret meeting?" Gironi asked when they met in front of the *Palazzo Longo*.

"Very well, thank you." Hunter was not willing to share any details yet.

"As your silence tells me you will say no more, let us go to Stefano's."

"Good. I am hungry." As Hunter had made several trips to Venice without accepting the invitation to visit Stefano, guilt pricked him as he followed Gironi into a narrow alley. Stefano and the scent of leather greeted them at the shop door. Hunter thanked him for supplying shoes after his dunking. They climbed to a room above where he introduced his wife, an adolescent son, and a small daughter. Hunter offered the conventional pleasantries he knew in Italian before sitting down to a meal of sardines, olives, noodles, and bread—a contrast to the feast at Lord Windsor's but served with more warmth.

After the meal, Hunter and Gironi descended to the shop. Stefano proudly displayed his creations, from fashionable to sturdy footwear. Hunter felt ordering a new pair of shoes appropriate. While Stefano traced the outline of his foot, Hunter asked what he knew of Girolamo Rossi.

At the name, Stefano looked up in surprise.

Gironi tensed. "Where did you hear of him? Everyone knows and fears his name. Many idle men will do anything he commands them to do."

"Barnes mentioned Rossi and Costa to me when I spoke with him." Hunter said. "So, he is a king of crime, as Biradi in Padua."

Gironi nodded. "I would hazard even Sior Biradi fears him." Stefano gestured proudly toward a rack. "My cousin crafted shoes like those for Sior Rossi."

"Where might one find him?" Hunter asked, thinking this might shock Gironi.

"Pray do not plan a face-to-face. Was our interview with Biradi not enough?"

"If your cousin can make him shoes, he may be kindly disposed to you."

Gironi reluctantly asked Stefano, then replied, "There is a tavern called *Mezza Luna* off *Campo Santa Margherita*. It is not far from the shoemakers' guild and their scuola. He can be contacted there."

"The Half Moon," Hunter said.

"Do not think I will leave you alone to wander in Dorsoduro," Gironi warned. "You consider too many dangerous acts."

Friday, 11 June 1574, Padua

Hunter had spent fruitless days trying to decipher the letter. Perhaps he had been wrong to believe that the cipher was based on a book. Or perhaps these books were not the right ones. He started again with Bishop Jewel's *Apologia Ecclesiae Anglicanae.* That produced no results. In the midst of expressing his frustration to Sidney, he hit upon an idea.

"I may have been going about this task all wrong," Hunter exclaimed, standing. "Instead of starting with one book or another, I should start with the message itself."

"But it is in cipher," Sidney said.

"Yes. And this idea may prove futile as well, but hear me out. If each letter replaces another, then the most frequent letters will be vowels, will they not?"

"Yes. But *t, s,* and *m* are frequent consonants in Latin."

"Well, I should look for the most common letters. Be the message in Latin or English, some patterns should emerge." Hunter shook his head in disappointment with himself. "Why did I not think of this before?"

"It may still prove difficult. The message contains no spaces, and you cannot be sure which vowel is replaced," Sidney said.

"I can do no worse than I have been. Pray excuse me." Hunter mounted the stairs, eager to start his task anew, when a knock sounded at the door.

Gironi answered it. Before him stood two disheveled men in need of shaving, the shorter one supporting the larger. After a moment of confusion, Hunter recognized Francis and Christopher, the servants of Ambrose Barnes.

CHAPTER 14

Resurfacing

"PRAY YOU, KIND SIR," FRANCIS SAID, "WE ARE SORE IN NEED. CHRISTOPHER burns with a fever."

Hunter bolted back downstairs, eager to ask the servants what they knew of the attack on Barnes, but realized they first needed care. "Pray come in."

"Lodowick, join benches together that we may lay him down," Sidney called.

Bryskett and Gironi scrambled to move the benches from either side of the table to a wall. Two steps into the room, Christopher's legs buckled, and Sidney caught him as he fell. Together, he and Francis lugged him to the benches. "Water," Sidney called out. "Lodowick, pray run to Saint Francis's Hospital for a physician. This man is on fire."

"Luca, pray bring a chair and water for Francis," Hunter said. "Are you in need of food?"

Francis nodded. After he was seated and given drink and bread, and while Sidney poured water into Christopher's mouth, Hunter asked, "Were you with Master Barnes in Venice when he was attacked?"

Francis nodded and hung his head.

"Can you tell us what you saw?" Hunter urged. "We seek to find his killer."

Francis took a deep breath. "Well, we came back to the house late. We saw lights inside and the lock broken. First thing we thought was burglars, and we were right. Master Barnes, he barged in and yelled at the man he saw stuffin' the candlesticks in a bag. He said 'Christopher, run for the watch,' but Chris didn't know where to run or what to say, not speaking their tongue.

"The man with the bag called out, and all at once there was five of them there, 'gainst only three of us. They pulled long knives, the kind they don't allow in Venice, and we all turned to run. All we had were bread knives. Master, he ran toward the canal at the end of the street. I thought that was wrong, 'cause there was nowhere to go that way. I yelled that out, but too late. The robbers were between us and Master." Francis paused, his face convulsed with guilt and regret.

"Did you see what happened to him?" Hunter asked.

Francis sighed. "I know we should've gone to protect him, but, to our shame, we run the other way. Three of them chased us, but we were faster, and they turned back. Guess they wanted things in the house more, thanks be to Our Lady."

"What did the men look like?" Hunter asked.

"One was a giant with a big beard. He chased us, but he couldn't run fast. Another was a real stick man, thin as you might like, but with that long knife, you wouldn't want to fight him. I didn't get a good look at the other one chasing us, 'cause all we wanted to do was get away from 'em, but he had light hair. The first man we saw, takin' the candlestick, had an ugly, bent-up nose, but he run after Master Barnes. Another one had red hair. That's all I remember."

The men who had attacked him, with two others, Hunter concluded. "You have done well to recall what you have. What did you do then?"

"Chris and me hid behind a stack of boxes for maybe an hour, then he says we should go back and see what happened. We did, slow and keepin' to the shadows. When we got there, the house was all dark. Inside, everything was gone—well, everything that was worth anything. We talked a little, then went outside and listened. We didn't hear nothin', so we reckoned they were gone. We wanted to see if Master Barnes had come to harm or got away. At end of the street, there he was, lyin' on that boat. We called and he didn't answer. Chris was brave enough to touch him and he was cold, so we knew he was dead.

"We didn't know what to do, fearin' those men might come back lookin' for us. Then again, we feared somebody might blame us for killin' him and takin' all the money and things. We did have money on us, you see, 'cause he had just paid our wages that day. That was good luck in a way. We went back and slept behind the boxes that night. The next day we went back to the house and saw you gentlemen there, with men that looked like the watch, so we stayed away. We knew a tavern, where Master sometimes let us go, that had rooms above. We knew the word for room and showed 'em our money. We lodged and ate there for near two weeks. Every night we paid what we owed for lodgin' and food, but after a bit the men who drank there got curious. They asked us questions, but we just said '*Non capisco*'— that's one of the things Master Barnes taught us. Then one of them asked '*Inglese.*' He could tell by the way we looked that we were, and he and the barman looked at us like maybe someone was asking about Englishmen. Besides, we were tired of pottage and our money was runnin' out. We counted up and knew we had enough to pay for a cheap boat back to Padua. About the time we left, Chris started to feel sick, but we took the boat last night anyway. Pray, masters, don't call the watch on us. All I've said is true."

"We will take care of you," Hunter said, not knowing if he could keep his promise.

Sidney had been listening. "Do you have other garments?"

"I thought we might find clothes at our lodgings in Padua, but there was a new door and lock. Chris remembered your servant had treated us well and said we should come here."

Hunter looked at Gironi and nodded his appreciation, then doubt assailed him. "Have you been to see any other Englishman in Padua?"

Francis shook his head. "Not yet. Thomas and Clarence, their servants, they mocked us for being new to Italy and not knowing as much as them."

Sidney again pressed water on Christopher. "Griffin, do you think we might have some apparel for these men?"

Madox looked doubtful "It may be best if we wait till the physician comes for Christopher. Harry may have a doublet that will fit Francis."

"Would you like a cup of wine?" Hunter asked Francis.

"You are too kind."

Hunter nodded to Gironi. "Not at all. You are providing valuable information. Do you know anyone who might have been angry with your master?"

Francis bit his lip as he accepted the wine.

"Did he argue with anyone in Venice?"

Francis took a deep draught. "No."

"What about here in Padua, before he moved?"

After pressing his teeth on his lower lip again, Francis spoke. "The night before we left, a man came to our lodgings and asked to see our master. He didn't speak English, so I had to call Master. When he asked the man's business, the Italian leaned close and whispered something in his ear. Master shook and asked him up to his chamber. I could hear them argue. After he left, Master Barnes said to pack the saddlebags; we would leave the next morning."

"Do you remember what the man looked like?"

"He was big, about Chris's size, and had a big warty nose. That's all I remember."

"Was he one of the men who were robbing your Venice lodgings?"

"No."

"You said saddlebags. Did you not take a boat?"

"Chris took a chest to the boat, but we rode to Megerra the next day and took a boat from there. Master said it would be quicker. I reckon that by ridin', there would be fewer folk to say when and where we were goin', too."

"Did you leave your horses at Marghera?"

"Aye. At a stable there."

"Why didn't you and Christopher collect them and ride back?"

"Master only paid part of their board. We didn't have enough for what was owed. Good thing that, for Chris was too sick to ride."

"Did you change houses when you arrived in Venice?"

"Four or five days later."

"Do you know that Master Barnes took his second lodgings under a different name?"

"He said to tell nobody, but I guess it doesn't matter now he's dead, God rest his soul. Master said not to call him Barnes, but Master Feenelly. I could tell by the way he said it that we shouldn't ask why. He was frightened."

Bryskett arrived at the door with a physician from the hospital. Sidney ushered him to the prostrate Christopher.

"Did Barnes say anything else about the man who came?" Hunter probed.

"I don't remember," Francis said, his eyes on Christopher.

Hunter longed to continue questioning, but as Francis's attention was on his companion, he judged it better to wait. "The physician may have questions about Christopher you can answer."

Saturday, 12 June 1574, Padua

The physician's dram of sedative produced a restful night's sleep for Christopher. The following morning, he was able to sit up and take nourishment. His companion Francis, without any drug, slept late into the morning in the storeroom Sidney's servants had cleared for them.

Hunter considered not accompanying Sidney and Hart into Venice, to hear the music of Gabrielli they had missed two weeks' before, but he decided that he need not stay in Padua if he could question Christopher that morning.

"Francis told me of events the night of Master Barnes's death, and of your hiding since that time. I wish to ask you of events longer ago," Hunter began.

"I hope I can recall," Christopher said.

"Francis said a man came the night before you left to take up new lodgings in Venice—a big man with a warty nose. Can you add any more to describe him?"

"Well, he spoke with a low voice. And this time he wore a hat with badges."

"This time? Had you seen him before?"

"Yes, he came about five days before to speak with Master Barnes."

"Francis didn't mention that."

"He wasn't there then. I forget where Master had sent him."

"Can you tell me what happened?"

"He came to our door and asked for Master Barnes and passed me a note to show him."

"Do you know what it said?"

Christopher's mouth opened in shock. "Though I can read a little, I would never read a note to Master Barnes."

"Perhaps your master told you the contents."

"No."

"So what happened with the big man the first time?"

"Master Barnes said he would talk to him in a back room, but I should wait by the door. I'm most as big as the man that came, so I guess he wanted me there in case there was trouble."

"Was there any trouble?"

"No. There were loud voices, and I stood up, ready to go in, but then that fellow came out. I guess Master put a flea in his ear."

"Did Master Barnes have any other visitors before that?"

"He and the other Englishmen here would visit back and forth all during the spring."

"What did they talk about?"

"Everything. There were merry jests. They talked about women servants at the college. They talked about politics and religion."

"Did they ever mention Master Sidney?"

"He was often there," Christopher said. "And when he wasn't, maybe they would talk about what he was doing and where he was."

"Any talk against him?"

Again, Christopher looked surprised. "No. They counted him a jolly fellow."

"Did Barnes visit anyone just before he moved to Venice?"

"Yes. An older fellow he called Doctor, not far from us."

Simmons. He would merit another interview. What had Barnes revealed to him? "What about visits before I arrived, before Master Sidney was captured?"

"That's a long time ago to remember. Just what I told you, other Englishmen."

"Any other visitors to your lodgings besides the Englishmen of Padua?"

"Well, there were the two friars."

Hunter sat up. Had the same friars visited Barnes as had visited Carollo? "What did they look like?"

"A pole and a ball." Christopher laughed, then stopped suddenly. "God forgive me for making a jest of his holy servants."

Hunter chuckled at the description while he tried to fit this information into the riddle of Sidney's capture. "When did they show up?"

"Just before the news that Master Sidney had been carried off down south and had returned." Christopher rested his head on his hand.

"You are sure it was before and not after?"

"I am. The day before he rode back with Captain Scarpa."

"What did they say?"

Christopher blinked a few times. It was clear he was tiring. "I don't know. Master talked with them in private."

"Any raised voices that time?"

"A few. There was not any laughing."

"Did they come before or after?"

"No, just that one time."

Sidney approached Hunter. "Are you ready to go?"

"It seems I must be." Hunter rose.

On the boat ride to Venice, Hunter tried to piece events together. A group of ruffians, known to Biradi and hired by someone unknown, attacked

Sidney the night before his arrival. Four of them carried Sidney to the Romagna, where they were met by others who cut their throats. Before Sidney and he rode back to Padua, two Dominicans, probably Alberto and his companion from Bologna, spoke with Barnes and Carollo. Had they met with Biradi too? Or others? Were the friars connected with Biradi or with the *romagnoli* killers? Could they have arranged Sidney's capture, then come to Padua to report the mission failed? They left Padua with Lucetta. Why only her? The English Catholics in Padua swore they had no knowledge of who might have hired Biradi's ruffians. Were they telling the truth or concealing it? A man came to Barnes with a threat, probably from Biradi, that frightened him, and he left Padua for Venice after speaking with Simmons. He moved from San Marco to Cannaregio and rented lodgings under a false name. Carollo was killed, or did that happen before Barnes left? He must try to write this all down in order. Was Carollo killed because he was a go-between, or because the friars brought orders to do so? If so, who gave those orders? He still believed Barnes hired the *bravi*, but he could not question a dead man. And he could not answer Sidney's key question— why would Barnes, Sidney's friend, have hired men to capture him?

But it was unlikely Biradi would undertake Sidney's capture without being paid in advance. Then, if Barnes had paid him, why rob and kill Barnes, except for the fact that he was rich? Did he owe Biradi money? Did he hold Barnes responsible for the killing of his men? Was that the reason Barnes was hiding in Venice? What had the big man with the warty nose said to Barnes?

While Hart and Sidney spoke to one another about art and Gironi and Bryskett shared a bottle of wine with Madox, White, and Fisher, Hunter rested his head on his arm and slept.

Monday, 14 June 1574, Venice

The evening conversation at Baron Windsor's revolved around the news that Charles IX of France had died on the last day of May. His brother had been proclaimed King Henri III in Paris, but would that proclamation prove good if he could not leave Krakow? If the news had reached Venice, it surely must have reached Poland, but no news from there had come to the Republic. Might Henry's younger brother Francis make a bid for the throne before he could arrive? He was already under suspicion for conspiring with Henry of Navarre. Could Henry Valois be king of Poland and France at the same time? Where would he reside?

While Sidney and Lord Windsor discussed French politics, Hunter's thoughts wandered to Caterina. He had to admit he desired her, yet he planned ways to remove her from her present occupation. How much would Signora Filippa ask to release her? Likely Caterina was in debt for lodging, meals, and expensive clothing. If Sidney and Gironi heard her sing, he hoped they would commend her to Lord Leicester. But taking them to hear her would require he admit his own visits to the brothel. How might Sidney react? If he arrived in England with a girl from a brothel, no matter how beautiful and talented, how would Lord Leicester react? It might complicate or injure the earl's relationship with Her Majesty.

Lady Windsor interrupted his thoughts. "Do you care little for the affairs of France?"

"Forgive me, Lady Windsor. My mind was wandering."

"I thought so. Perhaps, like me, you choose not to speculate what might happen, but are content to allow matters to take their course, then reflect upon them."

If only that were true. "Overmuch speculation may lead one to unnecessary anxiety."

Lady Windsor smiled, evidently taking Hunter's axiom as agreement.

"I offer speculation you both will find worth considering." Lord Windsor had evidently taken in their comments.

"What is that, dearest?" Lady Windsor asked.

"That His Highness may choose to avoid the Protestant states of Germany and take a longer route through Austria and Italy. In that case, I would expect him to visit Venice."

Lady Windsor's face lit up.

"I thought that might change your tune, my lady. Philip, you can see her imagining the receptions, the balls, the opportunities to dress in finery which will make other ladies jealous...."

Hunter rose to Lady Windsor's defense. "I must admit that the prospect of the King of France coming here excites me as well." He remembered the spectacles he had attended in Paris, and the figure of Henry III, who had then been the Duke of Anjou.

"I would look forward to such a visit also," Sidney said.

Their comments may have emboldened Lady Windsor, whose mouth curled briefly in a smirk before she said, "I could scarcely outdo you in strutting about in finery, my dear."

Lord Windsor glanced at the silver embroidery on his doublet and laughed. "You may be right, my lady." He turned to Hunter. "Have you discovered any more about the death of your friend Barnes?"

Hunter considered how much to reveal. He hoped general comments might satisfy the baron. "A few days ago, his servants appeared at our door in Padua. On the night of Barnes's murder, they had chanced upon thieves in their Venetian lodgings. The servants ran in fear. When they returned, they discovered their master dead."

"And they did not report it to the *Signori di Notte?*" Lord Windsor asked.

"Partly they feared they would be accused of the theft, partly they lacked the language to deal with Venetian authorities."

"So, they could not add any information that would allow you to bring his killers to justice."

"No." At least, no information Hunter was willing to share. His suspicions would not yet bear the weight of many questions.

Baron Windsor turned to speak with Sidney about a noble both knew at the Imperial Court in Vienna. The lutenist in the anteroom was playing 'Pastime with Good Company.'

Hunter decided to take a chance. "Lady Windsor, might you introduce me to your lutenist?"

"Indeed yes, Master Hunter. We shall make you a patron of the arts yet." She rose. "Pray excuse us, sirs. We go to speak with my musician."

"I should need a much greater income to be anyone's patron," Hunter said, following her into an anteroom off the *portego*. The lutenist stood as they entered.

"Master Hunter," Lady Windsor said, "this is Carlo."

Carlo bowed over his instrument. "I am honored."

"Carlo speaks a little English," she said.

"Your playing is skillful," Hunter said. "I enjoyed it."

"Thank you," Carlo said.

"I heard you play 'Lady Greensleeves.' Do you know many English songs?" Hunter could not ask the question he wanted to.

"My Lord and Lady sing songs. I find strings to sound for them," he explained.

"Do you learn the words as well?"

"Some."

"Do you know the words to 'Lady Greensleeves?'"

"Yes." He looked to Lady Windsor, who nodded. "You like I sing?"

"Pray do," Hunter said. He listened appreciatively. Carlo's version was the same as Caterina's, even the errors. He sang "discuresly" and omitted "all," singing only "was my joy." This was good enough to establish a connection.

CHAPTER 15

Fresh Currents

Tuesday, 15 June 1574, Venice

HUNTER HAD FINALLY PLUCKED UP COURAGE TO TELL SIDNEY AND GIRONI about Caterina, framing their brothel trip as a mission to rescue a poor girl from a life of sin. He reminded them that Sebastian Bryskett had introduced him to Signora Filippa's establishment on his first day in Venice, not mentioning his subsequent visits. Sidney accepted the explanation, but Gironi remarked that it had taken Hunter a long time to decide to rescue the girl. Hunter fumbled an excuse about the need to investigate Sidney's capture.

Zuan opened the door with, "Ah, Sior Hunter."

Sidney gave Hunter a skeptical look. Gironi said, "Your knight errant armor is a bit tarnished."

Hunter introduced his companions with a weak smile and, realizing a full confession would be necessary, tried to plan the best time for it.

Signora Filippa landed more blows to his metaphorical armor with her greeting. "Sior Hunter! Caterina is free now."

Even more sheepish, Hunter explained Sidney and Gironi were here only to hear her sing. Signora Filippa nodded knowingly and swept away to fetch Caterina.

"Everyone here seems to know you well," Sidney said smugly.

"I will explain later," Hunter said.

Wearing a light blue gown with a white bodice and underskirt, Caterina entered with a warm smile for Hunter, but when she saw the other two men, she opened a fan before her face.

"Caterina, I hope you are well and in good voice. I have brought two companions to hear you sing." After introductions, Caterina closed her fan, smiled, and curtsied.

"Dear gentlemens, I know only one English song."

"Pray sing us the song you sang when I first saw you."

Caterina smiled. "That is a song of Napoli."

"It was beautiful."

"I get my lute."

Sidney abandoned for the moment his questions about Hunter's relationship with Caterina. "Her English is not bad."

"A courtesan named Lucia, a favorite of our friend Baron Windsor, has been teaching her," Hunter explained.

Sidney's eyebrows rose. "An intimate friend?"

Hunter nodded. His friend might at least grant him marks for intelligence gathering in this bordello.

"She is quite beautiful," Gironi remarked. "That might please Lord Leicester."

"But her origin," Sidney objected.

"No doubt Edward has discovered her history during his visits here," Gironi said.

There was no use maintaining his pretense of innocence. "She comes from a poor farm..." Hunter began, but he stopped when Caterina entered with her lute.

"Pray sit." She led them to the benches beneath Danaë.

Signora Filippa drifted back to the reception room. "Wine?"

Never one to pass up an opportunity for profit, Hunter reflected. "Yes."

"*Tre*," Gironi said.

A servant arrived with drinks as Caterina finished tuning. As before, any uncertainty vanished as she became one with the music. Sidney and Gironi exchanged looks of amazement. Hunter was encouraged, but appreciation of her music was a long step from transporting her to Lord Leicester's house in England. At the end, they applauded, and Sidney asked for another, livelier song. Caterina obliged and was met with approbation. Gironi named a Venetian tune and Caterina sang it.

Hunter looked at his companions and asked, "Shall we allow Caterina to rest? Do you wish to hear more?"

"I think we have heard enough." Sidney turned to Caterina. "I thank you for your songs." He raised a hand to summon the serving girl and paid for their wine.

In the gondola back to the *Palazzo Michiel*, Gironi said, "We have heard and seen Caterina, but perhaps you can tell us how well you *know* her."

There was no use denying, Hunter decided. "I admit I have coupled with her. The act weighs upon my conscience."

"A pity you are not a Catholic," Gironi said. "You could confess to your priest and be shriven. As a Protestant, you must deal directly with God."

"Are you not a Protestant?" Sidney asked.

"I am a Protestant in England," Gironi answered, "but we are hearing Edward's confession, not mine."

"I swear I coupled with her only once," Hunter said.

"The guard and the matron seemed to know you well," Sidney said.

"I have been there more often, I admit. Once with Sebastian Bryskett, once when I bedded her, and another time when she was entertaining a Dominican friar." Perhaps shame, perhaps the intimacy and emotions of the encounter, kept Hunter from relating his most recent visit.

"A friar?" Sidney asked.

"Yes. He wanted her to scourge him, and when she refused, he began to whip her. I heard her scream and ran to intervene."

"So there *is* a bit of the damsel-rescuing knight in you," Gironi said.

"If it pleases you to say so," Hunter said with a grunt.

"I am sure it pleased her to be rescued."

"You have kept more than one secret. If Lucia is Lord Windsor's mistress, does she work there?" Sidney asked.

"She did, but she now has her own house."

"And what do you *know* of her?" Gironi seemed intent on discovering all Hunter's secrets.

"I have not known her carnally, nor, before you ask, any of the other women at Signora Filippa's. I met her on my first trip there." Hunter decided it was not necessary to reveal that Baron Windsor had passed a note from Lucia, nor the details of his visit to her. "But to the point of this trip. What do you think of Caterina and the possibility of Lord Leicester taking her into his service?"

The gondolier swung his craft into the Grand Canal and turned left, skillfully avoiding other boats.

"I am certain my uncle would appreciate her beauty and her singing," Sidney said, "but her origins weigh against her. And there is no time to write him for permission."

"How long has she been in the brothel?" Gironi asked.

"Perhaps six months," Hunter said. "She said she came from a poor farm, and her mother is Signora Filippa's cousin. She has no dowry. Although she does not want to work as she does, she has little choice. The matron is grooming her to serve English clients."

"Unfortunately, my uncle would be tempted to enjoy more than her voice," Sidney said.

"Although he does not have the appetite of a satyr, his cravings might match any he-goat," Gironi said. After a sharp look from Sidney, he added, "Begging your pardon, Master Sidney."

Sidney sighed. "You but speak the truth, though it pains me to hear it. It is said he has tupped many of the maids of honor at Her Majesty's Court."

The gondola glided past the *Fondaco dei Turchi* and turned into the *Rio di San Marcuola*.

"Lucia said Caterina and the other women there are in debt to Signora Filippa for their gowns, rooms, and board," Hunter said. "One would have to pay that debt to free her."

"How much might that be?" Sidney asked.

"We must ask Signora Filippa."

"Surely Lucia did not mention debts to Signora Filippa when you met her at the brothel," Gironi said.

Hunter had revealed himself again. He sighed. "No. I met with her at her request. She sought information about Barnes's killing on behalf of Signor Rossi." The mention of the criminal master appeared to silence Gironi for the moment. "We spoke about the possibility of Caterina leaving the brothel. We agreed that, though she might become a mistress to one man, it was better than the life she faced."

"Is she free of disease?" Sidney asked. "We could not introduce the pox into my uncle's home."

"The matron takes care to deny those with disease access to her women," Hunter said.

"How does she manage that?" Gironi asked.

The man seemed determined to unearth intimate details. "You are unusually curious of the ways of courtesans."

"So am I," Sidney said.

Hunter could not ignore both requests. "Fine, then. Other than looking for pox upon his body, it seems they are instructed to squeeze the cock of each customer to see if a foul juice flows out."

Gironi nodded sagely. "And you were treated so?"

Hunter exploded. "If you must know each detail, yes. I will let you examine my prick as well, you prying churl."

Gironi held up his hands. "Pray forgive me. I could not resist denting your gleaming armor. I am glad to hear that Filippa takes care of her brood."

"I hope such precautions suffice," Sidney said. "Yet every day she remains there is a further hazard."

The gondola turned left on the *Rio della Misericordia*, right into a narrow canal, then left again on the *Rio della Sensa*.

Hunter gave Gironi a hard look. "Now that we are to discuss the business of freeing Caterina, I will approach Signora Filippa tomorrow as to Caterina's debt, if Luca will accompany me."

"I shall be glad to."

Sidney chewed his lip. "I hesitate to anger my uncle, yet if we wait to free her, she may become polluted bodily as well as morally. Once we know the amount of her debt, I can draw that from the Strozzi bank."

Hunter's spirits lifted. "Then you agree we should take Caterina back to England?"

"If she proves free of infection," Sidney said. "I hate to think that such a soul should suffer to sell her body against her will."

"I have practical questions to solve, gentlemen," Gironi said. "Where is Caterina to stay from the time you pay her debt until she can depart for England? As you say, each day she remains at the bordello is a chance for disease. What if some infection she harbors now bursts forth a week from now, or a month?"

Sidney and Hunter looked at one another. Hunter had not considered beyond the task of convincing his two companions of the idea of taking Caterina to England.

"It will be too great a burden to ask Beatrice to share her chamber," Sidney said.

"No rooms remain at Pozzo della Vacca, other than hers," Hunter said. "And we cannot ask if she may stay at *Palazzo Michiel*." He would ask Lucia if Caterina might stay with her.

"Perhaps Christopher and Francis might relinquish their cramped storeroom," Gironi suggested.

"If both are well," Hunter said.

"If she does develop a disease, we would have to take her to the *Incurabili* hospital," Sidney said.

"And you would lose whatever money you pay her matron," Gironi said with a sour face.

Hunter felt compelled to say, without knowing how much remained of his allowance, "I will contribute ten ducats to paying her debt."

The gondola bumped against the embankment outside *Palazzo Michiel*, and the men climbed out. Hunter allowed himself a moment of congratulation, followed quickly by a fear that some impediment, either of infection or finance, might yet occur.

Wednesday, 16 June 1574, Venice

Signora Filippa pummeled Gironi with angry words so rapidly that Hunter could not catch any of them. When finished, she folded her arms in front of her and frowned.

"Signora Filippa is unhappy," Gironi said.

"That did not need translation," Hunter said.

Gironi related the matron's case. "She obliged her cousin by taking Caterina in, she found her tuition in English, she arrayed her with costly apparel, and the girl owes her not only money, but a year's service."

"Let us not argue with her. Ask what price she wants to release Caterina. We can negotiate from there."

Gironi spoke with Signora Filippa. "She says she must calculate her loss. She can give us a figure tomorrow."

"Perhaps this short conversation is best," Hunter said. "She may need time to accustom herself to the idea." He paid for the wine and left a tip.

As they stood waiting for a gondola, Hunter suggested, "Our time here was less than expected. We might go to Tintoretto's studio. As Lady Windsor is eager to show me his work at the *Scuola di San Rocco*, if I can provide her a visit to his studio, she will be filled with gratitude. I am to dine with the baron and baroness tonight."

Gironi raised an eyebrow. "Always to be on the best footing with the nobility. Let us go to his studio."

Tintoretto slapped down the brush he was holding and gave his visitors a sour look. This seemed Hunter's day for disturbing people.

"Pray forgive our intrusion," Hunter began. "Once again I hope to find a time one of your admirers might visit, an English baroness who lives in Venice."

When he heard the translation, the painter's countenance changed. As Hunter had hoped, he seemed to sniff a possible commission.

"He says he was once introduced to an English noblewoman at the *Scuola di San Rocco*," Gironi said.

"Probably Baroness Windsor. I know of no other English noblewoman in Venice, and she is a great lover of art."

"He says around midday is most convenient, because the light is not right then," Gironi said. Speaking more softly to Hunter, he said, "Might I suggest to him that we know a courtesan who could pose for him?"

Hunter was momentarily confused. "Who?"

"Caterina. In that way, she might help to pay off her debt in a more honorable way. She might feel less guilt about the expense to you and Sidney."

The idea of Caterina posing naked troubled Hunter until the image of her coupling with another man flashed into his mind. He banished it and focused on the logic of Gironi's suggestion. "Yes, you may, but tell him we have not yet presented the idea to the lady."

Gironi explained to Tintoretto. "He says he is looking for a 'Flora' to paint. We might bring her for him to look at, again at midday."

Hunter searched the artist's face for signs of lechery but found none. "Fine. But remind him again that we have not spoken with the young lady."

"He understands."

Sidney and Bryskett were seated near Lord Windsor at the head of the table, while Hunter found himself again sitting adjacent to Lady Windsor. The baron continued to speculate as to when and how Henry of Poland, now Henry III of France, would make his way to his native realm. Sidney said Ambassador Ferrier was eager that he come to Venice. When the baroness spoke of art, and Hunter mentioned a visit to Tintoretto's workshop, her squeal attracted the attention of all at the table.

"My dear," Lord Windsor said, "pray what is the cause of your delight."

"Master Hunter has spoken with Jacopo Robusti, the artist Tintoretto, regarding a visit to his workshop."

"But you have met Master Tintoretto before," her husband said.

"Yes, at the *Scuola di San Rocco*. But I have never been to his studio. When I met him, I was loath to ask for so private a meeting."

"It will be an honor to arrange such a visit," Hunter said.

"And it will be my honor to show you his works at San Rocco before we visit his studio," Baroness Windsor said.

Lord Windsor turned to Sidney. "You chose Veronese to paint your portrait, rather than Tintoretto." It was a question disguised as a statement.

"I did. When I looked at the paintings of both in churches and scuole, I judged Veronese more noble and elegant; Tintoretto more dramatic and spiritual."

"Your judgment agrees with many," the baroness said.

Windsor nodded. "I presume that, as a Protestant, Veronese's trouble with the Inquisition was a recommendation rather than a detriment."

Sidney's response was slow, as though recalling himself from a distant place. "It was no part of my decision." He smiled weakly. "Yet I gather that many devout Catholics in Venice were amused with Veronese's solution."

Windsor laughed. "Changing the title from *The Last Supper* to *A Feast in the House of Levi* was biting his thumb at the Inquisition, but they could not do anything about it. The Dominicans even accepted it for their refectory."

Hunter thought he was unlikely to see this much-discussed painting if it meant entering a Dominican friary.

"Venetians are devoted enough to Saint Mark and the Virgin," Lord Windsor remarked, "but they do not extend that regard to the pope."

"If the pope acted more like the Vicar of Christ and less like an Italian prince, they might render him more respect," the baroness said.

While the baron and his wife discussed the relations between Venice and the Vatican, Hunter noted with concern Sidney's eyes lose their focus and turn glassy. They closed as he slumped in his chair and slowly tilted toward a shocked Bryskett. Lodowick caught him and exclaimed, "He burns with a fever."

CHAPTER 16

With the Current

Baroness Windsor leapt up and dashed to Sidney. "Oh my, oh my!" She turned to her befuddled husband. "Quick, call Ernesto." She dipped a serviette in water and daubed at Sidney's forehead.

"Ernesto, Ernesto!" Windsor called.

Hunter strode to Sidney and touched his cheek. "Pray, madam, may we carry our friend to a couch."

"*Ernesto,*" the baroness addressed the entering servant, "*la camera verde.* He will lead you to the green bedchamber."

Ernesto and Hunter supported Sidney's shoulders and backed up a staircase, while Bryskett bore his feet. "This illness has come from that servant of Barnes," Bryskett said. They carried Sidney into an olive-colored room. No sooner had they arranged him in bed than Lady Windsor entered.

"This is the chamber we had hoped Master Sidney might stay in," she said, "but not under these circumstances. My lord will send for a physician immediately."

"Thank you, Baroness," Hunter said. "Lodowick, do you think we can take him to the *Palazzo Michiel*?"

"No, no," the baroness protested. "You must keep him here. And one or both of you must stay."

Hunter hesitated. He had planned to visit Signora Filippa, to discover her price for releasing Caterina, to visit Lucia to ask if Caterina might stay with her while he arranged to take her to Padua, and to withdraw funds from the Biondi bank. Yet if Sidney were to die, none of this mattered. "I shall stay."

"So shall I," Bryskett said.

Together, they removed Sidney's doublet and venetian breeches. After the physician left, prescribing a cold and moist diet of cucumbers, lettuce, and fish, and promising an electuary of honey with an infusion of wormwood and yarrow, the two friends watched alternately through the night, although both scarcely slept, waking at each moan or movement.

Thursday, 17 June 1574, Venice

Just before dawn, Sidney's call for water awoke Hunter. Bryskett was already lifting a cup to his lips. "You must beg pardon of the baron and baroness," Sidney said after drinking deeply. "And thank them for providing me a bed."

"I shall," Bryskett said. "I promised to tell Lady Windsor when you woke."

"Pray wait," Sidney said. "I am in no fit state to speak with her. Is there a chamber pot here?"

The friends helped Sidney out of bed so he might relieve himself. He stood unsteadily. "I fear I may need more rest. My head throbs."

Hunter felt his forehead. "You are still hot."

Sidney struggled into bed with their aid. "I am grateful, but do you not have tasks? Edward, did you find what the matron wanted for Caterina? If I write a note, Bryskett can withdraw funds from the Strozzi bank. And I should write the *Palazzo Michiel* to explain why I did not return last night."

"Let us stay by you until the Windsors stir," Hunter said. "Can we bring you sustenance?"

"Perhaps a piece of bread, and another cup of water," Sidney said.

As soon as Lady Windsor entered the green bedchamber, she took charge, ordering servants to fetch fresh linen, to run to the physician again, and to order the cook to prepare a tincture of borage and white willow bark, her preferred fever remedy. Hunter and Bryskett left for *Palazzo Michiel*, not only to deliver the explanation of their absence, but to gather a fresh shirt and stockings for Sidney.

Madox, White, Fisher, and Gironi greeted them with anxious faces. When they learned of Sidney's sickness, all wanted to go comfort him.

"You are too many to descend upon him," Bryskett said. "Let one or two go and take his clothing."

They tossed coins and determined White and Gironi would go. Gironi whispered to Hunter, "Not only will I content myself Sidney is well, I shall not have to face Signora Filippa again. You two may have that pleasure."

At the brothel, the matron named sixty ducats as the price for relinquishing Caterina. She insisted the girl was reluctant to leave and presented a paper, listing Caterina's debts for clothing, food, and lodging, plus a reckoning of her losses due to Caterina's future absence. When Hunter asked to speak with Caterina, she frowned but summoned her. While Bryskett negotiated with Signora Filippa, Hunter retreated to a far corner of the reception area.

Caterina beamed at Hunter. "I am grateful you came."

"We came to ask *matrone* if you may leave her service."

Her eyes lit up. "In truth?"

Judging from her expression, there was no need to ask the question, but he must for form's sake. "Do you wish to leave this house?"

"Yes." Then her face clouded. "But where will I go?"

"I am not sure. Perhaps to Lucia's for a time, perhaps to our lodgings in Padua, but we hope you will come to England."

Caterina looked uncertain. "Lucia, yes. Padua? England?" Her tone of fear increased as she named each more distant place. "*Matrone* say no trust English gentlemens. Men promise and promise, but they will not give good food, good bed, good clothes. Men will make you slave. Make you give fucks to everyone and beat you and take your money." When she finished pouring out her fears, she was trembling, looking with pleading eyes.

Hunter took her hands. "She was right to warn you away from evil men, but we are not evil. You must trust me."

"Will you swear to God, to Holy Mother, to all holy things?"

"I will. I swear I will not hurt you. I swear we will take you to a better place." Hunter hoped he could keep his promise. Would Leicester take her into his household? Would he treat her well? What could Hunter do if he did not? "Does not Signora Filippa force you to couple with everyone and keep your money?"

"She treats me well, but I do not want to give fucks to everyone."

"That is what I wish to take you from." Hunter embraced her.

Bryskett called from across the room; Hunter left Caterina reluctantly. "I have succeeded in negotiating the sum down to forty ducats.

And Signora Filippa promises Caterina will not serve other clients if we return tomorrow with the money."

Hunter returned to Caterina with the news. A smile lit her face. Then she frowned. "How much?"

Hunter did not want Caterina to think her worth as a person could be measured. "Do not worry about the sum. Your debts will be paid."

Again elation lit her face, followed by doubt. "May I keep my lute and some gowns?"

Hunter was unsure of the conditions Bryskett had agreed to. Surely Signora Filippa would not turn the girl into the world naked. "I hope so. I do not know."

"I ask *matrone*. I must thank her."

Hunter's emotions mirrored those of Caterina. He was thrilled that his plans to free Caterina were working but feared possible slips on the many steps before them. "There is much I must attend to. I hope to see you again tomorrow."

Bryskett confirmed that Caterina could keep several gowns and a lute. Thanking Signora Filippa, he and Hunter took their leave, Bryskett to the Strozzi bank and Baron Windsor's, while Hunter headed to the Biondi bank and Lucia's, to ask if Caterina might stay there. They agreed to meet at Lord Windsor's in three hours.

"Sior Rossi was pleased that you could tell him details of the killing and theft in Cannaregio," Lucia said, "but he wants more information before he deals with this Biradi."

Good news. Rossi might prove a powerful ally. "How can I help Signor Rossi?"

"He would know the items that were taken from the house."

Hunter could list a few, but Christopher or Francis should be able to compile a more complete list. "I will undertake that, though I will have to return to Padua."

"He is in no hurry." Lucia sipped her wine. "As to the Dominicans, Brother Alberto's short companion is *Fra' Iseppo*—you would say Brother Giuseppe. Both stay at the friary at Zanipolo. The friars brought the girl you saw, Lucetta, from Padua and took her to *Le Convertite*."

This was a name Hunter had not heard. "Pray what and where is that?"

"It is Santa Maria Maddalena convent on Giudecca. It is a new convent for reformed *meretrice*."

If Lucetta had taken orders, Hunter would be unable to ask her what she knew of Carollo, Barnes, and the Dominicans. "Is she now a nun?"

"No. She must wait a year until she can take orders."

"Might I speak with her then?"

Lucia frowned. "You would have to get permission from the abbess. She might well question your reasons."

Hunter had to agree. An Englishman asking to interview a former harlot would be unlikely to be allowed access. "I must beg a favor of you. I am disposing affairs to release Caterina from Signora Filippa's."

"Oh." The muscles around Lucia's eyes tightened.

"Yes. Master Sidney and I hope to take her to England to serve his uncle, an important nobleman."

Lucia looked suspicious.

"I assure you we have her best interest in mind."

Lucia appeared unconvinced.

"And I am not in love with her."

Lucia snorted. "What favor do you ask?"

"I hope that Caterina might stay with you for a few days until I may assure her a place in Padua."

"How many is a few?"

Hunter smiled his uncertainty. "Less than a week, I hope."

"And when would you bring her here?"

"Would tomorrow be convenient?"

"If Caterina remains in a chamber, unseen, and does not sing, she may stay for a few days. I do care for the girl. If she cannot accustom herself to life in a brothel, then your plan, if you can manage it, might prove better for her. I presume you will pay for what she eats here."

"For certain." Lucia's concern for Caterina was tempered with a concern that Lord Windsor and her other patrons not see or hear a beautiful younger woman.

"And you are to send me word before you appear at my door with her."

"To be sure. I am much in your debt." Hunter bowed to the courtesan. Two steps were settled—Caterina's release and her temporary stay with Lucia.

Hunter found Sidney sitting up in bed, still weak and fevered and enduring a severe headache. Gironi hovered behind Bryskett, who was giving Sidney a cup of water. Lady Windsor had forbidden Sidney to leave and provided another pallet so that Gironi could also stay overnight.

"I understand Signora Filippa has agreed a price for Caterina's freedom," Sidney said.

"Thanks to Lodowick." Hunter felt himself flush. "I must confess to careless reckoning. I said I could furnish ten ducats, but when I went to the bank, they would allow me to withdraw only seven. I will not be allowed more until the first of July."

Sidney sighed. "I am in a similar situation. With the thirty ducats, I shall have drawn as much as I might for this month. That leaves us three ducats short."

"I am able to contribute that amount from my own funds," Bryskett said.

"I shall repay you in July," Sidney said.

"You need not," Bryskett said. "It shall be my gift to Caterina."

"What are the plans to collect and transport Caterina tomorrow?" Gironi asked.

"Lucia has agreed to house her for a few days, until we return to Padua," Hunter said. "But I must let her know at what time I shall bring Caterina."

"I would think eleven o'clock may be a convenient time to collect her," Bryskett said.

Hunter knotted his brow. "I promised Lady Windsor I would stay with Sidney, but I must return to Filippa and Lucia to alert them of our plans."

Gironi spoke up. "You have run about the city all day. Allow me, as your supposed servant, to run these errands, as well as to fetch Master Sidney anything he needs. That will raise fewer questions with the baroness."

Hunter saw the sense in his suggestion. "Fine. I must write a message to Lucia and tell you where she lodges."

The swishing of Lady Windsor's gown warned them of her approach.

Friday, 18 June 1574, Venice

The day ahead looked both less and more difficult to Hunter. Sidney awoke without a fever, declaring he felt much better and need not impose further on the hospitality of Lord and Lady Windsor. As he would return to *Palazzo Michiel,* Hunter and Bryskett need not devise excuses for leaving their friend. On the other hand, Gironi had arrived late the previous night after visiting both Filippa and Lucia twice. Caterina could be collected at eleven, but no later. Important clients were to be entertained that afternoon. Lucia was also busy with clients, so Caterina could not arrive before five in the evening.

Sidney's friends delivered him to Madox, White, and Fisher, with instructions to keep him at rest. Bryskett, Hunter, and Gironi proceeded to the brothel, discussing the problem of what to do with Caterina between noon and five. Bryskett suggested the timing would be right to take Caterina to Tintoretto's studio. Hunter wished to take her to *Le Convertite* to speak with Lucetta but did not mention this to Bryskett. Both plans might frighten the girl. He would have to speak with her and gauge her mood.

Zuan met them with baskets and one box containing Caterina's clothing and personal possessions. He and Gironi began loading the baggage into a gondola.

Hunter and Bryskett mounted the stairs to the *portego,* where a gracious Signora Filippa greeted them. Perhaps she can hear the coins jingling, Hunter thought. Caterina stood slightly behind her in a violet gown, her hair done up and decorated with a coronel, her face the mixture of happiness and fear he had seen the day before. After greeting the matron, Hunter excused himself to speak with Caterina while Bryskett attended to business.

"I am glad you come," Caterina began.

"I hope this will prove a happy day for you," Hunter said. Perhaps this was a bit of a prayer, considering how she might react. "Your baggage is being loaded below to go to Signora Lucia's."

"We go there now?"

Hunter tensed. This was the first of several hurdles to clear. "Lucia is entertaining clients until this evening. She has agreed that you stay with her several days but asks that you stay out of sight unless she comes to you."

Caterina's smile faded and her brows creased. "Then where we go now?"

Hunter hemmed. "Do you know the painter Tintoretto?"

Her face lit. "Everyone know him. Famous painter."

Perhaps this would work out well. "My friends and I have met him. He likes to paint beautiful women. We told him of you. He would like to meet you." There, he had taken the leap, only slightly stretching the truth.

Her eyes widened. "Me? Today?"

"Yes."

"He will paint me today?"

"I do not know, Caterina. After we leave, we will go there." Hunter looked toward Bryskett. Both he and Filippa were smiling. "You may bid your matron good-bye."

The two women embraced, the men standing apart while they spoke. Caterina began to cry. Despite her matron's severe business instinct, Signora Filippa also lifted a handkerchief at her eyes, then dabbed away Caterina's tears. At a word, Caterina turned to Hunter.

As they climbed into a gondola, Caterina's lip trembled.

"Do not be afraid," Hunter repeated several times.

Bryskett spoke to her in Italian. "She is sad to leave in a way. She is excited and afraid about meeting Tintoretto. What have you told her?"

"That he wanted to see her."

"Let us hope he finds her a fitting subject. It is almost midday."

"I hope that will please her." Dread overcame Hunter. Might he ask her to disrobe? Would she think he intended to prostitute her in a different way? As the gondola glided along, he became as nervous as she.

At Tintoretto's studio, Bryskett handled the conversation with the artist. Caterina stood shyly behind Hunter. At one moment, she gasped. Hunter turned in a panic, but Caterina whispered excitedly, "He will pay me." To do what, Hunter wondered.

The artist summoned her forward, looked at her closely, spoke in soothing tones, and touched her hair. He nodded. After further words, Caterina loosened her bodice.

Hunter drew in his breath. He was demanding that she disrobe. Yet she was still smiling. What was going on? He caught Bryskett's eye and waved him close. "What is happening?"

"He thinks she will make a lovely Flora," Bryskett said. "He will pay her twenty-five soldi today to make a few sketches."

"Does he want her to shed her clothes?"

Bryskett laughed. "Not today. I explained she had just left a bordello and was afraid of the future. He could see her fear and spoke to her calmly. He wants her shoulders to be exposed. That is all."

Tintoretto seated Caterina on a stool, tilted her head, adjusted her gown, and turned to his palette and brushes. He placed a canvas on an easel and began to outline her portrait. He worked with marvelous speed for half an hour, then turned to the men and spoke.

"He wants to know if we can return later today, near four. The light will be better then," Bryskett said.

It was time for Hunter to explain his idea. "How long will it take to reach Giudecca from here?"

"That depends on what part of Giudecca."

"*Le Convertite.*"

Bryskett looked back in shock. "You cannot mean to take the girl to a nunnery."

"I hope she may speak with Lucetta, one of Carollo's harlots that the women at the Castelletto spoke of." Hunter explained what he had learned from Lucia.

"So you spoke to her of more than Caterina," Bryskett raised an eyebrow.

"I will tell you more later. I doubt that the abbess of *Le Convertite* will allow two men to speak with Lucetta, but if Caterina asks to, saying she knows her and wants to discuss convent life, then she may be able to find out more about the Dominicans who whisked her from Padua and if she spoke with Barnes."

"I shall explain to Caterina. I hope taking her to a convent will not frighten her."

"If it does, we will not go."

"Do you think her capable of such deception?"

"She worked at Filippa's for several months. That must have required deception." Hunter did not want to think about all the lies she had had to tell or consider the possibility that she had deceived him.

Bryskett nodded. "I think we can travel there and return by four." He turned to an impatient Tintoretto.

When Tintoretto handed Caterina coins, she thanked him several times, her face glowing. The moment she was outside the studio, she extracted her purse, dropped the coins into it, and exclaimed with excitement, "The first good money I earn. The first—" she searched for a word "—honest money."

Pleased to see her pleased with herself, Hunter said, "Yes. Honest money. You should be proud."

"Now I can sing and sit for painter." Her face suddenly clouded. "You and friend pay *matrone* much. I can give money to you."

"No, no," Hunter said. "It is, as you say, the first honest money you have earned. You must keep it." She was feeling generous and in his debt. This seemed the time to ask her to speak to Lucetta. He immediately felt guilty. He was taking advantage of the girl again, yet this might be the only opportunity to find out what the Dominicans had said to Lucetta. "Caterina, it is several hours before we can go to Lucia's. There is a hard request I will ask of you." Hunter glanced at Bryskett. "Perhaps my friend can explain better in Italian."

Hunter watched her face as Bryskett spoke. When he mentioned *Le Convertite*, she showed surprise and fear. Bryskett's reassuring words led her to relax into suspicious listening. He spoke of Lucetta and she asked questions. Finally, she pressed her lips together in determination and turned to Hunter. "You pay my debts. I do this for you."

"I am grateful," Hunter said. "And if it becomes too hard, you may come back without seeing Lucetta."

She nodded. "I will try."

CHAPTER 17

Diving Deeper

HUNTER AND BRYSKETT PACED UP AND DOWN BEFORE THE AUSTERE façade of the nunnery. Caterina had done well at the gate, saying the kind gentlemen had brought her from a brothel, but she was not sure she wanted to become a nun. Her conversations, first with the nun at the window, then with two others of greater authority, finally gained her entry.

"Perhaps she could act on a stage, as well as sit for painters and sing," Bryskett said.

"Not in England," Hunter said.

"True. I was thinking of Italy, of the Gelosi."

A distant *campanile* chimed three.

"She has been a long time. She must have gained access to Lucetta." Hunter went over the questions he had requested she ask. Would she remember all of them? Would Lucetta have answers? As the men turned back toward the gate, Caterina emerged. He rushed to her. "Thank you. Thank you. Was it difficult?"

"The abbess is hard. She say I will be damned if I do not become a nun." She looked at Hunter with worried eyes.

"Only God can damn a person, not an abbess."

Caterina breathed a sigh and smiled. "That is what I think. But I act sad and repent and say a talk to Lucetta might make me be a nun."

"Repentant," Hunter said automatically. "I beg your pardon. It is not time for English lessons. Did you see Lucetta?"

"Yes."

Bryskett interrupted. "We should start back to Dorsoduro. We can speak in the gondola."

They climbed into the gondola and settled themselves in the *felze*. As they pushed off, Hunter began his questions.

"What did she say about the Dominicans?"

"They were kind."

"What were their names?"

"*Fra' Alberto e Fra' Iseppo.*" She twitched. "I mean Brother."

"I understood. Why did they take her from Padua?"

"A bad man want to hurt her."

"What was his name?"

She hesitated a minute, trying to remember. "Biradi."

"Why did they take her and not the other girls?"

Caterina looked puzzled. She turned to Bryskett, who spoke to her at length in Italian. At the end she said. "I do not ask."

"When did the Dominicans take her?"

"When they come."

"I mean, did she remember a date? Was it before or after Captain Scarpa returned?"

Again, Bryskett needed to clarify.

"She is not sure. When news come men are killed, the brothers come. Speak to Carollo. Pay him her debt. Bring her to Venice to be safe."

That made sense. As the friars were from Bologna, they somehow knew of the murder of Biradi's men. They were not working with Biradi but came to Padua to warn Carollo and his women of the danger from him. But why were they in danger? They must have played a role in setting up Sidney's capture, so Biradi held them responsible for the death of his men. How did the Dominicans know of their involvement? According to Barnes's servant Christopher, they had arrived before Captain Scarpa returned, knowing everything about the attack. "Did she know an Englishman named Barnes?"

"She say no. But I think she lie." Caterina was showing more confidence after sitting for Tintoretto and talking her way into the convent.

"Did the Dominicans speak of Barnes?"

"Friars say little to her. Tell her she must go *Le Convertite*. She go. I think she is a simple girl."

"Did she tell you anything more about the Dominicans?"

"No. She is full of holy words. She pray for the friars and thank God. She pray for the other girls she work with. She say she will pray for me."

"Well, we all need prayers," Hunter said, disappointed. "You have been brave and done good work."

Caterina gave a broad, confident smile. "Now I work for Tintoretto. Get more money."

Monday, 21 June 1574, Padua

Beatrice's smile at their return became a frown when she spotted Caterina. She unleashed a stream of angry words at Gironi. Caterina turned to Hunter. "You say I will sing for gentleman. She say I should not come."

Gironi had predicted this would be a difficult homecoming. Hunter guided her to the cart that held her possessions. "Let Luca speak to her. He will explain it is Master Sidney's wish that you stay. We can unload the cart." It would have been better if Sidney had been healthy enough to return and Bryskett had not stayed with him in Venice.

They carried the first load past the quarreling pair to the central room. Francis and Christopher entered from the kitchen, dishcloths in their hands. They stopped abruptly to gaze at Caterina, affected by her beauty. Hunter introduced them and the servants bowed to her. Clearly Caterina's gown had convinced them he had brought home a lady.

"Where shall we take her baggage?" Christopher asked.

Hunter was unsure. "Let it remain here for now. Pray help us with the rest."

They followed Hunter outside while Caterina remained, taking in her new surroundings. Beatrice stood silent, frowning, with feet apart and arms folded. Gironi approached Hunter. "I need not tell you how Beatrice feels about Caterina. I told you it would have been better if she had changed into clothing less grand."

Hunter had to admit he was right. The stares on the boat up the Brenta were a reminder during their journey. He had made the situation worse by embarking on an English lesson on using *do* in negative statements. Gironi looked away in embarrassment as first Hunter, then Caterina, bobbed up and down saying "I sit," "I do not sit," "I stand," "I do not stand." The other passengers moved away from these mad foreigners. At least it had kept them from asking uncomfortable questions.

"She is willing to tolerate Caterina if it is Sidney's will, and if Caterina will help, as Christopher and Francis do. She even said she will allow her to sing for one hour each day. I hope that will improve things. The question of where she is to stay must be solved. Beatrice says she has only a small room for herself and her son and will not share with any 'woman of the street.'"

Hunter smiled at Beatrice. "*Grassie.*"

She huffed in behind Christopher and Francis, who carried the last of Caterina's boxes. Hunter paid the carter and followed them. When he entered, Beatrice was shouting at Barnes's servants. Although they could not understand her words, it was clear that they should get back to the pots and pans. She turned and gestured to the baggage.

Before Gironi could intervene, Caterina bowed to the housekeeper and spoke in calm, respectful tones. Was she begging pardon for the trouble she might cause? Best to let Caterina speak for herself, Hunter decided. He waved Gironi to his side. "I shall ask Christopher and Francis to abandon the storeroom. They believe Caterina to be a Venetian lady. We can store some of her belongings in our chamber."

"That may work. What will they say when they see her in an apron helping Beatrice?"

"By then it will be too late. They have few possessions, which they can store in corners of the main room. They can sleep on benches."

"I see no other solution, unless you take on two more servants."

Hunter smiled. "I have enough trouble with you, Luca. And I had forgotten you are my servant."

Gironi smiled back. "I am glad to hear that."

Why hadn't he thought of analyzing the enciphered letter before? With a list of the most frequent letters in the message before him, he had only to write the alphabet over the text at possible starting points to determine if the vowels lined up with those letters. If they did not, he discarded that attempt and moved on. But now Hunter had exhausted the starting points in the books from Barnes's lodgings. Could he have started with the wrong presumptions? Could some of the letters signify spaces? Could letters without meaning have been mixed in to foil attempts at deciphering? Should he have read the numbers at the top backwards? Backwards! Could he solve the cipher if he wrote the alphabet backwards over possible starting points?

Hunter lifted the pile of books from the floor onto the desk and began again with *De Imitatione Christi*. Using his system of vowel frequency, he worked more quickly through the possibilities. Within half an hour, he exclaimed, "Hoorah!" The most frequent letters in the message corresponded with vowels from a starting place in Cardinal Pole's *De Concilio*. He set about deciphering the message. With each line, his excitement grew. If only Sidney had been there to witness this. After another half hour, he lay down his pen with a crow of triumph. He rose from the desk as footsteps raced up the stairs.

Gironi burst in the door. "Are you in pain?"

Hunter laughed. "No, no. Look here, Luca. Here is a key to the mystery of the attack on Sidney."

Gironi looked at the page Hunter thrust at him. "You know I cannot read Latin. Pray what does it say? Who wrote it?"

Hunter sighed. "There is no signature, so that mystery remains. But I surmise it was written by a cleric, perhaps one of the Dominicans I told you about."

"What does it say?"

Hunter opened his mouth to begin, then said, "If you will allow me to keep you in suspense another thirty minutes, I will translate the message into English."

"You do this as a torture. I will make sure Francis and Christopher have cleaned out their closet so it is fit for Caterina. May they carry some of her baggage up here?"

"Yes. They shall not disturb me."

"Luca," Hunter called down the stairs. "Pray come up."

Gironi took the stairs two at a time. "I am grateful for your effort, but you might have spared yourself by telling me before."

Hunter smiled and handed the page to Gironi. "It was a good exercise. Go ahead, read."

IV-XXII-VII

> *Pray forgive the lack of formal greeting. If this missive were to fall into the wrong hands, it were best that neither sender nor recipient be identified.*

> *I acknowledge that your actions, as conveyed in your letter to me, were taken out of devotion to the Church and*

abhorrence of heresy. However, the means you employed were in error, and might even work to the detriment of the faith.

I had not heard of this Englishman before I received your letter. You believed that the Inquisition would be eager to apprehend and try him. In this, you are in error, and clearly unfamiliar with the proceedings of the Holy Office. We are not accustomed to seize any foreign heretic who happens to be in Italy, whether in the jurisdiction of His Holiness or not, unless he is attempting to make proselytes or openly profaning holy objects or buildings. If our authorities had taken possession of the Englishman, as you presumed they would, the already strained relations between the Holy See and England would become worse, to no purpose.

Due to your actions, taken without consulting the proper Church authorities, it was necessary to employ regrettable violence against Christian souls, no matter how sinful they might have been. Let this weigh upon your conscience.

If you seek to aid our Holy Mother the Church, you should aim to deteriorate relations between England and Venice. As the Most Serene Republic does not pursue heresy with the zeal it should, you must devise some way in which the Englishman you detest appears to threaten or bring dishonor upon Venice. Then they will be more likely to prosecute him.

After reading, I pray you burn this letter.

Gironi whistled. "It appears Barnes wrote someone, whom you guess to be a cleric, of a plan to carry Sidney into the Papal States, but he was rebuked."

"More than that," Hunter said. "Barnes supposed that the Inquisition would seize Sidney. Here is evidence not only that Barnes hated Sidney, but that whoever wrote this is responsible for the murder of Biradi's ruffians, the 'regrettable violence against Christian souls, no matter how sinful.'" He paused. "It might be the inquisitor or vice inquisitor, someone with enough authority to order the killing of Biradi's men."

"If one can be thankful for another's death, we can be thankful Barnes will not be able to—" Gironi referred to the translation "— 'devise some way in which the Englishman you detest appears to threaten or bring dishonor upon Venice.'"

"So I thought as I deciphered the message," Hunter said, "but Barnes may not be the only person with whom our cleric communicated. If he now knows of Sidney, could he not engage another to use Sidney to harm the relations between Venice and England."

Gironi sighed. "Indeed he might."

"I must speak again with Fitzwilliams about the Catholic clergy he knows."

A lush song floated up from Caterina, accompanied by her lute. Hunter caught the word *amore*. He and Gironi descended to find Christopher, Francis, Beatrice, and her son Giulio all standing transfixed, staring at the door of the storeroom, which now served as Caterina's chamber.

Francis turned to them, wide-eyed. "You did not say the lady could sing, master. Pray you, bid her come out."

Gironi gestured to Beatrice. "She also wishes to hear more singing."

Hunter strode to the storeroom and knocked. Caterina's song stopped. "*Si.*"

"May I enter?"

Caterina opened the door. She had changed from her gown into more humble attire. "Good afternoon, Master Hunter."

"An audience awaits you."

Caterina's brow wrinkled. She did not understand his words.

"Everyone would like to hear you sing. Can you come out?"

Caterina hesitated. "I do not know these people well."

"If you will make money singing, you must get used to singing before strangers. Besides, Christopher and Francis left their chamber for you and carried your bags. You will do well to please Beatrice."

Caterina considered his words for a moment, then nodded. "I will come." She followed him into the main room.

"*Ela canta ben,*" Beatrice exclaimed. She spoke to Caterina warmly and asked her a question. Caterina smiled and nodded. She began singing and Beatrice joined her.

169

Hunter turned to Gironi with a smile. If the two women knew the same songs, things promised to go more smoothly.

When the song ended, the men applauded. Beatrice and Caterina consulted again, then began another song, this time exchanging verses. Gironi explained. "In this song, the old woman advises the younger not to trust men, but she will not heed her because she is in love."

After the applause, Beatrice named another song. Caterina shook her head. Hunter feared that the mood of cooperation might dissolve, but instead, Beatrice sang a verse and refrain. She spoke again with Caterina, then both began the verse haltingly.

"She will teach Caterina a new song," Gironi said.

Hunter relaxed. The good will continued. This was an opportunity. "Christopher, Francis, pray accompany me upstairs, that I may speak with you. We shall leave the ladies to work on their song. Luca, pray stay with the ladies, as you know what they are saying, and ask Giulio to bring up three cups of wine."

When Barnes's servants were seated on stools, cups of wine in hand, Hunter cleared a space on his desk and took up pen and paper. "First, I thank you again for moving so that Caterina may stay with us. Master Sidney will be pleased."

Christopher took the lead. "It was our privilege to welcome such a lovely and skilled lady." Francis nodded with enthusiasm.

"I wish to ask you more about the goods stolen from Master Barnes's lodgings in Venice and Padua. Pray tell me in detail what was taken."

"That is what the other gentlemen asked," Francis said.

Hunter looked up in surprise. "What other gentlemen?"

The servants said they had been visited twice—first by the expatriates and then by Dr. Simmons and Captain Scarpa. Both times they were asked to tell of the night of Barnes's murder, to explain where they had been afterward, and to list the stolen items.

"Why did the Englishmen want a list?"

"They said it was for Captain Scarpa, but then he came" Christopher shrugged.

"Did the Englishmen ask about the friars?" Hunter asked.

Both servants shook their heads.

Did that mean they did not know the Dominicans visited Barnes, or that the friars had visited them as well? "Did Captain Scarpa?"

"No."

Scarpa probably did know that the friars had whisked Lucetta away to Venice. "Did the Englishmen ask why you moved to Venice? Did you tell them about Barnes changing his name? Did you tell them of the big man with the warty nose who came twice to see him?"

"They didn't ask about any of that," Christopher said. "Nor did Scarpa."

How much did the expatriates know? How could he ask them without revealing all he knew? Best move on to the inventory. "Pray list for me the items that were stolen, while I record them."

"That's not hard." Francis straightened with pride. "We've done it twice before, and I have a good memory." He began his list with candlesticks and other silver items, described missing clothing, mentioned lesser valuables, and ended with glass bowls Barnes had purchased in Murano a few days before his death.

Rossi should be pleased with this complete catalogue, whatever the uses to which he intended to put it. He would ask Gironi to translate it. "Your memory is indeed powerful," Hunter said. "I want to ask you again about the Dominicans, Christopher. Are you sure they arrived before Captain Scarpa, Sidney, and I returned?"

"Yes, I'm sure." Christopher said.

"We heard the friars talkin' angry," Francis said, "but Master Barnes said not to mind. It was later when the big man with the warty nose came that Master seemed scared."

"The second time," Christopher added.

"So Master Barnes never told you what the friars said, or why they were angry."

Both men shook their heads.

"Did the friars give your master a letter?"

Another exchange of glances. "No," Christopher said. "At least I never saw one."

"Did you ever see him looking at a paper and a book, and writing?"

Christopher shook his head.

Francis frowned. "Yes. One time I knocked at his study and went right in. He looked like he was copyin' out somethin'. He was angry and told me next time to wait till he answered."

"Was this in Venice or Padua?"

"Padua, a few days after the friars came."

So, they *had* brought the enciphered message to Barnes.

"Master Hunter," Christopher said hesitantly, fear in his voice, "what will become of us?"

Hunter and Sidney had not discussed this to any conclusion. Here were two masterless men, in a country where neither spoke the language. "Do you wish to return to England?"

The men exchanged glances. "We have no business here," Francis said, "but we are Catholic, like Master Barnes. He came here 'cause he hated the English Church."

"We asked the other English gentlemen, but they all have servants." Christopher looked expectantly at Hunter.

"As do I and Master Sidney," Hunter said.

Disappointment passed over Christopher's face. "I guess we had best return and bend ourselves to the English Church, but I don't know how we will get there, with no money."

Hunter had no clear idea either. If he and Sidney had not just expended a considerable amount freeing Caterina from the brothel, they might have been able to loan these two men funds to make their way home. "What talents do you have?"

"Aside from servin' a gentleman well?" Francis asked.

"Yes."

"We're both good with horses," Francis said. "And I can repair leather—not shoes, but bridles and reins and such."

"I can do a bit of carpentry," Christopher said. "I can read a little."

Not a very impressive list, Hunter thought.

"Francis forgot to say he can sing well," Christopher said.

"Not like the ladies did," Francis said. "Not the pretty Italian songs, but I know a few English catches."

"Caterina knows a few English songs," Hunter said. "You might teach her more."

Francis's face colored. "Some of the songs I know are not for ladies to sing."

"But you must know others that are suitable," Hunter said.

Francis nodded. "A few."

"Do not be shy. Tell them you can sing," Hunter said. If the problem of these servants remained, at least Caterina had been settled in Padua, he had obtained the list of stolen goods, and he had succeeded in deciphering the message to Barnes. He could count this a successful day.

CHAPTER 18

Drop by Drop

Tuesday, 22 June 1574, Padua

HUNTER SAT FACING THE CIRCLE OF EXPATRIATES. ALTHOUGH IT WOULD have been better to speak to them individually, he was anxious to return to Venice and show the deciphered letter to Sidney, so he addressed all at once in their lodgings.

"Much has happened in the month since I last saw you at Ambrose Barnes's lodgings," Hunter began. "I understand you spoke to his servants."

"Yes," Fitzwilliams said. "They told us of the attack."

Randolph sniffed. "A pity they did not show more courage and come to the aid of their master."

Hart raised a hand toward Randolph. "To be fair, James, they were outnumbered by men wielding weapons."

"May I ask how you heard they had come to Padua?" Hunter asked.

"Two ragged Englishmen stumbling about town were bound to draw attention," Fitzwilliams said. "At the university last Monday, a friend described the pair and I recognized Ambrose's servants. He said they were seen near Sidney's lodgings."

"I was surprised you did not send a message to inform us," Randolph said.

Hunter had prepared his defense. "Pray pardon me, gentlemen, but you may owe me thanks. Christopher had a raging fever when he arrived. I thought to contact you when they recovered, but Sidney and I left for Venice the next day, and he was still ill. A few days later, Philip developed a fever. He did not return from Venice because he is still suffering."

The expatriates took turns expressing concern and wishes for Sidney's health.

"The servants told me you asked for an inventory of the stolen goods," Hunter said.

"Yes." Le Rous spoke for the first time. "Together, they gave a complete list and description. We handed it to Captain Scarpa. I reckon the value of the possessions at over two hundred ducats. I understand the captain's men will question known receivers of stolen goods, and they will keep an eye out for apparel in used clothing shops, now that they know what to look for."

If Le Rous had given the list to Scarpa, why had the captain come later to question the servants? "As you have been in contact with the captain, did he suspect the servants of the theft?" Hunter asked.

"As everyone else in Padua, he suspects Biradi is behind the robbery, and the murder too," Fitzwilliams said, "though underlings carried out the deeds. Nevertheless, he intended to question Barnes's men the day after we gave him the inventory."

"Has Scarpa made any arrests?"

"Not that I know," Hart said. "He will need to gather evidence." The others grunted their agreement.

"If he can deliver Barnes's murderers to Venice, it will be a feather in his cap," Fitzwilliams said.

"Did Barnes ever say anything to you about a visit from two Dominican friars?" Hunter asked. No need to mention the letter yet. The men's eyes moved back and forth among themselves, as though asking one another who would answer.

"He did not," Fitzwilliams said.

"Did the friars pay you a visit, Roger? You are interested in the relationship between Venice and the Vatican, and you know several church leaders."

Fitzwilliams's jaw tensed. "Those interests are no reason Dominican friars should visit me."

Not exactly a denial. Hunter decided to stretch the truth to determine what the expatriates might know. "The servants said friars brought Barnes news of Sidney's transport and the slaying of men in the Romagna soon after it happened. I wondered if they told only Barnes or spread the news to others."

Randolph squirmed in his seat. Le Rous worked his fingernails. Only Hart appeared to consider the question.

"The servants did not tell us about any friars," Fitzwilliams said. Again, not a denial.

"And Vice Inquisitor Fascetti did not send you a letter?" Though Hunter addressed Fitzwilliams, he scanned every face for any reaction to the word *letter* but saw none.

"Why should he? I do not know the man personally."

"Forgive me, Roger. You mentioned him. I thought you knew him."

"I only know the man's name." Fitzwilliams folded his arms across his chest and frowned.

Hunter struck a pose he hoped would convey pondering. "I find it strange that the friars only told Barnes." No one rose to the bait. "Could it have been that Barnes was behind the attack on Sidney?"

Exclamations of wonder greeted his question.

"Why would he want to harm Philip?" Hart asked.

The same question of motive Sidney had raised. "I hope one of you might have some idea," Hunter said.

"One should not speak ill of the dead," Randolph said.

"Sidney had given no offense to Barnes," Le Rous said.

"I believe you should abandon that thought," Fitzwilliams said. "Besides, how did the servants know what news any friar brought to Ambrose? They understand neither Italian nor Latin."

"I imagine Barnes told them." Hunter realized he had almost been caught overstating the facts. "Pray forgive my suspicion, but someone was behind the attack on Philip Sidney, be he living or dead."

"That is doubtless true," Le Rous said, "yet Sidney's capture and Barnes's murder and robbery may be unrelated events. Why do you connect them?"

Hunter was unwilling to show all his cards. His questions about Barnes assuming a false name in Venice and the visits of the big man which led him to flee to Venice must be left unasked for the present. "Biradi's men were involved in both events. That argues a connection between Biradi and Barnes."

"But not between Barnes and Sidney's capture," Le Rous argued.

"As I have said before," Fitzwilliams said, "Barnes's display of wealth marked him as a man with valuables to steal. That was enough reason for Biradi to direct his men toward Ambrose."

"Do any of you know when and why Barnes changed houses in Venice?" Hunter asked.

"You are full of questions today," Randolph remarked. "Would you do Captain Scarpa's work?"

Caught off guard, Hunter said, "I merely hope to ensure my friend's safety."

Randolph raised an eyebrow. "By asking about Barnes's move in Venice?"

"None of us visited him there until the day that we found his body," Hart said.

No one had answered his question, but Hunter tried another tack. "One Englishman is grabbed and carted to the Romagna, and another is killed. I wonder that you are not afeared."

Le Rous snorted. "We have neither such important kin as Sidney nor such wealth as Barnes."

"And we have all been here near two years without incident," Randolph added.

"I have a question for you, Edward," Fitzwilliams said. "What have you been about during your week in Venice?"

Hunter considered for a moment telling him it was none of his affair. He hesitated, yet Caterina was here in Padua now, and they would soon find out. "I spent time at Baron and Baroness Windsor of Stanwell's palazzo, both dining and caring for Philip once he was taken with a fever. In addition, we visited Tintoretto's studio, and we found a girl with a beautiful voice to take to England to sing for the Earl of Leicester."

Raised eyebrows showed the expatriates had not expected such information.

"I dined once with the baron," Fitzwilliams said, never one to miss a chance to affirm his rank.

"Where did you find this singer?" Randolph asked.

Why lie? "In a bordello," Hunter said. "She did not deserve such a fate, so we rescued her from that place of ignominy." The shocked looks he received pleased him. Would any of them dare to ask how they had happened to be in a bordello?

Randolph could not resist. "How did you happen into that 'place of ignominy'?"

Hunter allowed himself a partial lie. "Lodowick Bryskett's brother, Sebastian, took us there to hear the girl and behold her beauty." That answer seemed to satisfy them. The morals of a relative of Lodowick's were none of their concern, it seemed. It was time to leave before any more questions knocked him sideways. "Pray excuse me, sirs, but I promised our housekeeper to return in time for supper."

Wednesday, 23 June 1574, Padua

He had learned little yesterday, Hunter thought, making his way to Dr. Simmons's house. He should have pressed them harder about Barnes's move to Venice. He was certain the expatriates knew of the Dominicans' visit to Barnes, but whether Barnes had told them or they too had been visited by the friars, he was unsure. His question to Fitzwilliams about a letter from the vice inquisitor was a guess, but the lack of reaction suggested it was wrong. Had any of them known of a letter to Barnes, there should have been a twitch or glance to reveal it. Perhaps his visit to Simmons would disclose more.

The servant Zorzi answered the door and ushered him into his master's study.

"*Salve*," Simmons said. "It has been a long time since you paid a visit."

"*Salve*," Hunter replied. "It has been. I hope you are well."

"You find me so. Would you care for a cup of wine?"

It was early in the day but accepting might smooth the road. "A small one." Hunter decided to proceed directly. "I hoped I might speak to you of Ambrose Barnes and what his servants revealed." He hoped this was vague enough to cover both what they had said about the killing and any suspicion that might have been cast upon Barnes for the attack on Sidney. "I understand you interviewed them with Captain Scarpa."

Simmons raised his thin eyebrows. "I translated for the captain. It was quite a tale they told."

"Did you believe what they said?"

"Most of it. Scarpa believed them."

"What steps will he take besides watching for the stolen possessions?"

"He sent descriptions of the killers to Venice. I should say 'presumed killers,' for the servants did not see the act. Scarpa recognized the descriptions and intended to question Biradi." He snorted. "I suspect he found that the men he sought were no longer in the Veneto, and that Biradi and others swore they were at the Ram's Head the night Barnes was killed."

Zorzi entered with two cups on a tray.

"I thank you for the wine." Hunter held up his cup in salute. "You do not expect that he will arrest anyone?"

Simmons returned his gesture. "He might, but *non omnia reus es punitur*. For example, the pimp Carollo is over a month cold, and no one has been charged."

It suddenly struck Hunter that Christopher and Francis, as potential witnesses, might be in danger. But now he had to attend to Simmons. Time to reveal a few cards. "Your mention of Carollo brings to mind something I discovered when I spoke to some of his women. They said when the news of Sidney's capture came to Padua, two Dominicans spoke with Carollo about danger."

"What danger?"

"I believe they warned him Biradi might seek revenge for the killing of his men, and that Carollo was involved."

Simmons's mouth twitched. He blinked several times. "That is odd. Did they say how these friars came by their knowledge?"

"No. Did the friars chance to visit you?"

"Why would they do so?"

That sounded like Fitzwilliams's response—not a denial, but a parry. "I do not know, but, as one Englishman had been attacked, they might have contacted other Englishmen in Padua to warn them. Barnes's servants said the friars visited him."

Again, Simmons blinked before answering. "I can believe the friars might speak with Carollo, if not to warn him, then to urge him to repent and mend his life. I am surprised to hear they visited Barnes, as he had nothing to do with that affair."

"Their visit and his murder make me suspect Barnes may have had a connection to the attack on Sidney."

Simmons shook his head. "Barnes was, as all the English scholars here in Padua are, Sidney's friend. He would have no motive to arrange any attack. I would look to the Romagna for those responsible, not here."

The same theory Fitzwilliams had voiced. Hunter considered mentioning the enciphered letter. No, he would say nothing until he had shown Sidney. "Why do you believe Barnes was killed?"

"My understanding is that it was a robbery that turned violent when Barnes discovered the robbers in the act."

Here was the same statement the expatriates had given. As Hart and Fitzwilliams were Simmons's tutees, one of them may have told him of Hunter's questions. "Did Barnes say anything to you about the friars' visit?"

Simmons blinked several times. "He did not."

He is unaware he signals his lies, Hunter thought. "Did he speak to you before he changed lodgings in Venice?"

"Yes."

"Why did he wish to move?"

"He complained of noise and expense at his lodgings. I believe you are mistaken to suspect Barnes. *Ut dixi,* he had no motive."

This interview was proving as fruitless as yesterday's. Both Simmons and the other expatriates were hiding information concerning Barnes and the friars, but he had no way to pry it from them short of the enciphered letter. Even then, they might deny knowledge of the letter, hold that he had not deciphered it correctly, or that Barnes had not been its recipient. Hunter rose. "I thank you for your time, Master Simmons, and your wine. Should you hear any more about Captain Scarpa's investigation, I shall appreciate it if you send me a message at Pozzo della Vacca."

"Be certain I shall," Simmons said. "*Vale.*"

Hunter spotted Carr at Luigi's. He might be the one Englishman in Padua who had not spoken to Christopher and Francis. "Good afternoon."

Carr's head jerked up from where he appeared to contemplate the stained table before him and he frowned. "What do you want?"

"I hoped to speak with you about events that have passed since I last saw you," Hunter smiled and sat opposite.

"We do not have time to discuss everything that has happened in the last three weeks," Carr said with a sneer.

"Perhaps I misspoke," Hunter said. "I hope you have not suffered any more at the hands of Tommaso Biradi."

"I have not. No thanks to you."

"I have not spoken with Biradi since I last saw you."

Carr snorted. "Do you intend to have a chat with Biradi about these past weeks?"

Hunter laughed. "That is not my plan, but I shall if I must."

"Be sure not to mention me, unless you say I told you not to see him."

"I shall." Hunter looked toward Luigi at the bar and held up two fingers. "*Due vini, per piacere.*"

"If that wine is supposed to buy you information, you are wasting your money," Carr snarled.

"I might supply you information, rather than the reverse," Hunter said. "Have any of your friends told you that Barnes's servants came to Padua a week ago?"

Carr's brows flicked up in surprise for a moment before his face resumed its sardonic expression. "I see little of them these days, but I have heard that the servants came to Sidney's lodgings."

"From whom did you hear?" Hunter suspected the news had reached Carr at the Ram's Head.

"That is my affair." Carr picked up the cup of wine Luigi placed before him. "You said you were giving rather than taking information."

"So I did. But if you already know what Christopher and Francis said about the night Barnes was killed and robbed, I will not bore you by repeating it."

"An indirect question. But I have not heard what the servants said."

Hunter related the story of Barnes's murder and observed fear cloud Carr's face. When he spoke of visits to Barnes by a man with a big nose, Carr's eyes revealed that he knew the man, though he denied it. Finally, Hunter mentioned the Dominicans. "When Biradi's men were killed in the Romagna, two Dominican friars from there visited Carollo, according to two women you said you knew."

"If they said so, then it must be so, but why do you tell me this?"

"The women said they spoke of danger to Carollo, as though he were connected to that affair."

"If he was, he was in danger of Biradi's wrath," Carr said.

"Barnes's servants say that the same friars, at the same time, visited their master. Why should they do that?"

"I have no idea." Carr drank.

"Does it not make sense that the friars were warning Barnes against Biradi's anger because he was involved in the attack on Sidney? Like Carollo, Barnes was later killed."

Carr was sweating more than the weather required. He was not as good a liar as the other expatriates, and he was certainly more afraid. Hunter chanced a question. "Did the friars visit you?"

"No," Carr said. "Using your logic, if they had visited me, I would now be dead."

"Did Barnes or the women ever mention the Dominicans to you?"

"Now you have switched from informing to questioning, Master Hunter." Carr drained his cup. "If you will not drink your wine, I shall do so, and listen to whatever other information you might give me."

Hunter chuckled. By his denials and avoiding answers, Carr had shown he knew of the Dominicans and the connections among Biradi, Carollo, and Barnes. "You are welcome to my wine." He rose, placed a coin on the bar in front of Luigi, and turned again to Carr. "I hope we may have more of a conversation when next we meet."

Carr grunted.

Hunter heard the shouting as he approached Pozzo della Vacca. In the doorway, Gironi knelt before Giulio, his hands on the weeping boy's shoulders. Behind Giulio, his mother was shouting, holding a cloth stained with blood.

"What has happened?" Hunter asked.

"Giulio says he and Christopher were attacked near the market," Gironi said. "He ran away and left Christopher in an alley."

CHAPTER 19

Odd Currents

AFTER THE BLEEDING FROM GIULIO'S NOSE AND LIP WERE STAUNCHED, Beatrice agreed that her son could return to show Hunter and Gironi where he had left Christopher.

Gironi related the boy's story as they hastened to the market. Beatrice had sent him and Christopher to the market. After they started back, a big bald man approached Christopher near Antenor's tomb and asked where he had bought the fine carrots and onions in his basket. Christopher had not understood, so Giulio translated. The man asked if they would take him to the stall and suggested a short cut. In the alleyway, another man coming toward them grabbed Giulio. After a short struggle, he let the boy go and turned on Christopher. Giulio ran all the way home, where his mother alternately cried over him and scolded him. He had arrived only minutes before Hunter came.

Giulio indicated the entrance to the alley, but was afraid to enter, pointing to a trail of blood leading into the darkness. Hunter drew his bread knife and stepped forward. A man lay in a heap halfway down the passage. "Christopher?"

The man groaned. "Aye."

Hunter and Gironi ran toward him, stumbling over a shopping basket and strewn vegetables, and knelt by Christopher's side.

Hunter felt a sticky wetness as he touched the servant's forearm. "You are wounded."

Christopher winced. "Cut up a bit. Must have swooned after he ran off."

"How long ago?" Fearing the attacker might pounce upon the boy at the alley's entrance, Hunter glanced back to see Giulio creeping cautiously toward them.

"Don't know." Christopher tried to sit up.

"Let us help you." Gironi and Hunter hooked their hands under Christopher's armpits, avoiding his injured left forearm, and pulled him to a sitting position. Gironi shouted to Giulio and explained. "He will run to the used clothing stall and get a cheap shirt to staunch this bleeding."

Christopher shook his head as if to clear it. "The lad is safe?"

"He is," Hunter said.

"I fear he and I shall get a chiding from his mother." Christopher glanced up and down the alley. "The eggs must be broken."

"You have more serious worries than smashed eggs just now," Hunter said. "Pray tell us what happened."

"A man approached me out there," Christopher gestured toward one end of the alley. "Giulio said he wanted to know where I bought the vegetables. He asked us to lead him to the stall and said this was a quick way to the market. About halfway in, another fellow comes toward us and grabs Giulio. I drop the baskets and go to pull him off the lad. When I get to them, he lets Giulio go, pulls out a long knife, and calls to the man behind me. The fellow with the knife was the smaller and closer, so I wrestled with him and took away his knife. He scudded away once I had it. It was a good thing I did, because his friend, the bigger one, was on me in a second. At least it was a fair fight. We were the same size and both had knives. He cut me a few times on the arm, and I cut him back. He gave me a pretty good jab here." He pointed to his left arm slightly above the elbow, where his doublet was soaked with blood. "He might have finished me off, but he slipped on an onion and went down. I stepped on his hand when he went after his knife and grabbed it. So, I had two knives, but had to move my foot to turn around. When his hand was free, he rolled away. I tried to kick him but mostly missed. He came up with a stick and thwacked me on the head. I lunged and stuck him good in the belly. He screamed and ran. I felt weak of a sudden and sat down. Must have swooned then."

Giulio arrived as Christopher finished his narrative and handed Gironi a well-worn linen shirt. He began to tear it into strips.

"What did the men look like?" Hunter asked.

"Didn't get a good look at the first one, except he had few teeth and rotten breath. The big strong one, he was bald. His head came straight out of his shoulders."

Hunter exchanged glances with Gironi. Christopher had described men they had encountered at the Ram's Head. Gironi shifted closer. "I will bind your arm to stop the bleeding, but we must get you home to remove your garments, wash your wounds, and bind them again."

As Gironi wound the bandage, Christopher winced. "I warrant Goodwife Beatrice will know some mending herbs." He bit his lips. "She won't be happy we lost her provisions."

Gironi turned to Giulio and gestured to the baskets lying in the alley. The boy sprang to them and began gathering the vegetables. He held up an unbroken egg with a cry of joy.

"Can you stand and walk?" Hunter asked.

"I think so." Christopher glanced about him with a worried look. "The knives are around here somewhere."

"I shall look for them and any provisions that may have fallen this way." Gironi wandered toward the market, scanning as he went, and returned with one knife, a portion of meat wrapped in cloth and two eggs that had landed in straw. He added his finds to Giulio's baskets. "That is as good as I can manage. Let us stand you up."

Together, they helped Christopher to his feet. A glint of steel caught Hunter's eye, and he laughed. "You were sitting on the second knife."

Walking back to Pozzo della Vacca, Hunter warned, "This attack was no theft attempt. You and Francis saw the killers in Venice and could bear witness to their crime, at least to their burglary. You two must stay in, I fear, or only venture out with Sidney's companions, who bear arms."

Saturday, 26 June 1574, Venice

Thank goodness Fisher and White had returned to Padua. Leaving two men who had a license to bear arms with Christopher and Francis eased Hunter's mind. The wounds in Christopher's left arm were mending, and they had not brought on a recurrence of the fever. Perchance that was owing to Beatrice's poultices. At any rate, Hunter need not worry about matters in Padua, though he was uneasy about the way John Fisher looked at Caterina. As he stepped onto the embankment before the *Palazzo Michiel*, his attitude changed. Before him, Griffin Madox and a servant of the French Embassy hauled a small chest through the door. Was Sidney leaving just as he was arriving to show him the deciphered letter?

"Heigh ho, Griffin," Hunter sang out. "Is Master Sidney returning to Padua?"

"Master Hunter, greetings to you. Sidney is not returning, but I am. He and Lodowick are going to Lord Windsor's soon."

At that moment, Sidney came through the door. "Edward! I am glad to see you back in Venice."

"And I am glad to see you. But why are you quitting the *Palazzo Michiel*?"

"I see you have not heard. The news came here first. King Henry is coming to Venice. The ambassador will need all the rooms here and more."

So Baron Windsor's prediction would come true. "When will he arrive?"

"No one knows for sure. He is in Vienna now and wishes to visit Venice and see its wonders."

"So, you are moving to Lord Windsor's?"

"We may tarry here for one or two nights. The baroness was kind enough to offer me a chamber where we might stay if His Majesty comes. I am heading there now to see if I may impose on their kindness."

"Good fortune for you," Hunter said. But, if accommodation at the French Embassy would cease in a few days, where was he to lodge?

As if reading his thoughts, Sidney said, "Come with me. I shall ask if you might share my chamber, at least for a while."

Hunter cut his eyes toward Gironi. "That might become quite crowded."

Sidney bit his lip. "Luca has a cousin in town, does he not?"

"I do indeed," Gironi said. He raised a hand for the gondolier to be patient. "I daresay he will have a bed for me. Might I offer a suggestion?"

"Pray do," Hunter said.

"If it is not now too late, I suggest we make haste to engage a house for the month of July. When word gets out that the king is coming, rents will fly high into the air."

"You are right, Luca," Sidney said, "and the news is fresh. The ambassador received it only this morning." He turned to Madox. "I imagine you, White, and Fisher might wish to catch a glimpse of the French King and the pageantry Venice will provide for him."

Madox smiled. "I daresay we would."

Gironi cleared his throat. "If I might speak for others, Beatrice, Giulio, Caterina, Christopher, and Francis will also wish to witness the festivities."

"They might," Hunter said," but where could everyone be housed?"

"If I might make a suggestion…" Gironi began.

"I am sure you shall," Hunter said.

"My cousin Stefano has connections through his scuola. I believe he might find lodgings for all July, assuming that is when King Henry will arrive."

"Well, if we must proceed quickly," Hunter said, "pray take the gondola to your cousin's home and marshal affairs so that all may enjoy the king's visit."

"Luca, if we need not rent a house for the entire month, but only the period of the king's stay, please do so," Sidney said.

"I shall do what I can." Gironi addressed Hunter. "Shall I keep our bags with me until you speak with the baron?"

"Pray do. And ask your gondolier to call some of his brothers, one to take Madox to the Brenta and another to row Sidney and me to *Campo San Polo*."

The gondolier put fingers to his mouth and produced a piercing whistle. Soon, two gondolas appeared from opposite ends of the canal. The men boarded their respective boats and set off. They had scarce pushed away when Hunter spoke. "Have you recovered completely from your fever."

"I have," Sidney said. "I planned to return to Padua in a day or two, but now I am unsure. Is Caterina settled in?"

Hunter related her arrival and how she won Beatrice over by her singing. He described the attack on Christopher.

"We must be vigilant," Sidney said. "Biradi seems intent on doing away with anyone who might bear witness to Barnes's murder. Did you report the attack to Captain Scarpa?"

"We did." Hunter sighed. "Alas, whenever Scarpa's men appear at the Ram's Head, the person they are looking for is nowhere to be found."

"At least Scarpa knows what mischief Biradi is up to."

"I have held my most important news until last." Hunter drew the enciphered letter, its Latin solution, and the English translation from his doublet. "I discovered the key to the message. Here is solid evidence that Ambrose Barnes arranged your capture and transport."

Sidney read the papers with knitted brows, then exhaled. "It seems your theories about Barnes were correct, yet I know not why he bore me enmity."

"You were a heretic in his eyes. It seems he hoped the Inquisition would seize and try you."

"Assuming this letter was addressed to him, we have solved one mystery. Another remains. Who sent the letter?"

"Some cleric who knows the workings of the Inquisition is my guess. I have no basis, but I suspect the vice inquisitor who questioned you. You said he seemed little inclined to discover who killed those who captured you."

"That's true."

"If he had ordered the killings, no investigation would be desired."

"At least I need no longer fear danger," Sidney said.

"Not from Barnes," Hunter agreed, "yet I believe danger remains."

"From whom?"

"When I spoke to the English Catholics in Padua, it was clear they were concealing information about Barnes."

"So you still do not trust them?"

Hunter posed a question. "Did you trust Barnes?"

"So far as I knew him, yes."

"As your other friends all left England for Italy, are any of them less sincere, ardent Catholics than Barnes?"

Sidney' brows furrowed again. "No."

"They all denied any knowledge of the Dominicans who appeared in Padua before we returned from the Romagna. According to Christopher and Francis, the friars warned Barnes of Biradi's anger. According to the whores, they warned Carollo and carried Lucetta off to Venice. Might they have warned others?"

"Perhaps my friends have no knowledge."

"And perhaps they were told to deny knowledge and find a way to use you to drive a wedge between England and Venice, though I doubt any will approach Biradi to do so."

"Are all equally suspect?"

"I am certain Carr and Simmons were lying. I'm unsure about the rest."

Sidney hummed thoughtfully. "Should I suspect Baron Windsor as well?"

"I have no reason to suspect him or his wife."

The gondola bumped against the quay on the east side of *Campo San Polo*.

When Sidney broke the news of King Henry's visit to Lady Windsor, she leapt to her feet in glee. She urged him, Hunter, and one servant each to move in immediately and stay throughout the king's visit. They thanked her liberally. Sidney whispered that such an invitation would relieve the pinch he felt on his purse.

When he returned at midday, Baron Windsor not only agreed, he ordered his servants to clear two rooms, and insisted they stay to dine. Hunter thought he saw relief on the baron's face. Having two young men at hand to entertain his wife might allow him more freedom to pursue his "business."

Wednesday, 30 June 1574, Venice

A few days passed without care for Hunter and Sidney. They partook of good food and fine wine. Baroness Windsor delighted in playing their guide. They accompanied her to the *Scuola di San Rocco* to see Tintoretto's works, to the *Scuola de Carita* to examine Titian's paintings, and to the *Scuola San Zuan Evangelista* to see the reliquary holding the miraculous piece of the True Cross. Hunter arranged a visit to Tintoretto's studio, during which the baroness was a fountain of praise and gratitude. She commissioned a small painting of her namesake, Saint Catherine. Whenever thoughts of Biradi, Caterina, Christopher and Francis crossed Hunter's mind, he quickly pushed them to one side, declaring to himself that he was on holiday. Gironi brought news his cousin had obtained lodgings for July from a landlord who had several houses available.

News that the Senate had voted a small fortune toward a reception for King Henry, due to arrive in a few weeks, swept the city. Baron Windsor reported that nobles scrambled to outbid one another to host His Majesty, or to provide him with a meal or an evening's entertainment.

It was evening, and Gironi should have returned from Stefano with details as to the location and terms of the house they might rent to accommodate all of Sidney's party during the royal visit. Worried, Hunter excused himself and set off for Stefano's shop to search for him. When he turned a corner into a narrow alleyway, his way was blocked by two men. He heard rustling behind him and started to turn. His arms were caught in an iron grip. As he prepared to shout, someone jerked his head back and forced a gag into his mouth. A hood descended over his head. A bolt of terror coursed through him. Biradi's men had followed him to Venice. He would suffer the same fate as Barnes!

Hunter struggled, kicking out and twisting from side to side, but he was lifted from the ground and held tightly by strong arms and hands as his assailants bound his hands and legs.

One man said, *"Tranquillo, tranquillo."* In a heavy Italian accent, another said, "Hunter. No fight, no hurt."

Despite the whispered promise, Hunter knew they would carry him to a dark alley and kill him. He kicked out with both feet, eliciting a cry of pain and curses from one captor. A club struck the side of his head and he went limp.

CHAPTER 20

Upstream

HUNTER FOUND HIMSELF SEATED IN A CHAIR. THE HOOD WAS OFF. BEFORE him sat a large man in a gold-braid-trimmed black doublet with graying hair, a closely trimmed beard, and steely eyes, who turned and spoke to a man on his left. Hunter followed his gaze and was surprised to see Gironi, his trembling hand clutching the bottom of his doublet. He tried to say, "Luca," but the gag was still in his mouth.

"Pray pardon me, master, for your injury," Gironi said. There was no irony in the term this time. "I said you would not come peacefully and begged to send a note, but they did not trust what I might write in English."

Hunter struggled to speak again. His eyes asked Gironi to explain.

"This is Signor Girolamo Rossi." Gironi gestured to the man in the chair, who nodded to Hunter.

Hunter's heart raced. He and Gironi were helpless before one of the most feared men in Venice.

Reading Hunter's eyes, Gironi said, "We have nothing to fear. We are his guests. He has a bargain to offer us." A quaver in his voice belied his words.

Hunter grunted. After a nod from Rossi, a tall man untied his gag and bonds. "Water," Hunter gasped.

"*Acqua, per favore,*" Gironi translated, then addressed Hunter. "Let me explain how you come to be here. *Padrone* Rossi is the man Stefano approached, through the officers of his scuola, about renting a house. When he heard an Englishman wanted the house, he asked for further details, and Stefano called me. *Il padrone* recognized your name. It seems you have done him a service by presenting a list of the articles stolen from Barnes, so he is well-disposed to hire out lodgings to us, at a cheap rate, in return for— further services."

Hunter swallowed and handed the cup back to the lackey who had served him. His fear subsided, but he said with a frown, "If you had come to explain this, there would have been no need for an assault."

"Master Rossi required I stay here. He likes to look a man in the eye when he makes a bargain with him." At a question from Rossi, Gironi explained in Venetian what he had just said.

"What further services does he want?" Hunter asked.

Gironi looked down, gathering strength to speak. "He wants us to present demands to Biradi."

Hunter's heart sped up again. "Demands?"

"He wants Biradi to pay him one hundred and twelve ducats, the value of the goods taken from Barnes's house in Venice, plus fifty ducats penalty for daring to operate in his territory."

As Hunter scrambled for a way out, his tone became bolder. "Why are *we* to present demands? Surely his men can carry a message. I do not even speak the language."

Rossi frowned at Hunter's tone and cast a stern glace at Gironi.

Gironi said something apologetic in Venetian, then lowered his head and dragged one foot in front of the other. "There is more to it. I told you that I left Venice of a sudden many years ago, after a youthful indiscretion with my master's daughter."

"Yes."

"Well, Venetian families have long memories. The Tartara, the family I was apprenticed to, heard I had returned. They approached Master Rossi and asked that he exact a price for dishonoring their name."

Hunter frowned. "So, I am caught up in your penance."

"You might look at it that way," Gironi said. "*Il padrone* will take care of my problem and let us have the house for this service."

"If we survive the service."

"I regret that my actions have put us in this situation, but you were the one who insisted we confront Biradi in the first place."

"What if we refuse?"

"We will have no house to rent in any part of Venice that owes allegiance to Sior Rossi, and you may have to explain to Lord Leicester why I was killed in Italy."

"Could you report the Tartara's threat to the Venetian authorities?"

"They would side with the Tartara. I might be fined, or locked in prison, or they might merely turn me over to the Tartara to do with as they will."

"In other words, we have little choice."

"Correct."

Again, a grunt from Rossi caused Gironi to stop and explain their English conversation.

"Are we to go to Biradi alone?"

"I did argue that we might not be able to speak a message to Biradi if his men kill us on the spot, so Sior Rossi has agreed to send along four of his followers. They might intervene if we are attacked."

"They *might*?"

"I fear I was playing a weak hand."

"When are we to approach Biradi?"

"He hopes we will return to Padua within the week."

Hunter sighed. "Tell him we agree."

Rossi broke into a broad grin when Gironi told him. He called a short, older man to him.

"His secretary will write out the contract," Gironi said.

"He writes out contracts? I am amazed if he turns to the law to enforce them."

"I suspect he has his own methods of enforcement, and it will include the terms of house rental."

Rossi spoke an order and a thin man left.

"What...?" Hunter began.

Gironi shook his head.

Soon the scribe showed Rossi the contract. He signed it and mimed that Hunter and Gironi were to do the same. Having no choice, they did so and received a copy. The thin man returned with cups of wine and Rossi indicated the signatories must drink to their bargain. With resignation, they did.

Friday, 2 July 1574, Padua

For two days, he and Sidney had discussed their situation again and again. Sidney was unhappy that they were now indebted to one of the chief criminals of Venice, but he recognized that Gironi's past sins compelled them. He insisted on accompanying Hunter and Gironi to the meeting with Biradi, but both, along with Bryskett, argued that the danger was too great. "This is *our* contract to fulfill," Hunter stated so often he lost count.

Money was another concern, though Sidney was able to visit the Strozzi bank on the first of July and withdraw more funds. Gironi had combined flattery and pleading with Rossi, who agreed to accept only half of the rent in advance, for the promise of the other half plus ten percent at the end of the month. Beatrice was down to her last lire, though her complaints to Sidney were mild compared with the comments directed at those who lodged in Pozzo della Vacca about the quantity of food and drink they consumed.

"We didn't understand her words," White reported, "but her hands and face spoke clearly. We have been on half-allowance since you left, save for Christopher."

Hunter regretted the abundance he had enjoyed at Baron Windsor's table, and vowed to be sure the servants received full measure while he and Sidney were in Padua. Word of Venetian accommodations that would allow all to witness the festivities of King Henry's visit cheered them.

Beatrice accosted Gironi with questions concerning the kitchen at the rented house. He confessed he had not enquired. She huffed and set about determining the minimum number of pots she would need. "Prepare yourselves for boiled eels on trenchers," Gironi warned.

Caterina had kept in Beatrice's favor by helping with meal preparation and backing the housekeeper's demands for tidiness, using English whenever Christopher and Francis feigned incomprehension. To them, she remained a mysterious Venetian lady. They couldn't understand why she exchanged her fine gowns and stooped to manual drudgery. She affected not to understand their tentative questions. She and Beatrice set aside an hour in the late morning for song. In the last few days, Francis had become bold enough to sing with them. Because they laughed at his attempts at Italian, he confined himself to joining in choruses of fa-la-la. They commended his tenor voice.

Christopher's and Giulio's wounds had healed during the time Hunter had been in Venice. Since the attack, Fisher and White always accompanied the boy to the market, both armed. As Christopher and Francis chafed at being housebound, they joined to make the party more formidable.

Sunday, 4 July 1574, Padua

The sun had not risen yet. Rain droned on the roof. Hunter tossed in his bed. This was the morning Rossi had promised his men would meet them near the Ram's Head. As Hunter had reasoned before, Rossi recommended a Sunday morning as an auspicious time. Biradi's men might be ale-washed or, if sober, attending Mass. As Hunter had done all night, he imagined possible outcomes for his meeting with Biradi.

He and Gironi might be attacked as they approached the tavern. Would Rossi's men be there to come to their aid? Hunter reviewed their faces in his mind: sloping forehead, rabbit teeth, bat ears, razor nose. What would he do if they were not at the crossroads near the Ram's Head? Well, then Rossi would not have fulfilled his part of the bargain, and he and Gironi could go back home without fulfilling theirs. Or perhaps he would go to the nearest church and give thanks. Bryskett, White, and Fisher were to accompany them to make sure Rossi's men were on hand, but could they repel an attack from Biradi? Would they be blocked from entering? Surrounded once they entered? Biradi had told them never to return. Did all his men know of that prohibition? At least he and Gironi would go armed. The possibility of being charged with carrying illegal weapons was minor compared with the prospect of lying dead outside the Ram's Head. How many minions could they kill or injure before being overpowered? Would it matter?

Hunter rolled over again and threw off the sheet.

If only Rossi had given them a note to hand to one of Biradi's men. Then, if he were not at the tavern, they could hand it over and retreat. How odd that he had written a contract for them to sign yet had not committed his demands to paper. Of course, the contract had been vaguely worded.

He felt momentary anger toward Gironi. If Rossi had not used the threat from the Tartara as a lever, would they be undertaking this errand? Gironi surmised that Rossi preferred to hazard the lives of an Englishman he did not know and an expatriate Venetian who faced revenge, rather than putting his own men in danger. That was not a comforting thought. Perhaps Rossi was testing their courage, Bryskett suggested. But to what end? Hunter could think of none.

There was no use trying for sleep any more. He would rise.

Hunter and his party tried to avoid the puddles as they approached the Ram's Head. Despite warm weather, all wore cloaks to keep their powder dry. Would the rain keep Biradi's men indoors? Would it keep Rossi's men from the rendezvous? Church bells rang nine. He turned and flashed a nervous smile at Bryskett, White, and Fisher. When he turned back, four men had stepped from the shelter of a doorway. Gironi let out a sigh, whether of disappointment that he and Hunter would have to brave it out or relief that Rossi's men showed pistols under their cloaks, Hunter could not be certain. The man he had dubbed Razor Nose signaled that the Englishmen other than Hunter and Gironi were to stay back, while he and his companions fell in behind them.

Two of Biradi's men slouching by the doorway pulled themselves to attention. The taller guard called to the approaching party, asking their business. Gironi requested an audience with Biradi. The shorter guard opened the door and shouted inside. He and his companion eyed Rossi's men priming their pistols. After a few tense minutes, a red-haired man came out, whispered to the guards, and spoke to Hunter and his companions.

"He asks for our weapons," Gironi said.

"Does he think we are fools?" Hunter asked.

Before Gironi could respond, a bass voice sounded behind them. Hunter made out "No" and Rossi's name. The redhead blanched and darted back inside. More moments passed. Six of Biradi's men filed out of the tavern, four of them bearing pistols in hand, the other two holding swords. Hunter recognized the man with a crooked nose and scar as one of his attackers, and guessed the redhead was another. If either side began shooting, Hunter feared a ball might enter him or Gironi. Crooked nose summoned them into the tavern. To do so, he and Gironi would have to pass between lines of Biradi's men. Hunter heard the crunch and splash of steps behind him, and more deep tones from Sloping Forehead

"Rossi's men insist on accompanying us inside," Gironi said.

"Thank God," Hunter whispered. "Will they allow it?"

"Rossi's man said only cowards demand they face defenseless men."

Redhead ducked inside again while the men on both sides stared at one another. He emerged in a moment and spoke over Hunter and Gironi.

"He says they are not cowards. We may enter if all cover their flash pans, adjust the dogs to a safe position, and lower their pistols," Gironi translated. "Biradi's men will sheathe their swords."

"Good for us. We never had a chance to draw out our pistols anyway," Hunter said.

The men neutralized their weapons on both sides, keeping wary eyes on those opposite. When all had finished, Redhead signaled Hunter's party might enter.

The tavern had fewer men inside than the last time Hunter and Gironi had been there. No one played cards, though two slept, heads on a table. Hunter counted six men in addition to those who had confronted them outside, but these had no weapons besides bread knives. Rossi's escorts and Biradi's men filed through the tavern door behind them.

"We are already surrounded," Hunter whispered.

"But not alone, thank God." Gironi nodded toward Rossi's men. "Just outnumbered."

Redhead motioned them toward the inner room where they had last spoken to Biradi. Hunter, Gironi, and their escorts approached the open door. Rossi's men peered in and told Gironi they would wait in the tavern's main room.

"A good plan to prevent an ambush," Hunter said. They stepped into Biradi's office. Bodyguards on either side of the door closed it behind them.

Biradi's lips curled in a silent snarl. He threw sharp, clipped syllables at Gironi, who swallowed before answering.

Hunter recognized the repetition of *"Padrone Rossi"* and the amounts of ducats demanded.

Biradi's jaw muscle clenched and unclenched as he listened, struggling to control himself. When he spoke in a calm, reasonable tone, Hunter understood his request that they return in a few days for their answer. They had foreseen Biradi might ask for a delay in order to arrange an ambush. Gironi recited the answer they had prepared, that Rossi required they make only one visit and return with his response.

Biradi's face grew red and his nostrils flared. Out of the corner of his eye, Hunter could see the bodyguards stiffen. He calculated how quickly he could draw his sword or pull a pistol. When Gironi finished, Biradi slammed his fist on his desk and unleashed a torrent of vituperation. Gironi blinked like a man struggling against a strong headwind and mumbled something in an apologetic tone. He turned to Hunter. "We should leave now."

Hunter needed no encouragement. He pivoted to face the door but caught his breath when the two bodyguards stepped in front of it. His hand edged toward his sword. The men's eyes followed the movement and their faces grew hard. Hunter let his arm fall to his side. Behind him,

Biradi continued railing. Gironi nodded, repeating, "*Si, si.*" Finally, Biradi paused and issued a one-word command. The bodyguards stepped aside and one opened the door.

Hunter breathed deeply and forced himself to walk slowly, rather than run, into the outer tavern. Rossi's men, flanking the doorway with their backs to it, turned their heads to watch Hunter and Gironi exit. The group began a slow march through Biradi's smirking minions.

Outside, Hunter's legs stopped trembling and he became aware of the rain trickling down his face. "You need not translate that Biradi refused Rossi's request."

"In very clear terms. He also said we were never to return, on our own or as messengers, on pain of death. He demanded that Rossi's men leave Padua." Gironi nodded toward a far doorway where Bryskett, White, and Fisher huddled. "Pray reassure our friends we are safe, while I relay to Rossi's men everything Biradi said."

Friday, 9 July 1574, Padua

The week had started with two letters from Hunter's Uncle Babcock, dated the third and tenth of June. He was delighted with the bargain struck for Signor Zordan's silk thread. He was also satisfied with the agreement for silk cloths in Venice, but disappointed that it seemed impossible to transport silk flies and their worms. He hoped to hear news of mulberry trees and a Venetian weaver. Uncle Babcock's wish for a weaver pricked Hunter's conscience. He had become absorbed in the machinations of Padua and Venice and neglected part of his mission. Hunter had written him of Gironi's success with the trees, but he would just now receive that letter, if the Channel cooperated. Gironi had mounted to bear a message to Zordan, stopping at villages near Vicenza to converse with tavern-goers about weavers.

A note arrived from Rossi, stating that Hunter, Sidney, or anyone they chose might move into the house in Dorsoduro as soon as they wished, but they must vacate within three days of King Henry's departure. Half the rent must be delivered to the *Mezza Luna* as soon as anyone began residence. So, Hunter concluded, criminals could be trusted to keep their word. As no news of the king's arrival in Venetian territory had come, Sidney preferred to stay in Padua. Provisions were cheaper there, and he still suffered from severe headaches every third day.

This Friday evening, headache abated, Sidney agreed to dine with the English expatriates at the Owl. Though Sidney urged Hunter to join him and Bryskett, it was clear he was not invited. With Gironi gone, Hunter found himself alone, ordering the mass of papers on his desk. He stacked his failed attempts at deciphering in a pile to be used as fire starters and secured the original letter in a chest. He responded to a knock on the door with, "Come in," and turned on his stool.

Caterina stood before him, smiling. "I hope I do not disturb. Chores are done. I think I need to practice English if I go to England."

Glad for her companionship, Hunter rose and pulled another stool opposite him. "I would be glad to speak English with you. Pray sit. It has been some time since we have spoken, but I can tell your English is improved." She wrinkled her forehead. "It is better," he explained.

"Thank you."

"I thought Francis and Christopher spoke to you in English."

"They do." Her eyes sparkled. "And Francis teach me—teaches me English songs."

"Oh." Hunter recalled Francis said many of his songs were unsuitable for a lady.

"Yes. He teach me 'Fairies' Dance' and 'Of All the Birds That Ever I See.'"

Hunter laughed. "I know that one." He broke into song, and Caterina joined him. When they finished, both laughed.

"You can sing with me and Francis," she said. "And he teach—he taught me a courting song I like."

Hunter felt his stomach tighten. Was Francis courting her? "How does it go?"

"The man sings, 'Will you love me, lady sweet,' and then woman sings, 'Fie away, fie away, fie, fie, fie.' It means go away. I like to sing that. I could not say such things at Signora Filippa's."

"It is a good phrase for a woman to know."

"Yes. I said it to John Fisher yesterday when he stand too close."

"Did he make advances to you? Do you want me to speak with him?"

"He say he want to hold me, but I say, 'Fie away, fie away, fie, fie, fie.' You need not speak. I can speak for myself."

Hunter smiled. Caterina was even more beautiful as a confident woman. "Tell me if he asks again."

"I think he will not. He left me." She shifted to one side on her stool. "Beatrice said we go to Venice soon. I hope I can sit for Tintoretto again."

"I am glad to see you so bold."

Caterina beamed. "I owe it to you and Master Sidney. You buy me from Signora Filippa."

Hunter felt queasy. Did she feel she was his property? "We did not buy you; we paid your debts." He heard horses whinnying in the stable and hoped Giulio would see to them.

She leaned forward and gazed into his eyes. "I do owe you much."

Hunter felt himself stir. It seemed that Caterina was not only confident enough to refuse advances, but to make them. Emotions swirled in him. He must not allow himself to succumb to her charms again. He had endured guilt for giving way to lust. He had sworn an oath to himself to help her to a better life. "You owe more to your sweetness, your beauty, and your voice."

"You are sweet, too," she said, her eyes still inviting.

Both straightened at the sound of shouting below.

"*Fogo! Fuoco! Incendio!*" Giulio cried.

"Fire!" Caterina said.

The horses screamed.

CHAPTER 21

Drenching

Hunter sprang to the door. "Fire!" he bellowed, bounding down the stairs. Madox and White clattered behind him. The screaming of the horses grew louder.

Beatrice ordered Francis and Christopher to the courtyard with large pots.

Hunter dashed after them. Smoke stung his nostrils. Flames billowed from the corner stall next to Dancer. He ran to his horse, grabbed his halter, and turned his head away from the flames. He stared into the horse's terrified eyes and cooed Dancer's name. He forced himself to open the stall gate calmly, though the heat threatened to singe his right side. Dancer bolted and ran to far corner of the courtyard.

Madox and White, farther from the conflagration, led their mounts out of their stalls. Madox held the halters of all three horses as White bolted back to plunge a bucket into the rain barrel. As Christopher staggered toward the fire with a kettle full of water, Hunter rammed a cookpot beneath the pump. Giulio worked its handle feverishly to fill the vessel. Francis seized a rake, yelled a warning, and pulled burning hay into the courtyard. Everyone jumped back amid sparks and flying stalks, then rushed toward the flaming pile. The men emptied pails and pots of water while Beatrice and Caterina flailed at the hay with wet blankets. Francis pulled another blazing load into the courtyard and all closed in to quench the flames. As the water doused this pile, a blackened stick with tightly wrapped cloth appeared. "A torch," Hunter cried, kicking it to one side. Several repetitions of raking hay and stifling each heap succeeded in extinguishing the fire. White threw a bucketful of water on a smoldering beam above the stall. Everyone stood panting in the dark, mud covering their shoes, clothing soaked, the smell of wet ashes rising around them.

"Thank God four horses were away," Hunter said, striding to where Madox hummed to the twitching horses. "I must stay a while with Dancer to calm him, and house him in Brownie's stall tonight."

"Lucky those days of rain filled our barrels," Christopher said.

"I will fetch Sidney and Bryskett from the Owl," White said. "A ride there may calm Billy."

Caterina walked to Hunter and the horses and began a soft Italian song. Beatrice joined her, while Hunter and Madox stroked the animals. White returned to a calmed Billy and placed a bridle on his head. Hunter thanked Caterina and led Dancer to the stall Gironi's mount had used. The horse shivered in disapproval of his new surroundings, but when Hunter tried to lead him to his former stall, he balked. "Well, old boy, you must choose one or the other," Hunter said. Reluctantly, Dancer allowed himself to be housed in Brownie's stall.

Leaving Giulio to watch that the smoldering hay did not reignite, the others returned through the kitchen to the central room of the house.

Hunter had almost passed the kitchen fireplace when he noticed a stack of burning papers fluttering. Drawing closer, he could see they were the deciphering notes he had left on his desk when Giulio raised the alarm. Disregarding his muddy shoes, he dashed up the stairs two at a time. His desk was clear. Not only the stack of notes, but his translations of the enciphered letter were gone. He glanced around his chamber, looking for anything else out of place. The peg on the wall where he had placed his holstered pistols to dry after the Sunday meeting with Biradi was empty. He had told himself several times he should put them away. Biradi had tried to disarm him and Gironi at the Ram's Head. Now, he was sure, he had sent one of his ruffians to throw a torch over the wall and set a fire in the stable so that Pozzo della Vacca would lie open to burglary. He strode to the chest where his purse and clothing were secured. The lock was not broken. He saw nothing else out of place other than his pistols and the papers missing from his desk. Cursing himself, he marched to the door and spoke to Madox, climbing the stairs. "We have been robbed."

"What?" Madox stood open-mouthed before him. "What is missing?"

"My pistols are gone and my papers are turning to ashes in the kitchen. I know not what else is missing. I pray you, look about your chamber and Philip's to see what may be amiss."

Hunter fetched a candle from his chamber and walked with Madox to the room he shared with White and Fisher. Madox paced about, opening locked chests, and lifting the lid of his writing desk. "Nothing missing that I can detect," the secretary said. "Our pistols were locked within our chests."

"Let us hope we find the same in Sidney's chamber," Hunter said.

A different scene presented itself when they opened the door. Mangled locks hung from three open chests. Clothing lay strewn about the floor. Madox uttered what Hunter assumed was a Welsh curse. "What was in the chests?" he asked.

"Clothing certainly," Madox said. He stepped over a doublet to peer into a chest. "I know he kept money locked in a small casket in one of these."

"He just collected funds from his bankers," Hunter said. "Let us hope he hasn't lost all of his month's allowance."

"I know not, and I hesitate to rummage through his possessions."

"Do you know where he kept his pistols?"

"There, I believe." Madox pointed toward saddlebags near the bed.

"Then they are missing, too."

"Perhaps he took them with him."

"I am certain he did not, for we had a difference of opinion about venturing out unarmed."

"His sword and Bryskett's hang on that wall." Madox nodded toward them.

"What about Bryskett's pistols? I do not know if he took them."

"Neither do I."

Voices below told them that Sidney and Bryskett had returned. Their dinner companions, drawn by news of the fire, accompanied them. Hunter had only an instant to decide whether to reveal the robbery or not. Sidney might prefer assessing his losses before the news became public, but speaking now would give him a chance to observe the reaction of the expatriates. "I shall tell all we have been robbed. Pray watch Beatrice and Giulio, Christopher and Francis. Look for signs they knew of this."

Madox nodded in agreement, and they headed downstairs. In the central room, the expatriates were already babbling questions, asking household members for assurances of their safety.

Hunter raised his voice over the hubbub. "Pray silence, gentlemen. I am sure Harry has already told you of our misfortune, but there is more. We have been robbed." He scanned the expatriates and saw only expressions of astonishment. Barnes's servants glanced toward the bags that held their few possessions.

"Let it not be so," Sidney said. "What is missing?"

"So far as Griffin and I could tell, several pistols. Pray go up and scan your chamber."

Sidney and Bryskett hurried upstairs. Madox followed, leading White to their chamber, assuring him they had not been robbed. Caterina and Beatrice ducked to their rooms to see if anything was missing. Christopher and Francis searched their bags.

"How could this happen?" Randolph asked.

"We were all quenching the fire," Hunter replied.

"Was the door not locked?" Le Rous asked.

"As we were all here till the moment Giulio raised the alarm, there seemed no need."

"Our bits are all here," Francis reported.

Caterina popped out of her storehouse room. "Nothing gone."

"It appears you and Sidney were the targets," Fitzwilliams said. "And the fire was used to draw everyone from the house."

"I agree," Hunter said.

"How long were you all in the courtyard?" Hart asked.

"Perhaps twenty minutes," Hunter said.

"Little time for a thorough search of the house," Le Rous said. "Was any money stolen?"

"Not from my chest," Hunter said. "Nor from Madox. I do not know about Sidney and Bryskett."

At that moment, both trudged down the stairs.

"Pray, what did you find?" Hart asked.

"As Edward said, my pistols are gone," Sidney reported.

"They would not be, had you taken them." Bryskett used an accusatory tone, touching his wheellocks.

"You and Edward were right," Sidney admitted.

"Did they take any money?" Le Rous asked.

"I fear they did. Near twenty ducats worth of Venetian coin and some crowns and shillings as well. I have only what is in my purse."

"Though my chest was pried open," Bryskett said, "my money remained safely hidden."

"Shall you be able to stay in Venice to see the festivities of the king's visit?" Hart asked, his brows knit.

"I can draw more funds," Sidney said, "but I shall be short ere this month ends." He smiled. "I understand moneylenders are not hard to find in Venice."

"But they will charge you five per cent," Le Rous said.

"Allow me to loan you money at no interest," Hart volunteered.

"I can do so as well," Randolph said. "I will ask no collateral, and you may pay me back in August."

"I, too, can advance you part of what you need," Fitzwilliams said. He turned toward Le Rous.

"And I," Le Rous said reluctantly. "Will you speak to Doctor Simmons and inform him of our friend's need?" he asked Fitzwilliams, who nodded agreement.

"You are all too generous," Sidney said.

"Nonsense," Hart said. "Your loss, divided five ways, is not a great burden for any of us."

Fitzwilliams cleared his throat. "May we view the courtyard?"

"You will spoil your shoes with mud," Hunter cautioned.

The expatriates shrugged off his warning. Christopher and Francis lit lanterns and led the throng into the courtyard. Hunter splashed across to retrieve the burnt-out torch and showed it to the expatriates, who, despite their bravado, stayed huddled at the side, out of the courtyard's puddles.

"Should you need somewhere to shelter your horses," Hart said, "we can keep them with ours for a few days."

"My Dancer seems settled now," Hunter said. "Moving him to new surroundings might cause more distress."

White and Madox also refused the offer.

"I shall see how Ned behaves when I lead him in," Sidney said.

"And I," Bryskett agreed.

The expatriates filed back in, offering comforting words in English and Italian to the residents of Pozzo della Vacca. Sidney and Bryskett led their horses around to the courtyard gate and returned to report that their mounts, calmed by Fisher, had entered their stalls after some hesitation.

"Gentlemen, I ask you to forgive our poor hospitality, but—" Hunter gestured to his clothes—"we need to see to our apparel and mop our floor."

The expatriates shuffled to the door with words of sympathy and encouragement. Leaving, Hart said, "Soon I hope to bring you funds to make good your losses."

As he removed his soiled shoes, Hunter drew Madox aside. "Did you see any hint that someone in the household expected fire and theft?"

"No. All seemed shocked and dismayed. They rushed to check their own possessions as soon as they recovered their wits."

Either all were better actors than he had observed, or they had no part in the burglary, Hunter decided.

"Here is John, fresh from the horses. Pardon me, but I am sure he will want to mount to our chamber to look over his things." Madox moved to join Fisher.

Hunter walked to where Sidney and Bryskett stood with heads together. "I suggest we draw cups of wine and repair to my chamber to discuss these events privily."

"If we hold our colloquy in my chamber," Sidney said, "Lodowick and I may retrieve our clothes from the floor and replace them in the chests."

As they cleared the apparel and folded it, Hunter said, "The aim of the theft appears to be to disarm us. Our pistols, shot, and powder are all gone."

"Why not swords as well?" Bryskett said, folding a doublet on the bed.

As usual, his theory did not account for all the facts, Hunter realized. "Perhaps a single thief, little time."

Bryskett grunted a neutral response.

Sidney held up the two halves of a small ivory case that had been broken open. "I regret the destruction of the casket almost as much as the theft of the money. Thank God I left funds in reserve at the bank."

"If the goal was to disarm us, they failed. Four of us still have our pistols. And why take Sidney's money?" Bryskett asked.

"Opportunity, I imagine." Hunter shook the dust from a pair of stockings. "If the thief was one of Biradi's men, he might have helped himself to what appeared valuable."

"I can only conclude that Biradi sent a poor burglar," Bryskett observed. "Why did he not take the casket, without prying the lock? It would fetch a good price. And why leave fine clothing?" He lifted a doublet from the floor and brushed it off.

"As for the clothes," Hunter said, "one man can only carry so much."

Sidney looked up from smoothing folded breeches in his chest. "Was anything missing from your chamber besides your pistols?"

"My papers," Hunter said. "They were thrown into the kitchen hearth."

"What papers, pray?" Sidney asked.

"My deciphers and some scrap. But I have the original locked in my chest and can solve it again."

"Our loss could have been worse," Bryskett said. "But this business of your papers seems odd. I can understand why Biradi might send a thief for money; that is his trade. And the pistols can be turned to cash. But so could swords. And why bother with your papers?"

"I have no idea," Hunter admitted.

Sidney pursued a separate train of thought. "Since the attempt on Christopher, one of us who has permission to bear arms has accompanied Christopher and Francis on their outgoings. Taking pistols makes no sense. Our swords would prove a handier defense."

"I must agree that this theft is difficult to fathom," Hunter said.

Saturday, 10 July 1574, Padua

Bryskett went to report the fire and theft and returned with Captain Scarpa and one of his men.

Scarpa greeted them with one of the few English words he had learned in their company. "Again."

Sidney chuckled. "I fear so."

Scarpa stepped around puddles in the courtyard to look closely at the scorched stall where the fire had started. He glanced up at the wall behind it and handled the remains of the torch.

Bryskett translated his comments. "An easy act, if one knew where the hay was stored. How many people would know that?"

"Everyone in the household, of course," Sidney replied.

"And all the English expatriates, I assume," Hunter added, "though I have never seen Carr nor Simmons here."

"They have been guests in the past," Bryskett said. He listed the expatriates to the scribe, who stood behind Scarpa, jotting down notes.

Sidney frowned. "Have him note those with us last evening. They could not have set the fire."

"Anyone who knew, including Ambrose Barnes, could have told Biradi the disposition of our lodgings," Hunter said.

Sidney led them upstairs, where Bryskett pointed out the broken locks on the chests and ivory case. He described the missing pistols—easy enough in the case of Sidney, as his initials were inlaid in ivory in the ball butts. Hunter drew a sketch of his, indicating a scorch mark on one wooden stock.

Scarpa interviewed the members of the household with Bryskett's help, and promised to question Biradi, though his manner suggested that nothing would result from it. He said he would leave interrogation of the English expatriates to their fellow countrymen. When Scarpa left, it fell to Bryskett to sooth the injured pride of Beatrice and her son. Sidney dealt with his men and Barnes's servants.

Hunter spoke with Caterina. She was unsettled by her conversation with Scarpa, though it had been the shortest, as she was a stranger to Padua and had spent the least amount of time in Pozzo della Vacca.

"Who is Biradi?" she asked.

Hunter explained who the criminal leader was and why he might want to hurt Christopher and Francis to keep them from identifying his men.

She nodded. Francis had told her of Barnes's murder. "Why did he want to kill Master Barnes?"

Hunter decided not to explain the details of Sidney's capture, merely saying that Barnes had dealt with Biradi and may have owed him money. He asked a question which had festered in his mind since he first met her. "You were afraid Signora Filippa might discard you because one Englishman did not like you. When the men were here last night, was one of them that man?"

"No. The Englishman who said he does not want me is old, with long gray hair."

Simmons, Hunter thought. "Do you know his name?"

"No. He said call him '*Dottore*.'"

"Did he speak Italian?"

"Yes."

He must visit Simmons again. Perhaps he could use this new intelligence to pry information about Barnes and the Dominicans from the tutor.

"You continue to suspect my friends." Sidney sat in Hunter's chamber after supper, sipping wine. "Yet they have offered to make good my loss."

"Well, your uncle directed me to keep close watch on your association with Catholics here, the burglary happened on a night you and Bryskett were lured away to dine with them, and they did not offer to rearm you."

"First, I was not lured away. I chose the day, after refusing previous invitations. Second, my lawyer friend, dining with them provides their alibi."

"Only partly. They may have told others you would be gone."

"Or Biradi's men may have been keeping close watch on our lodgings," Sidney set down his glass. "Should I ask my friends if they hired Biradi to burn the stable and steal my pistols?"

"I admit that is too heavy a cudgel," Hunter said. "But when I spoke to them last, while you lay in Venice, I was convinced they were withholding information."

"About what?"

"They refused to see any link between Barnes and Biradi, nor any connection between Barnes and your capture and transport. We now know Barnes was behind your capture. The enciphered letter proves that."

"But it does not prove any of my friends knew of his plan," Sidney insisted. "You said yourself Barnes could have told Biradi details of our lodgings."

Hunter was unwilling to discard his suspicions. He could mention the expatriates' denial of the visiting friars after Sidney's rescue, but it was difficult to link that to last night's burglary. "Did any of your friends appear nervous as you supped last night?"

"They were not. Until Harry arrived, our conversation was all about King Henry's visit to Venice. They were animated at the prospect of seeing the monarch and the shows Venice will provide him."

"Will they be in Venice?"

"Yes. Doctor Simmons has secured a short lease on the lodgings Barnes used. He and the others will stay there during the king's time in Venice."

Simmons again, Hunter thought. If he could secure the building from the Contarini now, there was a good chance he had done so for Barnes when he moved to Venice. "When will they move there?"

"Sometime next week," Sidney said. "But this discussion of my friends diverted me from my reason for bringing you a cup of wine. We need to discuss expenses that threaten."

Hunter sighed.

Sidney shifted on the bench. "Forgive my asking, but how much money do you have available to pay for this house we have leased and for its provisioning. After last night's loss, despite my friends' offer to make it good, I fear we may be short of funds."

Hunter had done his own calculations. Though he had not been robbed, his contribution to Caterina's debts and the promise to pay Lucia threatened to strain his finances. "I could contribute a few ducats to our lease. Will that be enough?"

Sidney shook his head. "I fear my reckoning was faulty even before last night. Your share, together with the contents of Bryskett's purse, will suffice to pay the lease and transport us to Venice, but I must somehow feed everyone once we are there. It is certain all grocers in Venice will raise their prices, if they have not already done so."

"Unlike you," Hunter said, "I withdrew all I am allowed for July. You said some of your funds remain."

"I can withdraw more when we reach Venice, but I will be short well before the end of this month. There is not time for a letter to reach my father before then."

"Do you have a solution?"

"It hurts my pride, but if we accept the Windsors' hospitality, then I will have four fewer mouths to feed—you, me, Bryskett, and Gironi."

"Who am I to turn down excellent food and pleasant accommodation?" Hunter said.

"I am determined to leave the Veneto in August," Sidney said, "and return to Vienna."

His friend had finally acknowledged he was in danger in Italy. Though inwardly thankful, Hunter decided not to voice this to Sidney. How much effort had it taken him to admit that he may have been wrong? "I am due to leave in August as well, if Captain Connors and the *Adventure* encounter fair seas." A shiver ran through him as he considered the reception he might receive. Would Lord Leicester feel he had done his best to safeguard Philip? Would he succeed in finding a silk weaver who would leave Italy? How would both his patrons react to his return with an ex-prostitute, no matter how well she sang? Sidney was not the only one who could make mistakes.

CHAPTER 22

Regal Waves

Monday, 12 July 1574, Padua

GIRONI BROUGHT GOOD AND BAD NEWS ON HIS RETURN. SIGNOR ZORDAN was pleased Uncle Babcock had approved the bargain with Hunter. He promised the silk could be delivered to Chioggia at a few days' notice. Gironi had found several weavers who chafed at the regulations limiting the cloth they could produce, but none were willing to leave Italy to move to a cold, remote island.

Hunter's buoyant hopes floated to a slimy mud bank. The mission would not be successful until the silk, the mulberry trees, and a weaver were aboard the *Adventure*. Sidney would not be safe so long as he remained in Catholic states. Venice and its dominions were too full of plots he could not fathom: Sidney's captors being slain, a strange robbery, the secrets the expatriates were concealing. At least he knew who had been behind Sidney's capture, if not the reason Barnes wished him ill. Perhaps the other expatriates were furtive because they had been his accomplices.

He hoped to squeeze more information from Dr. Simmons before leaving for Venice. Zorzi answered his knock and communicated through gestures that his master was occupied tutoring a student. He had not sent Gironi to set a time for this visit, thinking it would be better to give Simmons no advance notice. He sat in the antechamber wishing he knew enough Italian to ask Zorzi when Barnes or the Dominicans had paid visits to Simmons.

After ten minutes, the door to Simmons's study opened and Fitzwilliams walked out. His eyebrows shot up. "Master Hunter, what brings you here?"

"I hope to have a conversation with Doctor Simmons, if no other student has an appointment now."

"He does not." Fitzwilliams's face immediately registered regret that he had revealed that Simmons was free.

The tutor appeared behind him. "Ah, Master Hunter, returning like the proverbial bad penny. Farewell, Master Fitzwilliams. I shall see you again next week."

Fitzwilliams took his cue and left.

Simmons turned. "Enter, Master Hunter. I was sorry to hear from Fitzwilliams of Master Sidney's further misfortune. I gave a contribution to help our fellow countryman. *Zòrzi, vino per due.*"

Hunter seated himself in the study. "For Master Sidney and on my own behalf, I thank you for your assistance. Did Master Fitzwilliams voice any guess as to who was behind the fire and theft?"

"There are many burglars in Padua, most with a connection to Tommaso Biradi. I have not heard of the stratagem of stable fires before. I hope it will not become a *novus modus* of theft, lest the town be burnt to the ground."

"Amen." Hunter waited, unsure how to launch into his questions.

Zòrzi served the wine. After taking a sip, Simmons asked, "How may I serve you today, Master Hunter?"

"I understand you not only are helping Sidney, you have also rented Barnes's Venetian lodgings for you and other English expatriates during the king's visit."

"That is true." Simmons smiled the smile of one who knows more than others. "King Henri entered Venetian *terrafirma* on Saturday and was greeted by the Governor of Friuli."

Hunter refused to be diverted. "Tell me, did you engage Barnes's rental as well?"

Simmons sat a bit taller in his chair. "I did. I have a connection with the Contarini. I tutored one of their family."

Hunter hoped pride would go before a fall. "I assume Barnes told you threats necessitated his leaving Padua quickly."

Simmons blinked. "Threats?"

"His servants said a large man with a warty nose came to him directly before he resettled in Venice. Did he not mention this to you?"

"Master Barnes had voiced his desire for a new Venetian residence several times before I located one for him."

Not an answer to his question. "I believe this large man was a messenger from Biradi, delivering threats. When Barnes moved to Venice, he adopted the false name Feenelly. I suppose that was to keep Biradi from finding him."

Simmons leaned forward in his chair. "Why should Biradi threaten him? If he planned to rob Barnes, he would not alert him thus. He said nothing to me of a large man, nor of adopting a false name."

"I believe Barnes's death was more than a burglary. He was involved with Biradi in the assault and capture of Master Sidney."

"You still beat that horse, do you?"

"I have good reason. I discovered an enciphered letter that proves Barnes engaged the *bravi* who carried Sidney away."

Simmons eyebrows shot up. "*Mirabile dictu!* Do you have this letter?"

"Not on my person."

"Who sent it?"

"It was not signed."

"Are you sure it was sent to Barnes?"

"I found it at Barnes's Venetian lodgings the day we discovered his body."

"I should like to see this letter before I believe you. *Ut prius*, I know of no reason Barnes would wish Sidney ill. They were friends. You are full of suppositions, Master Hunter."

If Simmons attacked, Hunter would riposte. "Pray then, what is your theory for why he took a new name in Venice?"

"If he did, which I do not know, perhaps he planned to engage in activities he would not wish friends or family to know about. Venice has many courtesans."

Simmons was agile, but, as he had mentioned courtesans, Hunter made a thrust. "Would his friends disapprove of visiting a courtesan? Would *you*?" Hunter twisted an insinuation into the last word.

It was Simmons's turn to riposte. "Do *you* ask for a personal reason? I hear you discovered a young woman in a Venetian brothel and brought her to Padua. Of course, what you do with your concubine is your affair."

Hunter had not foreseen his line of attack. "She is not my concubine," he snapped. "I freed her from her brothel that she might live a better life in England."

Simmons pressed his attack. "Without a husband or relatives? What noble motives you have."

Hunter mustered only a weak defensive. "I hope her music will enrich the house of a nobleman."

Simmons smirked. "If that nobleman is Lord Leicester, he may appreciate more than her singing."

"I believe *you* have heard her songs." Hunter said.

The smirk vanished from Simmons's face and he stood. "I have answered all your questions I wish to, Master Hunter. In fact, I was not obliged to answer any of them. I must now devote time to packing. I journey to Venice tomorrow. Farewell."

All the way back to Pozzo della Vacca, Hunter chastised himself. Although he had scored a hit with his final question, he felt he had lost the match. He had let Simmons shake him with the word *concubine*. He should have asked Simmons again about friars. He should have stated directly that he knew Simmons had tasted Caterina's flesh. He should have said more about the contents of the enciphered letter.

Caterina greeted him at the door of their lodgings. "We have been waiting for you."

"Why?"

"Francis and I prepare entertainment to cheer all. Everyone is too troubled by the stealing." Caterina called. "Come! Come! Signor Hunter is here!"

The members of the household assembled. Caterina and Francis stood before them and glanced at one another, eyes sparkling. They sang four songs, two in English and two in Italian. Each met with shouts and applause.

"She has been teaching me Italian," Francis said.

"And he, English."

Both exchanged glances and laughed.

"We all benefit from your language studies," Sidney said. As all rose, he leaned toward Hunter. "I detect a fondness. I shall speak with Francis and warn him not to get too close. Pray do the same with Caterina."

"I shall." Hunter knew that they must wait a few more days to be sure Caterina was not infected. Despite his own affections for Caterina and a pang of jealousy, a solution to the question of what to do with Francis and Caterina sprang into his mind. If Caterina returned to England married, that would protect her from a future as Leicester's mistress. But would she be accepted into his household? Might he employ both Caterina and Francis as singers? If not, what would they do? He had no other connections with nobles or gentry who might engage them. How would a Catholic couple fare in Protestant England?

Thursday-Saturday, 15-17 July 1574, Venice

Sidney and his party, a dozen strong, had arrived on Thursday. A purse of money from the expatriates allowed them to pay half of their rent to Rossi and provision the three-story house in Dorsoduro. It had enough rooms to accommodate them all, with space to spare. Beatrice occupied the outer chamber next to the kitchen, Caterina the inner chamber. Caterina could not reach any other rooms without passing through Beatrice's chamber, an arrangement to keep her chaste during their stay in Venice.

Sidney, Bryskett, Hunter, and Gironi moved into the Windsors' palazzo, where the baron and baroness provided two chambers for them. Each day fresh news arrived chronicling King Henry's journey to Venzone, San Daniele, and Sacile, and describing the receptions provided at each stage by the noblemen of that region: coaches, mounted escorts, cannon salutes, banquets, music, and balls. In addition to those who hosted the king, nobles and gentry from northern Italy and farther afield gathered to swell his retinue.

"Like bees to honey," Sidney said at breakfast, responding to Baron Windsor's recital of the worthies who had hurried to welcome the monarch.

"Like flies on shit," Gironi whispered to Hunter.

"Why do you disparage the king?" Hunter whispered back.

"Did he not lead armies against the French Protestants? Did he not encourage the massacre in Paris?"

"True," Hunter admitted, "yet we have all come to Venice to see him."

"I, for one, have come to see the Venetian spectacles. There is no city in Europe can match her processions and shows."

"Pray, what do you speak of privily?" Baron Windsor asked.

"We marvel over the quality of those you list," Hunter lied. "Your mention of the Duke of Nevers particularly caught my ear."

"And the Duke of Ferrara mine," Gironi chimed in.

"Philip mentioned you met Nevers in Paris," Lord Windsor said.

"Indeed we did." Hunter remembered a conversation with the duke in his garden, and the relief when he appeared at the English Embassy.

"Perchance you may greet him again in Venice," Windsor suggested. "I am to speak with a senator this evening, in hopes of securing an invitation. If I do, I shall ask if I may bring guests."

"You are too kind," Sidney said.

Lord Windsor slapped his thigh and stood. "I must be about my business. You are free to tarry here, or to roam about the city."

"We plan to see the preparations," Sidney said.

"Then pray accompany me as far as the quay. I shall take my gondola and you may wander at will."

The four companions did wander, on foot and by gondola. At every turn they saw evidence of excited Venetians preparing for King Henry's visit. Servants stood in doorways filling lamps. Above, others beat carpets to hang from the balconies. Gondoliers polished the fittings and repaired scuffs on the sides of their craft. Men of rank crowded the shops on the Rialto, creating a brisk trade in silks, satins, and jewelry.

As Caterina had requested, the quartet visited Tintoretto's studio to ask if she might sit for him again, but they were told he was at the Lido, working with his rival Veronese to paint a great triumphal arch designed by Palladio. It seemed all the artistic talent of Venice had been summoned to welcome the king.

Gliding down the Grand Canal, they passed the *Ca' Foscari*, where the king was to reside during his stay. There, activity was doubled. Men balanced on the gunwales of boats, painting fresh stripes on mooring poles. Servants scraped dirt and mold from the balustrades above them. Carpenters hammered on a huge pontoon dock near *Ca' Foscari*, in anticipation of scores of gondolas.

By early evening, they had returned to the Windsors' palazzo, to share what they had seen with the baroness. The baron returned in time for supper. Hunter could see no signs he had spent the afternoon with Lucia, but Lady Windsor's frowns suggested he had. The baron brought news of the banquets, performances, boat races, and nightly spectacles planned. He bubbled with enthusiasm, telling that the king wished to see a battle between the Castellani and the Nicolotti. He speculated which senators would be granted the favor of accompanying King Henry to Mass.

After the supper chinaware had been cleared, and Baron Windsor had exhausted his store of news, he drew Sidney and Hunter aside. "When I mentioned that the baroness and I had been invited to the *Fondaco dei*

Turci to dine in His Majesty's presence and see the Gelosi perform, I did not mention how this will affect you, Master Hunter."

Could it be that the baron had convinced someone to include him among the guests? "Pray tell," Hunter said with a smile.

Baron Windsor's demeanor changed from sanguine to apologetic. "The Duke of Ferrara, that evening's host, requires accommodation for two of his courtiers. I fear, Master Hunter, that I must ask if you might find other lodgings."

That was the price of the baron's invitation, Hunter realized. "Of course, your Lordship. Master Sidney has rented a house with many rooms."

"You need not move at once," the baron said quickly. "It will take the king several days to reach here."

Later, after Hunter broke the news to him and Gironi, Bryskett spoke up. "I shall speak to my brother. I am sure he has a chamber he can make available."

"I would be grateful," Hunter said.

Gironi laughed. "If he can do so, he might rent it out for a huge sum."

Hunter gave a mock blow to his shoulder. "Do not give Sebastian ideas. His dwelling is closer to here than the Dorsoduro house."

Sunday, 18 July 1574, Near the Lido, Venice

Hunter bobbed in the gondola with Sidney, both Brysketts, and Gironi. Their gondolier, as many, had removed the *felze*, so that his customers might better catch a glimpse of King Henry's welcome at the Lido. He had rowed them into position early that morning, and had fended off other boats, who sought to push them aside and take their vantage point. Sebastian had forethought enough to bring loaves of bread, a pound of cheese, and two bottles of wine, to make the hours of waiting pass more quickly.

Each companion pointed out to his colleagues details on the arch: the coats of arms of France and Poland, Roman gods, and battle scenes reckoned to be Henry's victories at Jarnac and Moncontour, where, as Duke of Anjou, he had defeated Protestant armies. Many of the Venetians around them wore azure and yellow, the king's colors, to honor him. Sidney waved to German nobles who called to him from distant gondolas. Hunter spotted the English expatriates and exchanged shouted greetings. He was surprised to see Charles Carr next to Dr. Simmons. His friends must have taken pity on him and invited him along. Sebastian pointed out Veronica Franco, Venice's most famous courtesan, radiant in a light blue gown, blonde hair coiled on her head. He named men in scarlet robes on the Lido, a litany of noble families: Contarini, Loredan, Pisani, Bembo, Morosini, Cappello, Zane, Priuli...

"Enough," Hunter exclaimed. "How do you come to know this?"

"Useful information to have," Sebastian said.

They passed the time in a friendly argument about whether King Henry had arrived in Venice. Gironi held he had entered Venice when he set foot on the city's *terrafirma* domains eight days before. Both Brysketts made their case for yesterday, when senators and Venetian clergy had greeted him at Marghera and escorted him to a palazzo in Murano. Hunter argued that the king would only officially arrive when the doge, his council, and the patriarch greeted him under the triumphal arch on the Lido and accompanied him in the *bucintoro* to Saint Mark's Square. Sidney refrained from taking sides but raised points to refute each argument.

They had reached no conclusion when the murmur from the crowd in the boats and on shore grew louder. The cannons at the forts fired. A gondola bumped against theirs as its rower attempted to nudge his way forward to gain a better view, and their craft rocked with the impact. Their gondolier snarled at his fellow. Hunter turned to see that the boat was filled with Signora Filippa, Leona, and several of her ladies. He nodded to them, surprised he had not noticed them before. Their gondolier must have been creeping forward for some time, counting on the charms of his passengers to allow passage.

On shore, a group of clergymen in resplendent robes wound their way from the church of San Nicolò del Lido through the crowd of noblemen to their appointed spots to one side of the central arch. Sebastian Bryskett identified the two foremost, the Papal Nuncio and Venice's Inquisitor General, the latter in Dominican garb.

Near those two stood a Dominican Hunter recognized. He nudged Sidney. "Look, the vice inquisitor who questioned you. The one whose heavy eyebrows meet over his nose."

"I see, but I do not understand," Sidney said. "If he holds his office in the Romagna, what is he doing here?"

"I believe I know," Sebastian said. "I heard the Spanish Ambassador convinced the Master of the Dominican Order to appoint a representative to convey his greetings to King Henry. Someone not a Venetian. Is this the man you told me about, Ludovico?"

"He is. You seem to know everything, brother," Bryskett said.

Sebastian grinned. "I keep my ears open."

At the vice inquisitor's side hovered the friars who kept appearing at crucial times, Brothers Alberto and Giuseppe. Brother Alberto directed his gaze to the gondola of Signora Filippa and smiled at Leona. Then his eyes shifted and he looked directly at Hunter. His smile changed to a smirk of self-satisfaction and menace that reminded Hunter of a snake. For a moment, he reconsidered his conclusion that Biradi had been behind the theft of their pistols. Could it be that Brother Alberto sought to exact revenge for his humiliation at Signora Filippa's by using Hunter's pistols against him? Though he could not picture the friar pulling a wheellock from beneath his robes, there were plenty of *bravi* the friar might hire in Venice. Had he been in Padua last week?

His thoughts were interrupted by a trumpet fanfare. A galley surged across the water from Murano and glided to a stop at the dock not far from them. Cheering loudly, everyone stood in their gondolas, blocking Hunter's view. Soon, King Henry appeared, walking up a slope toward the arch under a gold canopy supported by Porcurators of Saint Mark's. Passing the Dominicans, he was greeted by Doge Mocenigo and Patriarch Trevisano. One by one, other officials of the city greeted the king. Hunter realized he too was cheering, though Henry, when Duke of Anjou, had directed assassins who began the Massacre of Saint Bartholomew's Day, which he and Sidney had barely escaped. He was less immune to the emotions swirling around him than he had believed.

"He is little changed," Sidney said.

Hunter remembered his first glimpse of Henry in Paris in 1572. "A bit older. Let us hope considerably wiser."

"May God answer your prayer," Sidney said.

His thought was not exactly a prayer, but Hunter promised himself to compose one that night. If Henry held tight to the beliefs he had championed two years before, it boded ill for the Protestants of France. "Look, Philip, behind him. It is the Duke of Nevers, just turning this way."

"You are right. I can never forget the ride through Paris he gave me, and his appearance at the embassy."

"Nor can I," Hunter said. "He must have traveled hard from Paris to arrive in time to welcome the king."

"The king wears mourning for the death of his brother," Sebastian commented. He glanced at Lodowick. "I wonder if it is possible to feel sadness at the death of your brother and elation that you have inherited his kingdom."

"As you are no king, I shall not have that conflict," Lodowick said. "I would feel only sadness."

The crowd quieted as King Henry and his party passed through the triumphal arch and entered the loggia. Hunter could faintly hear a choir of monks chanting a *Te Deum*. His attention flagged as the ceremonies he could not see dragged on. Finally, to increased babble from the crowd, King Henry, Doge Mocenigo, and a party of chosen nobles reemerged and boarded the *bucintoro*. Accompanied by galleys firing salutes, the ducal barge slipped from the dock and made its stately way to *Piazza San Marco*, hundreds of gondolas and other craft trailing in its wake. Hunter and his companion were thrown about as the gondolier, adding his curses to those about him, jostled for a favorable position among the press of boats. When they finally reached Saint Mark's, the companions had to clamber over a dozen docked gondolas to reach the embankment, as bells rang, cannons boomed, and crowds cheered. Unable to reach the square, they barged their way through the throng to a tavern in *Campo San Stefano*.

Hunter joined Sidney and the Bryskett brothers at the Windsors' for a late afternoon meal. They met secretaries of the Duke of Ferrara, men who had displaced Hunter in the palazzo. The baron and baroness exchanged descriptions of what they had seen in Saint Mark's Square for reports of the ceremonies at the Lido. The baron added to the debate concerning the king's arrival in Venice by telling with a knowing smile that His Majesty had ventured incognito from Murano the night before to taste the forbidden pleasures of Venice. Though Lord Windsor was elated to name the dignitaries he had encountered, his wife complained of the crowds, the noise, the foul odors, and her weariness. Hunter could sympathize. He longed for an afternoon nap. Through the plethora of images seen and related, his most vivid memory was Brother Alberto's ominous stare and mirthless smile. He drew Sidney aside to share his thought that the Dominicans might hire ruffians to attack them with their own pistols.

Sidney shook his head. "You are seeing danger everywhere again. One angry look does not signify murder."

Hunter tightened his brows. "And you are denying the evidence of the past months again. You made a promise to take greater care."

"I am staying at Baron Windsor's. Could there be a safer place in Venice? Besides, the assaults on me and my possessions have been in Padua, not Venice."

"Do you believe Venice safer? Barnes was killed here. I was assaulted and thrown in the canal. And you..." Hunter thrust a finger into Sidney's chest. "...you cannot swim."

Sidney pushed his hand away. "Did I not say, after the robbery, that I would leave Italy in August. Am I not to enjoy a few weeks here as Venice celebrates King Henry?"

"I also wish to enjoy these weeks, but I must keep you safe during that time."

Sidney threw up his hands. "*You* must keep me safe? I did not escape father, uncle, and mentor for you to tell me what I may and may not do."

"Someone must tell you that you may not do whatever you wish nor never detect danger. Whatever risks you take, you will still be the son and nephew of noblemen. That is not my situation. If I do not fulfill my mission, I am a second son who has not qualified as a barrister. I shall be doomed to copy merchants' contracts."

"So your mission, as you call it, is not about me, but your own position." Sidney spun on his toes and stalked away.

Hunter's heart beat fast. How had he let himself reach such a state? He cared for his friend's safety, yet he had just pushed him away. Perhaps he had just admitted a truth he had hidden from himself. Could he be more concerned with himself than with his friend?

Tuesday, 20 July 1574, Venice

Hunter slept late. He had been witnessing memorable spectacles for two days—regattas of boats with varied numbers of rowers; gondolas with singers serenading the king; at night, thousands of lamps hanging from palazzi, lighting the Grand Canal; a mock volcano spouting fireworks on a boat floating in front of the *Ca' Foscari*. Even after the lamps were extinguished, laughter and singing echoed in the streets. Sebastian Bryskett insisted they end each evening by visiting a tavern near his house for a few more drinks.

Today he left Sebastian sleeping and ventured out to meet Sidney and Lodowick Bryskett at a tavern in *Campo San Polo*. He had scarcely gone a hundred paces toward I Frari when Charles Carr stepped before him. "Good morrow, Master Hunter."

"Good morrow to you, Master Carr. I saw you at the Lido two days ago."

"I was able to convince Doctor Simmons and the others to include me in their party. Have you seen many of the celebrations?"

The two compared their observations of the events of the past few days.

"I hope you enjoy the remainder of your stay in Venice," Hunter said, hoping to bring their conversation to an end.

"I hope the same for you," Carr said, "yet I doubt the coming days will bring you joy."

What did the man mean? "I know no reason why they should not," Hunter said.

Carr's mouth curled into a smirk. "I do. I have a proposition that will ensure we both enjoy the rest of our time in Venice."

"Pray make your meaning clearer."

"I have valuable information that concerns you closely. I am willing to give you that information for five ducats."

"Five ducats! How do I know your intelligence will be worth that much?"

"I assure you that if you do not hear my words, you will pay a much higher price in the future. Not everyone in Venice wishes you well. You are in considerable peril."

"Pray whom do you mean? Is your information about the theft of my pistols?"

"As I said, good information has a good price."

"I do not have five ducats now, and I am late for a meeting."

"Are you not interested in my proposal?"

"I must think on it. May I meet you tomorrow?"

"There is an alley to the left of the Carmini. I shall be there at eight tomorrow morning. And the price then shall be six ducats."

"So be it. If I am not there by half past nine, you may assume we have no bargain."

"As I say, you will pay a higher price if you choose to remain ignorant." Carr turned and walked toward the *Scuola di San Rocco*.

As he watched Carr walk away, questions swirled. Had Carr been waiting by Sebastian's lodgings to intercept him? How had Carr known where he was staying? How had he convinced the other expatriates to allow him to accompany them? They must have agreed to pay his way. Was Carr's warning of danger true, or a ruse to pry money from him to pay a gambling debt? The theft of pistols was evidence someone wished him ill, but Carr would not say if his intelligence concerned that. Could he afford not to pay Carr?

Wednesday, 21 July 1574, Venice

Hunter, Gironi, and Sebastian Bryskett were awakened by loud knocking. They threw on robes and descended to glimpse Caterina, her face contorted with fear, beyond the servant holding the half-open door.

"Pray let her enter," Hunter said.

Caterina darted inside with a glance behind her and grasped Hunter by his shoulders. "The king was assaulted," she burst out. "You are in danger."

CHAPTER 23

Going under Twice

"WHERE? WHEN?" HUNTER ASKED.

Breathing hard, Caterina released her hold and answered. "Outside Filippa's. Few hours ago. *Bravi* attack king. *Bravi* dead. *Matrone* and women answer *Signori di Notte* questions. Lucia sent moor to warn me."

Sebastian shook a groggy head. "What time is it?"

"Bells say four," Caterina said.

"Why am I in danger?" Hunter asked.

Caterina grabbed him again and shook him as she spoke. "The money. The pistols."

"What?"

"*Bravi* have English money. Filippa say pistols belong you and Sidney."

Hunter's head whirled. The stolen pistols could not have surfaced in worse circumstances. "Have you told Sidney?"

"No. I come to you first."

"We must dress and run to the Windsors," Sebastian said.

Hunter lifted Caterina's hands from him and held them. "Pray stay. We shall be down in a moment."

Upstairs, Gironi, digging in a chest, extracted one of his worn suits. "You must not wear your clothes. Pray don mine to appear a servant."

"Praise to you for quick thinking." Hunter took the garments.

"I shall dress as a servant as well," Sebastian said.

"How did Lucia hear of the assault so soon?" Hunter asked.

"Rossi's men spend every night in the streets," Gironi said. "They track the king's movements and spread the news to every brothel and courtesan. They would have told Filippa about your missing pistols."

That made sense. King Henry had frequented one courtesan or another before his formal welcome on Sunday. Rumor said he had visited Veronica Franco the night of the regattas, two days before.

The three descended and hurried with Caterina through the quiet streets toward *Campo San Polo*. Scurrying behind the church, they encountered Carlo, the Windsor's lutenist, his hair unkempt and clothing awry. He grasped Caterina by both elbows and addressed her in frantic tones.

Gironi gasped. "He says Sidney and Bryskett were taken. *Sbirri* came and Lord Windsor gave your friends to them. We must not approach the Windsor palazzo."

They were too late. "Where will they take them?" Hunter asked.

"To prison, either the dank cellars or the attic of the Ducal Palace, 'the tiles'." Sebastian answered. "We must save ourselves and get out of Venice if we can."

Though Sebastian made sense, Hunter recoiled at the idea. "And leave them to face false charges?"

"I had thought we could flee with Philip and Lodowick," Bryskett said. "But we cannot help them if the Ten believe they are a danger to the Republic. Their trials are secret; their verdicts, final."

"But Lodowick is your brother. And the pistols and coins were stolen," Hunter remonstrated.

"Can they prove that is true? The Ten may decide they are lying, that they provided the weapons and paid the *bravi*."

"Their motive?" Hunter pressed.

"Sirs," Gironi interrupted. "You must not stand in the campo debating. The *Signori di Notte's* men are looking for you both."

Gironi spoke true. His pistols had been identified. As Lodowick Bryskett was seized, they would search for Sebastian too. Hunter stood paralyzed, unwilling to flee, but uncertain what he might do to help Sidney. Was this the information Carr had offered to sell him yesterday?

"Let us separate," Gironi said. "Sebastian may do as he wills. Edward, come with me to Stefano's. He can hide us."

"What about the others?" Hunter asked. "Madox? White? Fisher? Beatrice? Francis? The others?"

Hearing the names, Caterina spoke. "They were scared at the news. They ask, 'Do the *sbirri* know we are Sidney's people?' They ask, 'Should we stay? Should we go?'."

"We cannot leave them," Hunter said. "We must warn them to flee Venice. They may torture them to find me."

"Then it is safer if they do not know. Caterina should tell them to flee but not where you are," Gironi said. "Come now."

"Yes," Caterina urged. "I will warn. You go." She turned and ran into the shadows.

Hunter still hesitated. "Go to your cousin's, Luca. I must return to Sebastian's to fetch my dagger. We will need money, whatever we decide." If he could meet Carr, he might discover who stole the pistols. Hunter could pay him to testify and free Sidney and Bryskett.

Gironi sighed. "Be quick."

Hunter and Sebastian sprinted back to his lodgings. Breathing heavily, Sebastian warned, "Do not allow yourself to be captured. The Ten use the *strappado* to get confessions."

Hunter had heard terrifying stories of this torture. Pulling a prisoner up by a rope tied to his hands behind his back, then dropping him and jerking him up short of the floor, until he confessed or fainted from the pain of dislocated shoulders. "Will they do that to Philip?"

"He may be too important a prisoner," Sebastian said, "but Lodowick is not."

At Sebastian's lodgings, Hunter extracted his dagger and purse from his chest. He glanced at his sword but reasoned no servant would carry one.

"Let us pray the Ten are so busy hosting King Henry that they cannot mount a trial," Sebastian said. "He attends a service in Saint Mark's and a banquet today."

Loud knocking sounded below.

Sebastian's eyes widened in terror. "The *Signori di Notte* are here. You must escape through the window."

Hunter did not hesitate. "God protect you." He ran to the window, opened the shutters, clambered onto the sill, and contemplated the twelve-foot drop to the ground. The torches of the *sbirri* flickered from around the corner against the wall opposite him. They shouted to open the door. He took a deep breath and leapt.

Despite himself, Hunter let out a grunt as he landed. Immediately, voices and torchlight approached, still out of sight around the corner of the building. He turned and ran the only way he could, away from the agents of the Night Lord. Shouts and running footsteps followed him. He heard Sebastian's warning again. "Do not allow yourself to be captured."

He turned right down a broad street, then right again. His pursuers were no closer, but neither had he outdistanced them. At the next turning, he dodged to his left, then left again. He took the next right, down a narrow alleyway. Five paces and he realized his mistake. This *calle* ended at a canal. There was no way back. He ran on, hoping to find a narrow embankment at the end of the alley.

There was none.

Behind him, two men entered the mouth of the *calle*. He scanned the canal. On the other side, stairs led to an embankment. He thanked God he had learned to swim in Geneva, jumped in, and stroked toward the stairs. Behind, pursuers shouted their consternation. Dripping foul canal water, he pulled himself onto the stairs. He prayed the *sbirri* did not have pistols. Glimpses to right and left revealed no bridge nearby that they could cross. He darted down the first alleyway he saw and kept running across bridges and through small courtyards.

When he stopped to catch his breath, he heard no pursuit. He whispered a prayer of thanks and looked about him. The façades were familiar. He had just passed the house of the courtesan Lucia. If she had sent Edoardo to warn Caterina, perhaps she would help him. If he were wrong, where else might he turn? Stefano's was in Cannaregio, halfway across the city, with patrols between him and there. He looked up, saw a light in a window, and knocked.

Edoardo frowned when he saw Hunter. Lucia called to him, and the moor answered, "Hunter," in a solemn tone.

"*Entra. Entra,*" she called, hurrying down the stairs in a pale red nightgown.

Edoardo reluctantly allowed him to enter and barred the door.

"Caterina told me of the fire and robbing," Lucia said. "When I heard of the assault on the king, I sent word to her. Did she tell you?"

"Yes."

Fear suddenly flashed in her eyes. "Did you set men to kill the king?"

A chill ran through him. If she suspected him, she might turn him out or turn him over to the *Signori di Notte*. "No, madam. I do not know who stole the pistols or how they got to the *bravi* who attacked the king."

"Were you followed?"

"I swam a canal to escape a patrol," Hunter said. "They could not follow."

Lucia wrinkled her nose, as though just aware of Hunter's damp clothes. "I see you did. There is a fire in the kitchen. Come."

Lucia led the way to the kitchen and sat Hunter on a stool by the fire. "What has happened?"

While Hunter told of his morning, an elderly cook poured buckets of water into a kettle, swung it over the fire, and glared at Hunter.

Lucia shook her head. "You are in great trouble. What will you do?"

He had no better answer now than when he learned of Sidney's capture. He could try to flee Venice or stay and try to present evidence to clear himself and Sidney. Neither was a good choice. Running to save himself was not only cowardly, it betrayed the trust the Earl of Leicester had put in him. He had come all this way to look after Sidney's welfare. No amount of silk thread or weavers could make up for abandoning his friend.

But who could explain how stolen pistols had ended in the hands of would-be assassins? The members of the Pozzo della Vacca household could swear to the theft of the pistols, but the Ten might consider them part of a conspiracy. They were of insufficient rank to acquit men who had plotted the death of a king. The English expatriates had been there that night. If they could swear to the theft, it might sway the Ten. Captain Scarpa must have sent word of the theft to Venice, but that only reported Sidney's claim. None of the possible witnesses could explain how the pistols reached ruffians outside Signora Filippa's. He thought again of Carr. There was a thin chance he might hold the answer.

"I must try to reach people who can swear the pistols were taken in Padua," Hunter said, "and someone who may know how they came to Venice."

"Dressed like that?" Lucia said.

Loud knocking caused both to tense. In a moment, Edoardo appeared with Caterina. When she saw Hunter, she dropped the cloth bag she was carrying and ran to embrace him. "Oh, Edward, I think you go with Luca. Thank God you are here. They are gone. Francis, Madox, Beatrice—all. House empty. I not know what to do."

Hunter's heart sank. "They have been arrested." The fear returned that they might be tortured to tell where he was.

Caterina broke into tears.

CHAPTER 24

Sinking

"SIT. SIT," LUCIA PRIED CATERINA AWAY FROM HUNTER AND SAT NEXT TO her by the hearth. Both switched to Italian and spoke at length. Lucia turned to Hunter. "No one was at the house, but many things were there—pans and pots, chests of clothes. We do not know for certain they were taken. Perhaps they escaped."

"Pray God they did," Hunter said.

Stroking Caterina's shoulder, Lucia said, "You sit too, Master Hunter. Did either of you break your fast?" Neither had. She spoke to her cook, Margherita, who nodded and left.

Hunter considered his next step. Faint morning light now bathed Venice. To reach either Gironi or the expatriates, he would need to walk across half of Venice, crossing the Grand Canal by the Rialto Bridge or a *traghetto*. How many patrols would be searching for him? He must wait for nightfall. Could Lucia shelter him until then? Authorities would not connect her with him.

Lucia pointed to Caterina's bag and spoke to her. She looked closely at Hunter. "What are you thinking?" Hunter asked.

"I must know more," Lucia said. "Where are those you would reach?"

"Cannaregio."

She shook her head. "Too far. I must think again." Margherita returned with bread and cheese and Lucia sat pensively while they ate.

Hunter nodded at Caterina's bag. "What did you bring?"

"A gown," she said. "And my money."

What an act of vanity in such a dangerous time, Hunter thought. "Why in the world?"

Caterina reacted with surprise. "I can choose. Courtesan or servant."

Hunter realized Caterina's reasoning. She had come with a disguise. If she were the only member of the household who had not been arrested, patrols would be searching for her as well. "That is intelligent."

Lucia approached Hunter and pinched his doublet. "You are dry on this side. Turn."

Hunter stood to rearrange his stool and Margherita waved him aside. She swung the kettle out with a poker, poured dried beans into the boiling water, and swung it back over the fire. Lucia spoke to her. With a frown, Margherita stood beside Hunter. Lucia looked from one to the other and nodded. She spoke again to the cook, who answered with surprise and then disagreement. Lucia spoke more sharply, and Margherita left the kitchen.

"What was that about?" Hunter asked.

"Do not mind," Lucia said. "Just dry your right side."

Hunter looked at Caterina, who shrugged. He turned to Lucia. "I think it unwise for me to venture out before tonight. I hope I may shelter with you until then."

"We shall see," Lucia said. "Just now, I must change for the day. Caterina, pray assist me. Bring your bag."

With the women gone, Hunter removed his doublet and hung it near the fire. He sat, back to the fire, to dry his shirt, pondering again how he might reach Cannaregio. Taking a closed gondola to the expatriates' lodgings would be his safest course, if Lucia would not allow him to stay. Would gondoliers be on the lookout for an Englishman of his description? He need only speak to give himself away. Would the expatriates shelter him, or had the *Signori di Notte* arrested them as suspected accomplices? If only he had not sent Gironi to Stefano's.

After a while, Lucia and Caterina reappeared, both in dark blue gowns, with their hair arranged in horns atop their heads, trailed by Margherita, carrying a basket, and a smiling Edoardo.

"I am dry," Hunter announced.

"Good," Lucia said. "We now have a plan to help you."

"Pray, what?"

Lucia bent and pulled a smock and a brown kirtle from the basket. She advanced on Hunter and held them up to him.

He realized what she had in mind. "Oh, no!"

"Dear sir, do you wish to live?" Lucia asked.

Hunter sighed. He had to admit this was a better disguise than he might devise. "I divine one part of your plan, madam. Pray tell me all."

"Edoardo has been to Sior Rossi. He was glad to hear you are not arrested, and he has news to help you. We will go to him—two courtesans and their maid walking to *Mezza Luna*. Any *sbirri* looking for an Englishman will not stop us."

Caterina giggled and Lucia shot her a look.

Hunter rubbed the stubble on his chin. "Do you believe I will make a convincing maid?"

"Edoardo will shave you," Lucia said, "bathe canal water from your body, and paint your face somewhat, then help you into Margherita's clothes. You may need padding or pinning. I have wigs I wear for gentlemen who prefer black or brown hair."

"You seem to have thought of everything," Hunter said.

"Pray that I have. Your life may depend on it."

"I have one request. Though your English is good, I wish that my man Gironi might meet us at Signor Rossi's."

Lucia sniffed. "Sior Rossi had the same idea. He sent a man carrying worn shoes to fetch your Gironi."

The bell in the *campanile* of Santa Margherita rang half past eight. Hunter turned with wide eyes to Lucia. "Is the Church of the Carmini near here?"

"It is at the bottom of the campo," she replied. "Why?"

"I must to meet an Englishman there," he said.

She raised an eyebrow. "Dressed as you are?"

"It will not matter as long as I have money."

"Are you to meet him in front of the church?"

"No. A *calle* to one side of it."

"Could it be a trap?" Lucia asked.

"I do not think so. He spoke to me yesterday, before the assault on the king."

Caterina grasped his arm. "Every moment you are in the streets is a danger."

"He swore he had important information about the theft of the guns. It should only take minutes."

"Very well," Lucia said, "yet you endanger me and Caterina."

"Walk with me to the front of the church, then act as if you give me an order. I shall venture down the *calle* on my own."

The women reluctantly agreed. Hunter saw no one in the dark alley. Perhaps Carr stood just behind the bend in the church wall. He hurried as fast as his kirtle would allow to where the *calle* ended at a bridge. He mounted the bridge. No one on the opposite side. Could Carr be waiting in a boat? Only one boat tied to a post on his right. Perhaps Carr was late, or he had got drunk the night before and slept in some doorway. He glanced to his left and cried in surprise. Floating not an arm's length from the foot of the bridge was a corpse, blood staining the water near its head. For a moment, his mind flashed to the banks of the Seine, Huguenot corpses bobbing before him. He closed his eyes and shook his head. This was Venice, not Paris, and he feared he recognized the body. He descended, knelt, stretched out a hand to grasp the ankle, pulled the body to the bottom step, and turned it over. Yes, Carr. Crimson marks on his neck showed he had been strangled, but blood flowed from his left temple. He must have hit his head as he was thrown into the water. As he still bled and had not sunk, Hunter guessed he had been killed within the half-hour. Any information he had concerning the theft of the pistols died with him.

Who had killed him? This murder did not match the throat slitting of Biradi's previous homicides. Pursued himself, Hunter could not report this to the authorities. He must get as far away from Carr's body as possible. He turned and ran back to Lucia and Caterina.

"Did you meet him?" Lucia asked.

"In a way," Hunter said. "He was floating in the canal, strangled."

"*Madre di Dio.*" Caterina crossed herself. "What happened?"

"Death follows you too close," Lucia cut in. "We must not stay talking. Let us go to Sior Rossi without delay."

Hunter blushed as the men in *Mezza Luna* pointed, guffawed, and giggled. Regarding himself in Lucia's mirror, he had judged he was one of the ugliest women he had ever seen, and that was so much the better. He swallowed his pride and walked between Caterina and Lucia through the tavern to a large inner room. For a moment, the fear that Rossi might turn him over to the *sbirri* crossed his mind, but it was too late now. Rossi sat in a high-backed chair with arms, surrounded by several of his men. They subdued their laugher with difficulty.

Hunter felt relief when he spotted Gironi standing to one side of Rossi's "courtiers," apparently at ease. Then he was astonished to see, on the opposite side of Rossi, Tommaso Biradi, no longer a fearsome leader, but a captive with bound hands and slumped shoulders. If Biradi was now a prisoner, perhaps Hunter might ask him to explain Sidney's capture and Barnes's murder. Perhaps he knew of the pistol plot. "Has Biradi..." he began.

Gironi shushed him. Lucia and Caterina curtsied to Rossi. Lucia introduced her "maidservant." Rossi's comment produced hearty laughter in the room. He addressed a compliment to the women and dismissed them.

Gironi stepped forward to translate. "Sior Rossi says your appearance is much improved since he saw you last."

"I am pleased I can provide jollity at such a serious time," Hunter said. "I have news for Signor Rossi, but I pray that I may enquire how Signor Biradi has come here."

Hearing his name, Biradi frowned at Hunter.

Gironi spoke to Rossi, who nodded. "Sior Biradi came to Venice to see the celebrations for the king. He arrived here on the seventeenth, as King Henry reached Murano. Unfortunately for him, he did not take enough care after refusing Rossi's request for payment. He only brought four men with him. I can say only that all four have disappeared, and Biradi is now a prisoner. Rossi's earlier request for one hundred and seventy-two ducats has now grown to three hundred. He hopes that will be better received in Padua."

"In other words," Hunter said, "he is holding Biradi for ransom."

"I will not translate that," Gironi said.

"Has Biradi confessed to devising Sidney's attack and Barnes's murder?"

"Not in so many words. I will explain later. But what is the news you have for *il padrone*?"

"When I went to meet Carr, I found him strangled and floating in the canal beyond Carmini. We shall not know what he offered to tell me."

Gironi conveyed the news to Rossi, who appeared surprised. He barked an order to a man who scurried from the room. After a brief interchange with Biradi, he spoke at length to Gironi, who turned to Hunter again.

"Rossi may provide the information Carr hoped to sell. The men who drew pistols in the presence of King Henry were Rossi's men, but they were not working for him. He agreed a few weeks ago to hire them out for a large fee. The plan was that they would be arrested and name an Englishman as the one who engaged them to kill the king. They would bargain their information to escape execution."

Hunter stood gaping at Rossi. "So, he is behind..." Hunter began, his anger rising.

"Hold your tongue," Gironi warned. "The royal assault was not his idea, nor did he know that Sidney was to be blamed. As you recall, Sior Rossi is wont to draw up a contract, vague enough to be poor evidence, but good enough to insure both parties abide the bargain."

"Yes." Hunter wished he would get on with it.

"He is angry that his men were killed and wants the party to the contract to suffer."

"And who is that party?" Hunter demanded.

"You may read his signature yourself." Gironi nodded to the bat-eared man beside him, who produced a document and handed it to Hunter.

Hunter scanned the bottom of the page, where he found inscribed *Frater Alberto* and *Frater Giuseppe*. "The Dominicans!"

"The same."

Hunter's guesses fell into place. The Dominicans had spoken with Barnes and Carollo to warn them of Biradi's wrath and had whisked Lucetta from Padua. That meant Barnes, pimp, and prostitute were all connected with hiring Biradi to capture Sidney. The friars had brought Barnes the note chiding him, so they knew about Sidney's capture but were not responsible for it. The vice inquisitor they stood beside at the Lido was most likely the author of the note. He had ordered the slaying of Sidney's captors, but was now behind the plot to use Sidney's pistols to implicate him in an attempted assassination that would destroy the good will between Venice and England. Perhaps Brother Alberto asked that Hunter's pistols be stolen too, out of hatred for him.

"Have you read this contract? Will it clear Sidney?"

"I have. I believe it might, though it does not specify how the men will be employed. The contract will confirm that the friars engaged the men who were killed, not you or Sidney."

The law student in Hunter detected a flaw. "Is there any mention of the pistols?"

"No."

"The friars may say they hired the men for another purpose and have no knowledge of the weapons or the assault."

"That is true. Sior Rossi hopes we may find a way to link the pistols to the friars."

Hunter jumped at a possibility. "Does Biradi know of a link?"

"Alas, no. Sior Biradi denies all knowledge of the theft at Pozzo della Vacca."

"Carr might have contradicted that or confirmed my suspicion of the Dominicans."

"Neither Rossi nor Biradi knows about Carr's killing," Gironi reported.

Hunter was uncertain whether to believe them. "I am astounded that Rossi does not know of a killing so near here, though it may have happened just around eight."

"He sent a man to find Carr's body." Gironi's face was deadly serious. "Pray do not accuse him of anything."

Hunter saw the wisdom of that. "The contract with Brother Alberto is evidence that Sidney did not hire the men who threatened the king. But how can we present a defense to the Ten?"

"Sior Rossi believes they will not meet to consider the case against Sidney and Bryskett—and you—until the official ceremonies involving the king are completed. He has a good friend serving as one of the Ten this month, and he will send him a message later today."

"If Signor Rossi gives me the contract, I will present it to the Ten myself," Hunter said.

Gironi drew in breath through his teeth. "You will not be able to do that. First, you are wanted. Second, you do not speak Italian. Third, Sior Rossi is unwilling to give you the contract until after you perform a service for him."

Hunter was being squeezed again. "Another task? What service?"

"Deliver a message to Biradi's men in Padua, demanding—no, requesting the larger sum so that their leader can return to Padua safely."

"Will you come with me?"

Gironi sighed. "Alas, I must. If only you had studied Italian more."

"How are we to leave Venice, travel to Padua, and return without being taken by a patrol?"

Gironi turned and spoke with Rossi. "He says he will arrange for a boat leaving late tomorrow from Rio di Sant'Alvise. If you choose to return from Padua for the contract and put yourself in danger, another boatman in Marghera will bring you back."

Hunter stood calculating risks. Rossi had a contract that would help free Sidney, Bryskett, and himself. It would add to Scarpa's report of theft, testimony by the expatriates, and the letter to Barnes, indicating Dominican involvement. Could he obtain the other evidence? He had left the enciphered letter in Padua. The testimony of the expatriates was only a hope. Scarpa's report was somewhere in the Venetian chancery. Rossi's contract was there in front of him. If he did go to Padua, he could retrieve the letter and perhaps a copy of Scarpa's report. "Tell him I will deliver his 'request.'"

Rossi smiled, then spoke impatiently. "He says we must go now. Nicolotti captains are due here soon to plan their approaching battle with the Castellani," Gironi said.

"Does he control that as well?" Hunter asked.

"He is a *padrino*, a godfather, who is over squad captains."

Rossi snapped a comment.

"He says we must leave," Gironi said.

Hunter looked down at his kirtle and threw open his hands. "Like this?"

There was no need for translation. Rossi laughed and spoke to the man on his right side, whom Hunter recalled as 'bat ears.'

"He says Alvise will give you new attire and arrange to take us wherever we wish to go in Venice. He will send details of boats to the mainland to Stefano's tomorrow," Gironi said.

Alvise led them down a corridor connecting *Mezza Luna* with the used clothing shop. A dealer in such garments was Rossi's ostensible profession. As Hunter stood amid racks of used clothing, Gironi explained what he had gleaned. "I did not want to go into details before Rossi, but his men bragged about outwitting and disposing of Biradi's men. One, it seems, was the huge man with a warty nose that you mentioned."

"Am I wrong to feel joy that four of Biradi's underlings are no more?" Hunter asked. Bat-eared Alvise, oblivious of the English discussion, picked garments from the rack, held them up to Hunter, and shook his head.

"You must ask a priest, not me," Gironi said. "At any rate, you asked if Biradi confessed. He spoke of Carollo introducing him to Barnes, and of undertaking Sidney's capture and transport for a large sum. He was angry not only because his men were killed, but Barnes had only payed half the agreed price and was so foolish as to refuse to pay the rest when the plot failed."

"Foolish indeed."

"Biradi did argue Barnes's murder was a mistake of zealous men who were only meant to rob him."

"What did Rossi say?"

"He cared not a whit for an Englishman's life, so long as his domain was respected, and he was paid the value of the goods stolen."

The burden of ignorance lifted from Hunter. The mysteries of Sidney's seizure and Barnes's murder dissolved, and he was confident he understood who was behind the theft of the pistols. His relief was short-lived. Carr's murder was still an enigma, and over all loomed the problem of obtaining evidence of Sidney's innocence and presenting it to the Ten before they reached a fatal verdict.

"Aaaah," Alvise said. He nodded vigorously and handed Hunter a well-worn, unfashionable doublet and trunk hose that a servant might wear.

Thursday, 22 July 1574, Venice

Hunter spent a sleepless night in Stefano's storeroom. Though Stefano's wife had spread blankets on the floor, the room itself was so small that he had to sleep with his knees drawn up near his chest. The smell of leather was at first overpowering. The question of whether he could trust Rossi kept returning. The man had been party to the plot that resulted in the assault on King Henry. Might he extract himself from suspicion by betraying Hunter to the Ten? Would Rossi hand over the contract as promised or demand other acts? He itched to do something not dependent on Rossi to further Sidney's acquittal.

In the morning he could at last stretch, walk fretfully about the shop, and break his fast with the Piceninos. After midday, he argued with Gironi. "Why sit here idly when I could make my way to the expatriates and ask them for statements that the pistols were stolen?"

"And if a patrol stops you, what will you do? You may look like a servant, but if you open your mouth, you will be seized."

"Could you accompany me as far as the end of the *calle* where they stay? I can leave here with a pair of shoes to deliver, and play the noddy, as I would have last night, had we been stopped."

"You might play the fool in more ways than one if the *sbirri* see through your act."

"Then say I am mute. Or deaf and mute. I can smile as a fool then, and you will do all the talking."

"And if the expatriates bind you and turn you over to the *Signori di Notte?*"

"That is a chance I must take."

"Will you tell them of Carr's murder?"

"Not unless they mention it. I must concentrate on helping Sidney and Bryskett."

"Very well, Gironi said. "I shall stay at the tavern nearby to escort you back."

"Hunter!" John Hart exclaimed, opening the door. He stood frozen a moment, then glanced up and down the street before, stuttering, he invited him in.

"Bless you for your hospitality," Hunter said.

"Gentlemen," Hart called out, "Edward Hunter is here."

The expatriates filed into the central room of the house with troubled faces.

"We are surprised you have come," Fitzwilliams said.

"The *sbirri* were by earlier asking if we had seen you." Randolph said. "They asked us many questions about our friendship with Sidney, which we did not deny. They warned us not to leave Venice."

"They sought *you*," Le Rous said with a frown. "For your part in the assault on King Henry."

"They said Sidney and Bryskett were taken already," Hart said, face full of concern.

"It is on their behalf that I have come to you," Hunter said. "What did the *sbirri* say about Sidney's arrest?"

"Little," Fitzwilliams answered, "save that there was evidence he—and you—were behind an attempt on the king's life."

Dr. Simmons stepped forward with a solemn face. "Pray tell us what you have done."

Hunter spread his hands. "Gentlemen, you know Philip Sidney. I swear to you by all that is holy that neither he, nor I, nor Lodowick Bryskett, had any part in what befell King Henry two nights ago. The evidence they spoke of are the pistols that were stolen in Padua the night you dined with Philip. They ended up in the hands of the ruffians who assaulted the king."

All the expatriates expressed surprise.

"You all know that the pistols were stolen," Hunter pressed on. "I have come to ask if you would sign statements saying so, that I might present them to the *Signori di Notte*. I fear the Ten may condemn both our friends because of the pistols."

"No!" Hart cried. "That cannot happen. I shall be glad to write such a letter."

"Might that cast suspicion on anyone who writes such a letter?" Randolph asked.

What assurance could he give, with all Sidney's household arrested and under suspicion? "I am not sure. But, if any of you were suspected, would the *sbirri* not have arrested you when they came?"

"Master Hunter, would you excuse us a moment?" Simmons asked. "I feel we must discuss this before giving you our answer."

Hunter sat, his heel drumming the floor, while the expatriates retired to a room beyond. He could hear their voices, sometimes low and cautious, sometimes raised in objection, but he could not make out what they were saying. He longed to present the case that the Dominicans were behind the theft of the pistols, but he dared not do so until he had their statements and presented them to the authorities.

After what seemed to be a long time, Simmons led them out. He smiled at Hunter. "We all wish to help establish the innocence of our friends," he said. "We have penned letters concerning the stolen pistols, and I will accompany you to the office of the Night Lord to present them and add my own testimony. We fear if you go alone, you may be seized before you utter a word."

Hunter breathed a sigh of relief. He had succeeded in gathering evidence that might acquit Sidney and Bryskett and prevent his own arrest. "Pray when can you go?"

"I suggest we go now," Simmons said. "I know the way to the nearest office."

Hunter was grateful that their path took them by the tavern where Gironi sat, head lowered as they passed. He was confident he would follow to see what took place.

Outside the office of the Night Lord, Simmons hesitated. "I think it best if I go in alone, make a statement, and deliver the letters, while you remain outside. If I deem it safe, I shall come fetch you."

"That makes sense," Hunter said.

After Simmons entered the building, Gironi appeared at Hunter's side. "What is happening?"

Hunter explained.

"You are taking a grave chance," Gironi said. "Come with me now."

"If Simmons finds me gone, he may feel betrayed," Hunter said.

"I shall be gone, at any rate," Gironi said. "One of us must remain free. I shall tarry at the end of the *calle*."

Moments after Gironi left, Simmons strode out the door and motioned for Hunter to enter. He gave a broad smile. "All will be well."

Hunter walked from the bright sunlight into a dim anteroom. Strong arms gripped him on either side.

Simmons spoke in Italian. Hunter understood his name and the word *fuggitivo*. Sebastian's warning not to be captured rang in his ears. Now he was doomed.

CHAPTER 25

Deep in Locks

HUNTER STRUGGLED, BUT TWO MORE GUARDS MATERIALIZED, SHOUT-ing at him, pushing him face down, and binding his hands and feet. He shouted a curse and immediately realized that shouting did no good except to relieve his frustration at being helpless. The guards on either side laughed at him. They took his dagger and bread knife, carried him into a small room, and forced him into a chair. He sat, panting, his mind racing to devise some way out. Before him, an older man in an official robe sat behind a desk, a satisfied smile on his face. Simmons strode in and spoke to him. Hunter could follow a little of the conversation, recognizing his own name, *fuggitivo,* and *pistole.* Why had he been so foolish as to trust Simmons? How easy it would have been to follow Gironi's advice and leave. How ironic that he feared betraying Simmons. It was clear the tutor was betraying him to the Night Lord, who drew out a piece of paper and recorded his statement. Finally, the lord asked his name. When Simmons told him, the official stiffened and spoke sharply to him. While Simmons protested, he called his men, who leapt forward and seized the tutor. A jolt of satisfaction surged through Hunter, followed by a weaker pang of guilt. It was wrong to rejoice in another's suffering, no matter how deserved it was.

"No! No!" Simmons shouted. "*È un errore!*" He continued to yell as the guards dragged him from the room. The other guards yanked Hunter to his feet and followed them.

In the small, damp, windowless cell beneath the office, permeated with the smell of decay and urine, Simmons finally stopped weeping. Hunter lay bound, the cold, slimy stones of the floor pressing remorselessly into his side. He prayed briefly for mercy, but his need to discover the truth overcame the inner voice that warned him he should prepare himself for death. He ventured a question. "Why are you here?"

Simmons sniffed. "Some mistake. They will realize their error and release me."

"What mistake?"

Simmons's tone changed. Despite the darkness, Hunter sensed that Simmons sat up straighter and tightened his body. "I must say no more."

Hunter decided to try sympathy. "I am sorry you, too, are imprisoned on false charges."

Simmons snorted, but said nothing. Did the tutor somehow believe he had plotted to kill King Henry?

Hunter willed his voice to sound calm. "I pray you may help me sit up and lean against a wall."

The tutor's hesitation revealed reluctance. Perhaps he suspected a trick, but after a moment, he shuffled his way to Hunter, bent, and pulled him to a sitting position. "Can you push yourself back with your feet?"

"Yes." After several leg flexes, Hunter felt a damp wall against his back. He sat in silence for a long time, hoping Simmons might say something. Finally, he asked, "Why did you turn me in to the Night Lord? Is there a price on my head?"

Simmons snorted again. "Do you think I act out of cupidity? I am not so base."

"Then why?"

"My reasons are my own. I need not tell you."

Hunter's anger swelled. He checked himself from cursing the smug tutor, so sure that 'they' would release him. Simmons might change his mind if hours passed and no relief arrived.

After a short time, voices sounded in the corridor outside, and torchlight flickered under the door. Keys jangled in the lock and the door opened. The torchbearer entered, and Hunter was blinded for a moment after an hour of darkness. The Night Lord followed, not tall with authority, but bent in trepidation. Behind him a tall man, his black cape swirling, strode into the cell. The glance of the vice inquisitor cut across Simmons and Hunter like a razor. He spoke complimentary words to the Night Lord, who relaxed and smiled. Then he addressed Hunter in Latin, "We meet again, Master Hunter."

"We do," was all Hunter could come up with, but his mind whirled. This was the cleric who wrote Barnes, who had ordered the killing of Biradi's men and then used his authority to hide his deed, the man likely behind his arrest. "I gather you found a way to use Philip Sidney to serve your purpose."

A second of surprise crossed the vice inquisitor's face, then he smiled cruelly "I do not know what you mean. You and your friend have been captured and will be punished for your vile plot."

"I suspect you know more of the plot than I do," Hunter said.

The vice inquisitor's lip curled in a snarl, but before he could speak, Simmons fell on his knees before him. "Vice Inquisitor Fascetti, thank God you have come. Pray tell the captain he has made a mistake."

The vice inquisitor's snarl turned into a sneer. "I am unaware of any mistake."

"He said an accusation against me was found in a *bocca di leone*, that I was part of the conspiracy against the king."

Hunter had seen these lion's head sculptures on the faces of buildings, their mouths serving as slots where citizens could drop accusations against those who were a danger to the republic.

"Then such an accusation has been lodged."

"But I carried out your orders," Simmons whined.

The vice inquisitor cast a cold serpent's eye on Simmons. "My orders? How dare you accuse me of involvement in your heinous plot?"

"But..." Simmons began.

The vice inquisitor cut him off. "Lordship, you have done well to apprehend these Englishmen. They may only be pawns in a larger Protestant plot to murder His Most Christian Majesty and tarnish the name of Venice, but they shall pay with their lives." He wrinkled his nose. "I need spend no more time in this stinking cell. A reception for His Majesty has already begun. Let us both repair there."

"How can you deny me?" Simmons screamed as the door clanged shut. He sprang to the door and beat on it, weeping again. Hunter waited in the darkness. After a few minutes, Simmons yelled, "May God damn the whoreson knave to hell!"

Hunter suppressed his instinct to ask questions. Better to sympathize than to interrogate. "You feel betrayed."

"The dogs! *They* are the ones guilty of a heinous plot." Simmons breathed heavily "I should not have trusted him. They are responsible for this accusation."

Hunter knew how he felt. "You believe you know when someone is trustworthy."

"Yes. And they threatened excommunication. Ha. What irony."

Simmons seemed unaware of the irony in Hunter's last statement. As he calmed, Hunter asked, "How could he accuse you of being a conspirator?"

Simmons's mirthless laugh revealed he was involved in the vice inquisitor's plot. If he asked Simmons directly to reveal the conspiracy, would he close his defenses? Hunter told himself it did not matter if he learned the truth if he was going to die, but his desire to know compelled him. He waited for Simmons to speak.

After another long silence, Simmons asked, "Do you see any way out of here?"

"No," Hunter answered honestly. "But surely you will stand before a judge tomorrow. You have the letters from the other expatriates. Will they help?"

A rustle as Simmons changed position on the dank floor. "They would not help me or you."

"Did they not state the pistols were stolen?"

"They stated you and Sidney *told* them the pistols were stolen, but they had not witnessed the theft nor seen any evidence." Another short mirthless laugh. "I told them what to write."

Simmons had planned his betrayal carefully. "Why did you wish to harm us, or at the least not help?"

"I was doing the bidding of others."

"The vice inquisitor?"

"Yes. May God damn his soul."

Hunter waited, hoping Simmons would say more. Finally, he asked, "Why should he wish us harm?"

"At first he did not," Simmons said.

"At first?"

"It began with Barnes."

Though Hunter believed he knew part of Simmons's story, it was better to play ignorant and let his cellmate tell his tale. "Barnes was killed almost two months ago. How could he be connected with the assault on King Henry?"

"But for Barnes, the vice inquisitor would never have known of Sidney."

"You speak in riddles, Master Simmons. If I am to die because of some plan of Barnes's, or yours, or this vice inquisitor, I deserve to know that plan."

A rustling as Simmons adjusted his position again and settled next to Hunter. "If we are to die, I may as well unburden myself. It will make no difference." After a pause, he sighed. "This story is filled with irony."

"You may point it out as you tell it. You said it began with Barnes."

"It began when he received a letter from his father, telling of his appearance before the Privy Council, his humiliation, his being fined—all for being true to his faith."

Hunter could not stop himself. "There is no law against faith."

"No. Just against practicing it, against attending Mass, against the sacrament of confession." Simmons sounded hot.

Hunter had made a false step. This was no time or place for religious controversy, or for suggesting he was now serving as Simmons's confessor. "Pardon me for interrupting your story. How did Barnes react to the news?"

"With anger, of course. Especially against the Earl of Leicester, who took the main role in his questioning and deciding his fine. Barnes believed Leicester hoped to break his father with fines and buy his estate at a low price."

Considering what Hunter knew of Leicester, that was entirely possible. Here was the motive that had eluded him. He guessed the next step in the story. "As Leicester was in England and his nephew Sidney in Padua, Barnes decided to take his revenge on Sidney."

"Yes. You were right with your annoying questions about Barnes and Biradi. Through Carr and a whore and the pimp Carollo, he hired Biradi's men to seize Sidney and carry him to papal territory. He wrote the vice inquisitor of his plan just days before it took place, expecting Sidney would be tried for heresy and he—Barnes—would earn praise for his efforts."

This explained the section of the enciphered letter that rebuked Barnes. "But he was mistaken."

"Yes. The vice inquisitor was angry. He sent men to kill those who captured Sidney when they reached the Romagna, and he dispatched two friars to reproach Barnes. They wrung from him the names of those involved in his plan and foresaw Biradi's rage when he learned his men had been slain. They took the whore from Padua and warned Carollo and Barnes. The friars came to me and asked that I keep an eye on Barnes and dissuade him from any more foolish actions."

"Were those Brothers Alberto and Giuseppe?"

"Yes. How do you know them?"

Hunter loosed a close-mouthed chuckle. "You speak of irony. A courtesan identified them to me. She knew Brother Alberto well." Better not to name Signora Filippa and put Simmons on his guard. "How did the vice inquisitor know of you?"

"He knew I tutored English scholars from the university. I knew nothing of Barnes's plan until the Dominican friars came to see me."

"Did the other expatriates know of their visit?"

"Not immediately. I did tell Fitzwilliams later."

That explained their behavior when he questioned them. Hunter thought there was more to the story than Simmons was telling, but that was unimportant now. "Did Barnes flee to Venice after the friars spoke to him?"

"No. His folly continued. I believe he wished to redeem himself in his own eyes with a show of courage. He not only stayed in Padua, he refused to pay Biradi what he owed him. He said the men had not completed their mission and he did not owe him the remaining half."

"What made him change his mind?"

"After two threatening visits from Biradi's man, the pimp Carollo was found dead in the marketplace. Barnes came asking for help. As you know, I arranged for him to rent a property of the Contarinis at short notice. He left me letters, a signet ring, and other jewelry for safe keeping."

"That makes sense. Letters or his ring might help identify him as Barnes, not Feenelly. Was the letter from his father among those?"

"I do not know. I did not open the locked box."

"But he gave you a key?"

"Yes."

If Hunter could get to Padua, he might open that box and discover more of Barnes's secrets. But he was not going to Padua. He was headed to another prison cell, then death. His shoulders ached. "Pray untie my hands. I swear I will not harm you."

Rustling. Hunter sensed Simmons stretched his torso away, as though looking askance at him. "I am not as foolish as Barnes."

Hunter sighed and resumed his questions. "Did you know Biradi would kill Barnes?"

"I warned Barnes that might happen and tried to prevent it."

Was Simmons lying? Hunter could not see if the tutor blinked. Might he have told Biradi where to find Barnes? "Why did he not flee the Veneto?"

"He did not think Biradi's reach extended to Venice—that he would be safe here with a false name."

"We know he was not. What happened next?"

Simmons was silent for a time. This part of his story must be more difficult for him to tell. "Nothing, until news came that King Henry would visit. Then I had another visit from the friars. They delivered a letter in cipher from the vice inquisitor, asking if I would undertake a holy mission." He spat out the last two words.

"I am surprised he committed plans to writing."

"He must have thought the cipher secure. It could not be broken without the prayer book the friars brought. *There* is irony—using a prayer book to order foul deeds."

"Does the letter still exist?"

"Yes. Though the vice inquisitor asked that I burn it, for a moment I mistrusted him and preserved it. I should have doubted that villain further."

"What was the 'holy mission' he asked you to undertake?"

"I was to hire someone to steal your pistols and English money, then deliver the same to the Dominican brothers in Venice."

Hunter remembered Brother Alberto's smug smile at the Lido. "Did you ask why they wanted those things?"

"When I asked, they said it was better I did not know, but that this was a service to the Church. They also offered thirty ducats. I suppose I was trying to serve both God and Mammon."

Thirty pieces of silver. How fitting. "Did you hire one of Biradi's *bravi*?" He no sooner asked than he remembered Biradi's denial of the theft.

"I could not approach him. After his dealings with Barnes, he trusted no Englishman."

"Then who?" Hunter thought he knew the answer.

"Charles Carr was always desperate for money. We bargained until he agreed."

"Did he set the fire and steal the pistols?"

"Yes. He knew you were investigating and bragged he burned the papers on your desk."

Finally, that made sense. "Did he deliver the pistols to you or the friars?"

"To me. I curse myself for being so foolish, but the 'holy mission' was mine."

And the thirty ducats. Hunter considered withholding the news of Carr's death but decided Simmons's remorse might make him reveal more. "I discovered Carr's body in a canal this morning."

"No!" Simmons's cry of anguish echoed in the cell. "My soul is laden with more sin!" He sobbed again.

Hunter waited until he calmed himself. "Do you know who killed him?"

Simmons sighed. "He may have cheated someone at a gambling table, but I suspect the vice inquisitor or a subordinate hired an assassin to ensure his silence. It seems no act is beyond the Dominicans. No doubt they can hear one another's confessions, assign a penance, and grant absolution. Would that I could so easily obtain shrift."

Hunter had not seen a friar that morning, but one could have strangled Carr and ducked into the church of the Carmelite brothers. He decided to press Simmons. "So, *you* were behind the pistol theft that landed us both here."

Simmons moaned. "When I heard of the assault on the king and the arrest of Sidney, I knew what use the friars made of the pistols. I suppose that is another irony. They used the pistols to falsely connect you and Sidney to the crime, but the vice inquisitor used them to ensnare me as well."

"Did you deliver the pistols to the friars?"

"My servant Zòrzi did."

"Do the other expatriates know of your part in all this?"

"They know of Barnes, but not my part in the theft."

They tensed as footsteps sounded outside, followed by jangling keys. A guard opened the door, placed two cups on the floor, and threw in two half loaves of bread. He muttered something and was gone before Hunter could react.

"He says we will be moved to the Doge's Palace tomorrow to appear before the Ten," Simmons said.

Hunter's mood grew dark. Now he knew what had happened, but any satisfaction he felt was hollow. He would never be able to tell anyone. He did not know whether to pray for a miracle release or a quick death. "Do you think we both shall be executed so soon?"

Simmons began wailing again. Hunter allowed himself to join Simmons in his tears. After some time of sobbing, Hunter asked again, "Will you untie my hands, that I may eat?"

Simmons hesitated. "I will feed you instead."

Hunter awoke to a scratching sound. Had the guard returned? Was it morning? All hours were the same in this dark cell. His body ached. He shivered.

"What is that?" Simmons had heard it too.

The flicker of a lantern shone under the cell door. "Not a rat, at any rate."

The door swung open and Gironi stepped in, followed by a man holding a lantern.

"Luca!" Hunter exclaimed.

"Thank God!" Simmons cried out.

"Hush!" Gironi warned. "The guards may be drunk, but they are not deaf. It is almost midnight. We must hurry to the boat."

Hunter remembered. Rossi had promised a boat to take them to Marghera. "Pray untie me, Luca. My every muscle aches."

As Gironi knelt and fumbled with the knots, Simmons begged him. "For God's sake, take me with you."

"Why is *he* here?" Gironi asked Hunter.

"The vice inquisitor betrayed him as he betrayed me," Hunter said. He groaned as he slowly pulled his unbound hands from behind his back and shook them.

Gironi untied Hunter's ankles. "Then let us leave the scoundrel here."

Hunter stood. "No. His testimony can clear me, Sidney, and Bryskett. He can link the stolen pistols to the Dominicans."

"Will he do so?" Gironi asked.

Simmons grasped Gironi's arm. "Yes. Yes. Only free me now."

Gironi objected. "We cannot take him with us."

Hunter recognized the torchbearer as Rossi's man Razor Nose. "Can this man take him to Signor Rossi? There he would be safe from the *Signori di Notte*, and Rossi will ensure he testifies against the Dominicans he wants punished."

Simmons looked terrified, a man caught between a road leading to certain death and another that might have the same end. "I swear I shall tell their misdeeds to anyone who will listen."

"Before we send you with this man..." Hunter began, but stopped, as he did not know the proper way to address Razor Nose.

"Zaninno," Gironi said.

Hunter resumed. "Before we send you with Zaninno, you must give me the key to your Padua house, and tell me where to find the boxes with Barnes's letters, the letter from the vice inquisitor, and the prayer book that will decipher it."

Simmons handed over his ring of keys, explaining the locations of the boxes and which smaller keys would open which cases. He even gave permission for Hunter to open his lockbox, in case they needed funds.

Gironi extracted a handkerchief from his sleeve. "We must make sure Master Simmons reaches Sior Rossi." He gagged Simmons and bound his hands behind him. He turned to Hunter. "Have you your purse?"

Hunter had given no thought to money since he had been seized and was astonished to feel the weight of his purse in his breeches. "Yes."

"Good." Gironi led them to a water door opening onto a canal.

"Praise God you were a locksmith's apprentice," Hunter said.

As they stepped outside, Zaninno extinguished his lantern. A gondola floated before them in the light of a waning moon. A roar of laughter sounded from above.

"How did you get the guards drunk?" Hunter whispered.

"Their captain left to attend a reception. Since the mice will frolic when the cat is gone, they are drinking with Rossi's men to the success of the Nicolotti," Gironi said. "Pray step into the boat and do not splash."

Muttering prayers of thanks, Hunter did so.

Friday, 23 July 1574, Venice, after midnight Thursday

After transferring Simmons and Zaninno to another boat a little distance from the office of the Night Lord, the gondolier made his way to the embankment just past the Church of Sant'Alvise, where he pulled alongside a wide barge lying low in the water. The unmistakable odor of fish wafted from it.

"This is where we get off," Gironi announced.

"I thought our gondolier was going to row us across the lagoon to Marghera," Hunter said.

"All craft leaving from this side of Cannaregio are being searched. We shall be obliged to lie under a canvas beneath a layer of fish."

Hunter wrinkled his nose. "At least it is better than being sent to live with the fishes by verdict of the Ten."

"And we must pay the boatmen eight soldi for the privilege," Gironi added.

Hunter paid the boatmen and crawled into a lidless box under a canvas. "Crammed into your cousin's storeroom, bound in a damp cell, and now voyaging under a blanket of fish."

"Beggars should not be choosers." Gironi crawled in beside him.

"Nor fugitives, it seems."

The boatmen shushed them and spoke to Gironi.

"Lie on your side, he says."

The two turned to one another and the boatmen lowered the canvas over them. In an instant, buckets of fish rained down. Both men covered their heads with their arms until the plopping of fish finished. Despite his distressful position, Hunter whispered a prayer of thanks as the boat pushed off. A little later, the boatmen spoke with others, who must be *sbirri*. Hunter and Gironi held their breath until they sensed from the rhythm of the waves that the barge had entered the open water of the inner lagoon. After ten minutes had passed, the fish were pushed aside, and a smiling boatman pulled back their canvas cover.

The breeze blew away some of the smell of fish, and the companions reviewed their plan. Hoping that guards were not also waiting in Marghera, they would proceed to the stables where Barnes and his servants had left their horses. Gironi offered a prayer that they had not been sold. They would pay the two month's fees for the horses and ride through the night to Padua, leave the horses at the stable with their own, and enter Simmons's house before dawn. Hunter would stay inside, reading such documents as he found, while Gironi determined how many eyes in Padua watched for Hunter.

Friday, 23 July 1574, Padua, near dawn

Hunter waited impatiently near the window for enough light to decipher and read the letter from the vice inquisitor. After the care they had taken to leave the horses at a Paduan stable, he dared not light a candle and reveal he was in Simmons's home. As he sat in the gloom, his nervous knee flexing up and down, the dark mood he had known in the cell returned. He would never return to England. Never see his family or friends. The worthy career he imagined for himself as an informer for Walsingham was not to be. He imagined his own execution. Heretics were drowned in the lagoon. Enemies of the state were beheaded between the pillars in the *Piazzetta* as the *Maleficio* rang. Surely the latter was preferable, if one had to die. Though innocent of the crime he was charged with, he was guilty of other sins: murder, fornication, adultery, false witness. If impure thoughts were as serious as Jesus had said, he was damned a hundred times over. The words of Rossi swam into his mind. He need not return to Venice. He was free now. Within a night's ride, he could be out of Venetian territory and headed north. He would see his family again. Why should he not follow that course?

This was temptation, he told himself, with Rossi in the role of Satan. He could not abandon Sidney, Bryskett, and the others of the household who had been arrested. Though they might still face execution if he returned, their deaths would surely be on his soul if he fled. If he could present the evidence he was gathering to—whom? A fugitive could not approach the Ten and demand an audience. He could not even request a hearing before a Night Lord. Could Baron Windsor aid him, or would he turn him over to the authorities, as he had Sidney? Could he go again to the expatriates? Would they hold him responsible for Simmons's arrest? Perhaps he could approach Sidney's noble German and Bohemian friends. Hunter wished he had had an opportunity to meet them, so that he might know whom to approach. Rossi, the Tempter, had said he knew one of the Ten. Dare he trust this criminal overlord?

He shook his head, smoothed out the enciphered letter, and opened the missal to the page indicated. Enough light filtered through the window for him to begin his task.

An hour later, when Gironi returned, he had not only completed deciphering the letter, he had scanned Barnes's letters and found the one excoriating the Earl of Leicester. Hunter turned to Gironi eagerly. "What have you discovered?"

"I believe we may make our way to Pozzo della Vacca. After asking the news from Venice of many in the marketplace, I heard only of fabulous fireworks, regattas and glassblowers on rafts in the Grand Canal, of King Henry's visit to Veronica Franco, of the honors heaped upon him by the doge. I asked about an assault upon His Majesty and was told 'Yes, they arrested some Englishmen,' as though that story was closed. I made bold to ask one of Scarpa's guards as well, jovially asking what miscreants he was searching for now. He only named a few of Biradi's men."

Hunter let out a deep breath. "Then I must not have been declared an outlaw yet."

"Let us hope the guard revealed all he knew," Gironi warned. "What progress did you make?"

"The vice inquisitor's letter is deciphered. It asks Simmons to obtain pistols from those Englishmen the bearers of the letter will mention, along with English coin, and deliver the same to the bearers in Venice. He calls it, as Simmons said, a 'holy mission' that will separate Venice from the heretic queen, for so he dubs Her Majesty. I have found at last, in a letter from Barnes's father, his motive for despising Sidney."

"Excellent. Did you open Simmons's strongbox? We have little money after paying for the horses."

"Not yet. Let us do so now."

Hunter and Gironi approached Pozzo della Vacca cautiously, wary of any guards who might have been posted to watch the residence. Seeing no one, they entered and proceeded to exchange their clothing, still smelling of fish, for fresh garments. Hunter retrieved the enciphered letter to Barnes from his chest and wrapped it with those from Simmons's house in a linen shirt. He packed them with care into a bag, along with his own garments. If by chance he might be able to appear before the Ten, he would not do so in a servant's attire.

Loud knocking at the door interrupted his preparations. Racing to the window, he gasped to see Captain Scarpa and two of his assistants.

"*Gironi! Untero! Aprite!*"one called.

CHAPTER 26

Treacherous Eddies

HUNTER DASHED TO THE LANDING, ALMOST COLLIDING WITH GIRONI. "They know we are here. Let's escape through the stable."

Gironi shook his head. "Men are there as well."

"But you said they didn't look for us."

Gironi's shoulders drooped. "The guard was wilier than I reckoned." The knocking came again.

"Our only weapons are your dagger and bread knife," Hunter said.

"They will not avail us."

"Of course not," Hunter said. How could he think they would prevail against Scarpa and his men? Why add a true charge of assault to a false one? "We must open to them."

Full of resignation, they descended and opened the door. Scarpa stepped in and greeted them, smiling. Hunter turned to Gironi in consternation.

"He says he is glad he found us."

"I am sure he is," Hunter said. "He will gain some glory."

Gironi shushed him, as Scarpa continued. Gironi relaxed and began to smile as well. "*Grassie, grassie.*"

"What...?" Hunter began.

"He was troubled when he heard of Sidney's arrest, and wrote a letter to attest that the pistols were stolen, that he had seen the forced locks himself, and that Sidney had not armed the king's attackers."

All tension drained from Hunter. "*Grazie, grazie, Capitano.*" He reached to shake Scarpa's hand.

257

Scarpa spoke again, and Gironi translated. "He planned to send the letter to Venice today when his lieutenant—that man there—reported he had spoken to me in the market."

"But the men at our stable?" Hunter asked, still fearing he might be arrested.

"They were looking for horses, to see if we were here. I explained where we left them," Gironi said.

"Then he has no orders to arrest me?"

"I shall not ask him."

"Pray invite him to come with us to Venice. He can speak to those in the *Signori di Notte* and present our evidence."

Gironi spoke again to Scarpa, who replied with a frown. "He has affairs he must attend to today. He bids us ride to Venice with his letter, and pledges to follow on the morrow."

"Pray tell him that Sidney may be tried by then," Hunter said.

Scarpa shook his head and spoke and Gironi related, "King Henry is to witness the Grand Council and sign the Golden Book today. Tomorrow he is to visit the Arsenal. The members of the Ten will be too busy to meet as a court until he leaves."

"I pray he is correct," Hunter said.

When Scarpa asked where he might find them in Venice, they looked at one another uncertainly. Rossi's headquarters, Baron Windsor's, the expatriates', and the rented house in Dorsoduro were all impossible. "We shall have him ask for Stefano the shoemaker, near *Palazzo Longo*," Gironi suggested.

Hunter and Gironi rounded the corner near the Ram's Head.

"I wish one of Scarpa's men had come with us," Gironi said.

"I do as well," Hunter said, "but we may owe Rossi too much to reveal his secrets."

"Perhaps they will be discovered when Scarpa investigates our disappearance at the hands of Biradi's men," Gironi speculated.

"You are too melancholy," Hunter said. "After all, we bring news of their captain."

"Have you not heard what happens to messengers of bad news?"

"I have." Would Biradi's men murder them in cold blood? They should have told Scarpa of this mission.

No one guarded the door of the tavern. "We are not expected," Gironi said.

"Surprising them might be good or bad," Hunter said. "One wakes a sleeping dog at his peril."

As they walked toward the door, two men emerged. Someone had been keeping watch after all. Hunter recognized Stick Man, who asked their business. Gironi handed him the letter, declaring it was a message from their master. He looked at it carefully, pointed to the seal, and shook his head. "*Non il suo sigillo.*"

Gironi encouraged him to read the message.

Stick Man hemmed a moment. The request was beyond his abilities. He signaled them to wait and disappeared inside. After a few moments, the snarling bartender, holding the letter, barged through the door to confront them.

Hunter's hand went to the kitchen knife he had gathered at Pozzo della Vacca, but Gironi reached to stop him and spoke calmly to the bartender. He growled a few words in reply and twirled back into the tavern.

"Let us go while we may," Gironi said.

Both backed away several steps before turning. "What did he say?" Hunter asked.

"He cursed the demand and asked if we expected he would pay. I told him that we were only messengers and the letter had instructions of where to deliver the money. He said we were lucky to be alive, but no one would kill without Biradi's direct order."

Hunter let out a long sigh. "I care not who asks what, I shall not return there again."

Saturday 24 July 1574, Venice

Hunter's heart raced. He could see figures in black marching solemnly to a scaffold between the columns in the *Piazzetta*. He knew they surrounded Sidney and Bryskett. "Faster! Faster!" he called to his gondolier. The rower stood puzzled. He did not understand English. "*Vite! Vite!*" he said. No, that was French. He could not remember the Italian words. The gondola seemed no nearer as the prisoners mounted the scaffold. The *Maleficio* rang. The sun gleamed off the executioner's sword. He had to reach the *Piazzetta* with his documents. But, sensing a lack of pressure on his shoulder, he realized the satchel containing the vital evidence was gone. What had he done with it? Why were they no closer to the shore? The gondolier grasped his shoulder and shook him. What was the matter with the man?

Hunter raised his head from the table, Gironi softly calling his name. In a flash, he remembered nearly falling from his horse on the way to Marghera, paying the wide-eyed stable boy to keep quiet about their return, falling asleep in the *sandolo*, and waking to stagger to the *Mezza Luna*.

"Time to break your fast," Gironi said.

"Thank you." His heart still racing, Hunter walked unsteadily to the piss pot in the corner, relieved himself, and returned to find two morsels of bread and a mug of watered wine. Gironi sat across from him. "What's o'clock, Luca?"

"Near eight. The sun has been up some time."

Hunter shook his head to clear it. "Have you seen Rossi? What is the news of Sidney?"

"Rossi should be here in an hour. The men have heard nothing of any hearings or trials of Englishmen."

"That is a relief." Now Hunter was thinking clearly. "When Rossi gives us the contract with the friars, we shall have a set of papers to clear our friends." He raised a finger for each bit of evidence. "The letter to Barnes connects the vice inquisitor to the killing of Biradi's men and the desire to drive a wedge between Venice and England. The letter to Simmons asks him to steal pistols and English coins. Rossi's contract shows the friars hired the king's assailants. Finally, Simmons will testify against the Dominicans, and Captain Scarpa will swear to the theft as well." As soon as he had stated his case, the lawyer in him spotted its weaknesses. The letters were in cipher, unsigned, and undated. Simmons had not given the pistols and money to the friars, Zorzi had. Finally, how and to whom could he present his evidence?

"Eat up," Gironi encouraged him.

"Has Scarpa arrived in Venice?"

"I do not know. He said he would arrive today and search for us at Stefano's. I do not expect him soon."

Of course not, Hunter reasoned. "Perhaps he will know how to get our evidence to the Ten."

"Perhaps. Rossi also has a connection with one of them." Gironi gave a wry grin. "An odd link between judges and criminals, but not without precedent."

"You have a cynical mind."

"You accused me of melancholy yesterday."
"Then I accuse you of both today."
"I fear no penalty if I plead guilty."

An hour later, Hunter and Gironi stood before Rossi, who sat enthroned as before. Gironi spoke at length, while Hunter stood impatiently, worrying about Sidney, Bryskett, and others of the Padua household. Had Caterina remained free? Where was she?

Finally, Gironi turned, frowning, to relate the situation. "Rossi has heard no news of trials. As Scarpa suspected, those in high office are all occupied with King Henry's visit. He is pleased we have evidence against the friars and the vice inquisitor, but he has changed his mind about the contract."

"What?" Hunter exclaimed.

"Pray remain calm. As he hired men to the friars who tried to shoot the king, he fears he may be tried as an accessory."

It was sound reasoning, but not what Rossi had promised. Hunter felt used again by this captain of crime. A line of defense came to him. "Could he not declare the friars wanted his men to escort and protect the vice inquisitor?"

Gironi relayed the suggestion. Rossi pulled on his beard and replied. "He will consider this and let us know tomorrow."

That was the best Hunter might do for now. "Can he deliver our evidence to his friend of the Ten?"

After another conference, Gironi explained. "His patron cannot receive such information directly from him. Their connection must remain secret."

"Then to whom can we present our case?" Hunter asked in exasperation.

"He says we must find our own way, and..."

"We are used again," Hunter interrupted. "He wants us to help his revenge against the Dominicans but will not help us clear Sidney."

"I won't translate that," Gironi said. "Can we present him a path?"

Hunter ran through the options in his head. After he and Simmons had not returned, the expatriates would not trust him, nor would they have any connection with Venetian aristocracy. Baron Windsor would, but he had allowed Sidney and Bryskett to be whisked from his palazzo.

Rossi had just refused to use his link to the Ten. A desperate idea came to him, unlikely to succeed, but all he could think of at the moment. "I know the Duke of Nevers, who travels with King Henry. If I could reach him, I am sure he would hear me out."

Gironi looked at him skeptically. "And how might we reach him?"

"I do not know, but pray tell Signor Rossi."

Gironi was surprised that the suggestion was not met with immediate dismissal. Rossi pulled at his beard again, then smiled and spoke.

"He has a plan..."

Before Gironi had time to explain further, bat-eared Alvise beckoned them to follow him down the corridor to the used clothing shop. There, he opened a wardrobe and took out a nun's habit.

"What is happening?" Hunter exclaimed.

"I shall tell you as you change," Gironi said.

"Change?"

"Yes. Rossi will not allow either of us to stay here. You will be taken to a nunnery on an island in the lagoon for safe keeping today and tomorrow. I shall go to Stefano's and await Captain Scarpa."

Alvise held the habit up to Hunter and frowned. He spoke to Gironi, who held the garment at Hunter's shoulders. Alvise fetched a knife, knelt, and began to let out the hem.

"Why such delay?"

"Rossi's plan to reach the duke is to use the mock battle of Nicolotti and Castellani on Monday. As a *padrone*, he will marshal the squadrons of Nicolotti, and can place you in one. The duke and king will view the battle from *Palazzo Foscarini*, on the Nicolotti side of the bridge. You should be able to slip from your group and reach Nevers."

Hunter did not see how he could accomplish this. A Venetian plebian presenting himself to guards protecting the king and his retinue would be dismissed out of hand. Yet, this was a plan to get him closer to the Duke of Nevers than any he could think of at the moment. Alvise tugged at his breeches and signaled he should undress and don the nun's apparel.

Hunter did so reluctantly. At least he would have ample time to think of what to say. "Will the nuns not unmask me when I speak?"

"Those who deliver you will state you are under a vow of silence." Gironi looked closely at him. "Your face must be shaved before you go." He spoke with Alvise, who nodded and trotted away.

"Thank Rossi for his plan, unlikely as it is to succeed," Hunter said. "And pray ask him to arrange that Simmons is also in the group of Nicolotti beside me. If I do reach the duke, he must be with me. Also tell Scarpa. I pray he may have a better idea how to reach the authorities with our evidence."

"You must hope I am not arrested as I go about your tasks. One hoist of the *strappado* and I will tell them whatever they want. Where will the papers be?"

"I will keep them. Ask those who take me to the convent to request pen and paper, that I may make a copy I can give you, in case I am arrested or unable to reach the duke."

"If you cannot, I will be unable to as well."

"Then give the copies I make to Scarpa when I return." Doubt assailed him. "When will that be?"

"Sunday night."

"Pray try your best to locate Caterina and those of the household who are captured. And, if you can go with one of Rossi's men to watch the expatriates' lodgings, point out Zorzi to him. If Simmons's man can testify to handing the pistols to the friars, our case will be stronger."

"You speak as though you will be in a court."

"I wish that were so." Hunter sighed. "But we must do whatever we can to make any room a court."

Alvise returned leading another man, bearing a shaving mug and razor.

Sunday, 25 July 1574, Venice

Hunter rose from the *prie-dieu*, stretched his legs and rolled his shoulders. He had been kneeling for over an hour. The desk had not been designed for writing, so he allowed himself frequent breaks. He was almost finished making copies of the documents. Despite a few odd looks, the abbess and nuns had left him alone in his windowless cell. He had kept the most devout posture he could imagine on those moments when they brought food and water. The boatmen must have presented him as a penitent sister who had many sins to pray away. Perhaps he was not the first man or woman Rossi had sent to this convent to avoid arrest.

He had had time to consider, then reconsider, possible words to say to gain access to the Duke of Nevers. As soon as he had settled on one phrase, a doubt entered his mind and he devised an alternative. So much depended on how far his squadron of Nicolotti fighters was positioned from the palazzo where the king would watch the battle. How many guards would stand between him and Nevers? Would they be French or Italian? Might they simply arrest him and hand him to a long-boat captain? What if Nevers did not accompany the king? What if Rossi went back on his word again? Despite his weariness, he had not slept. Worries, the hard bench that served as a bed, thunder and lightning, and, he was sure, giggling in the cell next to his, had kept him awake. The stories of male visitors to nunneries must be true, at least here. The midday meal, if you could call it that, had been served. Gironi had said he was to return Sunday night. He hoped the gondolier would not wait until nightfall.

The sun was setting over the lagoon when Hunter made his way to the landing, concentrating on walking as a penitent woman, head bowed. He waited to be helped into the gondola. The changing hues of orange and red reflected off the waves, the dark outlines of the towers of Venice, and the twinkling of lights newly lit in windows made the return journey a thing of beauty. Hunter soaked in as much as he could, a cankerous worm in his head whispering that this might be the last sunset he would see. He prayed for God's help.

When the gondola slipped to the embankment near the Half Moon, Hunter disembarked awkwardly in his nun's habit and toddled to the tavern. One of Rossi's retainers opened the door for him. As he entered, Caterina sprang from a seat and rushed to him. "Luca has been taken!"

CHAPTER 27

Into the Maelstrom

"No," Hunter gasped. "When?"

"Earlier today."

"Where?"

"Near Stefano's shop."

Hunter pummeled Caterina with questions. "Was Stefano taken as well? Where is he? Did he see Captain Scarpa? What did Gironi tell him? Does he have a way to contact the Ten?"

Caterina shook her head in confusion. "Pray say again."

Hunter repeated his questions one at a time, and Caterina provided what answers she could. Stefano had not been arrested, but she thought his shop was watched. Luca must have been taken to the prison in the Ducal Palace. She knew nothing of Captain Scarpa but would ask Sior Rossi. He remembered what Gironi had said, that after one drop of the *strappado* he would tell them whatever they wanted to hear. How long would it take for him to face the torturer? What would he say? He knew the nunnery where Rossi had hidden him, their plans to gain access to King Henry, and where he might be found. How much time did he have before the Ten knew where to arrest him?

Hunter recalled himself. "I am glad you are still free and safe. Where have you been?"

"Signora Filippa."

Hunter's throat tightened. "Did you...?"

"No. I sang. I did no fucks. Only..." she pointed to her open mouth. "Rossi said to *madame* to keep me safe."

Could she get the pox from sucking a penis? Hunter hoped not. Did Filippa keeping her safe mean Rossi thought Sidney and he might still escape Venice and take Caterina with them, or did he have other plans for her? "Is there news of Sidney?"

"No. All talk is the *battagliola* tomorrow. Because Gironi is gone, I must say words between you and Sior Rossi." She turned and spoke to a man standing by Rossi's inner door, who waved them in.

It appeared Hunter was not to have a chance to change from nun's garb. He trailed Caterina to the inner room. Rossi chuckled when he saw him, and the others in the room followed his lead. Hunter pushed back his veil and coif and stood as tall and unperturbed as he could. "Pray give him my thanks for keeping me safe and ask him for news of Sidney and Captain Scarpa."

Caterina spoke to Rossi and listened to a lengthy reply, then turned to Hunter. "Still no news of Sidney. No news of Scarpa. No news of Francis, Christopher, Beatrice or Sidney's servants."

Caterina had remembered to ask of the other members of the Pozzo della Vacca household. Hunter felt ashamed.

"He say you will stay in house, but not here. Ten offer money for you. Tomorrow you will come here and wear Nicolotti color. Join group of Alvise, near bridge."

So, a reward was offered for his arrest. Still, it seemed, Rossi had decided not to turn him in. Best concentrate on the morrow. "Pray ask him if Doctor Simmons will be in that group."

Rossi frowned and spoke.

"He does not remember," Caterina said.

An evasion if he had ever heard one, Hunter thought. "Pray tell him Simmons's words are needed to achieve his revenge."

Caterina's brows furrowed.

"Say Simmons must speak for Rossi to punish enemies."

Caterina nodded and spoke with Rossi.

"He will put Simmons with you, he say."

"Good. One last thing. Will he give me his contract with the friars?"

Rossi hesitated, but he barked an order to Zaninno. In a moment, he appeared and handed Hunter the paper he desired. There were the friars' signatures. There was no way they could deny hiring the would-be assassins. Tonight, he would copy the contract.

Rossi was speaking.

"He say you leave now. He have things to do. Zaninno will lead us to a house to hide," Caterina said.

"Both of us?"

"Yes."

By the time Hunter had changed into his servant's clothing, the sun had set. Zaninno escorted them into a gondola and spoke orders to its rower. Caterina's sharp intake of breath caused Hunter to ask, "What is the matter?"

"We go near *Campo San Cassan.*"

Hunter recognized the square he had first entered with Sebastian Bryskett, a hive of prostitution.

"Why are you afraid?"

"I fear to end there."

Hunter held her close. "We are there only for a night," he said, though knew that might not be true. "I will copy the contract and give you all the important papers."

To her look of doubt, he explained, "Gironi was to keep a second copy of letters and the contract to prove Sidney and I are innocent of the assault on the king. They show the friars planned stealing pistols and money to blame us. Because Gironi is taken, I trust you to keep the papers. If something happens to me, you must show them to the Duke of Nevers or Scarpa or whomever you can." She shivered, whether at the thought of his capture or approaching such august men, he could not tell.

"I will do my best." She nestled in his arms.

When they arrived, Zaninno led them through a narrow *calle* to a house with crumbling exterior. An old woman with sagging jowls and breasts and bright red lips and cheeks opened the door for them with a leering, tooth-gapped smile that changed to a frown. Zaninno bid them a curt farewell and gave instructions to make their own way to the Half Moon in the morning. His posture said he had many more important things to do before the battle. The odors of sweat, urine, and sour wine grew as the worn-out harlot led them upstairs to a small chamber with no furnishings other than a large bed with no canopy and gray linen.

"Are we to stay here?" Hunter asked. "It is unseemly."

Caterina remonstrated with the hag, who laughed and shrugged. "This is all she can offer."

The woman closed the door and left before either could say more. They stared at one another. Caterina burst into tears. "No, no, no! No stay this place."

Hunter understood. This dirty room and its rancid fumes reinforced her fears of failure and deprivation. "Signora Filippa's house is not far from here. Let us appeal to her for a night's shelter."

Though Caterina's face remained clouded with doubt, she nodded. "We will try."

Zuan greeted them with a frown and signaled they were to wait on the ground floor. In a moment, Signora Filippa descended in a foul humor. She loosed a torrent of angry words on Caterina, who passed them on. "She have no space for me upstairs, she say. Fra Alberto come later for Leona. You fight with him before. She no want fight. No want trouble. She say we are trouble."

"Say we are content with anterooms or closets for the night. I desire only pen and paper and a pallet on the floor," Hunter said. He extracted a silver ducat from his purse and passed it to Caterina.

After another discussion, Signora Filippa relented.

"You stay down here with Zuan. He will find room. I share with Leona until friar will come. Write and keep out of the way, she say."

Zuan frowned, but led Hunter to a storeroom near the water entrance, with racks of wine on one side and a straw mattress and a stool on the other. This must be where Zuan stole a quick nap on slow days. He thanked the guard and sat, relieved for a moment before fears assailed him once more. If Signora Filippa knew of the bounty for his capture, he might be awakened in the night by the *sbirri*.

He had had little time to worry before Caterina appeared. "Signora say come to her chamber. Pen and ink and paper there."

Hunter was surprised, yet thankful Signora Filippa was an educated woman. With thanks to her, he sat in the anteroom and began to copy the contract. Caterina sat beside him, watching as he wrote. "Can you teach me?"

"To copy, yes," he said. "If we both survive and reach England. But to read and write will take a long time."

"I will work hard," she promised.

Hunter allowed himself a vision of a peaceful future at one of the Duke of Leicester's houses, sitting by this beautiful woman and teaching her to read. When he finished the contract, he sprinkled pounce over the fresh ink and shook it into a pot on the writing desk.

"Pray tell me what the papers say," Caterina asked.

Hunter went through each document explaining who had written and received each and what they said. When he finished showing her the contracts, she frowned and pointed. "This here. Their names. They are not on the copy."

True. If she were to show this, it would be dismissed as evidence without the signatures of Alberto and Giuseppe. The contract was the only signed document he had. "You are right." His mind raced. Rossi had given him a copy of a contract mentioning the delivery of his message to Biradi and the house rental. He must have done the same with Brother Alberto. Either he or Brother Giuseppe must have that copy, unless they burned it. A desperate plan occurred to him. "When will Brother Alberto come to Leona?"

"I will ask," Caterina said.

"Let me come with you."

Hunter was grateful Zuan and Signora Filippa were occupied elsewhere as he followed Caterina to Leona's chamber. There, he explained his plan to them. Leona at first objected, then, after Hunter gave her a *zecchino*, she smiled and laughed at his idea.

Lying under Leona's bed, Hunter rolled on his side to relieve his cramped shoulders. At least he was not bound tonight. He hoped no more bottles of wine would be needed than those they had removed from the storeroom. If Signora Filippa discovered him, he feared she would throw both him and Caterina into the street. A bell in a nearby *campanile* chimed midnight. He should not have long to wait. Above him, Caterina and Leona giggled like schoolgirls.

A knock at the door and a question from Signora Filippa. Leona answered, "*Sì.*" In a moment, Brother Alberto's voice sounded. Hunter followed the events. Alberto's surprise when Caterina spoke humbly and apologetically. His delight at finding he would enjoy the favors of two women. Leona's cooing from the antechamber as she and Caterina helped the friar out of his clothing. Her playful jesting as she suggested a game. After some questions and answers, the friar agreed. The moment of deception approached. Caterina sang a few teasing notes from one corner of the chamber; Leona, from the other. This was the agreed sign. Hunter carefully poked his head from under the bed. Brother Alberto, blindfolded, naked, and displaying an erection below his paunch, darted first one way then the other, following the voices in his attempts to seize one woman or the other. Hunter slid out and crept past the friar and into the antechamber. He shut the door. A search of the friar's garments revealed no papers. How foolish to think Brother Alberto might bring the contract with him. He had to take the next steps and brave it out.

Every muscle in Hunter's body tensed as the gondola slid next to the embankment at *Campo San Zanipolo*. Leona had promised to prolong her encounter with Brother Alberto, but could she combine flagellation, sucking, and coupling to occupy the friar so he did not discover his missing garments? Caterina was to participate in the beatings but had sworn to avoid the other activities. He hoped she would be able to keep her promise. At the door of the Dominican monastery, he knocked for admission. This was the moment he must act his best. He hoped his Latin was up to the test, and that he could pronounce it in the Italian manner.

"*Salve*," the porter said. "What is your business, brother?"

"I come from Vice Inquisitor Fascetti," Hunter claimed. "He has sent me to fetch documents from Brother Alberto's cell."

"Enter." The porter ushered him in, then paused. "Why has Brother Alberto not come himself?"

"The vice inquisitor has need of him this night." Hunter hoped he sounded convincing.

"What is your name and monastery?"

Hunter had prepared for this question, choosing a city far enough away. "Brother Paul of Santa Maria Novella in Florence." That should keep the porter from speaking Venetian. He prayed he could not ask questions in Florentine Italian.

"Has the vice inquisitor given you a letter?" the porter asked, continuing in Latin.

"No. If I must return for one, you shall taste his wrath as well as Brother Alberto's."

The porter dropped his air of authority. Evidently he knew the vice inquisitor well enough to wish to avoid his anger. "This way."

Hunter followed him upstairs and down a hall, where the porter opened a door. "Will you be long?"

"As long as it takes to locate the papers. You need not stay." Hunter feared the porter might offer to help, and every minute would increase the chance he might speak Italian.

The porter lit a candle before leaving. Hunter was disappointed to see an empty desk but spotted a bulging satchel next to it. He extracted the papers and flipped through them. Licenses to preach in certain dioceses, introductions to Dominican monasteries, letters of recommendation. Yes! Finally, he held the contract in his hand. The friar had not destroyed it. God knew why, but he gave Him thanks. He folded it, pushed it into the doublet he wore beneath Brother Alberto's robes, and snuffed out the candle. Now to return to the brothel before its owner missed his apparel.

"Did you find it?" the porter asked.

"I did," Hunter replied. "the vice inquisitor will be pleased."

"Very well," the porter replied.

Hunter reeled with relief as he walked back to the waiting gondola.

Hunter left the friar's robes in the antechamber. He heard snoring from the room beyond and slowly opened the door. The friar lay with his limbs entwined with those of Leona, who stared impatiently at the ceiling.

Caterina rose, adjusted her clothing, and walked quietly to him. "Is Signora Filippa in her chamber?"

"Both she and Zuan," Hunter whispered.

"Did you get the contract?"

"Yes." Hunter handed her the copy. "Where can you sleep now?"

"Julietta said I may rest in her anteroom," Caterina said.

"I must to the storeroom," Hunter said.

"I think as I lie in bed. You can fall in the water in the battle tomorrow. Do you have a case to keep the papers safe?"

Hunter realized Caterina had thought further ahead than he. "No."

"I know were madam keeps her candles," Caterina said. "You can drop wax on cloth and wrap and seal the papers."

"Caterina, you are a worthy woman. I will do as you suggest. Pray help me find both candles and cloth."

Hunter spent several hours of the night dripping candles onto a length of linen and smoothing the warm wax into it. Finally, he wrapped the cloth around the documents and sealed them in with more wax. Ready to face the morning, and exhausted, he lay on the mattress and fell asleep.

Monday, 26 July 1574, Venice

"I do not know why Rossi does not turn you in for the reward," Simmons said.

He and Hunter stood in their assigned places in Alvise's squadron on the crowded embankment after marching into place with trumpets and drums. They faced the battle bridge and the *Palazzo Foscarini*. Both wore dark blue tunics, chain mail, gloves, and helmets provided by Rossi, and carried arm-long canes cut from the reeds of the lagoon. To their right, partisans stomped on makeshift stands chanting "Ni-co-lot-ti! Ni-co-lot-ti!" Spectators sat and stood on balconies and rooftops. To their left, across the canal, the bands of Castellani massed in front of the Carmini church and called insults as their supporters chanted. The canal was full of gondolas, all moored at a respectful distance from the bridge so as not to impale falling combatants.

"He wants me alive long enough to present my evidence against the friars responsible for the murder of his men." Hunter gave Simmons a retaliatory look. "He keeps you alive for the same reason."

"Rossi made that clear to me," Simmons said.

"He needs both your words and my documents," Hunter said. Those that Caterina had tucked into her bodice would also serve, but he had sworn her to secrecy unless something happened to him. "I wish we had news of Sidney."

"As they say here, 'Nessuna nuova buona nuova'."

"I noticed you spoke only English when we were in prison."

"I had no time for ornate rhetoric then."

Those around them began a scurrilous song insulting the fighting skill and manhood of the Castellani. The Castellani across the canal made rude gestures in return. When the noise died down, Simmons spoke again. "Though I may forfeit my life for supplying those pistols, Rossi promised he would petition for clemency."

Hunter made no comment on the value of Rossi's promises. "Quite the stakes to wager."

Simmons took a deep breath and blew it out. "If I do not confess my part to the authorities, I face certain death from either Rossi or Biradi."

"Biradi?"

"Though Rossi holds him captive, they both desire revenge on the vice inquisitor for the loss of their men," Simmons explained. "If I do not swear to Inquisitor Fascetti's deeds, both have sworn to hunt me down."

"I thought Rossi had killed Biradi's men."

"No. He only holds them until he is paid the ransom."

"A strange partnership," Hunter said. "Did Rossi say anything about Captain Scarpa?"

"No."

"His word would help our case."

"Pray tell again how you plan to reach your duke?"

Hunter opened his mouth to speak but a roar arose from all sides. Above, King Henry III of France strutted onto the balcony of the *Palazzo Foscarini*, flanked by French and Venetian noblemen. Hunter recognized the narrow face, the thin mustache, and the small beard under the lower lip. The king had changed little in two years. Hunter spotted the Duke of Nevers and his spirits rose. The man who might save him was within reach. The cheering continued for some time as the king nodded to the crowds. Finally, he held up his hand for silence. All eyes turned to the *piazza del ponte*, the crown of the bridge that was the goal both sides hoped to occupy. Rossi, as one of the *padrini*, or godfathers, and his opposite number from the Castellani, strode to the center of the bridge and gave short speeches praising the king, then each introduced one fighter, a champion from the Nicolotti fishermen and another from the Arsenal workers of the Castellani, to engage in one-on-one combat to show His Majesty the skill of Venetians.

Both sides of the canal, as well as the spectators standing in gondolas, erupted into shouts, encouragement, and insults in equal measure. The fisherman drew first blood from his rival, and the *padrini* called a halt and declared him a winner. Taunting whistles from the Nicolotti deafened Hunter.

During a short diminution of sound, Hunter reminded Simmons they should wait until six of the twelve scheduled individual matches had been fought before they struggled their way through the crowd to the courtyard of the *Palazzo Foscarini*, the area designated for care of the Nicolotti weary and wounded. That would be before the *frotta*, or general *mêlée*, began. Depending on whether Frenchmen or Italians were on guard there, either he or Simmons would appeal to speak with the Duke of Nevers.

Another two-person match began, amid resumed shouting. An *arsenalotto* won the second match for the Castellani, and the mocking whistles flew across from their side of the canal. Another *padrone* took Rossi's spot and three more man-to-man combats took place, ending with a one-match advantage to the Nicolotti.

"Only one more match to go," Hunter whispered.

"Let us begin to make our way now," Simmons urged.

The suggestion made sense. Both men turned from the canal and began to push their way toward the palazzo. Some act on the bridge, unseen by either, caused those around them to roar with anger. They surged forward, carrying Hunter and Simmons toward the bridge. Hunter turned away from the bridge but could make no headway against the human tide. Two men he faced snarled at him, no doubt an accusation of his cowardice, grasped him roughly, and turned him toward the bridge. At its apex, men slashed and flailed with their canes. The pressure of those behind brought the foremost face-to-face to match their strength trying to push one another off the span.

Hunter felt himself carried inexorably along the *fondamenta*. The few moments his fellow Nicolotti had spent giving him lessons on thrusting and slashing would be of no avail in this mass. Neither would his skill at fencing. He had reckoned to be out of his squadron before any skirmish began, but he was powerless against the pressure. He lost sight of Simmons. If he could work his way to the edge of the throng, he might jump into the canal and pull himself back along the embankment. As he tried, a press of screaming Nicolotti cut him off and compelled him to turn. The pressure of the zealous throng forced his steps higher up the arch. He fought panic, telling himself he could bear any stroke he received. Two men on his left lost their footing on the edge of the bridge, grasped those next to them, and, with a howl that rose above the *mêlée*, all four tumbled into the canal, leaving an opening. Hunter darted into the space, glanced down the canal, and saw the thin form of Captain Scarpa standing in the fourth gondola from the bridge. Thank God he had arrived. He raised the cane in his hand to signal the captain. A surge behind him pushed him to the edge. He teetered there a moment before a fierce forearm blow to his back sent him headlong into the canal.

The dark water closed around him, blocking the screams of those above. He sank until his hands were buried in the ooze. He waited to rise, but his helmet and mail weighed him down. How deep was this canal? Mixed with growing terror came an awareness of irony. He was floundering in a Venetian canal for the third time, with the clothing supposed to keep him from harm now threatening to drown him. He fumbled at his helmet and his face pressed into the mud.

CHAPTER 28

Striving toward Shore

ON HUNTER'S THIRD ATTEMPT, HE UNFASTENED THE CHIN STRAP OF HIS helmet and pushed his face and shoulders from the canal bottom, but his legs slipped in the muck when he tried to stand. Kneeling in mud, he was still underwater. His lungs screamed for air. He reached an arm over his head and felt his fingertips break the surface. He made another effort to stand, but again the slime defeated him.

A staff struck him in the back and sharp metal gouged his shoulder near the wound he had suffered in Yorkshire. Was a Castellano trying to push him under? Panic gripped him. Then he felt himself being hoisted. His head surfaced and he gulped in air. As he dangled at the end of a boat hook, two laughing men leaned from the side of a gondola, grabbed him under his arms, and pulled him into the boat. He sat for a time gasping, as one of the men wiped the ooze from his face and hands, chattering all the while.

"*Grazie, grazie,*" Hunter kept repeating. Slowly, he became aware of his surroundings. Shouts and splashes sounded from the bridge. The man on the prow of the gondola was fishing other fallen fighters out with his boat hook. Scarpa! He had seen the captain just before he fell. He stood in the gondola and looked to where he had seen Scarpa, but witnessed instead groups of men leaping from gondola to gondola, threatening one another with knives. The crowds on both sides of the canal berated them. What had happened to Scarpa? The gondola tilted under his feet. Its crew was pulling another drenched combatant from the canal. The man who had cleaned him pointed toward the embankment. He was right.

277

It was time for Hunter to get off and make his way toward the *Palazzo Foscarini*. He clambered from boat to boat over the tightly packed gondolas, steadied by those in each craft. When he reached the embankment, two Nicolotti helped him up. Another squadron surrounded him, this one less tightly packed than Alvise's. At his foot, a fighter pried a small paving stone loose and hurled it at the squabbling men jumping from boat to boat. Roof tiles and curses rained down on them. The mock battle was turning into a riot.

Hunter took stock. He was drenched in foul-smelling canal water, traces of mud still clinging to his doublet and venetians. He had lost track of Simmons and failed to make contact with Scarpa. Despite the probability of being turned away or arrested, he must try to reach Nevers and clear Sidney and Bryskett. He could only hope the Ten had not found time to condemn them.

He began to push his way through the Nicolotti squadron, then joined others, most dripping with canal water and blood, who shuffled into the courtyard of the palazzo. Companions crowded around each one entering, asking their condition. Men squatted or lay about the courtyard as wives and mothers cleaned and dressed their wounds. Hunter spotted Caterina, waiting here as arranged. She smiled and started toward him. From another corner, Simmons also walked toward him. Their eyes met in an awkward moment of recognition.

Hunter remembered Simmons was the client who had rejected Caterina. In order to save their feelings at this juncture, he introduced them as though they had never met. "This is Caterina, who has helped our cause. Caterina, this is Doctor Nicholas Simmons, who will come with me to speak for Signor Sidney."

"*Multe grassie*," she said, then asked Hunter, "Are you hurt?"

"No. Only wet."

Simmons nodded to Caterina, then addressed Hunter. "I feared you would not escape. Is she to come, too?"

"No." Hunter did not explain. "Pray help me shed this tunic and shirt of mail." Together, Caterina and Simmons pulled the tunic and linked armor over his head. "My thanks to you both. Caterina, pray wait here." His eyes told her she must keep the copied papers safe. She wiped slime from behind his left ear and his right cuff and retired as requested.

"I have wandered past the guards," Simmons said. "There are four: one each from France, Savoy, Ferrara, and Venice."

So, the dukes of Ferrara and Savoy were watching with the king, as well as Venetian officials. Might the Venetians there be members of the Doge's Council, perhaps members of the Ten? Hunter straightened his apparel, the doublet and venetian breeches he had brought from Padua for this meeting, now soiled with muck and canal water. Simmons at his side, he advanced to the guards at the palazzo entrance and addressed the French guard. "I pray that my companion and I may be granted an audience with His Grace the Duke of Nevers."

The Savoyard guard on his right stifled a laugh, then regained his stern expression. The French guard asked, "Who are you, that you should ask access to His Grace?"

"Edward Hunter, an Englishman who was his guest in Paris."

The guard raised his eyebrows, doubting such a drowned rat could be telling the truth. "We have orders to admit no one. Move away."

Why had he thought he would be allowed to approach anyone in the royal party? His escape from the *sbirri* and from prison, his shameful disguises, his burial by fish, his ride to Padua and back—all had been for naught.

"Are you deaf?" the French guard said. "Move away." He nodded to the Savoyard beside him, and they grasped Hunter by the arms.

Behind the guards, another man advanced. Hunter's heart leapt with joy. "Captain Ducasse!" he called. "We met in the English Embassy in Paris."

Captain Ducasse drew closer and peered into Hunter's face. "Yes. I remember."

"I and my companion are here to right an injustice," Hunter claimed, struggling against the guards' hold. "Messieurs Sidney and Bryskett, who were also at the embassy, are falsely accused of the assault on His Majesty. I beg that we may present our evidence to His Grace, that they may be cleared of that false charge."

Ducasse pondered a moment. "Release him for the nonce. I shall speak with His Grace. Wait here."

The guards complied, glaring at Hunter. Heart beating, he whispered an aside to Simmons. "Do you speak French?"

"Late to ask, but I do. I can plead Sidney's case and seal my own fate in English, French, Italian, or Latin."

"I pray your testimony will gain you a pardon," Hunter said.

They waited in silent impatience until Captain Ducasse returned. "His Grace will see you." Hunter sighed with relief. He and Simmons followed the captain up two flights of stairs to the level on which the king and his guests watched the mock battle. Shouting filtered through the balcony to the anteroom where Ducasse signaled they should wait.

After a minute, the Duke of Nevers hobbled toward them with his wounded, uneven gait. Hunter and Simmons bowed a knee to him. "I am surprised to see you here in Venice," the duke said, "and among an army of working men. Pray what is your story, Monsieur Hunter."

Hunter explained his presence in Italy, the false arrest of Sidney and Bryskett, his own peril, his presence among the Nicolotti as a method of approaching the duke, and his accusation of the vice inquisitor. He introduced Simmons as a witness to the deceit practiced by the Dominican friars.

Nevers nodded. "You make serious charges against others. Because I knew you in Paris does not mean you are telling the truth. Before Doctor Simmons proceeds, I believe it will be fair to summon the men he will accuse, so that they may defend themselves." He spoke to Ducasse while Hunter and Simmons exchanged worried glances. Neither had seen clergy near the king.

Ducasse returned, followed by the Dominicans. The Vice Inquisitor Fascetti frowned, Brother Alberto stared at Hunter with icy anger, and Brother Giuseppe's eyes darted anxiously from Simmons to the vice inquisitor.

"Doctor Simmons," Nevers began, "your friend says you can testify as to the plan to assault His Majesty."

Simmons seemed to wither before the baleful stare of the vice inquisitor, but he cleared his throat, swallowed, and began. "Your Grace, these two friars came to me in Padua and delivered a letter from the vice inquisitor asking me to engage a thief to steal pistols and English coins from Messieurs Sidney and Hunter. The man who committed the theft was murdered this morning. I was to deliver the pistols to the said friars in Venice. I understand those pistols and the money were found on the ruffians who assaulted His Majesty and the Duke of Ferrara a few nights ago."

Fascetti sniffed and said, "I have never seen this man before."

Rustling and indistinct speech alerted Hunter to others approaching from the balcony. Two Venetian senators in fur-trimmed red robes entered, the elder bald-headed with a long white beard and sallow cheeks, the younger with a dark beard and long hair covering his ears. A portly cleric followed, then noblemen clad in velvet suits with cloth of gold capes.

Hunter guessed these were the Dukes of Ferrara and Savoy. Finally, in mourning black, King Henry III of France. Hunter and Simmons fell to their knees.

"Rise, rise," the king said. "As there is a lull in the battle while peace is restored below, let us all hear what is said about the attempt on Duke Alfonso and myself."

With a shaking voice, Simmons repeated his story. When he finished, King Henry said, "These are grave accusations." He turned to the vice inquisitor, inviting his response.

"Your Majesty, these Englishmen seek to save themselves and their friends by accusing others. I am sure you recognize this as a ruse criminals often employ. The English have for centuries been enemies of the French. Now they are also a nation of many heretics. These men and their friend Sidney are part of a conspiracy to aid French Protestants and cause turmoil in Your Majesty's kingdom by slaying, God forbid, Your Most Christian Majesty. They persuaded their countryman to make a show of theft so as to distance themselves from this heinous act. Now they devise lies, as heretics will, to attack the Holy Mother Church." Brother Alberto wore the smirk he had shown at the Lido; Brother Giuseppe wore a nervous, unconvincing smile beneath frightened eyes. Fascetti addressed the Venetian senators. "I advise you to seize these two and bring them quickly to trial along with their companions already in your custody."

Two French guards stepped toward Hunter but paused to look at the king. Rather than signaling an arrest, he regarded Hunter with raised eyebrows, inviting his response.

Hunter recognized the vice inquisitor's rhetorical tricks. Flattering the king, he played upon French prejudices against the English and fears of the Huguenots, who raised armies against the king's authority. Hunter had seen cases argued before Queen's Bench in Westminster Hall, but he had never pleaded a case himself in any court. Now he must argue for his life and that of his friends against an experienced opponent. "Your Majesty, I thank you for judging this case."

The king raised his hand and turned to the Venetian senators. "I have no authority here, except by your leave."

The older senator spoke. "Though this matter is to come before us this evening, as it concerns Your Majesty most directly, we would welcome your judgment."

"I had not mentioned this before, Senator Malpiero, as I thought these English lies would be dismissed," Fascetti broke in, "but secular authorities have no jurisdiction over clergy."

The senator shot him a cold look, "That may be true of petty crimes, but am certain the Ten does not view attempted murder of a king in that category. You may appeal to them."

Senator Malpiero must be a member of the Council of Ten. Hunter's mouth was dry. If he could convince King Henry, he could likely effect the release of Sidney, Bryskett, Gironi, and any others of the Padua household who were imprisoned. "Your Majesty, I have proof of what Doctor Simmons has said." He began to unbutton his doublet. "I have here evidence. Copies of the letters sent to him, a contract to hire those who threatened you, and a message from the captain of Padua as to the truth of the theft there." He pulled the wrapped and sealed documents from his doublet. The smirk on Brother Alberto's face changed to a worried frown. Brother Giuseppe bit his lip. The vice inquisitor remained impassive. Hunter held the dripping packet in his left hand and reached for his bread knife. A tensing of everyone caused him to stop. He breathed a prayer of thanks, saying, "I dare not bare a weapon in the presence of Your Majesty, but I pray you command one of your servants to break the seal on this packet."

The king nodded to Nevers, who nodded to Captain Ducasse. He ran a knife along the line of wax on the packet and extracted the papers inside. Hunter gasped in dismay. Water dripped from the papers. The document facing him had only a few legible lines, then the ink ran into a meaningless blur.

CHAPTER 29

Crosscurrents

BROTHER ALBERTO BLURTED OUT A LOUD LAUGH, THEN IMMEDIATELY muted himself under the vice inquisitor's icy glance.

Ducasse handed the wet documents to Hunter along with the sodden missal. He pried the pages apart. Each was the same, a blur of illegible ink. Had he not sealed them well? Had they broken in his fall, his hoisting, the shedding of his mail coat? Scarpa's sealed letter fell from the set of papers. Could its contents still be readable. He handed it to Ducasse, who broke the seal and handed it back. Scarpa's words were as damp and smudged as the rest. He looked up at severe faces.

Simmons burst out. "Your Majesty, I am no heretic, but a loyal Catholic. As God as my witness, I acted in good faith on the instructions of Vice Inquisitor Fascetti. Though his letter is ruined, I pray you believe me."

"Your Majesty, these are empty words—desperate lies without evidence to back them," the vice inquisitor said.

Hunter regained self-control. "Your Majesty, I had feared an accident such as this. If you will order a man into the courtyard, he will find there a radiant young woman with golden hair who holds copies of the documents. I pray she may be fetched here, that I may present my evidence."

"Another irregular English trick..." the vice inquisitor began.

The king raised his hand to stop Fascetti, then smiled. "A radiant girl, you say? Let us see this fair creature." He turned to Hunter and his face changed from leering satyr to stern judge. "I hope her evidence proves more sound than yours."

Ducasse left. The vice inquisitor turned to the Venetian cleric and spoke in Italian. Who was he? A papal legate? The Venetian inquisitor? The senators muttered to one another. Simmons dared a whisper. "You did not tell me the woman kept papers as well."

"I hoped we would not need them," Hunter replied.

"Our lives depend on your defense," Simmons said. "I pray you have the skill to speak eloquently."

Ducasse returned, followed by Caterina and Captain Scarpa. Hunter allowed himself a moment of hope at the sight of the captain, as both fell to their knees before the king.

"Rise, both of you," he said.

They stood uncertainly, unsure of his French words but responding to his gestures.

The king smiled at Caterina and raised his eyebrows questioningly at Scarpa.

"*Gregorio Scarpa, capitano di Padova,*" he said.

"Pray give me the papers you have," Hunter asked in English.

Caterina looked uncertainly at the men around her.

"*Sì. Sì. I documenti,*" Senator Malpiero urged.

Blushing, Caterina reached down her bodice and pulled out folded papers. The king allowed himself a lecherous chuckle. At a signal from the senator, she handed them to Hunter.

He took deep breaths to calm himself as he ordered the documents. He must not fumble with shaking hands and drop them. Neither must he fumble his words.

He nodded to those before him, to include all. "Your Most Christian Majesty, Your Graces, your reverences, honorable sirs." He hoped he had used the correct respectful forms of address and spoken them in the right order of precedence. "I pray your indulgence and patience as I present each piece of evidence here. The first letter was sent to Master Ambrose Barnes, an English scholar in Padua and a Catholic, who was murdered in Venice May twenty-eighth. In it, the writer admits to approving the murder of four subjects of the Republic of Venice and encouraging Barnes to use Master Philip Sidney, a gentleman on whom Your Majesty's late brother bestowed the title of baron, to cause enmity between Venice and England. The original was written in cipher, but I provide deciphered copies in Latin and English."

Uncertain of the propriety of handing the papers directly to the king, Hunter passed them to Nevers. The vice inquisitor, looking over his shoulder, said, "This letter has no signature, nor salutation, nor date. It does not mention Sidney. It may have been written by anyone at any time. Its decipherment may be false." He turned to the senators. "Surely, such a document would be dismissed by the Council of Ten."

They nodded their agreement.

"My Lords," Hunter said. "Those things the letter lacks argue it is authentic. If one were to forge a document, he would include details to point positively to its writer, but a careful author engaged in a plot would not only encipher the contents, but he would speak subtly and not sign a message which might later prove his guilt. I invite Your Majesty to have another decipher it. I can provide him with a key."

The frown on the face of the vice inquisitor and the puzzled looks of his other auditors showed Hunter he had planted a seed of doubt in their minds. He continued. "The second document was given to Doctor Simmons by these two friars only a few weeks ago, as he can attest." He gestured toward Simmons, who nodded. "This letter was likewise enciphered but solved by Doctor Simmons using that sodden missal provided by the brothers. It clearly asks him to hire a thief to obtain the pistols and English coins that were found on the hired ruffians who assaulted your sacred person." Hunter handed the second letter to Nevers, who had handed the first to the king.

"Can you name this thief?" the king asked Simmons.

"Charles Carr, Your Majesty. The man who was strangled this morning."

Captain Scarpa raised his eyebrows in recognition of the name and the king gave him an enquiring look. He stuttered a few sentences, and the younger senator said, "The captain knows this man—an Englishman who consorted with low-born gamblers and miscreants."

The vice inquisitor gave a snort, but otherwise remained silent. Hunter judged that any objection he might make concerning the letter would echo those he made earlier, to less effect, as the recipient stood before him and the missal used to decipher it was at hand.

"The next is a letter from Captain Scarpa. You can examine his seal on the original, which was spoiled in the canal, and he is here to swear the contents of his message are correct. He states the circumstances of the theft of the pistols and money."

Senator Malpiero interrupted to ask Scarpa to confirm what he had written. Hunter caught the Italian words for fire, theft, and pistols. The senator related Scarpa's testimony into French for the king, who nodded sagely. The vice inquisitor's eyes shifted. He evidently decided not to contradict an agent of the Republic.

Hunter presented his last document, the contract between the Dominican brothers and Rossi. "Finally, an original contract between these friars and a Venetian, one of the organizers of this mock battle, whom you may have seen on the bridge—a contract to hire two men, those who dared assault Your Majesty and His Grace the Duke of Ferrara. You may clearly see the signatures of both brothers at the bottom, and a date at the top."

The vice inquisitor spoke up. "Pardon, Your Majesty, but this Englishman cannot prove that the men hired were the same ones who were evil enough to attack Your Majesty's sacred person."

Hunter was ready. "Master Rossi can, if he is called before the Ten." He pressed on. "Each of these documents tells the story of a plot, not by Englishmen, but by these clerics, to cast blame on honest men and sow discord between Your Majesty's kingdom and Her Majesty, Queen Elizabeth, between this Most Serene Republic and Our Queen, all by risking Your Majesty's life."

King Henry took a deep breath and regarded the Dominican friars sternly. He pointed to Simmons. "Did you meet with this man, as he claims?"

"We did meet him once, to warn him to beware the wrath of criminals," Brother Alberto said.

"Sì, sì." Brother Giuseppe nodded eagerly.

"That is true," Simmons said, "but not only that once. They came again, the time I spoke of, with the letter."

"Do you deny this second meeting?" the king asked.

Brother Alberto's eyes were those of a cornered beast searching for an exit. "No, but he cannot prove Brother Fascetti wrote it."

"We shall come to that." The king held up the contract. "Are these your signatures?"

Brother Alberto was not finished yet. "This document was provided by a Venetian dealer in second-hand clothing, a man of dubious reputation."

The king pulled back his shoulders and cast a harsh expression at the friar. "That does not answer my question. Is this your signature?"

Brother Alberto hung his head. "Yes, Your Majesty."

Brother Giuseppe nodded as well.

"And you paid the amount specified in this contract?"

"Yes, Your Majesty." Brother Alberto's voice grew faint. "I hope you might hold the man who agreed to supply the assailants as guilty as those who paid for them."

"That is for the Ten to decide," the king said. He turned toward the vice inquisitor. "Do you deny you wrote these letters in cipher?"

Vice Inquisitor Fascetti maintained his imperious bearing, though with difficulty. "I beg patience of Your Majesty. I would have to examine them closely, as well as any alleged solution to the cipher."

"Did you instruct these brothers to deliver letters you wrote to both Simmons and the other Englishman?"

The vice inquisitor glanced down at the back of his hands. He could not lie to a king. "Yes."

Brother Giuseppe fell to his knees, shaking. "Your Majesty, I beg for mercy. Brother Alberto and I followed the orders of our superior, both as messengers and when we conveyed the pistols. I beg you spare us." He began to weep. "May God forgive me. I pray He may forgive me my sin of this morning."

Everyone around him, except the vice inquisitor and Brother Alberto, drew in breath. Simmons bowed his head into his hands and muttered, "No, no."

Surprise on the king's face hardened into anger. "Are you confessing to the murder of this Carr?"

Brother Giuseppe nodded and continued to sob.

King Henry turned to the vice inquisitor. "Did you order this killing?"

"I only stated that the man had served his purpose," Fascetti said.

Giuseppe raised his head in shock. "No, no. You said, 'He could ruin everything if he tells what he knows. Would that his words are choked off before he speaks and does great damage to the Holy Mother Church.'"

The vice inquisitor began boldly, but his voice cracked before he finished. "Those words were not an order."

"Then you admit saying them?" the king asked.

Fascetti lowered his head and gave the faintest of nods.

"I must again refer your cases to the Council of Ten." The king handed the documents to the younger Venetian senator. "The friar's confession speaks for itself. As for the other two, the evidence presented here casts doubt on the guilt of the Englishmen and indicts these *reverend* brothers." His final words carried weighty irony.

Loud cheers announced renewed fighting on the bridge. King Henry turned as though his role of judge was finished. Nevers, Ferrara, and Savoy looked at one another, and all turned toward the two members of the Council of Ten.

Senator Malpiero waved the noblemen back to the balcony and signaled the Venetian guards, who marched forward to take charge of the Dominican brothers. Vice Inquisitor Fascetti maintained his dignity; Brother Giuseppe continued to blubber as the guards pulled him to his feet; Brother Alberto fixed Hunter with a stare of cold hatred. The Venetian cleric, whoever he was, turned his back on them and resumed his place on the balcony. After the guards marched the friars down the stairs, the white-bearded senator spoke to Scarpa in Italian, who exchanged looks of apprehension with Caterina. The younger senator stepped toward them and Simmons, and guards followed all three down the staircase. Malpiero turned and addressed Hunter in English. "You must come with me."

"You can speak English?" Hunter said, astonished.

"I accompanied an ambassador to your land at the time of King Henry," the senator said, "but we have no time now. The Ten may be starting your colleagues' trial."

"Then let us go. Where have Captain Scarpa and the girl gone?"

"They go before us to speak to the Ten. I pray you, allow a guard to bind your hands. You are still a wanted man in Venice. If you walk free, explaining may delay us. The guards at the Doge's Palace will let us pass if you are bound."

Hunter's shoulders tightened. He had evaded arrest since Gironi had freed him. Was this a cunning trick, such as Italians were rumored to employ, designed to secure him without a fight? He looked deep into the old man's eyes but could detect no guile. "I shall."

The guard tied his hands behind him, removed his bread knife and purse, and they proceeded to the courtyard. The two halberdiers who fell into step behind them, and the worried glances they received from those in the courtyard did little to dampen Hunter's fears. Malpiero led them through the *Campo Santa Margherita* to a canal where two gondolas waited. As they pushed off, Hunter prayed that he was truly going to free his friends, not walking into his own capital trial.

At the entrance to the Doge's Palace, Senator Malpiero spoke with a guard and turned to Hunter with open mouth and raised eyebrows. "Quickly, we must climb to the tiles. Your servant is in the *strappado* chamber." He spoke to the younger senator. "*Enrico, porta gli altri nella Sala della Bussola.*"

Hunter's heart pounded as they dashed across the courtyard and up a narrow staircase, both from the rapid ascent and from fear that Gironi was suffering severe pain on his account. "Why will they torture him?" he asked as they climbed. He immediately regretted as the senator paused to catch his breath before answering,

"They will ask him where to find you," Malpiero gasped.

"Then we must show them I am found."

They continued their climb, then wove their way through a series of rooms, Malpeiro signaling guards to let them pass. Ahead, a cry of agony shot through the air. In a moment, they entered the *strappado* chamber. Gironi stood on tiptoe atop a set of stairs, his arms stretched grotesquely behind his back, bearing almost his full weight. The rope from his bound arms rose past a balcony full of observers to an opening high above.

Senator Malpiero shouted a command, and the guard pulling the rope released it slowly.

Gironi groaned as his arms resumed their normal position. He spotted Hunter and forced an ironic smile. "Good timing."

The senator spoke at length with the guards and one man on the balcony, who must have been the attending physician. The guard who had been hoisting Gironi secured the rope and untied his hands with apparent regret.

"Have you been tortured?" Hunter asked.

"No more than you saw." Gironi flexed his shoulders back and forth and grimaced. "They were about to begin in earnest."

"Thank God."

"I thank Him indeed. But now it appears you are captive as well."

Hunter hesitated to say his bound hands were only for show, as he was not sure himself. "Senator Malpiero has brought me to testify to the guilt of the vice inquisitor and the Dominican brothers."

"Then you reached the duke."

"Not only him, but King Henry."

"Good. Now you move in exalted circles." Gironi rubbed his wrists.

The official torturer snarled at the Englishmen.

"He warns that prisoners are not to speak to one another," Senator Malpiero warned. "I must to the Ten." He dashed down a staircase.

Hunter and Gironi closed their mouths, aware again of their position. Guards herded them down in silence, one before and one after the prisoners. At the bottom of the stairs, one untied Hunter's hands. "*Sala della Bussola,*" said another, pointing to a door in a wooden screen that extended into the corner of a larger room. They stepped through into that room, richly decorated with leather wall hangings and tapestries and a gilded ceiling that framed one large and several small paintings. Near a marble fireplace, Simmons stood with two men in rumpled, soiled clothes. "Philip! Lodowick!" Hunter exclaimed, bounding forward. He wrapped his arms around his friends.

"Simmons told us of your defense before King Henry," Sidney began. "And explained your part in the battle. Thank you for all you have done to clear us of false charges. Pray forgive my unkind words at our last meeting. You were right that I should beware and that one baleful glance did portend danger."

"It is I who should beg your pardon," Hunter said. "When I heard you were arrested, I feared my last words to you would be those I spoke in anger." They embraced again. "I hope Senator Malpiero is presenting the evidence to clear you. I regret I did not arrive sooner. As for me, I was clearing myself as well. Have you appeared before the Ten?"

"We have," Sidney said. "After some fumbling Latin, Lodowick served as translator with Italian."

"When they heard me and recognized my Genoese origins," Bryskett said, "they grew more dubious of our denials. Our fate looked dark."

"But, thank God, they must not have condemned you. You are here," Hunter said.

"As they questioned us, a senator arrived with documents, and we were ordered back to this room," Bryskett said.

"If we are cleared, we must be grateful to Doctor Simmons," Hunter said. "Had he not told me of the letter from the vice inquisitor and his own role, my defense would have lacked evidence."

Simmons interrupted. "Perhaps you should thank the vice inquisitor himself. Had he not betrayed me after I did his bidding, I would not have been imprisoned with Hunter." He shook his head. "Such irony. I regret

I ever trusted him. If I had not, Carr would still be alive. If the Ten condemn me, it will be a just sentence."

"I shall refrain from thanking Brother Fascetti," Sidney said. "It is he, rather than you, who should be condemned."

"They must first rule we are innocent," Hunter said.

"Caterina and Captain Scarpa went before the Ten as we left," Bryskett said. "Their statements should help."

"I pray they will. How have you both been treated?"

"Respectfully up in 'the leads'," Sidney said, "and the food was tolerable. Lodowick did not complain of his treatment in the prison below, though I am sure conditions were worse."

"The food was simple, but not rotten, and the cell damp," Bryskett said. "I long to change my apparel."

"The worst was the waiting, not knowing when we might be hauled from a cell to face questions," Sidney said. "We were fortunate that the Doge and *Signoria* have been obliged to wait upon His Majesty."

"We all were," Hunter said. "It allowed us time to ride to Padua, gather documents, and speak to Captain Scarpa."

"If God allows us to be released," Sidney said, "I hope to see the letter to Barnes that inspired him to seek revenge on me."

"It seems you know all of the story of our discoveries," Hunter said.

The anteroom door opened, and a guard summoned Hunter and Gironi. Hunter's heart raced at being called before the most feared tribunal in Venice. Despite the evidence, a death sentence from the Ten could not be appealed. He followed the guard into the large room. Above him gods and goddesses sat and flew in gilded ceiling frames. Before him on a rounded dais sat, despite the council's name, fifteen red-robed magistrates, including Doge Alvise Mocenigo, all stern-faced. He was heartened to see among them the two senators who had heard his defense.

Senator Malpiero spoke. Hunter heard his name and understood the senator was describing the pieces of evidence he had gathered. When Malpiero finished, a magistrate with a short gray beard and piercing eyes, who sat next to the doge, stood to begin his interrogation. Malpiero served as interpreter.

"How long have you been in Venetian territory, Master Hunter?"

"Since April twenty-second, just over three months."

"Are you aware of our laws concerning weapons?"

"Yes, my lord. Though my servant and I carried weapons to defend ourselves on the long journey from England, we stored them at our lodgings in Padua and did not bear them."

"How were the letters we have seen obtained?"

"One enciphered letter lay on the floor of Master Barnes's lodgings in Venice after it had been ransacked and Master Barnes killed. The other I gathered from Doctor Simmons's house, with his permission."

"How were they deciphered?"

Hunter described his method, and that of Simmons.

The prosecutor, or so he seemed to Hunter, held up the letters and their deciphered copies. "So these are copies written by you?"

"Yes, my lord. The originals became wet. The ink ran and became illegible."

"How did that happen?"

Hunter felt himself flush. "I fell into the canal during the *battigli-ala* today."

A few of the Ten allowed themselves a chuckle.

"Do you swear that you did not compose these letters yourself ?"

"I do. You may ask the vice inquisitor to confirm the contents and the manner of enciphering."

"We shall." The prosecutor held up the contract. "How did you obtain this document?"

Hunter hesitated. The contract the speaker held was not the one Rossi had given him. Hunter might say it was and keep his theft secret. However, if he lied, he might be discovered and his entire testimony thrown into doubt. "I took that contract from Brother Alberto's cell at the Convent of Saints John and Paul."

"You admit to the theft of this document?"

"I do, my lord."

The judges talked among themselves. Hunter's sweat mingled with the canal moisture still in his clothing. The prosecutor turned back. "This contract does not specify assault, only hiring three men for one week's service. Do you allege that the friars who signed this intended to employ the men to attack His Majesty King Henry?"

"I do, but you must ask them their intent."

"We shall do so." The prosecutor sat, but another man stood, shorter and more rotund than the first. Perhaps all served as prosecutors and judges at the same time.

"When did you learn you were wanted?" the second judge asked.

"Shortly after the arrest of Masters Sidney and Bryskett."

"When you knew that, why did you not present yourself, if you were innocent?"

Hunter cleared his throat to give himself a moment to think. "I needed to gather evidence to prove the innocence of myself and my colleagues, rather than merely pleading."

The judges mumbled to one another. Hunter wished Malpiero would translate those words as well. The shorter magistrate referred to a document. "On the twenty-second of this month, you were captured and imprisoned by the *Signori di Notte* in Cannaregio. How did you escape?"

Hunter considered a lie—that a careless guard had left the cell door unlocked, or that one had accepted a bribe—but Simmons had already been questioned. He looked at Gironi, who gave a quick nod of permission. "My loyal servant, Master Luca Gironi, released me and Doctor Simmons."

The interrogator turned to Gironi and spoke in Venetian. His questioning continued for what seemed like half an hour to Hunter.

When the judges appeared finished, one of their number stood and spoke, gesturing to them. His tone was more conciliatory than accusatory. Was this the member of the Ten who was Rossi's friend? Hunter wished he could understand what the man was saying. When he finished, a third judge, thin and long-bearded, stood and directed a question at Hunter. Malpiero translated. "When and where have you had dealings with Vice Inquisitor Fascetti, Brother Alberto, or Brother Giuseppe?"

Hunter rapidly tallied each encounter with the Dominicans. "I first saw the vice inquisitor in the Romagna, on the day after we found Master Sidney bound and gagged, and his captors slain. I later learned from his letter that he had ordered the killing of those men. I glimpsed him at the Lido when His Majesty arrived. I did not see him again until today."

Whispered comments passed among the Ten.

"I saw the two friars on my first day in Venice, in Saint Mark's Square and later conducting a woman from *Campo San Cassiano*." Hunter saw his interrogator raise a hand to interrupt and anticipated his question. "That was in late April, the day before this worthy council granted Master Sidney and his party permission to carry arms." The judge nodded. Hunter took a deep breath. He hoped his next statement would not engender awkward questions. "I next saw Brother Alberto alone. He was naked, scourging a woman at Signora Filippa's house."

The babble among the Ten told Hunter this was new information about Brother Alberto's character. The standing judge shot him the inevitable question. "What were you doing at Signora Filippa's?"

No use lying. "I had come to visit the woman he was scourging, the woman Caterina whom you have questioned." He hoped this gained him another point for honesty. "I saw both brothers in early June entering the *Scuola di Sant'Orsola* and again with the vice inquisitor on the day His Majesty arrived. Our paths did not cross again until today."

His interrogator turned to Gironi and asked the same questions. He seemed satisfied with Gironi's answers and sat down. The members of the Council of Ten conferred among themselves. The doge spoke a command to the guards and Hunter and Gironi were ushered back into the *Sala della Bussola.*

Sidney grasped Hunter by his arms. "Pray tell us what they asked you." Hunter related his interrogation. Then Sidney turned to Gironi.

"I was asked mainly to corroborate what Hunter said." Gironi sighed. "Strangely, that was what I was tasked to do, though to Lord Leicester." He gave a mirthless laugh. "I owe him a letter, though I have a good excuse for not writing."

"So do we all," Sidney said, "though we need not worry until we hear the verdict of the Ten."

Hunter sighed in his turn. "I was to report on your Catholic friends and further my uncle's dreams of a silk industry in England, not merely stay alive."

"If you are not alive, you cannot do either," Sidney said. "And if your defense convinced King Henry, it should have convinced the Ten and you should stay alive to write and negotiate."

Hunter did not want to disparage his friend's sanguine humor, but Gironi spoke up and voiced his thoughts. "King Henry did not ask probing questions. Edward has confessed to theft; and I, to unlocking their cell door. I explained how Rossi's men occupied the guards, so we are all still in trouble."

Simmons joined in the lamentation. "In testifying against Fascetti, I confessed to managing the theft of your pistols and escaping lawful custody."

Hunter wondered if his claiming to be a cleric was a crime. How serious was the theft of one letter? What was the penalty for escaping jail? He imagined himself rotting for years in a damp Venetian prison.

As the minutes passed slowly, each man sat silently with his own thoughts. By their faces, Hunter judged that each one was imagining dreadful possibilities. Even when he considered others, his thoughts were grim. What had happened to Caterina and Scarpa? What had become of the missing residents of Pozzo della Vacca? Had his testimony embroiled Rossi and his men so that they too would suffer for his mistakes?

Senator Malpiero opened the door. "The Council of Ten is ready to deliver its verdict."

CHAPTER 30

Clambering Out

ALL IN THE ANTEROOM SNAPPED TO ATTENTION.

"Ask no questions," Malpiero intoned.

Hunter asked in low rushed whispers, "Can you tell us what happened to Caterina? Are Sidney's other servants imprisoned? Have the Dominicans been charged?"

Malpiero shot him a disapproving glance. "Caterina has been released. I know nothing of other servants. The Dominicans will receive justice." He turned.

Hunter assumed a serious demeanor. He, Sidney, Bryskett, Simmons, and Gironi filed into the chamber and formed a line before the rounded dais where the Ten sat. The sharp-eyed official sitting next to the doge rose to address each man in turn, and Malpiero remained standing to translate.

"Baron Sidney and Master Bryskett, you are free to go, but you must leave Venetian territory by the end of August or face permanent exile. You may collect your arms and English money at the *Porta della Carta* at ten tomorrow."

Hunter silently thanked God for his friends' acquittal. Their reprieve boded well for him.

"Doctor Simmons, you have brought dangerous and forbidden weapons into Venice without permission to do so. You have conspired with those who endangered the peace of the Republic, whether unwittingly or not. You must pay a fine of forty ducats or serve one year in prison. You face exile from Venetian territory if you come before us again."

A heavy burden on the tutor. Nevertheless, Simmons's body relaxed. "Master Hunter..."

Hunter thought he was standing erect, but he felt himself straighten an inch taller when his name was called.

"...you are guilty of serious violations of the laws of the Republic. Though the value of the item stolen was small, any act of theft is reprehensible. You are required to pay a fine of twenty ducats or serve six months in prison. For escaping prison, you are to pay a fine of twenty ducats or serve six months in prison."

Hunter breathed more easily. The amount of the fines was high, but it should not be impossible to raise, though he might need to visit the Jews of the Ghetto.

"Master Gironi, for effecting the escape of your companion, you are required to pay a fine of fifty *lire di piccoli* or serve three months."

Hunter restrained himself from smiling at Gironi. Paying Gironi's fine would fall to him, but in the end it would be a matter of money, not of blood.

"Masters Hunter and Gironi, you are both to leave Venetian territory by the end of August." If Captain Connors and the *Adventure* arrived in time, he should be clear of the entire Adriatic, perhaps the Mediterranean, by the end of August.

The magistrate made a sweeping gesture that encompassed all the accused. "You are dismissed."

Guards Hunter had not noticed stepped behind them and marched them to a room with four doors then down a staircase. Hunter and Gironi gasped as they passed a sober-faced Rossi ascending, escorted by guards. Although the man was slippery, he had been a benefactor. When they reached the courtyard of the Doge's Palace, Sidney inhaled a deep lungful of air and expelled it. "I never expected to breathe free again."

One guard snarled at him and raised the handle of his halberd toward the door opening on the lagoon.

"No more speech," Bryskett warned.

Once they stood in twilight on the quay outside the palace and the door had clanged shut, they allowed themselves a quiet cheer and embraced one another.

"Let us give thanks to God at the basilica," Sidney said, "then, as I am one of the few of you who does not have a fine to pay, I shall buy us all a mug of wine at the nearest tavern."

Hunter's body stiffened for a moment. Sidney wanted to enter a Catholic basilica again, after clerics of that religion had contrived to blame him for an assault on a king. He swallowed his objection as the others walked toward Saint Mark's, reasoning that he had entered there to hear music a month ago, and that he had frequented popish churches in Paris. Of course, he should thank God for his release, and there was no Protestant church in Venice. He would accompany his friends, then offer his thanks again, alone tonight. "The man we passed descending was Rossi," he told Sidney. "I regret that my testimony has entangled him. I hope he avoids a hard judgment. He sheltered us all and provided the means for me to reach the Duke of Nevers."

"Simmons told us of this plebian leader of doubtful morals," Bryskett said.

"He is more a Prince of the Nicolotti than a plebian," Hunter said.

"Gentlemen," Gironi interjected, "I am sure there are ample reasons to regret your imprisonment, but I shall add another. You missed seeing Edward disguised as a courtesan's maid, a servant, and a nun."

Sidney and Bryskett laughed at the images.

In the basilica, the flames of the candles glittered off the gold mosaic tiles. Hunter for a moment imagined golden flakes of God's Grace were falling on them all. After praying, they entered a tavern to find Nicolotti and Castellani, their mock battle over, drinking one another's health.

"This is a strange city," Hunter remarked, shaking his head. "Only a few hours ago, these men were striving to maim one another." He began to turn his mind to the future. How would he find the money to pay all his debts: his fine and Gironi's, the silk cloth he had ordered from the Ventura family, the silk thread Zordan would deliver to Chioggia, the mulberry trees? Where would he find Caterina? Did she go to the lodgings rented from Rossi?

The comments of others showed they were following a similar train of thought.

"I hope to visit Stefano and assure him I am well," Gironi said.

"And I wish to do the same with my countrymen and scholars, *quam brevissime*," Simmons said. He must be feeling himself again, Hunter reflected, hearing the Latin.

"I am obliged to inform Baron Windsor of my release and ask if he has any news of my missing servants," Sidney said.

"May I suggest, gentlemen," Bryskett said, "that as night has fallen, we first determine where we shall sleep tonight. The key to the Dorsoduro lodgings rests with our pistols and money, to be collected on the morrow."

"I am doubtful of our reception at the Windsors," Sidney said, "or if they have space."

"I suggest we first go to the Half Moon to obtain a key and ask for news of Rossi's fate," Hunter said.

"If you will excuse me," Simmons said, "I have sampled enough of Rossi's hospitality."

"Indeed," Sidney said. "We need not all pursue the same path."

They downed their wine and left, Simmons to the expatriates' lodgings, the others to the Half Moon.

The Nicolotti were reveling outside the *Mezza Luna*. "*Ahh, l'inglese coraggioso!*" one man shouted. Those around him cheered and waved Hunter over to join them for a drink.

Hunter spoke to Gironi. "Pray tell them we shall return, but we have business first. Ask who might hold a key to rented lodgings."

Though men, still wearing the dark blue tunics, pulled at his sleeves and Hunter's, urging them to sit, Gironi made it clear they needed to see to affairs first. In the Half Moon, cries of welcome and invitations to imbibe were repeated, but interrupted by a cry from a corner of the room.

Caterina rushed forward and embraced Hunter, then Sidney. "You are free! Thank God!" She began to weep. "I feared you would die."

"We did as well," Hunter said. "But now all is well."

"We look for Alvise," Gironi said. "He holds the key to our lodgings."

"You can ask Rossi." She turned to the inner room door.

"He is here?" Hunter exclaimed.

"Yes."

"So, I shall finally meet this esteemed gentleman," Sidney said.

"You may speak with irony, but it will be wise to treat him with respect," Gironi warned.

In Rossi's inner room, as those outside, men crowded around tables celebrating a Nicolotti victory. Seated beside them were harlots, arms draped over the victors' shoulders. Rossi sat at a large table, surrounded by his squadron leaders. Nearby sat Alvise and Zaninno.

"Ah, Hunter!" Rossi shouted. He waved a hand to clear the bench opposite him for Hunter and his friends to sit.

Hunter introduced Sidney and Bryskett, then turned to Gironi. "Tell him we are pleased to see he is well and free, then ask about a key and any news he may have of the Dominicans."

Rossi shouted to a servant, who placed large beakers of Murano glass filled with red wine before the Englishmen. Sidney and Hunter waited impatiently while he spoke at length, Gironi and Bryskett both nodding and occasionally laughing. He sent Alvise to fetch the keys, then raised his hand in a gracious gesture to indicate that Gironi might relate his story.

"Sior Rossi assures us he was never in jeopardy. He explained to the Ten that he frequently hires men for a time, without questioning how they will be employed. He was shocked that these men had been armed and directed to assault King Henry."

Rossi sat with a smirk as Gironi spoke.

"He expressed outrage that they had lost their lives as a result of a Dominican plot and urged the councilors to judge the clerics severely. His friend Malpiero, an ardent patron of the Nicolotti, will argue for such an outcome. He expects to hear their verdict soon."

So Malpiero, not the councilor who had spoken in their favor, was Rossi's patron within the Ten.

Bryskett took over the translating. "Though the lodgings have been empty, he did not rent them to others. In view of our fines, he will graciously extend the rent due until after the first of August."

"Pray relay our thanks," Sidney said.

Rossi spoke again. Gironi shrugged and turned to Sidney and Hunter. "He says if we are in need of money to pay the fines, he can offer funds at four per cent, less than the Jewish moneylenders."

Hunter exchanged looks with Sidney. "I hope we may speak to him again in a few days, after we know our position better."

Rossi appeared satisfied. Alvise returned with a ring of keys, detached one, and handed it to Hunter with a warning.

"That is the last copy," Gironi said. "You must not lose it."

"I shall guard it well," Hunter said. "Another should be returned to us tomorrow with our pistols." A sudden thought struck him. "Alas, I left the chain mail and tunic at the *Palazzo Foscarini*."

Rossi laughed when Gironi translated, then wagged his finger at Hunter.

"His men returned the mail and tunic, but you owe him ten soldi for the helmet, unless you want to dive in the canal and retrieve it."

"Tell him I shall pay tomorrow," Hunter said.

"We thank him for his hospitality," Sidney said, "but we wish to reach the Dorsoduro house before sunset."

As they rose, a short man rushed in and made straight for Rossi. The Nicolotti leader smiled and turned to address the room, who cheered at his words.

"The Brother Giuseppe faces execution for his murder. Brother Alberto is to be branded on the forehead and stand for half a day between the columns of the *Piazzetta*, then face exile," Gironi said. "The vice inquisitor is banished from Venetian lands."

This was the way of the world, Hunter reflected. Though Vice Inquisitor Fascetti had ordered the crimes, those under him received the severe punishments.

~

The gondolas docked near the Dorsoduro lodgings. Hunter and Gironi leapt ashore and helped Caterina climb out, while Sidney and Bryskett, each carrying a lantern, disembarked. Hunter approached the house with trepidation. Though no one had reported the imprisonment of those staying there, Rossi had said it had been empty. He extracted the key from his pocket and inserted it in the door. It opened at his touch.

"The door is unlocked," he announced. As he stepped inside, a rustling from the kitchen made him freeze. He raised a hand to silence the others and slowly shifted weight from one foot to the other. Four steps in, a board creaked beneath him. Whoever or whatever was in the kitchen scrambled toward the small courtyard behind the house. Hunter raced forward, grasped a diminutive figure, and twirled it to face him. "Giulio," he gasped.

"*Signor Hunter, per favore...*" he began.

"Giulio, are you safe? Are the others safe?" Hunter asked eagerly.

Caterina pushed him aside to embrace the boy. After an expression of joy, she asked "*Francesco sta bene?*"

"*Sì,*" Giulio answered.

Gironi was at Hunter's shoulder, showering Giulio with questions. He turned smiling. "All the others are safe at Mestre. He came to fetch onions and carrots they left in their haste. He hopes we will come. They are without money at his mother's cousin's farm."

"Ask him to stay here tonight and tell us his tale," Sidney said. "Once we reclaim our possessions tomorrow, I should be glad to retire from Venice and stay at a farm on *terrafirma* for a few days."

Hunter said a silent prayer of thanks. They could all resume the lives they had led before the king's arrival, free of threats—even better, free of unknown foes. No mysteries gnawed at his mind. The motives of Barnes, Simmons, and the vice inquisitor had been revealed.

Wednesday, 28 July 1574, Venice

Sidney's dream of a rural idyll faded as the necessary business of life overtook them. They needed to collect their possessions at the *Porta della Carta*, but were unable to find a gondola, as all had been hired to bid farewell to King Henry. They trudged about Venice, hoping to thank those who had assisted them, but the Windsors and the expatriates had joined the flotilla accompanying the king. Bryskett left in search of his brother, and Gironi to visit his cousin. Hunter and Sidney slogged through the heat back to Dorsoduro, where Caterina told them Giulio had left for Mestre early to tell his mother that all was safe to return. Disappointed at the prospect that the household might abandon the farm and come back to Venice, Sidney sought solitude in a bedchamber.

Hunter had rarely seen his friend in such a melancholy mood. Perhaps he needed time to change his outlook from a prospect of death to the role of the young Protestant hope that Languet pressed upon him. Escaping that burden and the expectations of others might account for Sidney's gallop to Genoa and Florence, his friendship with Catholic expatriates, and even his presence in Italy in disregard of Her Majesty's license to travel.

Thursday, 29 July 1574, Venice

The next morning Hunter and Caterina threaded their way through the *calli* of Dorsoduro to acknowledge their debt to Lucia, then took a gondola to Stefano's shop to thank him and collect Gironi. She ordered a new pair of shoes for her trip, bragging she could pay for them with the money she had earned from Tintoretto.

The trio returned to the Dorsoduro lodgings to find all the former residents of Pozzo della Vacca settled in. Caterina rushed into the arms of Francis with an ardor that suggested much more than joy at seeing a duet partner. Madox, White, and Fisher embraced Hunter and Gironi and expressed their relief that they had come to no harm. Fisher and Christopher bowed their welcome. Beatrice greeted them with tears and wet kisses. She was as happy to see her kettles and skillets as Caterina was to see Francis. All were more eager to stay in Venice than return to Padua. Sidney acceded to the group's requests to remain in Venice, at least until the first of August.

Monday, 2 August 1574, Venice

Things were looking up, Hunter thought. After drawing his monthly allowance for August, he had almost enough to pay his fines to the Most Serene Republic. He borrowed the rest from Sidney, who borrowed from noble German and Polish friends. Both feared explaining the debts to their uncles might prove difficult. If Hunter could bring back a weaver and mulberry trees, it might soften their moods. He longed to return to Padua, hoping a letter from London might await him with a draft to pay for the silks. Nevertheless, he must still attend to matters here.

Lord Windsor greeted them like returning prodigal sons, as though he had not turned Sidney over to the *Signori di Notte*. The baroness seemed more sincere in her welcome. Though the baron offered rooms again, Sidney refused.

With Gironi, Hunter visited the Half Moon, where they were met with smiles by the men who stood by the door and were ushered quickly into Rossi's inner office by the rabbit-toothed minion whose name he had never learned. Rossi greeted them warmly but did not bid them sit.

After the appropriate salutations, Gironi said, "Master Hunter and I wish to thank you again for your assistance. We have come to return the key and pay what he owes for the lost helmet."

Rossi indicated the sum could be given to Rabbit Teeth and spoke to Gironi. "He says the English ship is due to reach Venice in two weeks."

How he had learned that so quickly Hunter could only guess. The man's information network was as extensive as that of Venice itself, it seemed. "I am grateful for the news."

"He asks, seeing how soon the ship will arrive, if you have considered your need for a loan. If it is for a short time, he is willing to charge only three and a half percent."

Hunter bit his lip. He did not have the money needed to pay for the silks and thread he had ordered. "Thank him for his generous offer, but I hope to hear from London before I enter into a loan agreement."

Rossi shrugged at the reply. In Gironi's next question, Hunter caught the word 'Biradi.' Rossi smiled as he responded.

Hunter raised his eyebrows in question.

"Rossi says he received the money he asked for, so Biradi is back in Padua. His men have been turned over to the Forty, another Venetian court, charged with the murder of Barnes," Gironi explained.

"So Biradi has lost three men to the Church and four men to the Republic in the past months," Hunter summarized.

"All because of the presence of Sidney in the Veneto," Gironi said. "And Rossi has lost two for the same reason. He suggests we would be wise to heed the advice of the Council of Ten and depart."

The catalog of those who might want revenge on Hunter and his friend was growing too long. "I thank him for his advice."

The Dorsoduro house bubbled with laughter and the smells of another celebratory meal as they entered. Caterina bounced up to Hunter and exclaimed, "Francis and I will marry."

Hunter reeled with the news. The pair had made themselves scarce during the past few days, but he had assumed only courting was taking place, which would end when Caterina boarded the *Adventure*. Now, with some relief, his idle thoughts of coupling again with her during the voyage could be cast away. "Congratulations,' he sputtered.

Francis appeared at her side. "I pray you will bless us, sir, and stand beside me with Chris at our wedding."

"I...I...Have you spoken to Sidney? He has the greatest rank among us."

"We have, sir, but he said it was you who planned to set Cat free from that house she was in."

Hunter cast a glance at Sidney, who smiled. He had dodged the request by tossing it to Hunter. "So you know Caterina's past?"

"Yes, sir. She has been honest with me. I love her all the more for that."

"Where is this wedding to be, and when?" Hunter asked. Their plans could not delay his departure. Were they to live in Italy or England? If England, how would these two Catholics manage? Would Lord Leicester be interested in a married couple as singers?

"We hope in a week," Francis explained, "in someplace with grapes."

"Bassano del Grappa," Caterina interjected. "My mother live near there. I want Francis to meet her, to get her blessing, to say good-bye." She began to sniff and tear up.

"Do you plan to stay there?"

"No, sir. She wants to come to England, and I want to go home. She says you have managed for her to sail with you and I can sail, too. There we will both sing for a great lord. I can help the carpenter on the boat and all."

Captain Connor knew nothing of Caterina, let alone Francis. But was he to leave Christopher here alone? Had Uncle Babcock told the captain he might bring a weaver, unlikely as that was? "What about the banns?" Hunter asked. Surely they could not be read three times in a week.

"Oh, Cat says the father there is a close friend of her uncle, and he'll marry us after just one reading, for certain after she gives him a bit o' money."

"Money?"

"Aye. She's been sittin' for this Tintoretto gent afternoons. She had me come along to see that, even if she drops her petticoat and shows her breasts, there's not tricks or chamber work."

Hunter looked at Caterina with new admiration. She seemed to have everything figured out. It was clear who would wear the breeches in this marriage. "So, you are asking me to ride to Bassano del Grappa with you?"

"A farm near," Caterina said. "If you please, sir."

"We must return to Padua first," Hunter said, in what he hoped was a voice of authority. "And I must leave on the ship as soon as she is loaded, whether or not you be married. I cannot wait for the banns to be thrice read."

"Yes, yes," Caterina nodded enthusiastically.

Hunter would not ask what plans they might have if the 'great lord' did not employ them in England. If they were allowed to sail, he would have an entire voyage to prepare them for that possibility. "Congratulations again," Hunter said, suddenly aware all eyes had been on him. "Let us celebrate!"

CHAPTER 31

Receding Shores

Wednesday, 4 August 1574, Padua

In Padua a message from Uncle Babcock said Captain Connors was bringing a letter of credit to cover the cost of the silks Hunter had agreed to purchase. A letter from Hubert Languet begged Sidney and his party to come to Vienna, a request Sidney gladly accepted. Despite his inclination to follow his own desires rather than being manipulated by Languet, he was eager to leave the Veneto. Languet could also provide a loan for his homeward journey. Beatrice was glad to return to her kitchen, but her lip began to quiver and her eyes to fill with tears every time her tenants spoke of their imminent departures.

As they had not been able to meet with the expatriates in Venice, Sidney invited them to Pozzo della Vacca for a farewell supper. They arrived in a joyful mood, each in turn embracing Sidney, Bryskett, and Hunter.

"We left Venice on the day King Henry did," Randolph said. "We followed the armada that accompanied him to Mestre, then trailed his retinue to Padua. I am sorry we did not greet you after Doctor Simmons convinced the Ten of your innocence and accomplished your release."

Hunter and Sidney looked at one another in surprise, then at Simmons. His eyes pleaded with them not to tell a different story, then he said. "Master Hunter was also instrumental. As I told you, he corroborated my testimony before both King Henry and the Council of Ten."

Hunter bit his lip. Though he resented Simmons taking credit for their release, he did not contradict him. Simmons could remain in Padua as the hero of the expatriates, rather than a plotter and betrayer. A glance toward Sidney and Bryskett communicated his decision.

"We are all so grateful you escaped the false charges of the vice inquisitor," Hart said.

"And I thank God Doctor Simmons was able to clear himself as well as you and Philip," Fitzwilliams said.

Hart's face was sober. "The vice inquisitor's acts have shaken my faith. The Church I love does not bear false witness and order murder. I hope His Holiness will see fit to defrock Brother Fascetti."

Randolph took a deep breath. "John and I have had long talks. We both considered abandoning our faith, yet neither of us can. I have known the Church's faults for some time, yet, since the Council of Trent, it is reforming itself. We both believe it is better to remain and be part of this reformation."

"Reducing the power of the Inquisition is one goal we agree on," Hart said.

"I can only commend your decision," Sidney spoke, "and I wish you success in your attempts."

Le Rous snorted. "I wish them luck as well. It is a labor greater than any of Hercules to cleanse a church of men who, despite their vows, are as filled with greed, pride, and lust as every other man."

Gironi nodded in agreement.

"I would have chided you with being a Cynic before last week," Simmons said to Le Rous, "but I must now concur."

Le Rous spoke again. "Perhaps we expect too much of our clerics. What man, Catholic or Reformed, would not lie, bear false witness against others, perhaps even plot their deaths, to maintain his wealth and position?"

Hunter caught Gironi nodding again. Did he know of Reformed clerics who had been guilty of such acts, or was he thinking of the Earl of Leicester?

"God calls us all to resist such temptations and humble ourselves," Sidney said.

Fitzwilliams lowered his head and spoke. "John's words prick my conscience. Though I did not lie to you when you asked about Dominicans, I knew that they had visited Barnes because he was behind Sidney's capture. He told me. Perhaps that would have alerted you and prevented the theft of your pistols."

"I knew as well," Le Rous said.

"And I," Randolph added. "Only Hart did not."

Hunter was about to say he had suspected when Bryskett spoke loudly. "Gentlemen, gentlemen! This is to be a celebration, not a convocation. Come, let us sit and drink. Beatrice has labored all day to prepare a feast for us."

His speech broke the serious mood, and all moved to the table.

Sunday, 8 August 1574 Padua

The bells of Saint Anthony's Basilica and the echoing bells of parish churches called the faithful to worship. Embraces between Sidney and his party and those who were remaining briefly in Italy had occupied the last fifteen minutes. Beatrice's tears and kisses left Sidney's cheeks damp.

"Stay safe until we meet again," Hunter told his friend.

"And you likewise," Sidney said, "If I am to avoid brigands, you must avoid pirates."

"I must trust to Captain Connors for that."

"I shall trust to Lodowick and my men to match any robbers."

"Let us speak no more of thieves," Bryskett interjected, "but of a reunion in London."

"You are right, Lodowick. I trust that by the time we meet, Edward will have softened up Uncle Robert so that my Italian sins will be forgiven." Sidney smiled.

"I thank you for the letters of praise you send with me," Hunter said. "May they tilt the scales in my favor as my report will tilt them in yours."

"Do not forget the weights my reports shall place upon the pans for both of you," Gironi said.

"I shall not. I have praised you as well." Sidney fixed Hunter with a heartfelt look. "You have earned more praise and gratitude than I can convey. Without your efforts, my life, and the lives of those who accompany me, would have ended. A chasm would have opened between Venice and England. Her Majesty as well as I owes you thanks."

Hunter flushed. "You veer to hyperbole, Philip. Pray stop or I shall blubber like Beatrice."

"Enough good-byes then," Sidney said. He threw his arms around Hunter one final time as their friends embraced around them. Sidney and his party mounted and, with a final wave, rode toward the *Porta Pontecorvo*, the gate they had used inauspiciously four months before.

11 August 1574, Bassano del Grappa

Caterina's ability to convince friends and relatives to bend rules for her continued to impress Hunter. The priest in her mother's parish had agreed to marry them after only one reading of the banns and a few ducats.

After Gironi mentioned to Caterina that their arrival in England with a silk weaver would help her chances of securing a position serving the Earl of Leicester, she had located an apprentice weaver named Francesco who might be willing to accompany them. In the village, everyone had noticed a steady improvement in a local weaver's cloth during the past few years. All agreed he was passing off his apprentice's work as his own. Though the lad had completed his term, his master was unwilling to release him and allow him to practice his craft in Bassano or to move to Venice. Francesco had been orphaned soon after he began his apprenticeship, and he had no one to turn to. When Caterina ordered the cloth for her bridal gown, she had convinced the lad that, if he left his master to join Hunter, he would face a future as the most skilled silk weaver in England. His eyes glowed at the prospect, but his shoulders sagged when he told Caterina he was in debt to his master. Gironi offered to pay the boy's debt, but the master refused to free him at any price. When Gironi reported his failure to Hunter and Caterina, her eyes lit with a plan.

Hunter and Gironi crept through the dark streets of Bassano, approaching the weaver's shop from the rear. Hunter stopped short and turned a troubled face toward Gironi. "One commandment says not to steal, another not to covet his neighbor's servant."

"This is no time to quote scripture," Gironi said. "After endless discussions, we decided to hazard the laws of Venice again. Caterina and her family have framed all. The weaver lies insensible after her mother drowned him with the town's grappa. Caterina, Francis, and Christopher wait, holding our horses, and now you decide to worry about your soul?"

"I know. I know. All promises to turn to our advantage if we get young Francesco to join us, yet I regret what we must do. It would have been better if the weaver had accepted your offer."

"But he did not." Gironi sighed. "I believe my master sent me with you to overcome your scruples. You have faced Biradi and Rossi, spoken before King Henry and the Council of Ten, eluded the *sbirri* through Venice and to Padua and back. Will your courage fail you now?"

"Those times I was in the right."

"Forgive me, Edward, but were you in the right when you mounted Caterina?"

Hunter hung his head. "I was not. I have tried to make amends by freeing her and taking her to England."

"Then consider this part of your plan to win her a better life. You know that arriving with Francesco will incline both the earl and your uncle to find a place for her, Francis, and Christopher. Pray move aside, open the lantern a crack, and let me assault this lock."

Hunter shifted to one side. Gironi was right in one respect. He had undertaken a mission to observe Sidney's friendship with Catholic students and see to his welfare. With qualifications, he could claim he had done that. They had said their farewells, and even now Philip's party was on its way to Vienna. Finding silks and a weaver for his uncle and Leicester had claimed less of his attention, but if their release of the apprentice was successful, he could count that mission fulfilled as well. Yet Le Rous's comment about the acts a man might countenance to enrich himself echoed in his mind. It was too late to stop now. He would pray for forgiveness later.

The lock clicked under Gironi's tools and swung open. In the lantern light stood a thin, frightened young man, clutching a bundle. It must contain all his possessions.

Gironi whispered to him. Hunter subdued his doubts and led them decisively toward the grove where Caterina and the others waited.

15 August 1574, Chioggia

The *Adventure* rocked softly off Chioggia harbor as the sun set. Hunter watched the small boats with boxes of silk thread pull alongside to unload their cargo. Gironi and Francesco joined him. The apprentice's fingers drummed on the railing.

"Almost done," Hunter said.

"Almost is not soon enough for Francesco," Gironi said.

Hunter smiled at the boy. "Tell him not to worry. We are no longer in Venice."

"But we are still under Venetian rule," Gironi said. He bit his lip.

Hunter must not show his own worry. As late as that morning, he had been unsure whether Gironi had succeeded in obtaining the potted mulberry trees, and he relaxed only when a boat containing his companion and the small trees sailed into Chioggia harbor.

The boats returned to the dock to collect their final load of silk thread. Farther down the ship's rail, Caterina and Francis started to sing in harmony. Surely this Venetian adventure was ending well.

A sudden cry from Francesco pulled him from his thoughts. The apprentice pointed north toward Venice and exclaimed *"Le barche longhe!"* Light from the torches near the prows of the long boats illuminated the red and gold flag of the Most Serene Republic. Behind, men with pikes and muskets stood in postures the opposite of serene.

"Damn!" Gironi swore. "The weaver moved more quickly than we thought." Caterina let out a scream.

They had one day's head start from Bassano. Caterina's mother had told the weaver they were going to Padua rather than Venice. That should have delayed pursuit longer, but it had not.

Captain Connors was at Hunter's shoulder. "We must set sail immediately. Your last boxes of thread must stay in Chioggia." He barked orders to his crewmen. Some scrambled aloft, some pulled in the lines that had lifted cargo aboard, some took their place at the capstan and began to weigh anchor.

Hunter clenched his teeth. They were leaving fifty pounds worth of silk on the dock. "How long?" he asked the captain.

"The long boats will reach us in about fifteen minutes," Connors said. "It will be a close thing. Depends on the evening breeze. We must sail toward them before turning into the Adriatic."

Hunter gazed up at the sails. When the sailors released them from the yardarms, they flapped listlessly. Caterina grasped his right arm. "We will be caught," she wailed.

"I think not," Hunter lied. Nearby, Francesco moaned into Gironi's shoulder.

Captain Connors continued to shout orders. In a flurry of activity, sailors scrambled down from the rigging and grabbed sheets to tighten the sails. A light breeze filled them and the ship began to drift slowly toward the approaching long boats. The helmsman shouted he needed more speed to steer the ship. The men at the capstan secured the anchor and joined the others to position the sails to catch whatever wind they could.

The long boats bore down on the *Adventure*. One of the captains shouted at them, and several of his men raised their muskets. "I don't understand Italian," Connors said with a smile, adding, "I hope we are out of range."

The sails snapped in a sudden offshore breeze, and the *Adventure* heeled to starboard and picked up speed. Muskets sounded on the long boats and balls of lead cracked into the bow and whistled over the deck. Everyone ducked. "Stay down," Connors ordered his passengers. To the helmsman, he asked, "How long before we make to starboard?"

"Two minutes," came the reply.

The *Adventure* and the long boats continued on a collision course. Hunter entertained frantic thoughts. Did the long boats have rams? He had seen no cannon, thank God. Surely they would turn aside before the *Adventure* plowed over them. What would drowning Venetian officials do to relations with England?

Another volley struck the ship. A sailor shouted and fell as he was hit. His nearby mates rushed to him. The *Adventure* began its turn to starboard, exposing its side to the long boats. "Man your positions," the captain shouted, followed by orders to adjust the sails. Little by little, the ship maneuvered toward the inlet that separated the lagoon from the Adriatic. Long seconds elapsed as the ship slowly turned and those on the closing long boats reloaded. Simultaneously, a tail-wind filled the sails, and volleys from both longboats raked the larboard side of the *Adventure*. Still gripping the lines, the sailors on that side ducked to avoid what might have been a deadly fusillade, but the long boats were so close to the ship that the shots flew at an angle too high to reach the deck. The *Adventure* picked up speed and slid into the Adriatic Sea.

"How fairs Higgins?" Connors shouted.

"His shoulder bleeds, but it is not bad," came the reply.

"Fetch the surgeon."

Drawing near the captain, Hunter suggested, "English ships may not be welcome in Venice for a few years." The *Adventure* slowly slipped away from the long boats, which turned toward Chioggia dock.

Gironi smiled. "They can't catch us, but they can fine the dockmaster."

"Can Venice pursue us with a galley?" Hunter asked.

"Not now," Connors said. "We are safe unless there is no wind in the Adriatic."

Hunter gave a prayer of thanks. Despite his sins, God had seen fit to bless and preserve him. He hoped Lord Leicester and his uncle would do likewise.

The End

Author's Note

The more I write, the more fiction and less history makes its way into my novels. The bare historical facts are that Phillip Sidney and his party did spend November 1573-August 1574 in Venice, where he lodged at the French Embassy, and Padua, where he lodged at Pozzo della Vacca. Veronese did paint his portrait (now lost) and the Council of Ten did grant his party permission to bear arms in Italy. Although Sidney travelled across northern Italy in March of 1574, later expressed a dislike of Venice, and wrote Languet he was "entangled in many affairs," the details of his actions and thinking during the time of the novel are unclear.

Henri Valois, newly King Henri III of France, visited Venice 18-25 July 1574. The details of his visit are closely recorded, including the mock battle staged at his request on 26 July.

Beyond that, I have constructed a web of fiction. No attempt was made on Henri III's life. Sidney was never abducted or framed for a crime. I have simplified several complex issues. The value of Venetian currency varied depending on how much silver or gold was in each coin and what the rate of exchange between those precious metals was. I found information on prices, not all from 1574, and guessed. Venetian laws on what silks could be woven where and by whom were also complex, so I decided it would add a bit more drama if Hunter were breaking some laws. I have been unable to find where Tintoretto's painting workshop was, so I have placed it in his house on the *Fondamenta dei Mori*. Likewise, I do not know where Baron Windsor lived.

In Padua, it is likely that some lower level official would have responded to any kidnapping, not the Venetian-appointed *Capitano*. Although several of the Catholic expatriates are real, and Sidney and Randolph witnessed John Hart's doctoral exam, where those expats lodged is unknown.

The entire underworld of the Veneto is an invention. Such a criminal network must have existed, and perhaps some articles about it have been written in Italian, a language which is not in my skill set. Some good books have been written about the lives of courtesans, but in the novel much of their lives and situations are guesses.

As to the maps, I found it devilishly hard to discover the borders of Ferrara and Romagna in 1574. The borders of the Italian city states shifted with wars and dynastic marriages. I have assumed the northern border of Ferrara at that time to be the River Po. If anyone can provide me more accurate information, I would welcome it.

I hope my italicization choices were not too confusing. Official names, such as *Scuola di San Rocco*, were italicized, but 'San Rocco' was not. Ditto *campi* and *piazze*.

If you enjoyed this novel, I encourage you to review it on either *Good Reads* or *Amazon*. Good reviews are one of the few ways independent authors can hope their books will reach more readers.

DougAdcockAuthor.com
Facebook.com/DougAdcockAuthor

Acknowledgements

I am in debt to a large number of academics who have written about fifteenth and sixteenth century Venice. I first want to thank those with whom I have corresponded personally: Professor Emeritus Robert C. Davis of Ohio State University, Professor Michael Knapton of the Università degli Studi di Udine, and Professor Guido Ruggiero of the University of Miami.

Many people in Italy provided me with material for this novel: Valentia Pippin at the Doge's Palace and Monica Zussa aboard the *Burchiello*. Ruben Alba Ecequil guided my wife and I around Padua and Jennifer Engel was our gracious hostess and guide in Vicenza.

My special thanks to Professor Davis and Jennifer Engle for helping me with the Italian and Venetian in this novel. Any errors that exist are mine, not theirs.

Many thanks to my beta readers: Holley Adcock, Penny Barnes, Professor Robert Davis, Carol Krapfl, Monica McCann, and David Smith.

Cathy Helms created another great cover and three maps to help readers. Tamara Cribley has once again done a great job formatting the novel both digitally and in print.

I have leaned heavily on these publications:

Clarke, Paula C. "Business of Prostitution in Early Modern Venice" *Renaissance Quarterly* 68 (2015)

Davis, Robert. *The War of the Fists* (Oxford, 1994)

—"The Spectacle Almost Fit for a King: Venice's *Guerra de' canne* of 26 July 1574" in *Medieval and Renaissance Venice* Kettel, Ellen & Thomas F. Madden, editors (Champaign-Urbana, 1999)

Knapton, Michael, ed. *Venice and the Veneto during the Renaissance* (Firenze, 2014)

Lawner, Lynne. *Lives of the Courtesans* (New York, 1987)

Molà, Luca. *The Silk Industry of Renaissance Italy* (Baltimore and London, 2000)

Rosenthal, Margaret. *The Honest Courtesan* (Chicago, 1992)

Ruggiero, Guido. *Binding Passions: Tales of Magic, Marriage and Power from the end of the Renaissance* (Oxford, 1993)

—*The Boundaries of Eros: Sex Crime and Sexuality in Renaissance Venice* (Oxford, 1985)

—*Violence in Early Renaissance Venice* (New Brunswick, NJ, 1980)

Printed in Great Britain
by Amazon

36121658R00189